A Boy's Name

by

Stephen Queen

Pen Press Pubishers Ltd

First published in Great Britain by
Pen Press Publishers Ltd
39, Chesham Road
Brighton, East Sussex BN2 1NB

ISBN 1-905203-02-0

Printed and bound in the UK

Cover photography by Joanna Anthony ©

About the Author

Born in 1977 in the town of Munster, Germany, Stephen Queen grew up as the son of Angelina and James Queen, a soldier in the 1st Battalion of the Royal Scots. Queen is their second youngest child of four having one brother and two sisters. Growing up in an authoritarian domain did not dampen Queen's optimistic outlook on life. Some of his life experiences to date would be deemed as unbelievable, however, he has taken all of it in his stride and has turned them into positive events.

It was in Queen's early twenties that he first became aware of the joys of reading literature, a milestone in this transition was an eagerly awaited visit to the cinema to see *Harry Potter and the Philosophers Stone*. Mesmerised by the film and the storyline, Queen is now a JK Rowling enthusiast, motivating him to put pen to paper and write this novel, allowing his thoughts to come alive. Queen has also conquered the *Lord of the Rings* trilogy and counts the author, Jeffery Deaver as another firm favourite.

Queen has often been asked if *A Boy's Name* contains any real events. His answer is quite allusive as this fictional novel is written by an author who believes that every writer subconsciously incorporates their own experiences into their work and that it is often impossible to identify where the reality and fiction intertwine. But in a world where these two parallels come together so often, does it really matter?

Acknowledgements

I would like to thank Pen Press for all their assistance and hard work in the publishing of this novel.

It is with much gratitude that I thank J K Rowling for unknowingly providing the inspiration that opened up this new world to me.

'To the Twelve who can!'

CHAPTER ONE
Family & Friends

When looking back on life I often wonder how on earth I turned out normal. How, after everything that happened, I was still able to stand and move forward. As you grow so do you learn and achieve. Some people grow faster and learn more than others. Some achieve little while others make life-shattering discoveries. All in all, life to me stands for one thing: "Living in Family Environments". Without real family and people to care for you and love you, you can't really live. Well, not in my opinion. I truly believe life is about living for the here and now. Saying what's on your mind and never standing down. One day you might wake up and think to yourself "I have a great life" but let experience tell you that it isn't always going to be the case. I was fifteen when life as I knew it suddenly changed. At that age I thought life was about hot chocolate and having fun, but it isn't.

As a child, life for me was great. Full of fun, games, holidays and parties. It was the swingin' twenties and we were comfortably off enough to enjoy it. I was living what some people would think of as "a wonderful life" and yes! They might be right. I had the most caring parents in the world, one brother who would have gladly given his right arm if I had asked for it. The family could have been bigger and it wasn't for the want of trying. Mum and Dad tried extremely hard but weren't able to give us a sister. Mum had so much wanted a baby girl.

As children, we never went to Mum for help or to sort out any problems. Sure, we would talk, but never about girls or personal things, and Mum so wanted to feel required. She knew she'd be fantastic; she wanted to give the advice that our Gran had given her and do all the girlie things that she had done. For some reason, however, after she gave birth to Gavin, my younger brother, the doctors told her she wouldn't be able to have any more children.

As I said, not for the want of trying; from day one she was always dragging Dad upstairs, sometimes for hours on end. It had even become a talking point at the dinner parties they regularly held. Now, if you had ever been to one of Mum's famous dinner parties, you wouldn't have forgotten you'd been there. The best food, the shiniest silverware and even the tablecloth cost a fortune. I'll always remember that massive walnut dinner table. Gavin will never forget it either; well, not after he was caught trying to clean his best bicycle on it. You would have thought someone was attempting to murder Mum. She must have been screaming for at least an hour. Poor Gavin never knew what had hit him. It took a French polisher two whole days and twenty six pounds to repair it. No one had ever told Gavin the story about how Granddad took five years to make the table, and how Mr Silverdale, a successful local shop owner, had tried to buy it for two hundred pounds, but after Granddad died, Mum couldn't bear to see it go.

We lived in a little town called Rockfield, about fifty miles west of Edinburgh. Having been born in the village and always having lived there I went to the local school. However, school wasn't the best source of conversation in our house. Mum always wanted us to go to the Manor Fees boarding school for boys in Ayr. Dad disagreed and made it very clear that it would never happen. He loved us more than any Dad could ever have loved his children. For him, children were the key to life; they were the one and only reason why he worked so hard. We loved him just as much, and were very grateful for his want to keep us close, although sometimes he took it a bit too far. It took over three years of nagging before I managed to get him to allow Gavin and me to sleep over at our friends' houses, and even longer to be allowed to go away for the weekend with friends. He was a very protective parent back then and I now understand why. He hoped we'd be a lifetime investment for him.

Throughout my childhood, just as I was dropping off to sleep, Dad would come in and speak to me. I don't know if he ever meant me to hear his words as I continued to pretend to sleep and listen to his gentle voice rumbling on. He would talk about the strangest things and it was almost like an escape for him. He once told me that when he was young boy his Dad never really showed him any love, and that's why he'd never let the same happen to us.

Some people would consider it quite unusual he would come into my room, sometimes for hours on end and speak to me in the darkness, but to me it was like looking forward to a bedtime story. Just that my stories weren't like the ones that most young boys got told. My stories were always different and, most of all, they were real. Not some fairytale about talking animals and monsters that didn't exist. They were true, real life stories about my Dad, and the adventures he had as a child. The occasional story would be about his work or about Mum, but no matter what, I just lay there with my eyes closed, trying to resist asking a question when he said something I didn't quite understand. When he was finished, he would give me a kiss on the forehead and creep out of the door, pulling it quietly closed behind him.

It obviously mystified my mother. One morning she came into my room just as I was waking up. She looked slightly furtive, and I knew what was coming.

"When Dad comes into your room," she began, glancing over her shoulder uncertainly, "what does he do, or say, to you?"

"He just talks," I replied, wiping the sleep from my eyes.

"About anything in particular?" she asked.

I sighed impatiently. "He just talks. Quite randomly. Just memories of his childhood, things... just things..." I shrugged. I could see the confusion on Mum's face, but I didn't want to say anymore.

"Like what things?" she pressed further.

I just looked at her. I didn't want to say anything more, and finally she got the hint. She stood up and brushed some imaginary specks off her dress before leaving the room. I felt mean and from that day onwards, there was always some kind of distance between us.

I never had the heart to tell Dad what had happened that day. I don't think Mum ever told him either, as he never stopped coming in at night to speak to me. It seems strange now but I never talked to Gavin about Dad's visits. In a way, they were special and something I wanted to keep private. I don't know if Dad ever spent time with Gavin like he did with me, but one thing's for sure, Gavin never mentioned that he did. Which in a way made his visits that little bit more extra special? If you've ever felt that warm feeling like holding a hot cup between your hands and feeling the warmth travel through your bones, that's what it was like, except when you get the feeling for real it's a warmth in your chest and not your hands. You'll know what I mean when I say it's a special feeling, and one that can't be recreated at the drop of a hat. It's a feeling that doesn't pass with time, but stays with you long after many other feelings have long since disappeared.

As a brother, Gavin was great and because we never had any other brothers and sisters we stayed very close. Apart from Alex, who was my closest friend at the time, Gavin came first in my life. There were only two and a half years between Gavin and me, so our interests were very much the same. Many of our friends had brothers about

8

the same age but none had the close relationship that we had.

Most of my friends would often say "you can't bring him with us" but it was always both or none. My friends very soon accepted this, and Gavin was always considered one of the gang. We had some fun times together, but like everything else in the world it didn't last like that forever. Times were due to change, and change they did.

In the type of village where we lived, you couldn't have the kind of open life that most in the big cities could. Everyone knew everyone, and we all lived in each other's back pocket. As kids we never worried about it much, but he who brought shame upon his family lived a long time before the shame disappeared. There was one time a young boy stole a caramel chocolate-bar from Greens the sweet shop and got caught. Although he'd never even gotten out the shop with the chocolate, Mr Green knew he'd tried to steal it, and called the police. Mr Archibald Irwin was the local police constable and what a police constable he was. At some point in every conversation you had with him you would hear the sentence "the gallows he'll be found the one who steals in my town." This one little sentence was enough to make any boy or girl think twice before carrying out even the smallest crime, but it didn't stop everyone.

The young boy who attempted to steal the chocolate bar was indeed a very sorry boy. He came from a poor family who lived on the far side of the town in a small area called the Blacksmiths Fire. No one knows for sure why it was given that name, but the story goes that it took its rise from when a group of blacksmiths moved into the area a few hundred years ago. They worked day and night to forge weapons for a great battle that took place. No one ever seems to be able to tell you which battle it was but our schoolteacher, Mrs Greenshields, said it was a battle between the McDonalds and the McPhersons, who had fallen out over a piece of land. It's said that at night the sky would be lit with fire that could be seen for miles around while the blacksmiths worked. After a year or so they eventually left, leaving a group of stone buildings behind. These buildings were very quickly taken over by peasants and claimed as their own. Although it may have changed slightly over the years, the houses left behind are still there and still being used.

The boy was called Jamie Richardson. His Dad had died a few years ago leaving him, his mother, his brother and two sisters alone. Mr Green asked that the boy be whipped and then made to work in the shop until he deemed his error had been corrected. Jamie was made to clean the floors and any other filthy job that Mr Green could find. Jamie's family suffered severely because of this. He was the only one in their family old enough and able to work and make money for the family to live on. One of his jobs was working in the fields during the summer months to cut crops. Some of his other work included looking after cattle and cutting down trees. Even after he'd done his work for Mr Green he went to work on the farm 'til late. We called him "The Boy who Never Sleeps" because it sure seemed that way.

It was one day while out with Gavin and the boys that I first met Jamie. There he was walking along Riverdale Road with a cow.

"Look, it's The Boy who Never Sleeps," shouted David, pointing and laughing as he attempted to walk past us.

"Don't you like playing with boys?" he shouted again. "Look, lads, he can't find any real friends so he plays with a cow."

The boys all started laughing as Jamie trundled past us awkwardly.

"Shut up and leave him alone!" I had expelled words that I knew could only bring trouble, and I didn't know why I had spoken. I didn't glance at Jamie, but I could feel some kind of connection. It was as though they had all been laughing at me. Everyone stopped laughing and looked towards me. In my mind, the image freezes at that moment; me standing there with everyone looking at me, including Gavin and Jamie.

"What's this then?" David snarled, pointing his finger at me. "Sticking up for poor beggars and thieves are we?"

"Just leave him alone, we have better things to do than laugh at a poor boy with a skinny cow." I bit my lip as I said it. I had lowered myself to a level that I knew I'd regret. Instead of sticking up for what I believed in, I'd backed down in the face of embarrassment.

"You're right," David said, "let's get out of here."

We turned around and walked back along the road towards the graveyard as Jamie continued to walk the other way with the cow. Still feeling embarrassed and ashamed, I dragged my feet, falling behind the others and couldn't help but think about Jamie. I felt so sorry for what I'd said, and for not sticking up for him. Just as I was following in self-pity, I felt a hand on my left shoulder.

"What's up?"

"Oh, Gavin, it's you"

"He's just a poor boy, why be concerned about him?"

I could feel the anger starting to build up and rage inside. The others had drifted on ahead so stopping and grabbing Gavin by the arm I attempted to speak to him. "I thought you knew better? Dad never taught us to treat people like that, no matter who they are."

"Sure, but why worry?" he replied casually.

"You just don't get it Gavin, do you? You know what kind of life he's had so why make it any worse? He isn't as lucky as we are."

"Well s-o-r-r-y," he mouthed without any consideration whatsoever, and ran forward to catch the others. The matter was dropped there and then and Gavin never mentioned it again, but the memory of that first incident with Jamie was one that never left me, and one that very soon came finding its way to bring us together.

The following day we were due to go to Grandma's house in Lanark. Our bags were packed and off we went. Dad had recently bought a car. It was pitch black with dark leather seats inside, which when you sat down on them made a deep crunching noise. The inside was cold and when you drove round a corner you would slide from side to side, but when we drove through the streets we knew we were the envy of the town. There were only a dozen or so families who had cars in the town, but that was soon to change over the next few years as industry kicked in.

The trip to Grandma's house took three hours by car. This was a lot better than the six hours by horse and carriage. Buses and trains only ran in the main cities so making your way around wasn't too easy. The journey always started with laughs and carry on. Gavin and I played this game called Blackbirds Out. Every time we saw a bird, we would get points. A blue tit was worth one point; a robin was worth two points and so on, but each time you saw a blackbird you stole the points from the other player. Gavin always had a keen eye for birds and would sometimes win by sixty or seventy points. It was the kind of game that just as you thought it was over and I had won Gavin would shout, "There's a magpie, that's fifty-five points". I would always make the joke that I allowed him to win, but, to tell the truth, he was always much better than me.

Not long into the trip and after all the small talk was finished, we found ourselves saying nothing for ages, and then just as I was about to nod off Gavin would give me a nudge and begin to ask something that had been troubling him. Gavin was never the kind of boy who made it clear when something was wrong or just bothering him. He would rather say nothing and suffer than come and ask someone for help. I remember this one time when he came to my room at about four in the morning. I woke up the minute he opened the door but, not knowing if it was perhaps Dad and one of his stories, I just lay still, pretending I was asleep, like I'd normally do. After standing for about ten minutes he sat down next to the bed. It's a funny feeling when you know something's about to happen and all you want to do is wait. After a few moments, he pulled on the covers.

"Are you awake?" he asked in a rather solemn and low voice.

Not wanting to make it obvious that I was really awake, I pushed myself up off the bed and rubbed the sleep from my eyes. "What is it Gavin?" I said in that kind of still half-sleepy voice.

"Do you promise not to tell anyone if I tell you something?"

Not even stopping to think I came straight out with my reply, "Of course not, is something wrong?"

"Nothing's wrong but I need you to help me." I could hear his voice start to break as he continued. "Do you know Margaret Mullholland? She's one of the girls in my class at school."

"You mean the small girl with the red hair?"

"That's her."

Now the name never meant a thing to me, but I knew there was a little red headed girl that quite fancied him.

"That's the one," he repeated heavily. "She asked me to kiss her today and I just ran away."

"Why did you do that?"

"You must swear you won't laugh."

"I swear, now come out with it."

"Well, it's just I've never held a girl's hand let alone kissed one before and I got scared."

I could feel my cheeks starting to swell just bursting to crack a smile.

Trying to keep myself composed, I started to give some words of wisdom. Although, if the truth be told, I'd never kissed a girl before either, but being the big brother I had to save face by giving advice, even if I knew I wasn't qualified to do so.

"A kiss is just a simple little thing, just like eating an apple," I said, trying to sound confident. At that, he stood up straight, at the same time grabbing me by the hand and dragging me out of bed. "Hold on, Gavin, what are you doing?"

"I want to see what you mean," he whispered as we walked along the hall and down the stairs. Still with my hand firmly in his, we entered the kitchen where he switched the light on, sending my eyes into slant vision.

"Sit down," he said. I took up a seat at the wooden table that sat proudly in the middle of the kitchen floor, while Gavin entered the large larder in the far corner of the room. A few seconds later he re-emerged with one of the biggest rosy red apples you've ever seen. Walking straight over, he pulled out one of the chairs and sat down right next to me. "I want to see, show me."

Looking at Gavin and looking at the apple, which seemed to be growing with every second, I put out my hand and lifted it from his. Holding it very tightly, I started moving it towards my mouth. I could feel my heart starting to beat faster and faster knowing that not only was my explanation of a kiss the most ridiculous thing I'd ever told, but I was now expected to carry it out. Pausing for a moment and looking at Gavin, I placed the apple on the table and just as I started to speak

Gavin looked at me and said one word. That's all it took, just one word and I knew that no matter what I had to carry out this task of the kissing the apple no matter how embarrassing it might be. "Help," that's all he said - H E L P. Four little letters and I was reduced to the smallest animal on the face of the planet.

I picked the apple back up conscious that my every move was being watched and scrutinised by my younger brother. Closing my eyes, I placed the apple to my lips and slowly started to kiss it. The only person I had ever kissed before was Grandma and that was only a peck on the lips. I opened my eyes to find Gavin with his mouth in his hands and not saying a word. As I pulled the apple away, I could feel the warm, sloppy slavers drooling down my chin and landing with a slump on the wooden table.

After a moment's silence, Gavin stood up and said, "Well, that was interesting."

I looked at him slightly confused. "That's all you have to say, is it?"

"I'm tired and going back to bed. I'll see you in the morning". At that, he walked away and started on back up the stairs. I followed behind and as we reached the doors to the bedrooms he stopped and, without so much as turning his head, he said "thanks," entered his room and closed the door. He never mentioned the apple conversation again, and I must admit I was extremely happy that he didn't.

About halfway into our journey, we would stop off at Mrs Cook's tearoom. I was never a great lover of tea or coffee but boy! Did I love Mrs Cook's caramel shortcake! There was this one time when I had fallen at the duck ponds whilst out with Mum and Dad. I cried and cried so much that Dad disappeared and came back hours later after having driven all the way to get me a piece of this fabulous cake. The minute we would walk in the door old Mrs Cook would have the hot chocolate poured and my cake just sitting within sight. She would never put it within hand's reach because she knew I would have eaten it before I'd had "some proper food" as she called it. The walls inside the tearoom were covered from floor to ceiling with recipes that had been left by customers over the years. From little scraps with untidy writing to large headed paper with bold italic text, she even had a recipe from Lord Littlewood, who was one of the richest men in the country. She always gave the best of meals and always made you feel welcome.

I think that's why I loved the place so much, because I felt safe and warm whenever I was there.

After we had been fed and watered, we were off again, and after eating so much food the only thing we could do for the next hour was sleep. We would wake up to the sound of Dad beeping the horn as we drove up the long red shale drive to Grandma's house. By the time we came to a stop, Gran would already be standing at the side of the steps with Jenny, who was Grandma's right hand lady and would often be taken as her sister, although she was much younger than Gran. Seconds after jumping out of the car we would be covered by Grandma's arms, she would grab us tight and all we would hear were the same sweet words we'd be told a hundred times before, "Look at my beautiful little boys."

No matter who or what, there's always something you remember about someone. With Gran, it will always be that light smell of honey and roses she picked up from working in the greenhouse. I always wondered why she kept such lovely flowers cooped up in a small overgrown greenhouse. So I asked her one day and Gran simply replied, "My dear boy, outside the wind blows strong, the rain falls hard and frost kills quicker than a strangler. Irrespective of the weather outside, I can enjoy myself by looking after my flowers in the greenhouse whenever like."

If Gran ever had one true love in her life, it had to be flowers; I think that's why she married our Granddad. Granddad Ian was a botanist and had worked with flowers all his life. They met at a flower show in Ayr and instantly fell in love. I never remember Gran and Granddad ever having an argument or even falling out with each other. We all went out one day to a picture gallery and there in the main hall was a picture that depicted their life in an instant. It was a large oil painting of an elderly man and woman standing under a tree in a massive field of flowers. They were inscribing their names on a tree above an inscription that they had previously made over forty years ago. Love can certainly last a lifetime if the people in love are strong enough to take the good with the bad and the bad with the good.

After the standard welcome from Gran, the first thing on my mind would be the bathroom. Not because I needed to go to the toilet but because in Gran's house she had the biggest bath I've ever seen. It was sunken about four feet into the ground and tiled completely with pure white stone. The taps were bright gold as if polished repeatedly while rows of bottled oils made from the Gran's roses stood proud along the rim nearest the wall. It was the custom for me to go for a bath before I did anything else, so Gran always had it ready for me on my arrival. I don't know how she managed it, but the water was always perfect. As I opened the door, the steam from the waiting hot water would rush into my face as it made its way   upward towards the high patterned ceiling.

In seconds, my clothes would be on the floor and me in the bath. I consider the thought now and can't imagine a child looking forward to having a bath in the way that I did, but it was bliss and heavenly. I loved lying there, as red as a lobster from the heat, stretched out in the water with a wet cloth over my face. It would seem like hours had drifted by and any cares that I had just seemed to be lifted away with the steam. But they were always ready and waiting to be collected again outside the door where the steam would meet the cold air and fall to form a small puddle on the large oak floorboards. On the far side of the bath was a small flight of steps. I would stand up and walk towards them climbing out step by step. Upon reaching the top I would find myself standing for a moment while the water would cool down and run slowly to my feet. After drying myself on the large towels sitting neatly on the sideboard, I would get changed and search for Gran.

Even though the house had over thirty rooms and that's not including the hidden ones, it was never a long search. There were only ever four or five rooms that Gran would use. If she couldn't be found in the greenhouse or the collection room, she would be in the kitchen, failing that her last hiding place would be the games room. After finding her we would all sit together and talk about what Gavin and I had been doing since we'd last seen each other. We never spoke much about Mum and Dad other than silly things like four word questions such as, "Mum and Dad been ok?" Questions like this to a young boy could only be answered by a one-word reply such as "yes."

The first day at Gran's never lasted that long for me. With all the travelling and the excitement, I would find myself falling asleep. I had my own very special bedroom. It had this massive door that took most of my strength to open up but when inside, boy oh boy was it worth every ounce of strength I could summon! The room was in the shape of a triangle with this tiny little bed right in the middle. I swear Gran must have had that bed made a few inches bigger every time we visited because it always seemed to be just the right size. Once, using my feet, I walked from each corner of the bed to the wall. It was just as many steps in every direction, almost as if someone had taken the utmost care to make sure the bed was placed just perfectly.

Scattered from wall to wall were games, books and toys of every sort. Dad said she'd been collecting them for years. Gavin's room was just as wonderful but that never stopped him from sneaking into mine and taking something. Somehow the next day it would be right back in the same place from where it had been taken. Gran never admitted she was the one who returned them and Gavin always thought it was me who found them again, no matter how hard he tried to hide them. It was one of life's little mysteries, and not the only mystery that I would come across in my lifetime.

CHAPTER TWO
Fish & Deer

The day after we arrived, Gavin and I would go fishing in the lake at the back of the house. To the left of the house was a small building and a stable block. Gran told me how the building was no longer used, and that the maids all lived in the main house now. Gran felt it unnecessary to have the maids live in the outbuilding when there were so many empty rooms in the house.

I think it was really because she didn't want to be alone in that great rambling house. Although Mum and Dad were well off, we had never employed a maid, a cook or a cleaner. Dad never liked to think he needed people to run after him, and I quite agreed, although Mum would have gladly taken the assistance. She said looking after us was like running a farm. I think she was trying to tell us we lived like animals.

The lake was massive and took over an hour to walk around. We had this little spot that dipped down into a small hollow where you could catch the sun or the shade depending on how you felt. It was the most perfect fishing spot that I had ever been to in my entire life. It was strange, however, because every time we returned empty-handed, having caught nothing, everyone else just seemed to smile. I should have known they were hiding something from us. It wasn't 'til one day when I accidentally overheard Jenny and Tom the gardener talking that I found out the truth.

"Have them boys not found out there ain't any fish in that water yet Jenny?"

"Sweet Jesus, no. It's been so long now since they have been fishing, that we don't have the heart to tell them."

"They'll find out sooner or later, and I don't want to be around when that happens."

I stopped and thought for a moment about all the times I'd seen Tom and Dad with fish they said they'd caught, when all the time they must have been buying them to make us think there was fish. So they all thought we'd been fooled? Well, two can play at that game. The very next day I spoke to William, who was Gran's chauffeur. I worked on Dad while Gavin did the same on Mum and together we managed to get enough money to enable William to go into town and buy us a dozen of the biggest fish he could find.

Later that afternoon we took our rods and bait and set off the same as we'd done time and time before. William had planted the fish in our fishing bay and all we had to do was sit back and wait. An hour or so later, after working out the extent of our plan, we ran back towards the house with a fish.

"Mum, Dad, look what we caught!"

I've never seen their faces look so surprised. "Well I never," Gran said.

We did the same for the next few hours and, after we'd exhausted our supply, we called it a day. We had nine of the best-looking trout you could ever hope to catch. Gran had them cooked and along with the others in the house we all sat down and ate them that night for dinner.

Later that day, I could hear Dad speaking to Gran. "If the boys were able to catch that amount of fish in only a few hours there must be hundreds of them out there, this could be a small gold mine." Dad's voice was excited. "Why don't you sell permits to fish? Think about it: if there's fish out there, there's money to be made."

The next day the sign was up and the news spread all round the town. By lunchtime we had people who had travelled miles to come and fish. Never had we thought it would get so out of hand. By midday no one had caught a single fish and tempers were starting to flare. We could hear people making all sorts of remarks. "We must be using the wrong bait," one group of men could be heard to say, while others started to get suspicious.

Later that day after everyone had left, we approached Gran, Mum and Dad in the main room. Just before entering, we flipped heads or tails to see who would tell of our hoax. At first, Dad was quite angry but very quickly he came to see that we'd got the better of him, and he liked that. As for Gran, well, she just laughed and laughed. In everything bad there's always some kind of good to come from it, and Dad always tried to find it. The next day he took Gavin and me and we drove to the West Coast. He took us to meet with a man called Mick. From his voice and appearance, I could tell he was an Irish fisherman.

Mick was an old-timer who had fished almost his entire life. After he became unable to go out to sea any more, he opened up a small fish farm. He would breed fish to be released into lochs and fisheries. I then understood what Dad was about to do. Following some bartering and a few white lies, Dad walked towards us with a smile on his face.

"Well boys, we've just bought ourselves two hundred of the finest brown trout you'll find anywhere in Scotland."

"Real live fish," shouted Gavin. "Honest, Dad? Real live fish?"

"We sure have boys and they arrive in the morning." Dad was always known for his ingenious business ideas, and I could tell this was going to be one of his best ever.

Just as he had told us, the very next morning the fish arrived. Loads of little tin containers each holding a precious cargo of fish. They were unloaded at the side of the lake and Mick could be seen pushing a large wooden boat out to

21

the centre of the water. He must have been out there for hours. From where we were, all we could see was the hood from his big green coat bobbing up and down. And every so often there would be a splash.

"What's he doing, Dad?" I asked.

"Before the fish are released, they need to grow a little bigger and get used to the water. Then we can set them loose for people to fish, after all no one wants to catch tiny little fish now, do they?"

It took a little time but the fishery really took off. Old Mick moved his breeding business to the estate and lived in the old stable block and Dad employed a few locals to help run the business and keep poachers away. To this very day, people still fish that water and have managed to catch some really big fish.

It's funny how life can turn around so quickly and especially when you least expect it; I can certainly testify to that. The rest of our stay at Gran's house would consist of long walks, picnics and, best of all, adventures. I remember this one time when we met a young boy called Mark. He was a local boy who would play in the woods that surrounded the house. We met him one day while out looking for deer. The deer would often come into the woods and travel as far down as the lake. Sometimes, if you awoke early enough in the morning, you would see them standing about by the water. They always looked so peaceful but at the same time always on their guard. There was one in particular that would emerge from the trees and slowly walk to the waterside where he would drink. A few moments later the others would then join in, but one always stayed close to the tree line as if on look out. We often played with Mark and had many good adventures in the woods with him until one day he just never came back. We never heard from him and no one we spoke to would tell us why. It still remains a mystery to this very day.

It was on our eleventh day at Gran's on an October

morning when I awoke and there through the condensation on the window I could see a small group of doe gathered by the water. It was such a peaceful morning. The sun was just rising and the sky was of a somewhat shade of red. You could see the grass glitter in the dew like a field of bright green emeralds. I found myself standing, face pressed against the cold wet glass, and imagining what it would be like to stand there with them, what it would be like to touch their brown coarse hair. It's at times like that when you can reflect on life and truly wonder about what could be, and what never will be.

It was on that morning that something changed for me, something that has haunted me ever since. While standing there oblivious to the real world and flying through my own thoughts and dreams, a sound rang out that travelled for miles, hitting against every wall, tree and hill it could find. Echoing and echoing as if it had happened several times. All except one of the doe took flight and stampeded towards the woods. The one that didn't move had a large ginger stripe along the left-hand side of its body. It stood still as if frozen in time before, suddenly and without warning, like a puppet having its strings cut it fell to the ground. Realising what had happened, I ran from the room and down the stairs. Almost running out the main door, I stopped and grabbed the large metal bell from the side-table that Gran used to help call us in for lunch. I unlocked the door and ran towards the doe ringing the bell as hard as my arms would allow. Three men emerged from the trees all carrying shotguns dressed in fur coats and boots. Upon seeing me running towards them, they stopped and looked at each other. There was me, a young boy in pyjamas with nothing on his feet, ringing a bell. As I charged towards them, I knew they had guns, but the men and their weapons seemed insignificant. It was the doe that held every ounce of my attention. I got within fifty yards of the men before they suddenly turned about and ran off into the woods.

Finally I found myself standing at the side of Ginger. I had prevented the poachers from claiming the underserved prize, but by the looks of it, the damage had already been done. I could hear myself say "Ginger.... are you ok, Ginger?" but nothing. I'd never called any of the doe by name before, but it seemed a respectable thing to do at the time. I sat down on the grass and touched her hair. It felt just like how I'd imagined, coarse but soft and it had stickiness like sleepy willows. Putting out my hands, I submerged them into the blood that was flowing onto the grass, forming a large dark red pool. Steam was rising from its warmth and I had visions of her spirit evaporating up into the sky. I'm not sure why but I felt compelled to place my arms around her and hold her tight. After all, her friends had all fled, fearing death, leaving her all alone. The tears started to stream from my eyes uncontrollably and my first ever feelings of sorrow fell over me, crushing every inch of my body.

Moments later, I looked up to find the entire family huddled around me. No one said anything as if paying some kind of mark of respect to this departed animal's soul. I lay there cold and wet with blood, not able to move or speak.

Dad was the first to break the silence. "Son, let's get in and get you cleaned up, eh?" He put out his hand and raised me from the ground. We walked back towards the house while the others stayed standing around the dead body of the doe.

I felt numb and disheartened as if part of me had died with her. When we entered the house Dad took me straight to a bathroom and sat me on the toilet while he ran a bath. Dad gave me a hand to get the blood soaked clothes off and I walked into the bath. I lay there, still crying, while he attempted to reassure me, then something he said struck a chord.

"Look son, in life we only ever have one guarantee, and no matter what anyone tells you, never forget that the only certainty a man has in life is that one day he will die. Death is only a scary feeling to the man who doesn't like the feeling of not knowing. No matter what religion tells us, no one knows for sure where we go. Or what happens to us when we die, but one thing is for sure, we all have a purpose."

After hearing those words, I understood something about life that day and about death.

The rest of that day I stayed in bed and didn't talk much to anyone. Not long after lunch time there was a knock on the door. "Can I come in?" It was Gavin.

It took a few seconds to summon the breath to talk, "sure," it wasn't much of an invite but it was the best I could do.

He sat down on the end of the bed and looked towards the floor. We never looked at each other and said nothing for what seemed like ages. Then Gavin stood up and walked over to the window. "I don't know why you're so upset, it was only an animal, it's not like it was a person or someone you knew for real."

It wasn't the time or the place to have an argument or to try and explain the feelings I was experiencing. The last thing I needed was for someone to tell me what I should be caring about and how animals are only animals after all. To this very day, I don't know exactly why I reacted the way I did but one thing's for sure; I never felt embarrassed or weak because I let it be seen by others.

Still standing by the window, Gavin turned and told me that Dad had decided to take us home. I could hear in his voice that he thought I had spoiled the trip for everyone, but I knew Dad just wanted me to be away from this place. The following day we packed up and left to go home. It was one of those journeys when no one says a word. The compact air inside the car was heavy with deep thought. Gavin was sitting as far away from me as he possibly could and never made eye contact the whole way home. The trip lasted a lifetime and I was glad when we eventually arrived home.

I took my bags upstairs and then immediately went for a walk. I needed to be alone and have some time to myself. I needed to think about the cruelty of death, and wanted to make sure I had dealt with my emotions properly; that I hadn't just stored them in a box in the back my mind to arrive back in my life at some later point.

CHAPTER THREE
A New Friend

I chose to walk along Old Edinburgh Road. This was a stretch of road that lasted for five whole miles before it made a single bend. Dad told me the Romans had built it many years ago. It was a road I had walked several times before but no matter how many times I would walk it, there would always be something new to see. Things that when you didn't pay attention you missed. For instance, one time while walking this road I noticed a small opening in the hedges on the side of the road. I jumped down the embankment and through the small entrance to find a path leading to a burn. It was only a few feet wide but all around was covered with blackberries and raspberries; it was a jam maker's heaven. How many people knew about that spot I don't know, but to the people that did it must have been a very special place indeed.

I was only a few miles along the road when I could see someone walking towards me. He must have been about half a mile away so I never thought much about it until he got closer. He was wearing brown tatty boots and old torn clothes hanging by their last threads. Quickly, I released who it was. It was Jamie Richardson. I had last seen him the day when I had tried to stop my friends teasing him as he walked down the road with a cow.

We came closer and closer until we were literally feet apart. I kept looking down and walked straight past him.

Being two different kinds of people, from two different social backgrounds, we would never normally stop and talk to each other but something somehow made me pause. I felt a kind of pull inside me as I rooted to the spot, my back still turned to Jamie. I listened but could hear nothing, not a single footstep. Turning around, I saw that Jamie had also stopped, and we were now facing each other but saying nothing. I started to speak but at the same point so did he.

"You go," he spoke quietly.

I looked at him, knowing what I wanted to say but feeling ashamed. "Sorry."

"There's no need to be sorry, you haven't done anything wrong," he replied.

"Oh, yes, I have, Jamie."

"You know my name? How do you know who I am?"

"Everyone knows who you are."

"Ah, the sweet shop, I suppose."

"Well... yes"

"It never happened the way you think."

"What didn't?"

"I never stole the chocolate."

"I never said you did."

"But that's what everyone thinks. I went to the shop that day, that much is true, but I never went to steal. I had worked all year long and anything I earned helped to feed us, but this one day I took some of the money I had earned to buy a chocolate bar for my sister Mary. It was her birthday and I always tried to buy her something. It was never much but at least it was something. I walked into the shop and picked it up; I never stayed in the shop long because I know I'm not welcome there. So I took it straight to the counter and paid for it. There was a young boy on the counter; I thought he was Mr Green's son. I paid him and started to make my way to the door when I heard Mr Green shouting from behind 'Stop thief!' I looked around but couldn't see anyone else. All I seen was that big fat Mr

Green running towards me. He grabbed me by the ear and pulled me into the small office at the back of the shop. The young boy who I paid just stood there and said nothing. He knew I'd paid for it, but made me out to look like a thief and a liar. As a result, I had to work for him for nothing washing floors and cleaning the store, and Mary never got a present.

"I later spoke to the boy who had caused me all the trouble. His name was Allan and he was indeed Mr Green's son. I asked him why he did what he did, but he wouldn't give me an answer. I confronted him in the storeroom one day and we started to fight. What I didn't know was that Mr Green was standing right outside and heard every word we'd said."

"That must have been that time Allan came to school with a black eye," I interrupted.

"That's right. Mr Green instantly stepped in and asked Allan to go upstairs to his room. He asked me to forgive him and told me how sorry he was for not believing me. Telling me to wait a moment, he went back into the shop. A few seconds later, he returned with a large bag of chocolate and sweets for me, and food for Mum.

"He told me I could go and promised to tell Constable Irwin that everything had been a big misunderstanding. Just before leaving he asked me to keep the matter quiet, to which I agreed."

"Why keep it quiet, Jamie? Mr Green was wrong to ask you to do that."

"Maybe, but he could always say I was lying; I was caught between the devil and the deep blue sea."

"It wasn't the easiest predicament, I can see that. You must have been so angry."

"You can say that again."

We started to walk back into town but stopped and took a seat on the old stone wall around Moore farm. We sat there for about an hour just talking. We were both about the same age and, quite surprisingly, we shared very similar interests. The only evident difference was our social background. We sat there like chalk and cheese; two boys who would be about to take an adventure through life but neither of us could have guessed what would be in store for us.

Walking back into town, before we said goodbye and went our separate ways, we agreed to meet up the following day. Opening the door into the house that night, I felt much better than I'd been feeling early that day. The whole day's experiences had geared me to becoming a better person and a greater man in life. On entering the front door I could hear Mum and Dad shouting.

"He's always been the one for you, all the time it's him and never Gavin or me!" It was Mum's voice. I stood there in the hallway and glanced up the staircase to see Gavin sitting on the top step, I could see he'd been crying.

I walked up the stairs and sat down beside him. For ages we listened to them arguing. Gavin didn't talk much; he just sat there with his head pressing against the spindles of the staircase.

"It's not your fault," he said, turning to look at me. "Mum's just sad because Dad pays you a lot of attention."

"You don't feel like that, do you?"

"Of course not! Dad spends loads of time with me, with both of us." At that, he threw his arms around me. "I love you."

I was taken aback slightly because this was totally out of character for Gavin. Something seemed wrong, Mum and Dad often argued but he'd never cried like this before. He either heard something I didn't or was just feeling very emotional. I very simply replied, "me too."

It was getting late so we made our way to our beds. I was just getting ready when Gavin knocked on the door and walked in.

"Do you mind if I sleep in here tonight?"

"Sure, jump in." My emotions had showed the last few days with the doe, but now it seemed like it was Gavin's turn. We both lay there looking up at the ceiling in deep thought. It took a while but Gavin eventually fell asleep, I found myself looking at him for a while. If you've ever looked at someone's face while they were asleep you'll understand what I mean when I say, "it's a cross between death and life". The expression on a sleeping face is innocent and pure; it's never judgmental or shows emotions of any sort. Even the most evil of men look harmless when sleeping.

I woke the following morning to find Gavin had gone. The smell of frying bacon was filling the room. I had not eaten much the previous day so I had an immediate attack of hunger. I jumped out of bed and down the stairs to the kitchen. The smell of food got stronger and stronger the closer I got. Opening the door, I could see Mum, Dad and Gavin sitting around the table eating a massive breakfast.

"Oh! One of the living dead has risen," said Mum whilst Dad added, looking at his watch, "Someone must have been tired last night."

"How? What's the time?"

"It's eleven thirty, sleepy."

"Oh no!" I remembered I was meeting Jamie at twelve o'clock. I ran back up stairs and into the bathroom. I brushed my teeth, and got washed and changed as quickly as possible.

"Where are you off to in a hurry? You've not even had anything to eat."

I grabbed a few slices of toast and disappeared out the back door. "I'll be back later; I'm away out with some friends."

"See you later," called Dad.

It's funny to think that yesterday Mum and Dad were going at it hammer and tong and Gavin was feeling really sad, but this morning all seemed as normal. That's the thing with families, anything can happen one minute and be the exact different the next. Being a family member is like playing a great big board game. You take the good with the bad and keep going no matter what until you can't go any more. I just didn't know how many more throws of the dice our particular board game had left.

I ran along the main street and into the common green where Jamie was standing under the massive silver birch tree in the middle of the common.

"Sorry I'm late."

"It's ok; I only just got here myself".

It's funny looking back at that first meeting with Jamie. For me, it was just like meeting any friend but for him it was different. It didn't strike me until later that day just how much effort he'd actually put into our meeting. He was wearing a new pair of boots and fresh clean clothes. I'd never seen him dressed like this before, but in this condition he would have passed as a rich man's son any day of the week.

"Well what shall we do then?" asked Jamie.

I thought for a second for something interesting, "Have you ever been on a tree-swing?"

"No."

"Well let's go then."

We walked out of town and towards the White Lady woods. The woods were lighter than usual as the leaves had started to fall from the trees. It would normally have been much darker as the light tried to find its way through the tangled mesh of branches and leaves that hung overhead in the summer. The woods were alive with noise. The magical music of the birds had disappeared leaving only the calming sound of the waterfall as it ran down and the river splashing against the large cobbles and boulders that lay on its bed.

We talked all the while we walked along the hard mud path, looking like two old friends with no cares in the world, happy and with everything to look forward to. Or at least that's what it seemed like then. Little did I know things were about to explode around us.

We talked about trivial things such as brothers and sisters, what our interests were until we reached the clearing, and there it was. This massive trunk of a tree, most of its branches had been destroyed over the years. Only a few remained at the very top, which must have been about a hundred feet in the air. All around the base were carvings of names from the people that frequented it. Over the years it had lost its glory and not so many people visited it anymore. The story goes that a young boy by the name of Harold had been killed when he fell off. He had run away from home and had met some of the local boys. They pushed him and pushed faster and faster and never stopped even after he had started to cry. They thought it has fun until he fell and broke his neck when he crashed against the rocks in the water below. They say his ghost still haunts the area to this very day.

Ghost or no ghost, I never let it put me off going, and in fact it made it all that little bit more interesting. We stood for a second admiring the view and then headed over to make sure it was still in working order.

"Would you look at that? It's fantastic. Much bigger than I imagined."

Standing at the side of the swing you could see the swollen roots of the tree bursting out all over the ground. The tree sat about eight feet away from where the land fell sharply to form a gully with a small river running through it. Jamie's impatience was written all over his face. The way in which his smile grew from ear to ear was amazing to watch. It was as if someone had just given him the best birthday present ever.

"Can we start?" he asked anxiously.

"Sure." I was about to preach about safety but before I could say another word he was away.

"This is great, look how high I can get." He was so good I couldn't help think he should have joined a travelling circus. He flew through the air being more adventurous with every swing. We played for ages and lost all track of time. Jamie had taken time to relieve himself behind the tree when I heard him shout. "What's the time?"

"It's coming up half past one."

"Oh God! I'm late! I have to be at work for two. Sorry, but I have to go." For those few hours, I had forgotten that Jamie wasn't any ordinary boy, and had all sorts of responsibilities to take care of. We ran the best part of the way back to town and we quickly made arrangements for when we would meet next.

I was starving; I'd only eaten a few slices of toast all day. I got home to the smell of baking. Mum had been busy making cakes and anyone who knew Mum would tell you she made some of the best cakes you could find. There was never a year that went by when she didn't win a prize at the summer fair. Boy, was I glad to follow those strong smells of lemon and hot treacle into the kitchen!

"Where have you been all afternoon? Get your face and hands washed and come and have some lunch, now. Hurry up!" The two most important things as far as Mum was concerned were being clean and being well fed. The lads hated it when Mum would ask them to get their faces washed. But they all knew good food was the reward.

The rest of that day was filled with questions from Gavin. "Where have you been then? I was looking for you with David and Richard but we couldn't find you."

I paused for a second, then, without thinking, mumbled a sentence, "Erm, I was out looking for you but we must have missed each other."

"I thought this morning you said you were going out to see a friend?"

"Well, yea, that's right, but he had to go home because he didn't feel too good."

"So who was it then? Anyone I know, was it?"

"No, no. Just a friend." I wasn't embarrassed about Jamie, but I knew my friends wouldn't understand why I liked him, especially Gavin.

"Ahhh, so it's like that then is it?" Before I could say any more he marched off.

Upsetting Gavin was the least of my concerns at that moment. I had school the next day and had a great pile of homework to get through. Mrs Greenshields was my teacher and, although we got on pretty well, she hated anyone who handed in their homework late. To most people school was an inconvenience, but to me it was a chance to drift into a second life. I was by no means the star pupil of the class but I was definitely in the top five. I loved to learn and made every effort to find out one new fact everyday. In my last school report, Mrs Greenshields compared me to sponge. She said that I "loved taking in information like a sponge soaked up water."

The following morning I was up bright and breezy. The bath was so hot I had to leave it a while, so went down stairs for breakfast while it cooled. Gavin hated getting up in the morning, and all you could hear were Mum and Dad calling to get him up. "I won't ask you again, young man!" Dad shouted abruptly. The thundering noise of Gavin stamping about upstairs rang through the floorboards along with his shallow grunts and groans. We walked to school that day in the cold. It was a wintry day and the ground stood rock hard. The sounds of the birds had disappeared leaving behind the low murmur of the fierce fires from the steel works in Blacksmiths Fires.

I only had a year left at school and Dad was hoping I was going to start working with him at Candermill Properties. It was a family run company owned by Dad and Uncle Simon. They owned a whole load of properties that they rented out to help build new ones. I never thought much about what life would be like after school but working with Dad wasn't a bad idea.

We arrived just as old Mrs Brodie started to ring the old heavy bell. Everyone knew that the minute she started to ring that bell they had to stop at once and line up outside ready to be counted in. The yard went quiet as everyone stopped playing and immediately started to form up outside the two red doors. Each door had a name plaque above it. That on the left had 'BOYS' and that on the right 'GIRLS'. Silently we would stand waiting to be allowed inside. School that day went in incredibly quickly and all too soon I found myself outside with Gavin and the lads ready to go home.

"So what did you get up to yesterday?" asked David in a slightly suspicious voice.

"Nothing much, just went for a walk." I turned to look at Gavin, knowing he would be bursting to say something but before I had a chance to throw him a killing stare his mouth was open and the words had started to flow.

"I think he has a girlfriend, boys."

"You what? Have you gone soft or something?" Although it came as a surprise, I was relieved to think they thought it was a girlfriend. It was complete nonsense but I preferred they thought that rather than them knowing the truth.

Standing there looking around, I realised that my circle of friends was soon going to change. It wasn't a rash spur of the moment decision but was one that had been stirring around in my thoughts for a long time.

"Well, what are we doing then?" asked David, sitting on what was left of the big old tree that once stood outside the front of the school. It had been cut down because there were too many accidents with people falling off it, or so the headmaster said. We all knew it was because when you stood on the very last branch you could see straight into the girl's toilets.

"I know," Richard shouted, "we can go fishing!"

"Don't be stupid, it's far too cold and the fishing season's almost over."

"Well, you think of something then and don't call me stupid." Richard wasn't the cleverest person in the world and it showed. No matter what they decided I knew I wasn't able to stick around. I had arranged to meet Jamie.

"Sorry lads, but I have to go; I have so much homework tonight."

"Well, don't let us keep you, teacher's pet, run along and be a good boy." David was always a loud mouth and hated the fact that I enjoyed school, so his remarks came as no surprise.

With a shrug of my shoulders I turned and left, with Gavin closely behind.

"You're such a liar! You don't have any homework; you did it all last night."

"Well, maybe I don't but I have other plans."

"So all of a sudden you like to keep secrets from your brother, do you?"

"It's not like that, you wouldn't understand."

"So who is she then, eh?"

"It's not a girl; I'm just busy with something, that's all." We walked the rest of the way home not saying much. I hated not telling him the truth and I knew he would find out sooner or later, but now wasn't the time.

We arrived home and I quickly ran upstairs while Gavin went to the kitchen.

"What's for dinner Mum?" I could hear him ask.

"You'll just have to wait and see," Mum called from the back of the larder.

I was changed and on my way back down the stairs when Gavin was making his way up. "You ain't going to see a girl like that, I hope?"

I laughed his snide remarks off as though I'd thought he'd said something funny. On entering the kitchen, I could see Mum had started to put the dinner out on the table.

"Did you have a nice day at school?" Mum always asked this question but I had the impression that it just came naturally to her. I often thought I could say anything after that question and she wouldn't really hear what I had replied.

Dinner consisted of cooked ham and potatoes with a slab of bread that could have made a good doorstop. I ate as quickly as my teeth would chew, so I could go out to meet Jamie. When I finished I could hear my stomach screaming, as though I had just attacked it with a bombardment of oversized lumps of food. But I ignored that as I tore out of the door so as not to be late.

CHAPTER FOUR
Work Experience

Just as we had agreed, Jamie was waiting there.

"How you doing?" he asked, grinning.

"Just grand."

"Do you feel up to doing some work?"

"What kind of work?"

"I have a small job to do before I can call it a day; I'm supposed to milk the cows at the Riverdale farm."

I never gave it a second thought and before you could say a word we were off. It took about ten minutes to get to the farm but it passed by extremely quickly, while the thoughts of milking cows ran wildly around in my head. Jamie was explaining how it was done, but I was finding the whole thing far too amusing to listen to him.

The smell from the farm was disgusting; it was rich with ammonia that lingered around like a bad shadow. We entered a large, barn-style building and inside were two long rows of metal stalls each holding what looked like a hundred cows. Right along the middle was a large hanging metal structure. It had loads of pipes and glass bottles hanging from it. The smell inside, although still disgusting, was slightly different; it had a dry, musty kind of taste that made you cough if you inhaled too quickly. As we walked down the middle of the building, I could see that the cows were all facing the other way and seemed to be eating.

"You ready for you're first milking then?"

I looked at him with apprehension, then, in a slightly uncertain voice, answered, "Of course I am."

"Just wait a second and I'll be right back," shouted Jamie, as he walked into a room at the far end of the barn. A few seconds later, the noise of machinery starting up rang throughout the entire building. The bottles started clanking and the hoses pulsed up and down with strength. It was as if the barn was coming alive. The cows didn't seem startled at all; they just continued to eat without so much as turning their heads.

"Impressive, ain't it," said Jamie, emerging from the backroom. "Mr McNeil spent his life savings on this new technology. He owns this farm. He said he will knock the competition for dead with all this stuff." I remember thinking that if it worked half as good as it looked it must be pretty impressive. "Just grab those suckers and I'll show you what to do."

I reached up and grabbed a thick black rubber hose that had four suckers on the end it and handed it to Jamie. He knelt down on the smooth polished stone floor, pulling me at the same time to do the same.

"All you have to do is stick a sucker on each teat and the machinery does the rest," he yelled over the noise. After Jamie put the last sucker in place he pointed behind us. "Look!" The large glass bottle nearest us was filling with milk. It was amazing. "You see, it's easy. Grab another set and give it a shot."

I reached up for the second time and grabbed a set of suckers. Slowly kneeling down at the next cow, I put the suckers under the metal bar and reached for the cow's udder. The uncontrollable shaking of my hands was worsened by the heavy pulsing of the hose. Slowly, I placed each sucker in place until all four were on.

"I've done it!!" I shouted excitedly. "I've milked a bloody cow!" I turned to see Jamie had already finished the whole of the left side and had started on the other.

I walked down the building watching the bottles fill with the pure white milk. I had drunk milk hundreds of times but I'd never imagined for one minute this was how it ended up in the bottle on the breakfast table.

Jamie glanced up from beneath a cow. "Grab another one then, we don't have all day."

I started at the other end and in no time all the cows were being milked. What a marvellous sight it was to see. The horrid smell had long since disappeared, overpowered by all the excitement, and I found myself gazing at the bottles which were now nearly completely full. Just as the last bottle was about to overflow, Jamie ran into the back room again and the machinery died a sudden death. The hoses ceased to pulse and the only noise now came from the cows that were still chewing on their food.

A few seconds later, the sound of squeaky wheels turning seemed to grow closer and closer. Seconds later, Jamie flew out the backroom on a somewhat rusty looking trolley.

"Bet you never thought milking a cow could be such fun," he screamed as he came winging towards me. I just laughed and watched as he came to a stop almost crashing into the shelves holding the milk bottles. "All we need to do now is get the bottles on the trolley and empty them into the tank."

The bottles were large and weighed a ton. I felt embarrassed watching Jamie throw the bottle onto the trolley with ease while I struggled to lift even one. "Don't worry you'll get used to it," Jamie said in an attempt to make me feel better.

After three trips with the trolley we had emptied all the bottles into a large drum ready for collection. We then had to rinse out the bottles with a large water hose and some special soap that felt like sandpaper. The temptation for Jamie must have been too great because just after bending down to soap out some of the bottles he suddenly attacked me with a great whoosh of water.

"You think I'll let you get away with that, do you?" Lunging toward him I grabbed the hose and before I knew it the water was going all over the place. We laughed and shouted while we soaked each other, then all of a sudden the water went off.

"What in God's name's going on in 'ere? Jamie you ain't 'arf got some explaining to do."

I stopped and stood still watching while Jamie ran towards whom I could only presume was Farmer McNeil. They both walked out of the room, Jamie dripping with water, and stopped just outside the door.

"Sorry, Farmer McNeil. I was just showing my friend how to milk and I just got carried away."

There was a slight pause but then suddenly the building erupted with the thundering laughter of the huge farmer. "My dear boys get yourselves inside an' Mrs McNeill will get yer both cleaned up, now get going, I'll sort this mess."

Farmer McNeil peered round the corned and looked at me as though scanning me from top to toe. "You an' all, boy, get going."

We ran out the barn and simultaneously started to laugh. "I thought he was going to go crazy, he looked ready to explode."

"You've never met Farmer McNeil before, have you?" asked Jamie.

"How'd you know?"

"He's a bit scary if you don't know him. But he's really harmless. He's been like a Father to me."

Mr McNeil was about seven feet tall and built like a bull. His hair was dark brown and very heavy looking with curls. His head seemed to be far too small for his body and he wore several layers of very tight fitting clothes.

We walked toward a large farmhouse that was centred in the middle of a cobbled courtyard. There were chickens, goats and all sorts of other animals just walking around.

Just as we neared the large front door, it suddenly bounced open to reveal a large woman dressed in a blue skirt and shirt with a large white apron wrapped around her. Her light chuckle snowballed into coarse laugh as she saw the state we were in. "What on earth have you boys been up to?"

"Sorry Mrs Mac but we got a little carried away in the milking house, and had a fight with the hose."

"Stop talking and get yourselves inside before you catch the death of cold." She hurried us along a wide tall hall before hustling us into a room with a large log fire. "The both of you wait here a moment, I'll be right back."

We stood there dripping on the shiny wooden floor and seconds later the larger than life woman came thundering back into the room. In her hands she had two massive towels held tight against her chest. "Right, boys, get your clothes off and get dried, shout when they're all off and I'll come and get them." At that, she turned and walked out of the room closing the massive door behind her.

Jamie immediately started to get undressed, throwing his soaking clothes on the floor. He looked over at me and paused before speaking. "No need to be embarrassed. You don't have anything I ain't seen before, or don't have myself."

With my face bright red and feeling rather stupid and slightly scared, I started to get undressed, taking my time to see if she actually meant everything. Jamie obviously had no problem with being naked in front of people, but I'd never even seen Gavin naked let alone anyone else. I found myself standing there with Jamie who had absolutely nothing on but drips of wet cold water on his skin, bare to the world and I felt uncomfortable. It's funny, thinking about it now, but all it took was one look at Jamie and I realised I had nothing to be scared or worried about. It's true what they say: "A man measures himself according to the men around him." In this situation, I could clearly see that Jamie and I were both on the same scale.

I proceeded to strip down to the bare essentials and walked casually over to the wooden seat where Mrs Mac had placed the towels. Jamie was already engulfed in a large blue towel that covered him like a large cloak from head to toe. I wasn't sure if he was drying himself or pretending to be some kind of ghost. I dried off in front of the fire, which was now turning my naked skin scarlet red from the heat.

As I had the towel around my ankles and was drying my feet, Jamie's head popped out from the top of his towel at the same time his voice bellowed, "Mrs Mac, we're ready". Without giving me time to think, Mrs Mac opened the door and started collecting the wet clothes from the floor. If I had previously been embarrassed, I was certainly even more so now. I grabbed the towel, which was lying at my feet, and quickly covered myself. I could see Jamie ready to burst out laughing because he knew he'd caught me off guard.

"I'll take these clothes to the mangle and then hang them up to dry in front of the fire, and then I'll fetch you boys something hot to drink."

The second she walked out the door Jamie exploded in laughter. Tears streaming from his eyes while his hands kept trying to keep his towel from falling down. "You should have seen your face; it was the funniest thing I've seen in ages."

Although still embarrassed at having just exposed myself to Mrs Mac, the funny side shone through and I couldn't help but laugh myself. We took up a seat by the fire wrapped in the towels and talked about the day's events, Jamie bursting into laughter every now and then when the thought of Mrs Mac seeing me bare naked came back into his head.

No matter what would happen in the years to come

that was truly a day to remember and I've never forgotten it since. We'd only been sitting a few minutes when Mrs Mac arrived back holding two big mugs of sweet hot chocolate in her hands and our now semi-dried clothes draped over each of her arms. I couldn't stop thinking this must have been a woman who never stopped working all day.

"Here you go boys, get this into your stomachs and you'll feel much better." Like a mother would hang stockings up on the fireplace at Christmas, Mrs Mac hung our clothes on the sleeper-like mantelpiece to dry. You could see the steam rise from the clothes as if they were cooking, but in no time they were bone dry and ready to wear again. After we had drunk the chocolate and had eaten a whole tray full of homemade fruit biscuits, we got dressed. Mrs Mac appeared once more and whisked away the damp towels from the floor.

"Come on then, boys, you'd best be getting yourselves home now, it's getting late," said Mrs Mac as she left the room.

That day was truly one of the best days of my life. I'd experienced a whole load of new things that I would never have considered doing if it wasn't for Jamie. Somehow that day he'd spun me around to seeing life differently. I saw how the simplest things in life could make a person happy without the need for riches or fanciness. We walked back into town still laughing about what the last few hours had brought and departed at, what was now, our usual place.

"Well, thanks again for a great time. It's been a day to remember."

"It's nothing, but it's your turn to think of what we're doing next."

"I sure will, see you tomorrow."

"Yeah, see you." At that, we turned and walked our separate ways. The rest of the walk home felt as if it only lasted a few minutes and although the sky was dark, the world seemed to be clearer now than it had ever been before. I felt a massive smile on my face the size of a rainbow stretching from ear to ear and couldn't help but feel jolly.

CHAPTER FIVE
The Big Dinner

Mum had supper ready when I got home but Mrs Mac's fruit biscuits had more than filled me up.

"Your supper's ready," Mum announced on hearing the door close. I walked into the kitchen to see a feast of bread and jam strewn all over the table. Mum, Dad and Gavin were all sitting around it just ready to start.

"Well, don't stand around, sit yourself down." Said Dad, pointing to an empty seat. Not wanting to disappoint anyone, I sat down and slipped a plate into position from the pile that sat neatly one on top of the other in the middle of the table.

"So, what have you been up to these last few days? I've seen neither hide nor hair of you," asked Dad as he waved a slice of bread.

"Oh, I've just been out and about, nothing special." I could see Gavin's eyes squint towards me waiting to see if he could discern any weakness in my words. He knew something was going on but wasn't quite sure what. I wasn't going to be able to keep Jamie a secret. Sooner or later, they would have to know so this was going to be as good a time as any. I scooped up some of Mum's homemade plum jam and plopped it onto my plate, making a conscious effort not to make eye contact with anyone before coming straight out with it. "Is it ok if I bring a friend home for dinner on Thursday?"

The deep sound of food being chewed stopped and the clatter of knives being simultaneously laid on the table dropped the room into silence. Now, I'd purposely asked my question openly without directing it to anyone in particular, but I knew Dad would be the first person to speak. "Of course you can, son."

"Is it anyone we know?" Mum followed in her nosy, upper-class voice.

"No, it's a new friend. No one you've ever met."

The conversation never went anywhere after that. I ate a little food then asked to be excused. I left the table and floated upstairs still full of glee from the day's events. It seems somewhat strange when considering it now, but after seeing Jamie standing there brass necked and naked with not so much as a care about what I may have been thinking I understood that my body wasn't something to hide or be embarrassed about. As a child I was a late developer, so my body and manhood was always something that I considered extremely personal. But today showed me it was nothing to be worried about and when standing next to Jamie I could see that, even as a late developer, I wasn't that far behind.

Before stepping into the bath that night, I stopped and stood in front of the large rectangular mirror that hung on the wall. It was about three feet wide and seven feet long, so standing in front of it you could see your entire body in full as though looking at someone else. In a composed position, I scoured every inch of visible skin and for the first time I experienced my first emotions of what I could only describe as sexual. I could feel a warm swelling in my chest and a sudden urge to relax. Without going into too much detail, it was that same night that I understood my manhood had more than just one job to fulfil.

Thursday came all too quickly due to the fact Wednesday was full of questions and sly comments from David and the others. Gavin had decided to wait and say nothing until we would arrive at the dinner table. Getting home from school, I was full of nerves, not because I was worried but because I couldn't know for sure what was going to happen; I could only guess. No matter what, Dad was going to be fine but Mum and Gavin had minds of their own. Knowing Gavin's sentiments from our previous engagement with Jamie, I could almost guarantee how he would react with his look of disbelief that I had brought this poor boy to our dinner table, and Mum would be the one to speak constantly, fishing for information while watching his every move.

I felt apprehensive; my heart was beating quickly and I jumped when suddenly the doorbell rang. I paused at the door before opening it and seeing Jamie standing there ready and waiting. Except on this occasion he was standing dressed in a pair of dark blue trousers with a matching shirt and shiny black shoes that had little metal buckles on the front. His face and hair were gleaming as if he had spent all day polishing himself.

My steps towards him slowed down and became almost baby-like. A feeling of anger had started to drain all the good from within. I had expected to see the Jamie that I had started to know and become friends with, but instead here was this person standing who looked very like Jamie but at the same time didn't look like him. There was something very familiar about him. I approached but before I could speak Jamie had beaten me to it.

"Well I'm ready if you're ready?" he said. I sensed a sound of nervousness in his voice. I wasn't quite sure why but he seemed to have an itch about him. It was as if he had planned this day for years and it had finally arrived.

"You didn't have to go to any trouble, Jamie, it's only dinner at my house," I said, slightly crossly.

"You know what Mums are like," he explained. "I told her I was going to dinner at yours and she wouldn't let me leave until I was presentable - as she calls it."

I looked at him searchingly, as his words didn't quite ring true but he just smiled back at me.

"Are you going to invite me in?" he nodded to the door. I smiled, banishing my doubts.

"Of course," I swept my hand toward the front door.

"It's an impressive house," he nodded in appreciation, and I again felt the gnawing of doubt - or surprise. Instead of being overwhelmed he seemed just appreciative. As though he could easily become accustomed to such grandeur - or already was?

"It's the family home," I shrugged, trying not to sound big headed. I wanted to play the conversation down as I knew the only reason why I was living in this large house was because I was born wealthy and not everyone was as fortunate as I was.

Jamie glanced at the marble front steps then transferred his gaze to the polished wooden floorboards in the hallway. Mum must have been watching for us to appear at the bottom of the street because the moment we walked in the front door there she was waiting to greet us, staring at us in surprise.

"Mum, this is Jamie."

"Nice to meet you, Jamie," she gasped, a smile quickly replacing her odd expression. "I must just check the food," she said, turning quickly towards the kitchen.

We walked into the main room where Dad was resting. He was sitting legs crossed with one arm over the back of the chair and the other lying across his legs. He allowed us to watch him as he attempted to look casual, as if pondering a clue in a crossword, before he looked over at us.

"Hello there, son," he greeted in a rather inquisitive voice. "This must be our dinner guest for this evening."

"Yes, sorry Dad, this is my friend Jamie."

Dad seemed very surprised when Jamie turned around from looking about the room. He paused for a moment before speaking again, seemingly wrong-footed by something. It was unusual for Dad, who always had something to say. "Erm, hi, nice to meet you," he said finally.

I could see Jamie twitch his head towards me with a stare. Giving his attention back to Dad, Jamie replied, "Thank y-y-you sir."

"I hope you have a healthy appetite because there's enough food been cooked to feed the entire town."

"I haven't eaten much all day sir," he said agreeably.

"Well, let's get some food into you then." Dad stood up and, directing us to follow him, we walked through the hall and into the dinning room.

The table was laden with all Mum's finest table-ware and the food looked fit for a king. I'd never asked to bring someone home for dinner before, but I never expected Mum to go to all this trouble. I would think twice before asking again. It wasn't that often that we used the dining table, as it was normally reserved for Mum's parties and other special events. Jamie stopped at the sight of the table and almost tripped over himself as he attempted to string a sentence together.

"Well you weren't wrong, Sir, when you said there was lots of food."

Dad smiled, but not before I saw that he had been staring at Jamie intently. I frowned as we all took our seats, although Gavin hadn't put in an appearance as yet. Mum stood up and went to call for Gavin.

"Gavin, we aren't going to wait all night for you to join us, now hurry up and greet our guest."

Even before she had a chance to finish Gavin's reply was already echoing down from above. "I'm coming! Just wait a minute."

"That boy," huffed Father, taking a deep breath, "You try to make him take a bath and it's an uphill struggle, but then for some unknown reason he decides to take one when you least expect it." His absence now became clear; he was under the impression I was having a girl come to dinner so he was attempting to look good.

From where we were around the table, it was clear that Gavin was drenching himself in Dad's after-shave because its stale musty smell had managed to drift down stairs and overcome the smell of the food. Mum must have been thinking the same as me because a large smile had appeared on her face. I could see her attention turn towards Jamie who was still trying to snap shot memories of the fine display of Mum's cooking that lay before him.

"So Jamie, did you have a good day at school today?" Hearing the question we both turned and looked at each other trying to magic a mutual answer. Just as we were about to answer, the footsteps of Gavin could be heard coming in behind us. Mum suddenly interrupted us by directing her attention at Gavin and saying, "well, about time, the food's almost stone cold."

As his steps came closer I sat anxious to hear what he was about to say. He walked to my left, around the table and took up a seat next to Dad. As he dropped into the seat, I could see him staring at Jamie. He appeared to be trying to put a name to the face and looked somewhat surprised, as if he couldn't recognise him.

Of course, he had never seen Jamie looking like this; in fact, he never even knew his real name, only his nickname. The combination of him thinking Jamie was going to be a female and then not recognising him was the cause of his confusion. Before he had a chance to say anything, Dad, who was still trying to make an impression, began to say Grace. We'd never been a religious family but he must have thought it proper to act this way. The minute he said the words "let's eat" we all attacked the awaiting banquet. For someone who hadn't eaten such a meal, Jamie sure managed to carry himself with style. The conversation came in small short bursts until the main meal was over and the food had started to settle in our stomachs.

I could see Jamie glance every now and then at Gavin as if trying to recall were he'd seen him before. At the same time, Gavin was doing exactly the same. Mum was now hurrying around the table collecting the dinner plates, only not with her usual pace.

"That was one heck of a meal."

"Well, thank you Jamie," Mum replied with a smile. "I wish these three appreciated it as much as you. I've got some deep apple pie for pudding so I hope you've saved some space." Mum left the room, plates in hand, and headed into the kitchen leaving us guys together.

Gavin took immediate control of the conversation. "So where do you live, Jamie?" This was it, the point where everyone would find out who the person behind this false exterior was.

"I live in Blacksmiths Fire," he answered, without so much as flinching. "You know me as the Boy Who Never Sleeps."

I gasped in amazement at this sudden admission. Instantly, Gavin shut up in disbelief. Mum reappeared seconds later with the apple pie, placing a massive slice on each plate as she walked around the table. "Anyone for fresh cream?" she asked, now holding a large jug in her hand. There was no reply from anyone, including Dad who was still comprehending the words that had just been so perfectly spoken towards them.

"Have I missed something?" Mum enquired and stood waiting for a reply.

Dad simply answered, "Not at all dear, Jamie was just telling us he lives in Blacksmiths Fire."

"Oh... Oh, that's nice." Mum sat back in her chair still holding firmly onto the cream jug and just as Gavin and Dad had done she too looked at Jamie in disbelief. Clearly they were all wondering how such a smartly dressed and well-presented young man could come from such an uncommon part of town. All questions after that died a sudden death and we settled back to finishing the delicious pudding that now lay before us.

Just as Mum took to her feet again, Jamie also stood up. "I'll give you a hand if that's ok?"

Mum must have thought heaven had opened its gates and sent an angel to earth because she'd never had such an offer of help in many years, well, at least not from Gavin or me. A smile crept across her face as if she'd been pleasantly surprised by Jamie's offer. "Well, thank you very much Jamie."

Feeling somewhat redundant and slightly embarrassed at the fact that I'd never made such a suggestion myself, I took to my feet and joined in clearing the table. During the trips back and forth to the kitchen, Mum and Jamie seemed to be having a conversation and had even both started to laugh at one point. Gavin stayed glued to his seat watching and paying close attention to every detail. I couldn't help but think forward to the next day and to what Gavin might be telling the lads at school.

I tried best to bypass such thoughts and concentrated on the there and then. After the table was cleared, we went through to the main room and Dad suggested we play a game of backgammon. I don't quite know what Jamie and Mum were talking about, but whatever it was they seemed to be getting on like two mice in a cheese factory. Dad also seemed to be having a great time, I think partly because he had beaten me twice in a row and was proceeding to do it for a third time. The conversation really started to pick up momentum and in no time the backgammon was abandoned.

I expected Mum and Gavin to be asking the questions, but it came as a surprise when it was Jamie doing all the asking and questions. To be frank, it wasn't only a surprise, it was also extremely frightening. He not only held and kept control of a conversation but also displayed knowledge of our family and of local affairs that was amazing, too amazing. He also, either accidentally or not, mentioned one Margaret Mulhullond in the context of being Gavin's girlfriend. A fact that wasn't known to Mum or Dad - and I hadn't really acknowledged it myself.

Gavin, slightly surprised by the question, looked directly at Jamie and after a second or two replied, "Very well, thanks. We've arranged to meet on Saturday."

"Well, you kept that quiet," uttered Mum in amazement. She'd always wanted us to find a nice girl each whom we could take home for her to talk to.

"I obviously didn't. *He* knew," Gavin nodded his head towards Jamie who seemed slightly abashed, but couldn't apologise for asking after Margaret and Gavin as he knew he would just dig the hole deeper if he did.

"Well, you'll need to bring her here on Saturday to let us see the lucky girl," Dad said finally, covering the awkward silence.

I'd only known Jamie now for a few weeks, but in this short time we had some of the most fun packed times of my life not to mention some crazy experiences. However, in all the time we'd spent together I'd never seen this side to Jamie before. He'd never been to school as far as I knew yet he seemed very knowledgeable and was very well spoken. It was a side that I liked very much but to say I was intrigued was an understatement. What intrigued me even more was the fact that Gavin and Jamie seemed to be getting on well. I had half-expected to find them at each other's throats, but they were laughing and talking; in fact, if I'd been a stranger peering in the window from outside, I would have thought this was a perfectly happy family.

As it was early December, the nights came in fast and before we knew it, the evening was over.

"Well, Jamie, it's been a pleasure but I'm sure your mother will be wondering where you've got to. Wait a second 'til I get a coat, son, and I'll join you in walking Jamie home."

"You don't have to go to any bother, Sir."

"First things first, Jamie, you don't need to call me sir, the name is Thomas. And, secondly, it's no bother at all."

As we walked out of the door, Mum signalled Jamie and gave him a kiss on the forehead and thanked him for coming. "You're welcome any time, Jamie."

Halfway down the street, amidst the golden twinkle from the flickering streetlights, I noticed the first flakes of snow starting to fall. "Look it's snow," I shouted, "it's snow!"

Before we had even reached the end of the street, the snow had started to fall quite heavily and I could feel the flakes land on my hair and melt into my scalp, dribbling down the back of my neck. We danced along Shepherd's Lane, Dad included, and watched as children appeared at windows with eager parents over their shoulders to watch the first snow of the season. I loved this time of year, although I had never previously given it much thought. Christmas was near and it was snowing. How perfect.

We got as far as the common green and Jamie insisted we allow him to go the rest of the way himself. By the look on Dad's face, I could see he was slightly relieved. He thanked Jamie for coming and welcomed him back anytime. Dad started to walk away giving us a second to talk.

"Well thanks for coming, Jamie."

"The pleasure was all mine," he replied in a gentlemanly kind of way. "It's your turn to come to mine next time. How about Sunday dinner?"

Without even realising what I did, I turned to look at Dad, as if to seek his approval. Upon seeing my hesitation, Jamie added, "my Mum makes a great Sunday dinner, if it's ok..."

Without letting Jamie finish, Dad turned around with a snowy smile and said, "Sure he can."

There was something special in Jamie and slowly but surely he was showing me bit by bit what it was. We shook hands and as he ran off across the common which by now had at least and inch or so of snow Dad grabbed me, pulled me close to his side and we talked about this and that as we walked back to the house.

"You seem to have found yourself a good friend there, son," said Dad in a genuine-sounding voice.

Looking up at him and blinking as the snow fell into my eyes, I answered, "you know what? I think you're right."

As we entered the house, Mum was armed with two mugs, one with dark coffee for Dad and the other with hot chocolate for me. Dad was a lover of coffee and there was rarely an hour that went by when he never had a cup in his hand. The same could be said about hot chocolate and me but every boy is entitled to love hot chocolate.

As I was getting changed for bed that night there was a knock, and Gavin's head peered around the now opening door. "Well, that was a surprise," he said. "When did you become friends with Jamie?"

It was late and not the time for one of Gavin's meaningful conversations. "Not that long ago," I replied while pulling the covers over my head and finished with, "turn the light off on your way out."

He moped for a minute then about turned and mumbled as he closed the door behind him, "well, that's just fine, go to sleep."

CHAPTER SIX
The Hardware Shop

I lay for a few moments but found myself not able to sleep, turning restlessly every minute or so. After a while I got up and watched the snow out of the window as still, like me, it fell restlessly. I imagined myself being able to fly and soar through the air like a bird dancing with the flakes of snow and chasing them towards the grounds with acrobatic manoeuvres and speed. At some point whilst drifting about in fantasy I must have fallen asleep because I recall waking up in the small chair near the window with a rather stiff neck. It was about six fifteen in the morning and the chances of being able to get back to sleep were very slim.

I got up and changed, but school didn't start till nine so I wrote a small note for Mum and decided to go for a walk. It was still dark as I left the house and the snow lay crisp, brilliant white, pure and untouched before I became the first person in the street to make footprints in it. The subtle crunching sound followed by the deep compacting moan with every step brought the memories of last Christmas flooding back. On the common, there was nothing left uncovered. Every blade of grass and each branch on the bare leafless trees were covered. The tip of the rising sun catching the cold air made the whole place twinkle and feel rather magical.

I remember bending down and picking up some snow from the ground, and recall the feeling of coldness drifting through my skin and racing up the bones of each finger. All sensation disappeared as the numbness took over while I formed the snow into a neat round ball perfect for throwing. Taking aim, I launched it at a nearby willow. On impact, it exploded with a shower of snow against the tree. Mum would have gone crazy if she knew I had ventured outside without any gloves, scarf and woolly hat. I hated the way she would try to wrap us up when the snow arrived as if it was some kind of evil killer, but I'd noticed she wasn't being so protective over us lately.

I took to the main street and peered into the faintly lit shop windows, which had started to frost up on the inside. The Priestfield toyshop was the envy of many a child in our town. With all its shelves stacked to the ceiling with every toy you could think of, it was truly a magical place. As I stood there, I recalled Dad taking me into the shop on my eighth birthday to select a toy. Just before we entered, he stopped, lifted me up and whispered in my ear.

"Anything you want is yours, and you have all day to choose, so take your time." I took his words quite literally, because we were there for about two hours before I made a cast iron decision. In the end, I selected a model submarine that was made of metal and that actually floated when placed in water. We only visited the duck ponds once every few month so the only water the submarine ever saw was that at bath time.

This Christmas the window had a display of small cars in it, and a full size railway track. Most days you would find a handful of children gazing at the toys and fighting to get front row view. The only thing that came anywhere close to the wonderful toyshop was Mr Green's sweet shop, a place where every flavour of sweet and chocolate bar could be bought. I spent much of my pocket money as a child there and never regretted it for even one minute.

I was walking from window to window looking at the displays when all of a sudden I stopped. My attention had been arrested by a figure moving in the background of the hardware shop. It was dark but the sun had just started to appear and was creeping through the shops back window, shedding a haze of light inside. There was someone standing half crouched over something on the floor. I stood up on tiptoes in an attempt to get a better view, but boxes inside the window were blocking my view. I stood poised and watched, as the figure seemed to be struggling to lift up the object.

I pushed myself up onto the ledge of the window and tried to balance from swaying back and forth by attempting to suck onto the window with cold hands. Just as I became glued to the glass the figure leaned back heaving something over its shoulder. I could feel the chill of the cold air in my lungs as I inhaled a deep breath. It was a BODY! The fright took my feet from under me and my face fell into the glass with a BANG. I felt a trickle of warm blood run from my eye while trying to stand up. Suddenly I noticed the figure move quickly towards the front door. I grabbed my bag and ran as fast as I could towards the end of the street. My heart was thumping more than it had ever done before in my entire life. Looking back to the sound of the shop bell ringing, I saw a figure emerged from the shop doorway and onto the snowy road. I considered diving into one of the allies, but I'd made a breadcrumb trail in the snow that would have lead the figure straight to me.

The combination of the fright and the cold made me out of breath. I could feel a painful stitch, which arrived with an evil stabbing in my side. My pace slowed down to a jog, as the pain became almost unbearable. Ahead I could see the light of the town church and mustering every ounce of might I ran as fast as I could in through the large wooden metal studded doors and into the cold still hall. Collapsing behind the doors I pulled off my wet snowy shoes and made for the front of the church where a Christmas display had been built, lit with the glow of huge candles. I hid behind the long red velvet curtains and stood as still as possible, trying not to send any movement up through the thin fabric. My heart was still pounding and the lack of breath was making my head start to ache. If it wasn't for the fact that I was too scared to do anything else, I think I would have been sick.

The doors swung open and in the darkness of the doorway I could see the same large man-like figure that had come from the shop. He took a few steps forward and paused while he looked from side to side for the slightest sign of movement. I could see his cold breath rise from the darkness as he took slow heavy breaths. Suddenly he stepped forward putting a hand on the corner of the stone wall, his face still engulfed by the darkness. The big knuckled hand definitely confirmed that fact the figure was male. No woman on earth could have had such large, manly hands. As I stood trembling, every limb feeling cold with the sensation of pins and needles running though them, the hand disappeared and the figure retreated back out of the doors taking its rising breath with it. Standing like a bird I hopped from one leg to the other trying to keep my feet from freezing on the stone cold floor. The sun was now streaming in through the circular stained glass window, shedding rays of colour into the church. I slipped my shoes back on and walking slowly along the side of the wall in the shadows of the darkness to arrive back at the front doors. Opening them ever so slightly, with the squint of an eye I peered out to see if the coast was clear.

I don't know for how long I had been standing there but the street had now started to fill with people going to work, and there were children playing in the snow. I walked out into the middle of the street not knowing what to do next. It was dark so what I thought was a body could easily have been something else. There was more than likely a perfectly good explanation, but the visions of death and murder kept ringing in my head along with the sound of the shop doorbell and that massive, shadow-casting figure. I felt lost and looked for a familiar face to confide in, but searching around I couldn't find anyone.

I started to walk to school still half dazzled, re-enacting the events in my head. I kept wondering what if...? I considered going straight home to tell Mum and Dad, but if I didn't know for sure what had happened, how could anyone else believe me? Telling Constable Irwin was a no-no all together. He would take it one of two ways. He would consider me either a lunatic, and have me committed for being insane, or he would launch a wide scale manhunt for "a manly figure" which was the only description I could provide! I decided not to tell them until I was a hundred percent sure myself.

Sitting in class that day, the Christmas atmosphere was ripe, but you would never have known I'd noticed the snow and buzz of excitement. I was glued to my thoughts and the only interruptions came from the constant flicking of paper at my back from Gavin. Trying to concentrate was near impossible and I was awoken more than once by the howling shrieks of Mrs Greenshields. If it weren't for the fact that this was pretty odd behaviour for me, I would have had the ruler over the back of the neck as she often did to those falling prey to the sleep bug in her class.

Once again it had started to snow very heavily, and on days like this we weren't allowed to go outside for lunch, but instead had to sit in the classroom no matter how much moaning there was.

The end of school came that day with me standing up screaming after being shaken from a day dream by old Mrs Brodie shaking her bell in the hallway, which took me straight back to shop door opening again. The entire class silenced at the sight of me being scared to death and screaming out like a lunatic. I can't even recall the words I shouted, but my fear was written all over their faces including Gavin's, who was also showing signs of immense embarrassment. A cold sweat had started to make me feel slightly dizzy so as the class starting to make their way to the door I sat back down. Only a couple of seconds had rolled by when I could sense the overcast shadow of Mrs Greenshields standing above me.

"Is something wrong?" she asked in a concerned voice.

I raised my head up and paused for a second while I contemplated telling her of the morning's events.

"Nothing's wrong, Miss. It's just been a hard week."

"Well try and contain yourself whilst in class and get some sleep." She trundled back to her desk as I made my way to the door.

Just before stepping out into the hall I stopped and turned. Mrs Greenshields looked up and waited for me to speak. I was just about to confide but when my mouth opened all that came out was, "see you tomorrow, Miss."

"And you too," she replied.

I walked along the now empty corridor to the sounds of my own footsteps, turning occasionally to make sure I was alone. I got to the front gates of the school to find Gavin standing there alone.

"What was all that about? You've been acting funny all day."

"Um, nothing, I'm fine. I just never got much sleep last night. I had a sore head."

He looked right through me, knowing that I'd just blatantly lied. "Well, if you ask me, it's something more than just a sore head." As we walked home, Gavin took every opportunity to use me as target practice by pelting me with snowballs. I never had the will or the power to fight back, which only added to his already very suspicious thoughts.

At home that night, I never talked much through dinner. In fact, I didn't eat much either.

"You not got anything planned with Jamie today?" Dad asked.

"No, not till tomorrow." I had arranged to meet Jamie on Saturday morning but didn't feel like getting into a family conversation. I only lasted a few minutes at the table when I asked to be excused. I watched as Mum and Dad looked at me, concerned as if I was a boy with a crisis. While going up the stairs I could hear Gavin burst into conversation, telling Mum and Dad about how I'd acted at school. It wasn't even six o'clock and I had taken a bath and was ready for bed.

I'd only laid down for a few moments when there was a knock on the door and Dad's voice whispered through the crack. "Son, can I come in?"

"Sure, Dad." As the door opened, the light from the hallway entered the room. Dad sat next to the bed with his back to me like he would do when he talked to me as I slept. The thin line of light that came through the door shone between us like some kind of divide.

"Are you ok?"

"I'm fine Dad, honest."

"Gavin told us you weren't feeling too good at school today."

"Honest Dad, I'm ok, I just had a sore head but I feel great now."

"That's why you're in your bed at six o'clock, is it?"

I wanted to tell him, my voice had upped a few notes as my eyes started to glaze with tears, not only because I felt scared inside but because I hated lying to him. I imagined the ray of light from the hall that divided us was a shield of some sort that repelled me from being able to tell the truth.

"Well, son, if you need to talk."

"Yes, I know where you are, Dad."

Dad left the room, pulling the door closed behind him, deleting the light and returning the room to darkness – a darkness that swallows everything in its grasp and turns even the most colourful of objects to mere soulless shadows. I watched as the walls of the room swirled with patterns caused by the falling snow and the few clouds remaining in the presence of the ghostly white moon. I couldn't hold back any longer and the tears welling up had started to overflow. I pushed myself into the corner of the wall and held onto the pillow. I felt rather insecure and couldn't help but feel afraid. The images of that shadowy body and that massive hand kept flickering time after time in my mind. I wasn't sure what to do next, but one thing was for sure, I couldn't sit back and watch as this horror took control of everything good I enjoyed.

CHAPTER SEVEN
Daydreams & Nightmares

After some time, I eventually fell into a rather restless sleep, only to find myself back in the main street. I was standing there watching myself clinging onto the window of the hardware shop. As I watched myself peering through the large glass window, I shouted to myself to get down and run away, but I wouldn't listen. It was as if the other "me" couldn't hear anything. Although I was there and able to see, I wasn't able to interfere, I wasn't able to warn myself away. My shouts had turned to screams as I watched myself slipping off the thin window ledge and falling into the snow. Looking down and crying loudly, I could see the fear in my own eyes as our sights crossed. I wanted to grab myself up from the snow and run. Run as fast as I could and never look back, but I wasn't able to follow as with tremendous speed the other me sprinted with all his might down the street to safety. It was only when the bell, that high-pitched ringing bell, struck out into the cold air that the dream ended.

Out of breath and soaking with sweat, I awoke. My pyjamas and bed covers felt warm and damp. My heart and breathing thundered like battle drums in unison. What was happening to me? Or more to the point, what was wrong with me? After standing at the side of the bed scared and confused, I convinced myself that the danger, although only in a dream, wasn't there. I took off my pyjamas, pulled off the bed sheets and turned the cover over.

I climbed back into bed and drifted off back to sleep. It seemed like only a few minutes had passed by when Gavin shouting from the doorway woke me up.

"Wake up, wake up, Gran's here."

His words seemed to go into my ears then linger about in my head until a few moments later they were registered and I understood what he'd said. Gran was here! Gran never liked to travel and the last time she was here was well over eight years ago when Mum had been really poorly. I jumped out of bed and ran halfway out into the hall before I remembered I had taken my pyjamas off during the night and was about to run down the stairs naked. I stopped turned around and was about to dive back into my room when out of the corner of my eye I noticed a girl looking up at me. It was Anna, Jenny's daughter. She was about the same age as me and we often played together when we went to visit Gran. I always had a soft spot for her but treated her more as a sister than a friend. When she noticed I could see her watching me, she turned away rather embarrassed. She went about the same colour as I felt, although I was the one that had just bared himself for the whole world to see.

I got changed as quickly as I could and went down stairs to find Gran, Jenny and Anna along with Mum, Dad and Gavin. As I stepped across the doorway everyone turned and looked at me, everyone, that was, except Anna. She was still clearly far too embarrassed.

"The dead awakens," remarked Dad with a lift of his eyebrows. I glanced at the clock to find it was almost ten o'clock.

"Well, come in and let me see how you've grown," Gran bellowed as she stood up. I walked over towards her but before I had the chance to do anything she'd grabbed me and placed a kiss on my cheek.

"You're getting big," she said at the same time sending her eyes towards Anna as if trying to bring her attention towards something.

"And you're looking really well," I replied and actually meant it, for Gran looked truly fabulous. She'd always been a very beautiful woman, especially when she was younger. I wasn't quite sure what made it stand out today of all days, but there was something. Perhaps it was her long light sandy coloured hair or her overly warm face and seawater blue eyes. Whatever it was, it was working. We sat down and talked for only an hour, but during those sixty minutes every care that lay heavy on my shoulders seemed to lift off and allow me to relax. Pity it was only like that for sixty minutes though.

"But I didn't know you were coming," I added, perplexed. Gran just smiled and patted my hand.

Mum shouted me through into the kitchen where she'd poured out a bowl of soup and some buttered bread.

"Now, you get that lot into you, and I don't want to see you move until you've finished the lot. You hardly touched your dinner last night, and you had no supper."

I couldn't help it if I wasn't hungry, but before I had the chance to answer back she had already left the kitchen. I was sitting there dipping the bread into the soup and slurping away when Mum re-entered with my bed sheets and pyjamas bundled in her arms. Before she even opened her mouth I knew what she was going to say.

"Was everything ok last night? Did you have a slight accident?"

"You what? You don't think I wet the bed?" As she struggled for words, I quickly leapt to my own defence. "I never wet the bed, it was hot and I was very sweaty, that's all."

"No one said you did. I was just wondering, that's all."

"Well, it didn't sound like just wondering to me. I've got to go; I'm going out with Jamie this afternoon."

"But your Gran is just here, you can't go disappearing so soon."

"I've made arrangements; no one said Gran was coming so I wasn't to know."

I couldn't believe she actually thought I'd wet the bed! She made me feel about five years old, like a naughty boy wetting the bed all the time. I'd never wet the bed in my life and didn't intend to start now. I spoke to Gran and told her I was going out for a while and would speak with her later.

She just smiled and with a small kiss she said, "I'll see you later."

I pulled on a coat and left the warmth of the house to enter the bitter, face-clenching cold of the outside. Dad had heavily sprinkled salt crystals on the steps in case Gran had wanted to go outside so as to stop her from slipping, which made a sound like broken glass when you walked on it.

I made my way down to the common green to meet Jamie at the same time reminiscing about the hardware shop. I couldn't wait to tell Jamie all about it. At last, I could confide in someone about what I'd seen and not feel stupid. The common was full with kids of all ages, running about throwing snowballs at each other, shouting and screaming with laughter. If there was one snowman there must have been a hundred. Everywhere you looked you would see one. Each and every one was decorated with fruit, vegetables and clothes, making them look truly fantastic. On entering past the large steel gates, I could see two fairly large snow walls that had been built on each side of the path about thirty or so feet apart. There were no heads showing until I was about halfway through, when all of a sudden I was under attack. Snowballs coming from all angles, all shapes and sizes whizzing by with speed and force. I managed to survive with only a few direct hits only to see Jamie in stitches, crying with laughter at the sight. He had been subjected to the same bombardment only a few minutes previously so knew only too well what was coming.

"How you doing?" he yelled as I approached brushing the remaining snow from the front of my coat.

"Not bad, Jamie, and you?"

"Can't complain. So far so good. So what's on the cards for today?"

"Well, I must admit I haven't given it a second thought."

"Too busy wrapping presents and thinking about Christmas."

"No, quite the opposite! I've had much greater things to think about." We walked out the far side gate of the common to prevent any repeat of the snowball warfare and kicked our way down Weavers Road.

"So come on, tell me then," asked Jamie said with a hint of excitement. "What is it you've been thinking about?"

I stopped and pushed Jamie against the wall at the same time giving him a look of seriousness. "You must swear you'll never tell anyone what I'll tell you."

"Sure."

"No, I mean it, you have to swear."

Spitting in each others hand then shaking together, Jamie swore that he would never tell a soul what I was about to impart and keep it strictly to himself or suffer a painful death by being cooked slowly alive rather than tell anyone. His look of excitement had cleared and the wrinkles on his forehead showed his expression of concern. I knew I could trust him but still I felt slightly foolish about the whole thing.

I started to explain what had happened and how I almost died of fright when Jamie suddenly interrupted.

"What did your Mum and Dad say, and what about the police?"

"Well," I paused.

"What! You haven't told them yet? Are you crazy?

You have to let them know. What if this nutter knows who you are and comes looking for you?"

"Well thanks very much, that certainly cheered me up no end. That's what I expect from my Gran, not my best friend."

Jamie stopped and gave me that same glancing look as he did on the Thursday when I introduced him to Dad. I grabbed him by the arm as he turned away and pulled him back around to look at me face to face.

"Why did you do that?"

"Do what?"

"That stare thing."

"Oh that! It's nothing, sorry."

"You don't need to be sorry; you just need to tell me why you did it."

"Well, it's just you said I was your best friend, and well, it's been a long time since I had anyone tell me that."

"Oh." Blushing slightly and not knowing quite what to say, I gave a simply reply, "Well you are, aren't you?" We looked at each other and with a smile I could tell we both understood each other. That day was my first lesson in true friendship and it taught me that it's not just material gifts that as a person you can give, but also emotional ones, like the gift of friendship or love.

Having been slightly side-tracked, I composed myself once more and continued telling Jamie about the terrifying events.

"Gee, I would have been scared to death if that happened to me."

"Be glad it didn't, because it's hard to concentrate or sleep with thoughts like that on constant replay in your mind every minute of the day."

"We have to do something," he said in a voice shrouded in mystery.

"Easier said than done."

"Where there's a will there's a way. First things first,

we have to go to the hardware shop to look for clues." The sudden urge for adventure was written all over his face.

"Who did you call the crazy one? Me or you? Because if you think for one second that I'm going anywhere near that shop you're sadly mistaken."

"Oh don't be a cry baby and get a move on." The mere thought of going back to that shop made my skin come out in goose pimples.

I stood and watched as Jamie trudged off in the snow and briefly considered the possibilities. If I didn't do anything and stopped thinking about it, it may just go away. But, on the other hand, it could haunt me forever. I could hear my inner-self shouting words of abuse and telling me not to be such a sissy and get on with it. I knew there was only one thing to do and whether that decision was right or wrong, well that's just the way it goes. As Jamie turned and shouted some more, I pressed onwards trying to follow the footsteps he had made, preventing my feet from becoming any wetter than they already were.

We made our way to the main street where the customary decorations and streetlights now hung fabulously in view. With the snow lying thick and crunchy all around it really felt like Christmas, prompting that warm, tickly feeling to return inside. From the far end of the street I could see a group of carol singers making their way towards us accompanied by the usual sounds of Christmas tunes flowing from them in heavenly verse. I could feel myself wanting to join in and soak up some of their happiness and joy, but I was brought back down to earth by Jamie pulling on me to look through the hardware shop window. With the singing going on in the background and coming closer, we peered through the large window and glared at the people walking around inside. Most of them were holding large pots and new sets of dinnerware in their hands. I could smell a whiff of fear propel itself from me, and my fingers started to tremble slightly as the realisation of possibly seeing that man again came over me.

From where we were, we could only see part of the shop and before I knew it Jamie was dragging us inside for a closer look. Like a child not wanting to go to bed, I put my heels firmly in the snow and refused to move.

"Come on, we've talked about this, we have to go inside. Look, there's a lot of people inside so nothing is going to happen. Just take it easy and let's get a move on."

I loosened up and hurried in behind Jamie, keeping very close indeed. As he opened the door the large bell jangled and flashbacks came ripping though my mind, making me run backwards and bang into the group of carol singers who had settled behind us, dispersing them as though I was a gunshot. Instruments were sent flying up into the air, the singing turned to screams and shouting as I slid and came to a stop on my backside. Half-dazzled, I looked up to find I was the subject of a lot of angry looking stares - and a rather concerned look from Jamie. In the shop doorway, I could see a few spectators laughing at the sight of me covered from head to toe in snow and the rather disgruntled looking faces of the carol singers.

Amidst the people in the doorway I could see someone familiar. The faint outline of a man, a man who had captured my dreams and thoughts for the last few days and who was standing there right in front of me. In the background of the crowded door he was there, overcast by shadows, but there was no mistaking it, it was him. Reality suddenly struck a cord and self-preservation kicked in. Fear had once again opened a door into my mind and the whiteness of the snow matched the colour of my face. Like a jack in the box, I sprung to my feet and ran. I ran as fast as I could go without looking back. Just as a wild animal would, running from a hunter and feeling every ounce of fear that went along with it. I never once looked back and kept running; even after I had entered the house I was still running up the stairs and only came to a stop when the bedroom door was firmly closed behind me.

Out of breath, panting and wheezing, I fell behind the door after my legs collapsed. The sounds of footsteps running up the stairs fused with a heavy knocking on the front door. The footsteps had come to rest outside the door that I was now slouching behind and I could hear the voices of Mum and Dad.

"Just go in and find out what's going on." Mum hastily said to Dad.

"Stop overreacting, I'm sure he's fine."

If I just lay there and allowed them to find me like this there would be all sorts of questions to answer. The front door had not yet been answered so there was still some time to smooth things over as long as the door was being knocked by Jamie and not someone else. Looking up at the wooden shelf on the wall I pounced up and grabbed a football. Returning to the door, I opened it and looked at Mum and Dad with a false look of surprise.

"What's going on?" I asked.

They both stood looking somewhat puzzled and confused. "It's just that you seemed to be going up the stairs really fast and when your mother called you never answered."

"Sorry, Dad, it's just that the boys are waiting, were going to have a game of, em, snowball." Snowball! What on earth made me say that I don't know, and Mum and Dad looked just as bewildered as me? "It's a new game like football but played in the snow."

"Oh, well, just try and be careful then," Dad replied, looking at Mum and not knowing quite what to say.

The door knocked heavily again for the third time. I ran down the stairs and opened it to find Jamie standing there jumping up and down with excitement or the cold, one of the two. Pulling the door closed behind me, I signalled with my other hand for Jamie not to say anything.

We walked to the end of the road before we uttered a single word to each other. The moment that first word was set loose was like a horse being untied in a field after being stabled for years, everything went crazy. Jamie was firing questions from every direction, bombarding me into total disarray.

"Stop," I was shouting. "Just slow down a minute."

"Slow down! I've never seen anyone run so fast in my life. You were off like a speeding bullet. I don't reckon anyone could have stopped you." His words of encouragement didn't distract me from what I had just done and in no time I knew it would be headline news in the town's gossip union.

We took refuge in an old cart that had been lying on the side of the road for the last few weeks. It was believed it belonged to a Romany Gypsy traveller and it was considered to be very unlucky to remove or enter it without their permission. This point seemed very minor in the current situation and it seemed a good place to sit and talk.

"What happened to you? Why on earth did you run like that?"

"It was the bell. I've been hearing it ever since that morning. It keeps ringing over and over in my head. Whenever I hear that sound it brings everything flooding back."

"But why did you run? It was as if you'd just seen a ghost; you should have seen your face. What was it? What made you go like that?"

"It was him! I saw him standing there, right in front of me."

"Who was it then? Was it someone we know?"

"I have never seen his face, only his figure, only that same black shadowy silhouette of a huge man. I felt sick and my mind went into overdrive. All I could think was to run and not look back."

"Well you certainly did that alright. What did your

parents say when you went rushing in the house? I was at the front door banging for ages."

I explained about the silly excuse I had quickly invented and Jamie took one look at the ball which I was still clenching rather tightly in my hands and burst into fits of laughter, making the cart rock from side to side.

"And they believed that? Boy, they must really have thought you were acting very strange."

"Well, they did look at me rather funnily, I must say."

We sat for a while longer and I told Jamie about the events during the night and how Mum thought I'd wet the bed, which only added to the reams of laughter being expelled by Jamie. It's true what they say; laughter's a good cure for most ailments. Jamie tried very hard to convince me to return to the hardware shop but retreated upon viewing the ghastly expressions on my face. We agreed to leave our investigations until the next day, giving me a chance to settle after what I considered to be a great ordeal.

CHAPTER EIGHT
An Evening At Home

Not having planned anything for the day and as the snow had started to fall again whilst we were inside the cart; we decided to go back to the house. As we turned the corner, the wind picked up and the snow became fiercer. We'd only just stepped into the house when Mum come running towards us.

"My dear boys! You're alright," she coughed. Mum always overreacted and this was no exception. "There's a storm brewing out there and your Dad's been out looking for you two."

At that moment, the main door swung open embellishing the hall with a swooshing gust of snow followed by a rather windswept Dad at its heels. He struggled slightly to close the door before turning around and taking off his coat, he noticed us standing with Mum. "Thank heavens you're both here."

"We're fine Dad. It's only snow."

"Only snow, only snow," he harrumphed. "If only you had seen the power of the snow and the life that it can so easily take without so much as care in the world, without so much as the slightest bit of remorse. It's all fun to play in the snow but remember this if you never remember anything else I ever tell you, the both of you. The snow is made by Mother Nature and she's the one woman, the only woman whom a man bows down to, except your mother that is," taking a quick glance to the side where Mum was standing. "Anything to do with that lady who controls the elements you should take heed of. She has taken more lives than war and hatred ever has, and will continue to do so."

At that, he walked into the kitchen and I could hear the sound of a kettle being filled, followed by Dad shouting us through. "Who's for a cup of hot chocolate then?"

This was a stupid thing to ask in my company because very scarcely did I ever say no to such a Godly drink. "Jamie and I will both have one please, Dad."

"Take a seat and I'll bring it through when it's ready."

We walked into the main room where Mum had rested herself next to Gran. She was very pale and fragile looking, which I automatically put down to her being worried and never thought much more about it.

"Gran, this is Jamie. Jamie, this is my Gran."

"Pleased to meet you," Jamie said, taking what resembled a small bow.

"And you too, Jamie." Gran replied with a curious look before casting a glance towards Mum and Dad. I inwardly rolled my eyes in frustration. Everyone had the same curious reaction when they met Jamie, as though they had seen him before somewhere.

We sat down on the seat across from Mum and Gran, at which point Dad appeared carrying a golden tray adorned with five mugs and a biscuit jar. Being the proper gentleman, he set down a mug for both Mum and Gran before slipping the tray onto the table next to us and telling us to help ourselves.

"Dad! Where's Gavin? And what about Jenny and Anna?"

"Your dear brother is out on a date; he's gone to that young girl's house for dinner. Now, what was her name again?"

"Margaret Mullholland," Jamie answered.

"Oh that's right. Well, he should be back later hopefully, if the snow dies down, that is."

"Thomas, dear, give Mrs Mullholland a telephone call and make sure Gavin won't attempt to walk home by himself, he left the number on the sideboard in the hallway."

Dad stood up and proceeded to enter the hall, but then stopped and turned towards Jamie. "Jamie, is there anyone you would like to phone and let know you're here?"

"No sir, we don't have a telephone at home." I knew Dad hadn't asked the question out of spite but out of pure and utter kindness. He wasn't to know if Jamie had a telephone in his house or not, but Dad being Dad, he had to ask.

"Does your mother know where you are, Jamie?"

"Yes sir, I always tell Mum where I'm going."

"Good. It's just if the snow doesn't stop soon you may very well have to stay here tonight." At that, he turned into the hall and we heard as he lifted the receiver and asked the operator to be connected. Before we had the chance to listen any more, Gran took the opportunity to talk to us.

"So, boys, I hear you were playing snowball today. Your Dad tells me it's a new game like football." Both Jamie and I looked at each other and immediately burst into laughter.

Gran and Mum were looking at us bewildered. Because we were laughing so much they started to laugh at us laughing. By the time Dad had re-entered the room, the tears of laughter were streaming from all eyes.

"Well, what did I miss then?" Dad asked with a Cheshire cat smile.

"Nothing, Dad, nothing at all."

Still smiling, he sat next to Mum and told her what Mrs Mullholland had said. "I spoke with Mrs Mullholland and she said it would be quite alright for Gavin to stay at their house tonight and she would make sure he was brought home in the morning." Mum looked at Dad and before she had the chance to say anything Dad interjected. "She has assured me he will be sleeping in the spare bed in the boys' room with Margaret's brother, to which I thanked the dear lady and wished her a goodnight."

A relieved look appeared over Mum's face while Dad's held a small, almost hidden grin. I could remember some of the stories he told when I was asleep about some of the things he had got up to when he was younger, so I knew exactly what was causing him to smile.

"Dad, where's Jenny and Anna?"

"Oh sorry, son, I forgot you'd asked that. They're upstairs sorting the room for Gran and unpacking her clothes." I remember thinking she must be staying for some time if they were unpacking clothes and sorting a room as they must have been upstairs for hours.

"Well, dinner won't be cooking itself," Mum announced, while taking rather heavily to her feet, closely followed by Gran, "wait, dear, and I'll give you a hand."

They both moved off into the kitchen giving us the sound of pots and pans banging for the next ten minutes. As Dad had disappeared from the main room and both Jamie and I were slightly restless, we made our way to my bedroom where we could at least find something to do. On our way up the staircase, I could hear Dad and what seemed like Jenny talking.

"Thanks for coming to stay, Jenny, you don't know how much we appreciate it."

"Think nothing of it Thomas, you know how important this family is to Anna and me, if anyone should be grateful it's us."

"Nonsense, that was in the past and you know I would never hold you to any sort of past debt."

"I know, Thomas, and for that you will surely go to heaven."

"Things might not go as we all hope. I pray that all will

work out, but we must be prepared for anything that may come."

At that, Jenny seemed to catch us out of the corner of her eye, causing her to distort the conversation. Trying to make it look as if we'd never heard anything, we talked as we walked up the rest of the stairs and simply asked Dad to call us when dinner was ready. Whether he believed that we had just arrived or just accepted things, I didn't know, but something fishy was going on. We entered the room and sat on the side of the bed.

"Well I wonder what all that was about?"

Jamie seemed just as puzzled and offered very little reply. "I don't have a clue."

We sat for a few moments contemplating what had just happened. Jamie was first to break the thought filled silence. "Families...who'd have them? They are the strangest things in the world if you ask me."

We looked at each other in agreement but deep down inside it was bothering me. I knew something wasn't right. I could feel it, and the more it lingered inside of me the more I would question things.

Jamie had made his way to the window and just like I had done on so many occasions, he admired the view. You could see almost the whole town, or at least all of the rooftops of the houses in the town, that was. Sometimes on a good day you would just be able to see the Roman cliffs if you looked hard enough. But tonight in the darkness all you could see was a sheet of falling snow. You could only see about ten feet out of the window before everything became white. The snow was certainly hurtling towards the ground very fast indeed; it was now clear why Mum and Dad had been worried.

"I think you'll be sleeping here tonight."

"Are you sure you don't mind?"

"Of course I don't mind, you would do the same for me, I'm sure of it."

81

"That I would," he answered, still watching out the window.

We were talking some more about the hardware shop and what we would do next when the voice of Dad came hurtling up from below. "Dinner's ready, boys."

I was starving and didn't need to be told twice, and by the looks of it neither did Jamie. We made our way towards the door and, as I stepped out into the corridor, I bumped into something. It was Anna.

"Oh I'm so sorry Anna, I didn't see you there." We were standing barely a few inches apart, the smell of her perfume bounced from her body and mixed with the air where we stood.

"It's fine, it was my fault."

"No, it wasn't. I should have been thinking more about where I was going and not so much on food."

"Honest, it's fine, I'm ok." I turned and proceeded down the stairs with Jamie who was obviously reading too much into things as he was blowing kisses as me and make funny noises. At the sight of the redness creeping up my neck and into my face he realised I was utterly embarrassed so quit with the fooling around, but that wasn't the last I would hear about it.

We entered the kitchen and Mum noticing that my face was red, immediately piped up, "are you feeling hot? You're looking rather flushed."

"I'm fine Mum, just hungry," I said dismissively.

Jamie's face was beaming and I could tell he wanted to let everyone know about what had just happened. As we took up our places at the table, Jenny and Anna arrived, taking their seats.

"This looks lovely," said Jenny while Anna stared down at her plate trying to keep all eye contact at a minimum.

As per usual, Mum had made far too much food and put it down to us not feeling as hungry as usual. "It must be

the weather, people don't eat as much in the cold," she
said, rather convincingly.

"I thought Gavin was supposed to be bringing Margaret
to dinner here tonight, Dad."

"Well, that's what we had hoped, but your brother forgot
Mrs Mullholland had already asked him last weekend to
have dinner at their house, so he'll be bringing her here
next Saturday instead."

"Oh well, that will be interesting."

We sat around the table and had some meaningless
conversation for the next hour saying nothing much about
anything. Taking a minute, I glanced at the faces that sat
around the table and watched them. I watched as they ate
and talked. I watched the expressions that appeared on
their faces. It's truly an amazing thing to do and I highly
recommend it. It gives you a chance to view the innermost
parts of a person. You can very easily imagine how they
would react under different circumstances. I found myself
drifting into a daydream. I knew what was happening but
couldn't summon the power to prevent it. For some reason,
I wanted to see where it was going to take me.

I found myself drifting out through the front door and
along the snow-laden street until yet again I found myself
floating towards the hardware shop. But this time when I
arrived I was on the inside of the shop and looking out the
window towards myself. I watched as I clung to the outside
of the window like some kind or rock climber scaling a cliff
face. My eyes were pierced and looking right into the
darkness at what I knew was the shadow of the man behind
me. I trembled with fear and watched as I slipped and
banged my head into the window. The noise behind me
was like that of something being thrown to the floor followed
by heavy footsteps that came closer and closer. I didn't
dare turn or move a muscle. My eyes still fixed on the
window, I watched myself clambering out the snow and
running towards the end of the street. I started to feel faint

and light-headed and knew that any minute I was going to pass out. A large blackness moved across my left-hand side, half eclipsing my body in coldness. I could hear the sound of a lock being turned then it struck. The shop bell rang out sending my body soaring backwards.

I looked up and found myself lying on the kitchen floor with the faces of Mum, Dad and Jamie standing over me. Everyone else was standing up and glaring over the table at where I'd come to rest. "Are you alright?" Dad was asking, while Mum was feeling my forehead for the signs of fever.

I climbed to my feet; all the time wondering what had happened, let alone trying to think of something to say to Mum and Dad to prevent them from trying to call the doctor. "I'm fine, honest Dad I'm ok, I think Mum's been putting too much brandy in the trifle again."

"I think we should call for the doctor, Thomas," panicked Mum. "He looked very hot when he came down to dinner."

I could see Dad looking at me and contemplating the idea. "Dad, I'm fine, and anyway the weather's too bad to get the doctor."

I saw him take a fleeting look out of the window at the snow that was still rocketing towards the ground. "Very well, but if you don't look any better in the morning I'll do as your mother thinks best."

The feeling of relief swelled over me like a cherry tree in bloom. I could see from his face that Jamie realised I'd had a close shave.

CHAPTER NINE
A Change of Life

"Can we be excused Mum?" I asked putting on a rather exaggerated perky voice.

There was a pause in her reply as she walked towards the sink carrying a pile of dirty dishes. "Very well."

Without any further questions we took flight towards the bedroom. Upon entering, Jamie immediately commenced with a bombardment of questions. "I take it you had another vision again."

"I wouldn't quite call it a vision, but yes, I suppose so."

"What happened? What made you fall off your chair like that?"

We sat down and I explained how I'd found myself inside the shop watching as the other me peered in. Jamie, understandably, gasped. "Your Mum might be right, you should see the doctor and see if he can do anything."

"Sure thing. I'll take a packed suitcase so I don't have to stop off on the way to Ravenstruther mental asylum."

Jamie looked as if he knew his suggestion was ludicrous. Looking around, he quickly grabbed a pack of playing cards from the desk. "Let's play."

As he removed the jokers, I couldn't help but feel scared. What if there was something wrong with me? It was hard even to contemplate playing games when my mind kept wandering back to the hardware shop. It was as if something inside was trying to show me something. Taking me nearer and nearer, as though trying to persuade me to be an onlooker from close up. That's not what I wanted. I didn't want to see anything that looked remotely like a dead body. I just wanted to be able to sleep at nights and forget the whole thing had ever happened.

We'd been playing cards for well over an hour when, for some reason, the conversation turned to girls.

"So do you have a girlfriend Jamie?"

"Me? No. I am always too busy to be fussing around girls. That isn't to say I've never had one in the past, that is." I didn't know who he was trying to convince, himself or me. "What about you?" he asked in return.

"Can't say I have. I've never thought much about girls to tell you the truth." As he raised his eyes towards me I knew instantly what was about to follow.

"What about Anna?" Before being asked that question, I had never recalled thinking about Anna much. But now, with the question dangling right in front of me, I felt an overwhelming feeling inside. A feeling very similar to the ones I'd recently become friendly with in the bathroom. She was indeed a beautiful girl, and one of the things I predominately noticed when I'd bumped into her earlier before dinner, was that she now had breasts! I remembered because they softened the blow when we bumped.

"Yes," I said. "She's very nice." This was a rather simple and straightforward answer to a question that I took well over two minutes to ponder over, but it certainly showed I was somewhat interested.

Jamie could see I'd taken time to consider my answer and quickly came back with a deeper, more sexually explicit question. "So would you, you know, have sex with her?"

I looked at him in surprise. "I've never really kissed a girl, let alone done that."

"It's not a bad word that'll bite you, and it'll be happening soon enough," he replied rather seriously.

"What do you mean?"

"It'll be happening soon enough! We're men now so sooner or later we'll have to be looking for a wife, and thinking about children."

Reality started flying through my head with tremendous speed. Jamie was right. Gavin had already started dating, and he was younger than I was, and it wasn't going to be long before I was leaving school. I looked at Jamie with concern written all over my face. For the first time in days, all thoughts of the hardware shop had vanished and this new evil of darkness was swooping down towards me and attacking the very place I'd been protecting for so long, my heart. This evil darkness was a key; slightly rusty through age but never the less it worked its way to unlocking my heart and leaving it to become prey to the devouring women of the world and most of all love.

"If you ain't ever kissed a girl you've got some catching up to do."

"Yes, but how do I do that?" I asked, conscious of the fact that my heart was rushing and my hands were shaking.

"Leave it with me," he said mysteriously.

I wanted to ask more, I wanted to know how he could help, but something stopped me from asking any further.

It was getting late and right about now felt like a good time to go for a bath. Jamie had not planned on staying the night so he didn't have any pyjamas or anything with him.

"Jamie, follow me." We walked towards the main bathroom at the end of the hall. "I'm going to take a bath; you can go next if you want."

Jamie looked around the bathroom, exasperated while stringing a few words together. "Sure thing."

I started to run the bath and made sure there were plenty of towels. There's nothing worse than coming out of a bath and you don't have a towel to hand. Admittedly, this was one of my very few pet hates. Jamie was sitting on the stool in front of a mirror situated to the left-hand side of the door, and he was looking at himself as though in a daydream. He seemed to be thinking about something... something that I was going to find out about very soon.

The bath was now full and as I started to take off my clothes I called over to Jamie and told him he could use the small dark brown coloured tooth brush. It was mine but things like using another person's toothbrush never concerned me much. My concerns over being naked in front of people had evaporated now so it didn't bother me to get undressed in front of him. Just as I was climbing into the bath I heard the door handle turn. Without thinking about it, I twisted around to see who it was. The door opened, blocking Jamie behind it but leaving me in full view of Anna, who had just walked straight in. Jumping into the bath would have been the sensible thing to do, but instead I just froze. So too did Anna. I had quickly moved my hands to cover anything that might have been hanging about only to feel that it didn't want to hang about any more. On the contrary, it wanted to do anything except hang around.

"Oh. Dear God I'm sorry, I didn't see you come in, I'm so sorry." Her face was now scarlet red. I just wished she would go, an uncontrollable monster was being unleashed under my hands and the embarrassment was unbearable.

As she turned and ran away pulling the door closed behind her, Jamie fell to the ground in stitches of laughter, while I quickly fell to the water and suitably controlled the monster from brewing any further. I didn't think anyone had noticed what had started to react under my hands but it didn't matter, because Jamie thought the whole episode was the funniest thing he'd ever seen.

"The second time in one day," I said, meaning only to speak to myself.

"What do you mean?" asked Jamie.

"Remember I told you I'd had a nightmare and took my pyjamas off last night?"

88

"Yes," he replied, still laughing.

"Well, when Gavin told me Gran was here, I was so excited to see her that I ran half way down the stairs before I realised I had nothing on. Only, by that time, Anna had already caught more than an eye full as she stood looking up at me from the hallway."

The sounds of laughter worsened and echoed around the bathroom with force. I didn't fancy staying in the bath long so I very quickly found myself climbing out, at the same time pulling the plug and allowing the water to swirl rapidly down and out of the plug hole. I grabbed a towel and wrapped it around myself before giving the bath a quick clean and turning the water on again for Jamie. I changed into my blue and white striped pyjamas and started to brush my teeth while Jamie settled into the fresh hot water.

I remember glancing over at him, his eyes still red and puffy from laughing and thinking how much he had started to change my life and the way I thought about things in such a little space of time. After combing my hair, I picked up my clothes along with Jamie's, that he'd so neatly placed on the floor, and made my way towards the door.

"There's a clean towel and a pair of pyjamas at the foot of the bath for you." My words had fallen on deaf ears as on turning around I found Jamie to be total submerged in the water, so I left him knowing he'd find them himself.

I walked down stairs with the dirty clothes in the hope that Mum would clean Jamie's so as to be ready in the morning. I entered the kitchen but Mum was nowhere to be seen. The only person there was Jenny.

"Dirty clothes to be washed, I suspect."

"I was hoping Mum would wash Jamie's so he had something clean to wear in the morning."

Jenny took one look at the bundle of clothes and stepped forward to take them from me. "Your Mum decided to go to bed early so give them here and I'll make sure they're nice and clean for you. I hope you ain't gone and left anything in the pockets, I know what young men are like for keeping horrible things in their pockets."

I knew I had nothing in mine but the thought had never crossed my mind whether Jamie would have anything in his. "Let me check Jamie's, Jenny, to make sure."

"Don't you think he should be the one to check them himself?"

I knew she was right. How would I feel if someone had gone through my pockets? But I was doing it to be helpful, not nosy. "It's okay Jenny. He won't mind."

"Very well," she said, putting the clothes on the kitchen table.

Making sure not to come into contact with any underwear, I put my hands into the pockets of Jamie's trousers; all of them were bare except the back pocket. I had pulled a photograph out of what appeared to be Jamie with a large group of people. It seemed to be a family picture, but it couldn't be. Everyone in the picture was smartly dressed and it seemed as if this was a picture of a very wealthy family indeed. I was staring at the picture when Jenny had caught sight of it.

"How do I know that face then?" she queried. She had pointed her finger towards the man who stood to the right-hand side of a woman and whom Jamie was standing between. Everyone else in the photograph looked younger than Jamie did, but it didn't add up.

I placed the photograph on the table and handed the clothes back to Jenny who was still asking her the same question. "How do I know that face?" she muttered over and over again.

I left her standing poised in the kitchen with her finger on her bottom lip trying to put a name to the face. I lingered outside the kitchen in the hall for a few moments and found myself thinking about Mum and why she'd gone to bed so early. It wasn't like her and she didn't seem to be acting as usual. Suddenly, I heard someone racing down the stairs. By the time I'd moved into the hall Jamie was already down the stairs and pulling his pyjama top over his head.

"My trousers! Where have you put them?" His voice was shaking as if he was about to cry with fear.

"I gave them to Jenny, she's going to wash them for you," I hurriedly answered back. "If it's the photograph you're worried about, it's ok, I put it on the kitchen table."

A sudden wave of relief washed over his face and I could see the air in his chest expel making him slouch forward slightly. "So you saw the photograph then," he asked, sounding slightly disheartened.

"Well, I never really looked at it that much, I just took it out your pocket so that it wouldn't get destroyed when your trousers got washed, that's all."

As Jamie hung his head, I had a sense of foreboding. I could see he was about to tell me something... well, something big. "I think it's time I told you a little bit about myself."

We walked into the kitchen and took up a seat each at the table. Jenny who had overheard the conversation stopped what she was doing and asked if we would like a hot drink. She made us both some hot chocolate then left the kitchen, leaving only the two of us. We sat in front of each other both clutching a large mug full with hot, steamy, frothing hot chocolate and I waited for Jamie to speak. It was obvious this was hard for him to do so I made no attempt to rush him.

After a few silent moments and at his own pace, he began to talk. "I wasn't always a boy in a poor family you know! I once, like you, lived in a house such as this. It was even bigger as a matter of fact and there was never a day that went by that I ever needed something I couldn't get. My Dad was a banker at the Royal Bank of Scotland in Edinburgh and we lived not far away from the castle. They were the greatest years of my life. Everything was perfect; Dad was a great man and Mum was just as wonderful. We lived a happy family life with my brother and sisters. I attended a boarding school called *Sir Richards*. It was an all-boys school and most of the teachers were men too. I had a great time there and learnt much about reading and writing, that's why I'm able to do many of the things that you can do without going to the school here. It was at boarding school that I first met girls and for the years that I was there I had many a nice run in with them. They seemed to take a shine to me, and no matter what happened I was always able to get a girlfriend. The girls came from the local village to watch us. They would come and watch as we played football and rugby on the large grass parks. Boy, were they fun days! Even now I think about them often.

"Unfortunately, all wasn't going to stay like that for long. All the happiness that I felt, all the joy and love that I had grown up with was about to be shattered, torn out by the roots and des-destroyed in a puff of smoke. While at boarding school, I was a very shy and pretty self-contained around the other boys. Some of them didn't like the fact that I got on well with the girls and they often called me names because they were jealous.

"As I said, I was very shy indeed and when it came to wash time, I always waited 'til the showers were nearly empty before going in. They never had baths in the school, only long corridors of showers. When you entered the washroom there was a long wooden bench right along the middle, with the shower corridor to the left. The room would always be filled with steam and the heat would make your face sweat the minute you entered."

Jamie stopped and took a sip of his hot chocolate, that wasn't so hot any more. I looked to do the same but I'd finished mine already. Placing the cup back on the table, he then continued.

"It was the night just before my thirteenth birthday and I'd made my way to the wash room like I would normally do. Most of the boys had returned to the dormitory so I considered it to be a good time to go. I walked in as the last two boys were leaving. I peered down the shower corridor to make sure no-one was still inside. Then I hung up my wash bag on the hooks above the bench and started to get undressed. As usual, all the showers had been left on so it was just a matter of going straight into the already hot water and washing.

"Just as you seem to, I also loved getting washed. I walked into the shower corridor and made my way to the middle. I brushed my teeth and then took out the soap to get washed. I had formed lather in my hands and had started to wash my hair. The soap had just started to be carried down over my face by the water when I heard a sound behind me. I turned to see what it was but when I opened my eyes they were stung by the soap forcing me to close them again. I tried to rinse my hair as fast as I could, sensing something was wrong. I hadn't managed to get it all off by the time I felt a hand on my shoulder. I turned round too quickly, making me fall onto the tiled floor. Looking up I could see three boys standing in front of me. They were all naked as if ready to take a shower but none of them had a shower bag or soap."

"I looked up at the three boys and asked what they were doing, but they just laughed. I could hear the laughter of another boy just outside the showers, making four of them altogether. I started to feel frightened and tried to get to my feet, but one of the boys kicked me back to the floor. Two of them then reached down, grabbing one of my arms each and pulled me up, while the other laughed at me and pointed at my privates, making gestures with his fingers, which made the others laugh again only this time even louder. The fourth boy had popped his head around the corner of the wall, telling the others to shut up and get on with it. I remember thinking "get on with what?" but I soon found out."

"The two boys then turned me around, pressing my face against the white wet tiles on the wall. Although it was hot, the tiles didn't seem to take in any of the heat... I could feel the coldness pass directly from them and into my face. I couldn't breathe and my heart was pounding so fast I thought it would explode. I struggled but I was a thin boy and the others were a few years older than me. The third boy came behind me and kicked my feet apart. He was rubbing himself against me while all the time he kept telling me I wanted it. I didn't want anything. I struggled and pleaded with tears but still they held me. The third boy then whispered in my ear, "*Are you ready?*" Before I had the chance to answer, it happened. I screamed with every ounce of energy I had left, only to have my head smashed against the wall, breaking the tile that my forehead came into contact with. I remember the blood running past my eye and down my cheek towards my chin, where it fell, mixing with the water at my feet and turning it from dark red to a pale light pink.

"The pain was unbearable but he kept moving backwards and forwards pushing his... his..." The tears had started to trickle down Jamie's face and I knew this was very hard for him to talk about. I was so intent on listening to what he was saying that my mouth hung open and my own eyes were watering in sympathy at his pain.

"Each of them took a turn at raping me, even the fourth boy from by the door came in and swapped positions with one of the other boys to take a turn. I tell you, I've never felt so much pain in my entire life. I couldn't speak let alone shout anymore. I gasped for breath but choked with the mixture of hot steam and fear. It didn't finish with them all raping me. After they had finished with the rape they allowed me to fall to the floor where they performed unspeakable things on me. I was crying like a baby. When they eventually left, I couldn't even summon the strength to stand. Not long after them leaving I remember looking at the steam as it travelled towards the ceiling and watching the blood float away from me and swirl down the plug hole. It was only a matter of minutes before I'd passed out. The next thing I remember was waking up screaming in the sick ward.

"Whilst unconscious, I'd been dreaming about it. Everything kept buzzing over and over in my head. I could see the trails of blood swirling down into the maze of pipes below the floor. The faces of the boys kept flying up towards me and hovering in front of my face one by one laughing with a evil smirk, the broken tile, the steam, the pain. I could see everything... but I couldn't do anything... nothing at all... and no-one came to help. When I woke up I was screaming. I could see Dad arguing with the headmaster, while Mum was standing next to the school nurse. I sprung up in bed out of breath and dizzy, looking everywhere around me... they had to be somewhere, but I couldn't see them. I was confused and very sore. I had to lie back down, as it was far too painful to sit up. Mum and Dad rushed over to my bedside throwing questions at me left right and centre.

"I was far too embarrassed to talk to them, even to look at them. I didn't want to do anything except cry and sleep, but every few hours I would awake screaming and shouting. It appears Mr Murray had found me. He was our English teacher and it was his night to do the rounds of the halls. We had to be in bed before eight thirty every night or hell mend anyone that got caught up after that. Mr Murray had found me just after midnight; he covered me in a towel and lifted me to the sick ward, where I woke up some hours later. My best friend Ian was allowed to come in and speak to me. It was him who told me about the rumours that were flying around the school. Everything from being attacked by a madman to having slipped and banged my head. Everything except the real reason, the truth. I confided in Ian and told him everything. I didn't know if he believed me, but he did what I couldn't. He told Mum, Dad and the headmaster what had happened."

"As soon as I felt up to it, the headmaster called in the local constable from the nearest town and with the two of them I walked around each classroom during lesson time. They asked me to look through the glass window of each classroom door and try to pick out the boys who had carried out the attack. I had given a description of the boys already, so when I picked the boys out it should have helped in the investigation. It wasn't long before I'd found the four boys. They were all in the same class and of the same age. Immediately the headmaster called them from their class and directed them to go straight to his office. I was allowed to stay next door while they were being questioned. The thought of being in the same room as them was too painfully overwhelming."

"After some time and some shouting, I heard the sound of doors opening. The headmaster called me back through into his office but for some reason he sounded angry. I sat there and listened to him telling me a completely different story. The four boys had said that I was in the shower with them when *I* had attempted to touch one of *them* in places I shouldn't have. As a result of this, the four boys said they turned on me and beat me up. But it was lies! I never touched anyone. I tried to tell them but they wouldn't listen. They blamed me and asked that I leave the school. Mum and Dad argued but the constable made it clear that the matter was now closed and I was lucky not to be arrested for attempting homosexuality. That last walk through the hallways was terrible. All them faces staring at me and calling me names, it made me feel sick. As I walked towards the main entrance I could see the four boys standing there... Stephen Turner, William Simpson, James Williams and Stuart Grierson. Names that I have never forgotten, and never will. They just watched and grinned as I was expelled and made an outcast; as they made me out to be a liar! A sexual deviant and pervert.

"Dad tried to pursue the matter, believing in me one hundred percent but his quest for justice was the ruination of our family. *I* was the ruination of our family because in his attempts to have the boys arrested, he never put two and two together. He never realised that the governor of the bank, Mr Grierson, was the father of Stuart Grierson, one of the boys who had performed the evil acts on me. As a result, Mr Grierson hatched an elaborate plan to frame Dad for the theft of over twenty five thousand pounds from the bank, which he himself had taken. The trail led straight to Dad, who couldn't prove otherwise and he was dismissed from his job. Our home was foreclosed on by bank and all the money we had in our bank accounts was claimed by the bank.

"Dad's face was in every newspaper across Scotland. He was front page for at least two whole weeks. The only reason Dad wasn't sent to jail was because of his excellent past record and the fact that the bank was able to recover more than enough money by stripping our assets. We were left poor and penniless, no home or money. All our possessions except our clothes had been taken from us. We moved to Blacksmiths Fire where we had to work night and day to keep a roof over our heads. My younger brother and sisters were all too young to work and Mum had to stay and keep watch over them. Only a few weeks had gone past and already Dad was showing signs of deep depression. He was fired from almost every job he managed to get and Mum and him never did anything except fight and argue. He and I got some work felling trees in the Macmillan Estate. We'd only been on the estate for two days when the boss took a disliking to Dad and his "upper class snobbery". On the Friday of our first week after we had finished work, we collected our wages from the paymasters' wicket and were on our way back to the workhouse when Dad stopped."

"I stopped also and looked around to see what he was doing. He just seemed to be staring at me. Then he told me that he had forgotten to put the lock on the axe shed. He said he would only be a few minutes and that I should go on ahead and get some dinner. Just before I turned away he called to me and asked me if I knew that he loved me. I told him of course I did, and he walked off into the darkness of the semi-felled forest.

"I saved him a seat at the table in the old shack that formed everyone's eating and drinking quarters and waited for him to get back, but he never came. I was about to go looking for him when someone walked in. He took a few small steps into the light of the oil lamp that burnt in the centre of the room, took off his hat and stood still. I looked towards him just as the rest of the men in the room did. I was the youngest person in the room, being only a boy and just over thirteen years old. The man raised his head and looked straight at me, pausing before saying anything, and I'll never forget the look he had in his eyes.

"'I'm sorry son,' his expression, while he spoke, was soulless and looked as pale and colourless as a washed beach pebble.

"'What is it?" I shouted. But I already knew. Deep down inside, I knew what had happened. The minute Dad turned and walked away from me I understood what he was going to do. You see, I'd watched him put the padlock on the axe shed and hand the keys in to the paymaster when we collected our wages. So I knew he wasn't going to lock it again.

"'He's dead!' I said to the man before he could say it himself. The man looked at me and told me they had found him hanging in the forest on their way back. Dad knew there was a third shift still to finish and he had hanged himself on a tree that covered the path they would have to use to walk back on. If that was supposed to be a dignified thing to do then he was very much mistaken. I hated him for what he'd done, taking the easy way out and leaving me to take the reins and control of something I knew very little about."

"They had cut him loose and laid him outside the shack covered in a white sheet. The only thing that spoiled the whiteness of the sheet was the grubby fingerprints that were visible along its hems. The moon had cast a bright light into the open yard, which highlighted the outline of his body from under the sheet with amazing details. I wasn't able to uncover the body and look at him, and instead watched as four of the men picked him up and carried him into the stable block. They told me to rest on my bunk; I tried to sleep wondering what I would tell Mum and the rest of the family but soon found myself lying in the stable block next to his body crying."

"I eventually fell asleep only to be awakened by the paymaster. He asked me if I would like the assistance of a horse and cart to take Dad home but I thought it would only make matters worse. We never had the money for a burial, making it pointless taking him home, so the paymaster was kind enough to allow me to dig a grave in the forest and lay Dad to rest there. The paymaster mustered a group of men to number fifteen all told including myself, giving the burial a proper feel to it. Although they never really knew him, they were kind and warm. The men planted an oak tree at the head of the grave, and told me to think about how beautiful the place would look when it was fully grown. That thought has stayed with me ever since.

"Mum cried for weeks after I arrived home and told her. As for me, well, I never had the time to stop and grieve, as I had to keep on working; I didn't have a choice. After all, we still had to eat and survive. Mum stayed in the house for much of the next few months, and I told people Dad had died when explosives went off at a quarry we were working in, killing him. I still think about him from time to time when I need help with something and the answer always seems to drop from the heavens, so I know he's up there thinking about us and watching over us. Life isn't always as it seems. I wasn't only raped and abused, I was chained into poverty. I suffered the death of a loving father along with the destruction of a family that my father had worked so hard to make and provide for, and because of what? Because of four boys, that's what. I shall never forget their names and when I return to riches I shall haunt hunt those boys down and make them regret what they did to me.

"You see, since that day, I have never been ashamed of my body, and I've never tried to hide it from anyone. If it wasn't for the fact that I was shy around other boys when naked, scared that I might not match the grade, Dad would still be alive and my family would not have been destroyed the way it was. I know it was my fault and I know I can't bring Dad back alive, but vengeance will be mine. That I swear."

Jamie had finished talking, the tears on constant flow from his eyes. I stood up and walked over to him and wrapped my arms around him.

"I'm so sorry Jamie, so sorry."

He turned around and looked at me. "I've never told anyone that before, but it feels like I've just sat down for the first time after having walked continuously for the last few years."

"You've held so much on your shoulders for far too long, Jamie." I so wanted to talk more to him and tell him how brave he had been, but my mouth was dry and I had what felt like an apple stuck in my throat. I'd never heard such a story in my entire life. I found myself thinking how easily things can go wrong and how little there is you can do about it sometimes.

I filled the kettle and put it back on the hot plate while Jamie remained seated at the table. I made us both another mug of hot chocolate, which we drank and then made our way upstairs to bed. I put my head around the door in the main room to see that Gran and Jenny were still up. By the looks of their eyes I could see they'd been crying, which suggested they'd overheard our conversation. Jamie was halfway up the stairs so I took a second to talk to them.

"Please don't say anything to him to let him know you heard. He would be so embarrassed if he thought you overheard." They both seemed to agree when they shook their heads as if unable to speak, and I left them sitting there, hankies in hand. I made my way upstairs to find Jamie was standing by the window. "You have the choice of any of the spare rooms if you like."

"If it's ok with you I'd rather sleep in here on the floor if you don't mind?"

"Of course. I'll just go and get you some covers." I quickly collected some spare covers and a pillow from the main towel cupboard and returned. "You're more that welcome to share this bed if you like Jamie."

"Thanks, but if it's ok with you I'll just lay here."

"Sure."

I turned off the light and we both said goodnight to each other before drifting our separate ways into the land of dreams.

CHAPTER TEN
Anna

It was a peaceful sleep considering the last few nights had been full of nightmares and horrid thoughts. My worries seemed to be very small compared to those of Jamie's. At some point whilst dreaming I could see him standing with me. I couldn't see anything else, just the two of us. Everything that surrounded us was a blur of dark grey and white. He was standing with his hands in his pockets, the photograph of him and his family protruding slightly from the left one. From the way his knuckles were formed through his trousers, I could tell he was clutching onto it very tightly.

"Don't feel sorry for me," he said. Then with a smile he disappeared into the grey and white background leaving me to continue dreaming.

For the first time ever, my dreams that night were totally different to what I'd normally dream about. They seemed to be brightly filled with colour and happiness. I found myself climbing over a stile leading into a large meadow full of hundreds upon hundreds of flowers. It seemed as if this was some kind of special or secret place where every rainbow in the sky came to rest. Like a holding area of colour just waiting to be sent beaming up into the clear silky blue sky above.

I walked straight to the middle of the meadow as if being drawn to something or someone. In the distance, I could see movement, but I was too far away to make it out clearly. Each step took me closer and closer until finally I was there. Looking down I found myself standing at the foot of a red tartan blanket, and there in the middle sat Anna. She was wearing a white dress, her hair held up by a white net and her feet bare. She never spoke a single word, but instead just smiled as she stretched out her hand. As I took hold I could feel her pulling me down towards her. We sat together and looked in each other's eyes. Hers were a deep chocolate brown accentuated by the light covering of freckles on her face. It was a wonderful sensation to do absolutely nothing except hold hands and watch each other. Time just seemed to be drifting away as the sky changed shapes above us.

As we looked at one another I could feel us being drawn closer and closer. Ever so slowly our lips came to touch. The feeling was amazing, unlike anything I'd ever experienced. It was as if I'd just taken a drink of ice-cold water after having been thirsty for a week. It wasn't the only feeling I had, however... At that very same moment, I found myself being awakened. It was strange, I felt great but yet I was waking up and not knowing why. Then I felt it again! Something was happening down below.

I got out of bed and stood for a second before putting my hand down inside my pyjamas. Feeling around, I found a damp and slightly sticky substance had somehow got on me. Quickly, I took my hand back out wiping it on the side of my pyjamas. My heart was beating and a lump had appeared in my throat.

"You've had a lovers' dream!"

I looked at the floor, remembering that Jamie was sleeping there. "What!"

"You'll be ok. It's just a lovers dream." Jamie sat up and rested his back against the wall. The moonlight half-lit the room allowing me to see his face as I stood there still thinking I was about to die any minute, having caught some mad incurable disease. "What were you dreaming about?"

I told him about the dream I was having and watched as he smiled before repeating himself. "A lovers' dream. I take it you've never had one before?" The words rhymed off his lips as though this was a regular everyday thing for him. I stared into the shadow of the room feeling ashamed, stupid, at the same time holding my pyjamas away from my body.

"What is it? What caused it?"

"Go and get yourself washed and I'll tell you."

I walked rather uneasily to the bathroom. On entering, I purposely left the light out, for fear of what I might find. I dropped my pyjama bottoms to the floor and leaned over the sink to get washed. The white polished porcelain felt cold against my thighs while the warm water restored me back to my former comfort. I removed my pyjamas altogether and quickly ran back across the hall and into the room. Jamie was standing next to the window. The snow had stopped and the night sky was full of stars and a bright full moon that gleamed down upon our little town.

"You feel better?" he asked as I took a new pair of pyjamas from the side dresser.

"I think so, but what happened?" I pulled on the new pyjamas and sat crossed legged on the bed looking at Jamie for answers.

Still stood by the window he explained all about sperm and how and why it's created. He also explained about how the body has ways of expelling it to make room for newer, stronger ones. Every now and then I found I was unconsciously touching myself, as if trying to add reassurance to Jamie's words. "You see, what happened to you is a natural thing that happens to all men. Put it this way, it's the first time it's happened to you, but it won't be the last time. Now let's get back to sleep."

"Thanks Jamie." I climbed back under the covers with a head full of thoughts. It wouldn't be the last time it would happen! The dream I didn't mind having, but I wasn't so keen to have the aftermath again. I wondered how Jamie knew so much about these things. I was almost sixteen and didn't have a clue, but as Jamie had already shown, he wasn't just your average everyday boy.

I lay back, my head firmly locked into position by the pillow, and gazed up into the ceiling. My head had become packed with wild uncontrollable thoughts of Anna. It was to those thoughts that I eventually closed my eyes to and fell asleep. I don't recall whether I had any more dreams that night but when I woke up in the morning I felt great. It was Sunday and the whole of the house was still asleep including Jamie. I got changed, only stopping to think about the two sets of pyjamas that now lay on the floor. If I were to give Mum the two of them to wash, she would surely think something was going on after the accusations about the bedclothes the day before. I folded up the second pair and put them back into the side drawer, knowing this would cause far less problems, and then continued on down to the kitchen. I collected Jamie's clothes that lay neatly on the table and carried them back up stairs sitting them on the bed for him to see when he awoke, then made my way back to the kitchen to have something to eat.

Toast with lashings of honey, nothing could beat it. I was on my third slice when Jenny entered the kitchen. She wasn't wearing her usual uniform this morning. I gathered it was because Dad didn't like the sight of it and more than likely told her to wear something more suited to our household.

"You're up bright and early," she said, filling the kettle. "You feeling alright?"

"Couldn't be better; as a matter of fact, I feel great."

She looked at me with an eye of suspicion, thinking I was far to jolly for this time of the morning. "Seven o'clock in the morning and you look as bright as a cockerel at day break."

105

I took her comment as a compliment and smiled as she took up a seat at the table while waiting for the kettle to boil. "So what have you got planned for the day, then?" she asked, rubbing her tired-looking eyes.

"Later, I'm going to Jamie's house for dinner, but I'm not sure what we're doing this morning. What about you, Jenny? What will Anna and you do today?"

"We have more than enough to keep us busy." At that, the whistle from the kettle interrupted the conversation and so she proceeded to get up and take it from the heat. "Would you like a drink?"

"No thanks," I replied, holding up the cup of milk I'd poured only a few minutes earlier.

The sound of people awakening throughout the house broke the silence that had held it softly. Quickly, the kitchen became a hive of activity. Mum and Dad looked as if they were dancing past each other as they moved around the kitchen. Dad was looking for the morning paper while Mum prepared to make breakfast with Jenny. Then Gran and Anna emerged looking baggy eyed and tired. Anna looked nothing like she did in my dream but Dad often said a woman looked like a dragon in the morning, and by the looks of it he was right. I had visions of Anna yawning and exhaling huge flares of fire and smoke any second. I laughed at the thought a little louder than I'd intended causing everyone to turn suddenly towards me with bewildered looks. I just smiled and made a quick exit back upstairs without saying a word.

CHAPTER ELEVEN
Expert farm hand

As I entered Jamie's room, he stirred from his sleep and half-sat up.

"What time is it?" he asked, wiping the sleep from his eyes.

"About twenty past seven, I think."

"Oh damn it," he cursed. "I'm supposed to be milking the cows at seven thirty." He stood up and grabbed the clothes off the bed and tried to break the world record for getting changed. Not even a minute later, he was ready and still continuing to curse himself. "Sorry but I've got to go."

"If you want, I'll come with you?"

"Well if you want, it might help make up for me being late."

"I'll just let Mum know and we'll get going." Jamie ran into the bathroom and washed his face while I went down stairs to tell Mum. Just as she was trying to force me to eat a plate of eggs and ham, Jamie appeared.

"If it's ok with you, would it be possible to miss breakfast? It's just we have to be going somewhere right now."

Mum looked at Jamie with an even more confused look than before, then at me. "Well on you go then, no point in being any later than you already are."

Grabbing our coats from the stand at the front door,

107

we ran outside and into the fresh crisp snow that now lay over a foot high on the ground. We ran the most part of the way to the farm throwing the occasional snowball at each other. When we arrived Farmer Mr McNeil was herding the cattle into the milking barn.

"Thank heavens for that," Jamie sighed in relief. "The cows aren't in the milking barn yet. Good morning John," he then shouted over the noise of the cows as we went jogging across the cobbled yard into the barn.

"I hope I 'aven't kept you boys 'anging about in the cold too long now, 'ave I?" A look of good fortune appeared on Jamie's face.

"Well, we only just got here ourselves, problems with the snow and getting out of bed."

We followed the last of the cows into the barn where Farmer McNeil was putting the chains on the pens behind them as they hurried in for their morning feed.

"Same drill as last time," Jamie shouted. At that, he darted off into the room at the other end of the building to start the milking machine. "Right, let's get them on then." Jamie was back and already hard at work. The last time I was here the cows were already in and ready to milk, but this time I noticed Jamie was giving each cow a wash before attaching the suckers. I'd already had my first lesson in milking the last time Jamie had brought me here so I was able to work a little faster this time. In no time we had all the suckers on and the jars were swirling with milk.

Farmer McNeil entered the barn from where he'd been watching us in the bottle room. "Well Jamie, either your friend 'ere's an exceptional quick learner or you is a great teacher."

"I think it's a bit of both," answered Jamie over the sound of the pumping hoses.

"When you is both done in 'ere, get yourself inside for breakfast, I'll go tell Mrs Mac we have an addition this morning. Only this time," he added, turning toward me, "I hope you isn't going to be flashing yourself at ma missus. And don't be going fighting wi' the water hose neither."

With a great big smile bursting to explode, he then left the barn, leaving me at the mercy of Jamie and his infectious laughter. "Remember what Mr McNeil told you now!" Jamie said, laughing hysterically. "Don't go exposing yourself in front of Mrs Mac now, I don't want you embarrassing me in front of these good people."

"Ha! Ha! You're dead funny this morning," I muttered, but quickly grew to see the funny side.

Jamie turned the pumps off and collected the bottle trolley just as he'd done the last time. We loaded the freshly filled bottles onto it before making our way towards the storage tank where all the milk was poured and stored ready for collection. We then unchained the cows that had now finished eating and with the assistance of Mr McNeil we hustled them back into the open straw filled barn at the other side of the farm. Mr McNeil had already cleaned the barn, as there was a great heap of dung piled just as we entered the door ready to be loaded in a giant sized wheelbarrow. The cows spread out into the barn each going its own separate way as if it had its own little spot.

"They're not so skinny when you're up close are they?" said Jamie. I looked at him not knowing if he was talking to Farmer McNeil or me. "I said, they're not so skinny when you're up close, are they?" he repeated.

I didn't have the foggiest idea what he was talking about.

"You don't remember do you?" I looked at him for an explanation then it suddenly became clear. The words floated back to me as if I'd only just spoken them. I could feel the heat pour into my face as it changed to scarlet red. 'Just leave him alone! We have better things to do than laugh at a poor boy with a skinny cow.' Word for word he spoke what I said on our first ever meeting.

"You know I never meant what I said, don't you?" I asked, hoping for reassurance. "I only said it to stop the others, that's all."

Jamie smiled. "I know, but it was funny. One of the cows had got loose and I was just bringing it back when I had the fortune of bumping into you lot."

"I wouldn't quite say it was fortunate, after all the others just called you names."

"Yes, but I met you and if it wasn't for that first chance meeting I would never have stopped and spoke to you when we passed each other on Old Edinburgh Road that day."

He was right, because if the truth were told, I wouldn't have stopped either if I hadn't been so embarrassed into it. Farmer McNeil closed the door to the barn then grabbed hold of the wheelbarrow.

"You boys clean da milking barn while I gets this mess cleaned up, then get yourself inside for breakfast." Farmer McNeil then set off, pushing the wheelbarrow towards the big dung heap at the far side of the yard as we walked back to the milking barn.

"You brush and I'll shovel," said Jamie collecting a much smaller wheelbarrow containing a broom and shovel. I grabbed the stiff broom and we walked along each stall cleaning the ones that the cows had left in a mess. "That's the thing about animals, they don't care where or when they go for the toilet," laughed Jamie, as I brushed a large wet cow pat onto his shovel. It wasn't long till we were finished and making our way to the farmhouse.

We were only half way across the yard when the smell of freshly cooked ham and baked bread could be smelled overcoming the strong smells that surrounded the farm. As we entered the house Mrs Mac was standing there still dressed in a white apron, as she'd been the last time we'd met.

"Shoes off, boys," she shouted. "And get your hands and face washed."

Jamie took us to a little side room that had a small white stone sink and a toilet inside. He turned the water on and washed his hands followed by a splash of water on his face. "The water's hot so be careful," he said slightly muffled by the sound of the towel that he was using to dry his face.

I followed Jamie into the massive kitchen. The floor was laid with large brown quarry tiles that swept under the rich carved oak kitchen units The cooker was so big I was sure you could fit an entire pig inside it. The food smelled so much fresher than at home.

"Well, sit yourselves down then," called Mrs Mac.

We each pulled out one of the heavy high-backed seats that were pushed under the table and sat down while Mrs Mac lay a breakfast down in front of us that was fit for a king. We were shortly joined by Farmer McNeil who, by the sounds of it, had fallen over when taking his boots off at the front door. As he lifted out a chair and sat down, he called to Mrs Mac to do the same. Removing her apron, she sat down and together we all ate.

"Well you've done us proud yet again Mrs Mac," Jamie murmured stuffing a hot buttered scone into his mouth. I ate silently, relishing every mouthful of such food - freshly made, baked, prepared then eaten.

Breakfast that morning lasted longer than a dinner would normally have done. When finished, we gave Mrs Mac a hand to clear the table.

"If you wouldn't mind putting the jam in the larder please," Mrs Mac asked me, directing me with her hand towards a large oak door at the far side of the room. "The light switch is inside, just stick it on the shelf with the rest of the jars," she added.

I made my way over to the large wooden door and walked inside reaching to find the light switch. The door had closed behind me making it difficult to find, but somehow I managed to catch a hold of the thin cord and gave it a pull. With a sharp click, the larder instantly took form.

As my eyes adjusted to the light, I gasped with fright and stumbled backwards falling against the door. The jam jar fell from my hand and dropped onto the stone floor causing it smash into a pulp clinging to its sticky contents. Hanging all around me were birds. DEAD BIRDS. Hanging upside down by their legs, and all staring at me with their dead black eyes and twisted necks. I was scrambling around the floor kicking the broken jar while trying to find my feet, then the larder door flew opened.

"My dear boy, I'm so sorry, I forgot all about the birds. I should never have let you come in here, I'm so sorry."

I looked up to see Mr and Mrs McNeil blocking the doorway. Farmer McNeil entered and offered a hand while Jamie watched from under the armpit of Mrs Mac.

"I'm alright," I panted. "It was just a surprise, that's all."

"We're that used to Jamie seeing dem birds that we never thought," explained Farmer McNeil as he sat me down at the kitchen table. "Here, let me take a look at that hand."

Before I had the chance to look myself Mrs Mac had taken my hand and was gently wiping it with a warm damp cloth. "You must have cut it on the jam jar, but it's not that bad." Slowly, she moved her fingers over the cut in the palm of my hand. "I'm just making sure there ain't no pieces of glass stuck in it. Keep this on it for a few days till it's better." I sat quiet and still as she wrapped my hand in a small cotton bandage and secured it with a safety pin.

She then put a plate of biscuits on the table and a mug of hot chocolate for each of us to eat and drink. Boy, was I glad it was my left hand that got cut. If it had been my right hand I might not have been able to drink hot chocolate! Now that would have been a disaster.

"So don't you have any children yourself, Farmer McNeil?" I asked, trying to make everyone feel better.

"Mrs Mac and me ain't able to 'ave sprogs... that was, until dis one showed up, that is." He reached over and grabbed Jamie with a hug. "When dis one showed up looking fa work it was like our long lost son 'ad come home. We both looked at the scrawny little boy who 'ad presented himself at the front door and we both knew we 'ad been gifted from above. We've 'ad his pleasure ever since."

Jamie shied like a young boy and tucked his chin deep into the crest of his chest, sending his eyes looking upwards and lip drooping down. "What are you two like?" he said, looking back up at the giant farmer.

"Well ya can't say it ain't true, now can ya?" Jamie smiled in agreement, then jerkily looked over towards the large Grandfather clock that stood proudly in the hall.

"Is that the time? We have to get going, we still 'ave loads to do."

"That will be 'have,' not 'ave', young man," shouted Mrs Mac with a motherly tone and look. "Just because this big oaf can't speak proper that ain't to say you can get away with it."

"Sorry Mrs Mac, but we best be off now, if I don't see you later I'll see you in the morning."

I made for the kitchen door but not before seeing Mrs Mac giving Jamie a kiss goodbye.

"Before you go you've got ya wages ta get first," bellowed Farmer McNeil. "If a job's worth doing it's worth paying for also." Jamie followed the farmer's large torso into one of the rooms just off the main hall then reappeared a few seconds later.

"This is for you," Farmer McNeil shouted flipping something into the air towards me. Throwing out my right hand, I managed to catch it. It was a coin.

"Sorry, Mr McNeil, but I can't accept, I never came to get money; I came as a friend to help Jamie."

"Data may very well be ad case but it's still yours, so let there be no more said about it and ad both of you get moving."

Jamie smiled and we walked out the main door and along the stone drive to the main gates.

CHAPTER TWELVE
True Goodness

Walking out of the gates, I remember looking back at the snow-covered farm and thinking how beautiful it was. All it needed was for Farmer McNeil and Mrs Mac to dress like Mr and Mrs Claus, surround them with a few elves and some reindeer and you'd have the perfect North Pole. I definitely had a vivid imagination, that's for sure. Mum was always telling me that, and in more than one way she was right. I never lied or anything like that, I just pictured things differently to how most other people did.

It was eleven thirty and the morning had vanished. "I go and see old Mrs Blake on a Sunday. I help her do some housework and things. She won't mind if you come along."

"Old Mrs Blake! You mean old Mrs Blake from High View Road?"

"That's her," he answered sounding surprised.

"But no one has seen her in years. Only people going in and out of her house."

"Well she's very much alive, I can tell you, but since her husband passed away she doesn't venture out of the house that much." As we walked towards High View Road at the top end of town, Jamie told me how he came to be working for Mrs Blake.

"As a matter of fact it was one day while walking along this very road it happened. I saw a dog running past me. I noticed it still had its leash on which was dragging behind its body as it ran. In the distance I could hear the sounds of shots being fired. I just presumed the dog had been out with its owner for a walk when it got a fright and ran off. I chased after it for well over an hour as it ran up and down every street and alley it could find before finally catching hold of it. It was a mixed breed dog with a blue and white collar that had a small silver tag hanging on it. It read, 'I AM JOE, 112 HIGH VIEW ROAD, ROCKFIELD.'

"Taking the leash, I walked him to the address and rang the doorbell, but there was no answer. I couldn't just leave, so I sat on the steps and waited. About half an hour had gone past when a woman walked up the path towards me. The dog started barking and jumping around.

"'Joey,' she cried. 'I thought I'd lost you, you silly dog.'

"'Sorry, Miss, but I found him running down the road.'

"She paused, her eyes upon me with a poached look before speaking. 'Thank you.'

"'It's quite all right,' I replied, then started to walk off along the path. I was just about to round the corner of the house when she called me back, 'you boy, come here.' I turned around to see the lady pushing the door open and moving inside. I stood for a moment not knowing if it was in fact me she had called.

"'Well I'm not leaving the door open all day,' she said poking her head around the door and waving me inside. 'Come along, you look both cold and hungry.' I retraced my steps back along the path, up the stairs and into the house.

"The smell inside was terrible. The entire house was covered in dust and rubbish. There must have been over a thousand newspapers piled up all over the place. I followed her into the kitchen where I watched as she filled a kettle, which was pitch black with charcoal as if it had been left boiling on the stove too long. She then walked over to the sink and put her frail looking hands into the dirty stale water that filled it. She moved them around for a second or two then pulled them back out with a cup in each. She placed the cups on the worktop and dropped a tea bag in each. I watched in horror as she asked if I took sugar.

"'Why don't you sit down, Miss, and I'll make the tea,' I interrupted. She gave me the same poaching look as she'd done at the front door then told me to bring it into the main room when it was ready. I emptied the sink and filled it again with clean hot water and soap. Looking around, I picked up all the dirty plates and cups that lay scattered around the dirty worktops and put them in the sink, including the ones the woman had pulled out after removing the teabags. I might have been cold, hungry and poor, but I had standards. And anyhow, I couldn't afford to get ill through eating or drinking from dirty cups and plates. Not when it wasn't necessary.

"I cleaned the dishes and put them on the sideboard to dry while the kettle boiled. Taking a look around, I quickly moved a cloth over the surfaces and picked the rubbish up off the floor putting it in the bucket. In a matter of minutes, it was looking more like a kitchen. The kettle started to whistle, so I poured some hot water into the silver teapot that I had just so nicely cleaned and together with two clean cups I put it on a silver tray. Looking around I found a sugar bowl and a fresh pint of milk. Putting everything together, I made my way out into the hall avoiding the piles of newspapers and looked through each doorway to find where I was supposed to be going.

"'In here, boy,' the woman's voice sounded sharply. I took a few steps backwards to the room that I had just passed and stared into the darkness. The room was pitch black as the curtains were drawn closed. I transfixed my eyes on the table in the centre of the room and I placed the tray on it. Without asking, I moved over to the curtains and pulled them open.

"'I asked you in for tea boy, not to go touching things,' she scorched.

"'Sorry, Miss, but it's pretty hard to drink tea if you can't see it,' I told her.

"'The names Mrs Blake and not Miss!' she snapped, at the same time offering a wicked smile. 'Did your mother never teach you any manners?'

"'She most certainly did, and the name's Jamie, I'll have you know, not boy,' I snapped right back. Here I was trying to help the old woman and she was constantly yelping at me, that's gratitude for you, I thought.

"She sat back in her chair and I knew she was waiting for me to pour the tea.

"'Sugar and milk Mrs Blake?'

"'Yes please, two sugars and just a touch of milk.' I handed her the cup, which after a quick sip she rested on the massive arm of the dark green leather chair she was sitting in. I looked around to see that this room was just as filthy as the kitchen. There was so much clutter and furniture all over the place. The biggest thing in the room was a great big maple gun cabinet full with pistols and shotguns.

"'You're a nice boy,' she unexpectedly said. We talked for the next hour or so and she told me how her beloved husband had died a year ago leaving her all by herself. She did have children but they died through illness when they were young. By the looks of it, no one ever went near the poor old woman, or if they did they sure never gave her much of a hand to keep the place clean.

"As I explained I had to get going, she stood up and collected the tea tray at the same time and she asked that I follow her. We moved back into the kitchen where she stopped and looked around.

"'Jamie! Was this you?'

"I knew what she was referring to but looked stupid as if I didn't know what she was talking about. 'Was what me Mrs Blake?'

"'Did you clean up in here?'

"'Oh that! Well, I just cleaned a few cups and things.'

"She put the tray down on the worktop and turned to face me. I could see the tears in her eyes and she walked over to a small cupboard in the corner. She took out what looked like a large tin box and opened it. She re-closed the tin and walked back over to where I was standing.

"'Here you take this, and if you ever want to come back round. You do so any time, you hear me?'

"I looked at my hand, which she had clasped very tightly. Inside she had placed fifty pounds. I tell you, I almost died of fright. 'Dear God, Mrs Blake! What on earth are you doing keeping money like this in your house?'

"'Don't you worry about that, you just get going.'

"'But Mrs Blake I've done nothing to deserve such a large amount of money.'

"'Large amount of money,' her voice squeaked with delight. 'My dear boy.' She tugged me towards the small cupboard where she'd just taken the fifty pounds from. She opened the tin once again, only this time in plain view and right under my nose.

"'Holy Mary Mother of God,' I exclaimed. The tin that was about the same size as two loaves of bread was stuffed full with money. There must have been thousands of pounds in it. I looked at her and wondered if she had gone crazy. 'Dear God. Mrs Blake, you can't keep that amount of money in the house.'

"'Are you going to tell anyone about it? Or try and take it yourself?' she asked with a serious and sudden stare.

"'I most certainly am not,' I replied angrily.

"'Well then, it's perfectly safe then, isn't it?' and with a snap, the tin was closed and placed back upon its shelf in the cupboard. Words had failed me. For once in my life, I was totally thunderstruck. I pleaded with her to take the money back several times but she just wouldn't have it. Instead she made me promise that I would come back and see her again. Almost with force, I made her follow me to the door and lock it behind me. 'Oh stop fussing and be on your way.'

"On leaving the house, I could feel my fingernails digging into the flesh of my hand as my grip on those fifty pounds tightened. I was holding more money in my hands than I'd ever held in my life. It was a year's worth of wages and would make life at home so much easier, but I couldn't spend it. Nothing I had done justified receiving such a huge sum of money. I spoke with John and Mrs Mac and they were able to arrange for a lady to go and see Mrs Blake twice a day every day of the week. The fifty pounds would pay the lady's wages for the next two years as it was only part time and consisted of less than twenty hours a week. The lady they chose was called Linda Lamb. She worked in the post office so was perfect for getting groceries and such like before going and seeing Mrs Blake. The only problem we could foresee was that Linda wasn't a dog lover. But, on speaking to her, she assured us that wouldn't cause a problem.

"Linda wasn't able to start until I'd convinced Mrs Blake it was a good idea. I told her the government had issued a new system that gave free assistance to elderly people. After a while she agreed, so I took Linda to meet Mrs Blake for the first time. I tried to get the house as clean as possible by spending as much time there as I could. I burnt all the newspapers that had lain piled all over the place along with the rest of the rubbish that filled the many rooms. After a quick dust the house almost passed as respectable. It wasn't that I didn't trust Linda, but I made Mrs Blake go to the bank and deposit the money that she had stashed around the house. The money in the large tin in the kitchen wasn't the only money she had hidden away.

"The day we walked to the bank was one of the most unnerving days of my life. Mrs Blake asked that I carry the money as we walked. I reckoned I held about three thousand pounds in cash, but when we got to the bank, boy did I get a surprise! The bank clerk looked at me rather peculiarly as we entered. But that worsened when I handed over the green shoulder bag that Mrs Blake had untidily tipped the money into.

"'I do still have an account here, don't I?' she asked the young man.

"'Oh yes, yes indeed, Mrs Blake,' he replied standing in his crisply pressed suit and clean swept back hair. He then collected the bag by stretching out over the counter and pulling it towards him. Upon opening it, his response was pretty much the same as mine. 'Dear God Mrs Blake, where on earth did you get this?'

"'Well, it's been lying around the house for such a long time that I hardly remember. James never did like the bank much when he was alive.' James was Mrs Blake's husband. The clerk slowly counted the money, taking his time to remove each and every crease and fold. On finishing, he disappeared and returned moments later with the bank manager. It was very clear that Mrs Blake was becoming very impatient.

"'Mrs Blake it's lovely to see you.'

"'Yes, yes. Let's just get on with it.' Receiving a taste of her displeasure, he quickly informed us of their banking procedure for cash amounts over five hundred pounds and how it had to be counted twice. We were held for a further twenty minutes before we found out the total amount and were able to leave. In total there was four thousand six hundred and eleven pounds. Mrs Blake asked for the eleven pounds back and deposited the rest. With a quick signature, the money was deposited and we were free to go. On the way home, she poked and prodded me into every shop we passed in order to buy me treats. Although I didn't want anything, I was forced to buy for the sheer sake of it. But I must admit the chocolate and boiled sweets were greatly enjoyed. We walked home and, after making her a cup of tea, I had to leave.

"Linda and Mrs Blake seemed to get on like a house on fire. I felt comfortable knowing that she was at least going to be well looked after for the next few years. I still continue to see Mrs Blake at least two of three times a week, Tuesdays, Fridays and Sundays mostly. Every Friday I meet with Linda when I pay her wages and she gives me information on the things that Mrs Blake wouldn't normally talk to me about."

"You should be really proud of yourself, Jamie, that's a very noble thing you've done." He had just finished telling me about Mrs Blake as we reached the front of her house.

Jamie walked in through the front door with me following closely behind.

"Is that you Jamie?" called out a frail elderly voice.

"Yes, Mrs Blake, and I've brought my friend I told you about."

"Well, come on then, bring him in," she called again with a hint of excitement.

I couldn't picture the house the way Jamie had talked about it because everything was so clean and tidy. It even smelled nice with the hint of spices in the air. We walked into the living room where in the green leather chair that Jamie had described sat Mrs Blake. She was a frail, old looking woman wearing black-rimmed spectacles. Her hair was long and silvery, her brown eyes large and strong while the outline of her thin body was visible under the light silky clothes she wore.

"I was hoping Jamie was going to be bringing a nice young lady friend with him, but you'll do just the same." Jamie had disappeared into the kitchen and I could hear the sounds of him preparing to make tea.

"I've heard much about you Mrs Blake. Jamie talks about you all the time."

"Yes, and you too, he's told me more about you then

you may even know yourself. I'm glad he's found a good friend to have fun with. Although it would be nice if he managed to find a nice young girl as well," she added. As Jamie returned with a tray of tea and biscuits, the conversation turned to Christmas.

"You must be looking forward to Christmas?" she asked.

"Oh yes, I love Christmas time, and what about you Mrs Blake? Are you looking forward to Christmas?

"I don't care much for it any more," she groaned while pouring tea from the silver teapot with her shaky hands.

"Linda said you haven't been keeping too well this week."

"Oh come now Jamie, you know all I need to do is sneeze the wrong way and she thinks I'm about to die any second."

Jamie looked at Mrs Blake and smiled. "Well, if you ain't feeling too good you make sure and tell me."

"Oh stop fussing and drink your tea."

We sat and talked for about half an hour in which time Mrs Blake had managed to force me into drinking five cups of tea and loads of sugar coated biscuits.

"Well, we'll give Joe a walk then we need to get going," said Jamie, at the same time standing up. Amidst the conversation and even though I'd been looking about the room, I never once noticed the dog that was laying alongside the green chair that Mrs Blake sat in. Jamie picked up a leather strap, which I gathered was Joe's leash. The minute the leash was in his hands the dog was up and at his side ready to go for a walk, quicker than you could say snap.

Following Jamie and Joe from the room, we went outside the house and walked down towards a small track. I'd never walked a dog before and my desire to do so must have been shining so bright because it only took one look at me and Jamie was offering me the leash. I slipped my hand through the loop and closed my hand tightly around it making sure there was no chance Joe would be able to get free. For an old dog he couldn't half pull hard. The small sharp tugs were like having Gavin constantly pulling me when he wanted something. For the first time that day, we never really said much. Jamie asked if I liked Mrs Blake and I answered by saying "yes" but we spent most of that short walk just thinking. There was even a point when I'd forgotten all about the dog and found myself thinking about Anna. I imagined I was holding her hand as we walked, searching for the rainbow colour filled field that I'd dreamt about, but I was soon distracted by Jamie who was shouting for me to turn back.

I turned to see he'd stopped; like some kind of form of telepathy, he knew what I'd been thinking about. "Stop day dreaming, lover boy, and let's get back."

With a smile and a slight look of boyishness from me, we walked back to the house. Upon removing the leash from Joe's neck he moved back to his position at the side of Mrs Blake.

"Well, it's time that we got going, but I'll be back to see you on Tuesday," Jamie said, picking up the tray of empty cups and carrying it back to the kitchen.

"It was a pleasure to meet you, Mrs Blake, and thanks for the tea and biscuits."

"The pleasure was all mine, I assure you." We exchanged a mutual look of appreciation as I left the room.

CHAPTER THIRTEEN
Dinner at Jamie's House

It was a little after three o'clock and we should have been thinking about getting back for dinner. I was going to Jamie's house for dinner and I knew Mum wouldn't have been very happy if I didn't go home first and get changed. We made our way back to my house where I got washed and changed into a pair of dark blue trousers and a matching shirt. Although I wore a tie, I knew only too well I would be taking it off the minute I left the house. I walked into the main room with Jamie close behind me to find it full of people. Everyone was sitting talking with raised voices as if disagreeing about something. We were standing just inside the room for six or seven seconds before anyone noticed us.

"We thought you two had got lost," called Dad in a sudden overcast voice that deadened all conversation. There was a short pause, after which Mum spoke.

"What have you two been up to?"

"Sorry, Mum, we have to get going. Jamie's Mum is expecting us for dinner."

"Well, you better get going then," both Mum and Dad replied as one.

We about turned and walked back out of the door. Just before pulling it shut, I turned to notice that everyone had started to talk again. As the door closed, I looked at Jamie in puzzlement.

"What was all that about?" I asked in the hope that perhaps Jamie had noticed something I'd missed.

"Beats me."

We walked back into the cold outside and followed the dug out paths keeping our feet from becoming wet. As we neared the main street I suddenly remembered for the first time all day about the hardware shop. The thoughts of dead bodies and mass murderers had somehow stayed clear of my mind all day. But now, now they had returned with a soul gripping vengeance that held tight around my throat. I stopped and stood still looking at the alley to my right knowing that it would take me down to the next street bypassing what lay beyond. Jamie had also stopped instantly, sensing something was wrong. Without so much as opening his mouth, he changed direction and proceeded to walk down the alley, taking me away from the horror and visions of death that had so rapidly reclaimed their position of front row in my mind. My sudden change of wellbeing was clearly visible and confirmed by the fact that Jamie asked if I was ok.

We walked through the streets under the ever-darkening sky and eventually came to stand at the start of Blacksmith's Fire. Although I'd never entered this place known for its gloom and sadness before, I'd passed it several times. The one thing that was predominately noticeable upon entering the street was how very little snow there was lying on the ground. The roofs were covered in thick snow except in places where flaming torch lights were standing. The street appeared to be straight and long before it curved around to the right as if following the outline of the Rockfield. The sky wasn't yet totally black but still the street seemed to be very dark, full of shadows and darkened doorways.

It seemed that down here the use of electricity hadn't yet been implemented, as almost all of the windows were flickering with the glow of candles and oil lamps. The sound of roaring fires came closer and closer the further we walked. I noticed that at the end of each drainpipe leading from the roof was a barrel that collected the rainwater. We were now deep into the street and I could no longer see the entrance when looking back. On either side, the houses merged with each other. They were all shapes and size, but still keeping the same dark, unwelcoming colour. Each house seemed to be joined by small, unlit passageways that tunnelled into the unseen darkened background.

"Here we are," said Jamie, stopping and pointing at the door that stood before us.

He walked forward and opened the wooden door, shedding a twinkle of light into the dark abyss of the street. From the doorway, we immediately entered into the main room. It was a small room with very little furniture. There was no carpet on the floor or pictures on the walls, but it was unexpectedly very clean and tidy. An oil lamp burned on the large wooden table that took pride of place in the centre of the room. Sitting in the seats around it I could see three children. One boy about eight or nine years old, and two girls around the age of twelve or thirteen. I looked at them, slightly strained by the lack of light, and could see that they were all dressed in the best of clothes. They surely didn't look like they belonged in such a house, but then I remembered what Jamie had told me. The only items they took with them from their old life in Edinburgh were their clothes.

"Is that you, Jamie?" a fresh voice called out.

"Yes Mum."

"Is your friend with you?" she called again.

"He sure is and we're both starving."

Starving! I thought to myself. If the truth were told, I was the exact opposite. The late breakfast from Mrs Mac and the biscuits at Mrs Blake's had already filled me up.

"Take a seat, dinner will be ready in a minute."

Being a lover of honey, I recognised its sweet smell as it lingered in the air. It was so strong you would have thought there was a bee's nest in the corner of the room. As we sat down, Jamie introduced me, and then put names to the faces that sat in front of me.

"This little rascal is called Paul; this is my youngest sister called Alice, and my other sister called Mary." All of them just gave a smile of welcome.

As my interest in girls was becoming stronger, I noticed that Mary, who was the older of the two, was indeed very beautiful and possessed many distinguishing features. She had long hair and a perfectly well formed face that was free of any visible blemishes. I tried not to stare but found myself occasionally looking over at her through the light of the oil burner. Jamie and I were talking about the day's events and what we could do during the Christmas holidays when Mrs Richardson came into the room holding a wooden board with what looked like a roast on it. The heat waves rippled from the meat carrying the smell of honey that had been lavishly basted all over it. It looked fantastic and smelled even better. As she lowered the wooden board onto the table, she glanced over towards me and paused, I think the darkness made her struggle to see me right. She walked around the table and stopped right next to where I was sitting:

"Well, come on then, let me see you properly." Placing both her hands on the side of my face, she held me and looked straight into my eyes. "It's nice to meet you at last, Jamie's been telling us so much about you, I'm glad to see you've grown to be a healthy boy, and I bet you like vegetables?"

"They're ok," I replied, as she about turned back to the kitchen.

"Sorry about Mum," Jamie whispered, "She doesn't get too many guests."

Only a few seconds had elapsed when she had returned holding a bowl of what looked like vegetables in one hand and a jug of gravy in the other. "Jamie, can you grab some plates from the shelf and cutlery please." Instantly, Jamie made his way through the same door as Mrs Richardson had done and soon after returned with a stack of plates and a handful of knives and forks.

All being seated at the table, Jamie passed out the plates and cutlery while Mrs Richardson cut thick slices from the still steaming joint of meat. "How many slices would you like?" she asked, placing a slice on pork on each of the plates in front of her.

"Oh, just one for me please, Mrs Richardson," I answered in a shy schoolboy voice which raised a few notes with every word. She held out a slice of meat wedged between a fork and the carving knife while Jamie gave me a nudge to hold out my plate. "Oh, sorry Mrs Richardson." I lifted the white non-patterned plate up towards the awaiting meat.

"Now help yourself to vegetables," she said, pushing the bowl in my direction. Using the spoon that sat in the bowl, I took a few boiled potatoes, some carrots and a few spoonfuls of peas.

It was a very unusual feeling being sat at the table and eating with Jamie and his family. It wasn't a horrible feeling but it was slightly strange, for some reason I felt right at home. We all sat, ate and talked at the same time. Jamie's family were very nice, and it was a pleasure to be in their company. Even If he hadn't told me about his life in Edinburgh, I would have guessed that something wasn't right when we sat down for dinner. They all spoke properly and they all ate properly, not like you would have expected of a real poor family. Apart from the décor and the presentation of the food, you would have known a mile away that they didn't belong there.

The meal seemed to pass very quickly and, although it wasn't followed by desert, it was still first class. I helped Jamie and his Mum clear away the table and followed them into what I thought was going to be the kitchen. As we entered, it became apparent that, although it was in fact the kitchen, it was also a sleeping area. On the left-hand side stood a small stove with an even smaller sink. There was a stand up dresser that had cupboards on the bottom half and shelves on the top with a small chest. On the right hand side was a staircase leading upstairs that had a single bed under it and another along the far sidewall. I looked around, trying not to appear nosy, taking in the smaller details. Yet again the cleanliness jumped out first and foremost. The beds and their covers looked crisp and the wooden floor was spotless. Under each of the beds sat neat piles of clothes, books and some small boxes. I handed the pile of plates that sat cradled in the crevice of my arm to Mrs Richardson.

"Thank you very much; you need to come around here more often."

For a brief second as we exchanged the plates our hands touched. I could have sworn that right then she was about to say something to me, but just as her lips moved Jamie appeared, pulling me back into the main room.

While we sat talking, Mrs Richardson brought up the subject of school. "Do you go to the local school?"

"Yes, yes, I do," I replied, slightly taken back by the question.

"It's just I think these girls have been out of school long..." Cutting her sentence short, she quickly looked at Jamie, not thinking about what she had said.

"It's ok Mum, he knows." Jamie's words had suddenly washed a relieved look over her face.

Not wanting the conversation to die I immediately started to talk. "That's a great idea! The school could be doing with some new faces."

Mrs Richardson smiled. "It's not that they haven't been learning while not at school because I've been teaching them here at home," she said conversationally, as if trying to defend herself.

130

"If they know half as much as Jamie does I'm sure they know loads more than the others of their age." Her smile returned and she continued to ask me questions. "How would I go about it?"

"You would have to speak to the headmaster but I don't see it being a problem, I can get Dad to speak to him for you if you like, he knows him pretty well."

"That's very nice of you. I would like that very much" I agreed to ask Dad knowing only too well he'd be more than happy to assist.

The night was drawing on and I had to think about getting back home. Jamie must have been thinking the same. He stood up putting his hand in his pocket and taking out a small pile of coins he told his Mum he was going to walk me home, at the same time giving her the money from his hand. Once again, I thanked her for the fine food and with a last glance at Mary I said good-bye to all.

"Here you," Jamie said as he closed the front door. "I saw you looking at Mary but she's out of bounds."

"There's no harm in looking," I laughed.

"As long as that's all it is; she's far too young for you and she's... my sister."

We walked back along the street with only the flaming torch lights to highlight the way until reaching the streetlights of the town. Taking the same side street to cut out passing the hardware shop, we arrived at the common green.

"I can find my way from here."

"If you're sure?"

"I am, thanks for a great day, it's been fun."

"Yes it has, I enjoyed it." We looked at each other and without stopping to think I put my arms around him. "Everything will turn out for best, you'll see."

As we embraced each other he never said anything. We let go and I could see a tear forming in his eye before he quickly turned around and headed out of the common green. "Goodnight. I'll see you on Tuesday," he shouted, disappearing into the still of the dark, cold night. It was strange: not for the first time, I had the strangest feeling Jamie wanted to tell me something. Something important.

CHAPTER FOURTEEN
Holiday Starts Early

I made my way back home up the marble steps and into the warmth of the hall. After hanging my coat and hat on the stand, I quickly slipped back on the tie that I'd taken off and put in my pocket shortly after leaving the house. I could hear the sound of people in the main room so walked in and took up a seat. Gavin was home and sitting between Mum and Dad while Gran, Jenny and Anna took up other seats in the room. Looking around, my sight landed upon Gavin. From where I was sitting he seemed to be sporting a black eye.

"What on earth happened to you?"

"Don't ask, it's a long story," he replied in a low gruff non-talkative voice. The rest of the room burst out in laughter. "So you all think it's funny? Well that's just fine." Gavin stood up and stormed off out the room, slamming the door heavily behind him.

"What was all that about?" I asked through the laughter.

"You'll need to ask your brother, I think," said Dad as the laughter lost pace to a giggle.

"Anyway, young man," interrupted Mum, "what on earth have you done to your hand?"

"Oh, it's nothing, I fell earlier, cutting it on a piece of glass, but I'm fine, honest. I'll take the dressing off in the morning."

"Very well, but it's time for your bed, you have school in the morning."

"I know, I know," I grumbled, feeling slightly embarrassed as Anna was sitting close by. Jenny must have noticed me looking at her because she asked Anna to make her way upstairs but never mentioned the word bed. We both walked out of the room and made our way upstairs. We never spoke, as Anna made sure she stayed at least three steps behind, and as I entered my room she walked past keeping silent. I was about to close the door when I found myself uncontrollably moving back into the hall.

"Goodnight, Anna," I watched as she stopped and contemplated the thought of turning around.

"Goodnight," she lightly answered without looking, and then continued to walk on towards her room.

My head went all light and airy, her words floated about inside like clouds. I was in love. I could feel it deep down inside and knew there was something special between us. I'd known Anna for years, ever since we were young, and we always got on really well, but this was different. From the moment I saw her at the bottom of the stairs, I knew something between us had changed. Still dreaming, I got into my pyjamas, turned off the light, rolled back the covers and slipping inside. The coldness of the sheets sent a sharp gasping shiver down my back causing me to freeze solid for a brief second. The day had been fantastic and that little word of goodnight from Anna had made it perfect.

I felt like a man, it was like a sudden transformation. That morning I woke up as a boy, just a plain run of the mill boy, but as I prepared to sleep I felt myself fired into the rough and tumble of manhood. I had urges to do things I'd never thought about before. I had started to take refuge in the fact that I had two good hands, or at least one at the moment, which helped in cooling some of the overwhelming emotions I had started to feel. I lay and tried to recapture the dream from last night in the hope I would find out how it ended. I had a good idea about what sex involved but I wanted to know more. After a while, I managed to keep my eyes closed and drifted like a log on water into a deep sleep.

Waking just after seven, the morning had come extremely fast. It felt much darker than normal and looking out the window it became clear why. The snow had started to fall once more, only this time it was much worse than it had been in the previous days. The paths that had been cleared in the street were now completely re-covered and topped with a few extra few inches. Judging by its speed and thickness, I could tell it wasn't going to stop in a hurry. I also knew that getting ready for school was going to be a pointless exercise. In this weather, there was no way school would be open and with only a weeks to go until the holidays, I knew the chances were that school would shut down altogether until after the New Year.

With this in mind, I never even bothered to get changed before going downstairs to the kitchen. The house was swathed in a dull bleak darkness. Most of the windows were half covered in snow, sending a chill through the air. Approaching the kitchen, I could hear the sound of the kettle whistling and voices. Curious, I stopped just outside the door and listened. It sounded like Mum and Jenny, but they were speaking just above a whisper, making it difficult to hear them. After the sound of cups being stirred came to a halt, I pressed my ear against the cold wooden door and listened. Mum sounded concerned about something. More than once I heard mine and Gavin's names being mentioned. Something wasn't right, it hadn't been right for days now. Everyone seemed to be whispering or just stopped talking whenever I entered the room. I wasn't sure what to do and felt slightly confused. Should I ask what was going on? Or wait till Mum told me herself?

I stopped thinking and walked into the kitchen, acting as if I hadn't heard anything. As I could have predicted,

Mum and Jenny closed their conversation the minute they heard the door opening and turned their heads to see whom was entering.

"Good morning," they both said in unison, looking more than a little suspicious.

"Have you seen the snow outside?" I asked.

"I don't think you'll be going to school today," Mum smiled.

"I reckon they'll close the school now till after the holidays and you know what that would mean, Mum, don't you?" She looked as if waiting for the answer. "It means you'll have us under your feet for three weeks instead of two."

They both smiled and started to have some idle chitchat. I didn't feel very hungry, probably due to the masses of food I'd consumed the previous day, but I was surely thirsty. I took a large glass of milk and went back upstairs where I climbed back into bed and tried to sleep a little while longer.

I'd only been back in bed for about ten minutes or so when I realised trying to get more sleep was useless. I was far too much awake and found myself torn between daydreaming about Anna, thoughts of the hardware shop and questions floating in my head about Mum. Thoughts rushed through my head, making concentration very difficult. I got back out of bed and after getting washed I got changed and thought about what I could do. Sitting on the side of the bed, I could hear what sounded like crying coming from Gavin's room next door. I made my way to his room door and listened outside for a minute before knocking. A sniffling muffle came from inside, so I opened the door and made my way in. Gavin was sitting up in bed, his eye still blackened and his face damp from tears. It looked as if he'd been crying for some time, as there were wet patches on the collars of his pyjama top where the tears had landed after making the short journey down his face.

"What's wrong Gavin?" I waited for a reply but nothing came, he never even moved his head or raised a single hair on his brow. He just sat there staring at the covers and occasionally wiping the tears away that continued to roll down his disheartened face. I'd never seen him like this, even the last time on the stairs he wasn't as upset as he was now.

I stood for a few moments before saying anything else. "Gavin, what's wrong? If you don't tell me I can't help."

After asking for the second time and with a firmer voice, he looked at me. "It's nothing. I'm just feeling sorry for myself."

"I think it's a little bit more than just feeling sorry for yourself."

"No, honest, that's all it is. I'm just a little upset at the moment, but it's nothing."

At this point in the conversation, I knew he wanted me there. If he didn't he would have long since told me to leave. "What happened to your eye?"

He lifted his hand and touched it, as if he'd somehow forgotten all about it and making sure it was still there. "Oh, that was Margaret."

"How? What happened?"

"Well everything was going just fine. Mrs Mullholland had made a great dinner that we all enjoyed, after which we went to Margaret's room. We sat and talked for a while and everything was going just fine. We talked about school and the snow amongst other things and after the conversation started to dry up a little I moved closer to her. We sat looking at each other for a while and occasionally muttered a sentence or two, which didn't really mean anything. The time was right, or so I thought, to give her a kiss. I held her hand and looked deeper into her eyes than ever before. I could feel myself being drawn closer and closer to her lips, and I could see the same was happening to her. My heart started to beat fast and I could feel her warm breath hitting my face. It was great; I was ready to deliver my first kiss. The kiss that I'd been thinking about for so long. Everything was perfect, and now was the time. Just as we were about to touch lips I could feel her grip on my hand get tighter. We had almost kissed under what was the most perfect moment, when suddenly and without warning her younger brother stuck his head around the door.

"'Mum,' he shouted at the top of his voice. 'Mum, Margaret's kissing Gavin in her room.'

"I turned back around from the door to look at her as her brother ran off to tell his Mum, when the next thing I see is her fist flying towards me. All I remember is Mrs Mullholland picking me up off the floor.

"To say I was embarrassed was an understatement. I wished that the ground would open up and eat me that instant. The heat on my face was hot enough to fry an egg. Mrs Mullholland, after having words with Margaret and telling her it wasn't ladylike to hit someone, started to laugh. After her Mum had gone, she told me how sorry she was but it didn't make me feel any better. She said she got a fright and didn't know what to do. I told her the next time she should just calm down and think before she sends her fists flying. I never had much time to say anything else because before I knew it she'd placed her lips on mine and she was kissing me. I always thought I'd be the lead in my first kiss, but it never worked out like that. I just sat there, opened eyed and watching as she kept me close to her and kissed me. She had her eyes closed but somehow I could still see into them. I could see how everything was going to be just great.

"After the kiss, the throbbing pain from around my eye just seemed to disappear. She let go and opened her eyes and we just sat there. I felt so light, as if my legs had disappeared and I was just floating on the side of the bed. I moved close to her and we kissed again, and that's how things went on for the rest of the night before we went to bed. I stayed in one of the spare rooms but it wasn't very easy to sleep. I found myself wanting to be with Margaret, but knowing I'd just have to wait till the morning. I guess you think it's stupid?"

"No not at all! I think it's a great thing, but if you enjoyed it why are you crying?"

"Well, um, I suppose I'm just too happy."

I looked at Gavin, sensing he was lying, but something told me not to pursue the issue just now. Instead, I told him something that I knew would cheer him up: I told him about school being cancelled. Like clicking on a switch, I saw him automatically light up and his face sprung alive like a flower opening in the sunshine.

"I'll see you down stairs, I'm going to get some breakfast."

"Sure thing." I left Gavin to get changed and went to the kitchen to get something to eat. I wasn't very hungry but the smell of food being cooked had made me want some. I entered the kitchen to find Mum, Dad and Gran. They were all tucking into a fried breakfast. It not only smelled good; it looked good too. I pulled up a seat and Mum asked if I'd like any. After handing me a rather large plate of fried food that seemed to be spilling over the side, she sat back down. Gran didn't seem to be acting the same way as she normally did. She looked bland and very tired. It was as if she had just woken up and hadn't prepared herself to come down stairs. I'd never seen her look like this before. Looking at Mum, she seemed to be in the same condition. Mum never put a foot out of the door unless she'd put on her makeup and done her hair. It was as if they hadn't been to bed all night, but I didn't remember seeing Gran when I was up earlier. On the same note, however, I hadn't gone into the main room before.

After a rather tuneless and non-conversational breakfast, I took myself into the main room. The room was rather messy with crystal glasses and empty wine bottles sitting everywhere. On the floor lay the family photo albums scattered all over the place. Some of the photos had been taking from the books and had been torn into little pieces. I walked around the room looking at the floor and wondering what on earth had taken place in here during the night. I couldn't make out what was on the photos, as the pieces were too small. Things were very peculiar indeed and it seemed to be getting stranger and stranger by the minute.

Just as I was about to bend over and pick up some of the torn photos, Gran entered. "Come now, leave that mess alone," she called firmly. "I'll have it cleaned up; you go and find something fun to do."

By this time, Gran was kneeling down on the cherry red coloured carpet and had started to pick up the photos. I didn't know what to make of it, but one thing was for sure, I'd do my best to try and find out what on earth was going on. I walked back up stairs to my room and sat by the window gazing out at the snow as it still fell rapidly to the ground. On days like this there was never much you could do to entertain yourself, and I very quickly found myself wishing school was open. I sat about the house with Gavin for most of the day. Gavin seemed to be very interested in how Jamie and I had been getting on. He even suggested coming out with us one day.

I told him about some of the things we'd been getting up to, and I saw the green-eyed monster of envy streak across his face. This made him even more eager to be involved in what we were doing and he kept asking when we were next meeting up. It wasn't that I wanted to keep Jamie to myself or for any reason of greed that I wouldn't tell him. It was just I'd only really known Jamie myself for a few weeks and Gavin was one of the boys who'd made fun of him before. I would have to speak to Jamie before committing myself to allowing him to come with us. It was a kind of strange week all round; I had fallen in love with Anna even though she didn't know it yet, and Gavin had fallen for Margaret. Things were certainly changing in our lives, and it felt great.

The snow never stopped all day and continued right on into the night. Anna never ventured out of her room much that day at all. I wasn't sure if it was perhaps because she felt a little shy around me or if, like Jenny said, she wasn't feeling too good. I was supposed to be going out with Jamie the next day but if the snow didn't stop I wouldn't be going anywhere. Dinner came and went and it wasn't too long after that I found myself pulling back the covers and going to bed. I wondered if Gavin had started to examine his body in the ways that I'd been doing. Mum and Dad never really talked to us about the matter of sex or self-gratification. I knew that many people deemed it to be a disgusting thing that only bad little boys did, but it wasn't, I was sure of that. How could something that felt so good be so wrong? And it wasn't dirty or sordid. I had only done it in my own company, so it never hurt anyone. As I had realised after my first lover's dream, it wasn't perhaps the cleanest thing to do, but it was a small inconvenience compared to the enjoyment it brought. I often considered speaking to Dad about it, but wasn't sure how to bring up the subject.

I decided to say nothing and keep it to myself. I thought it would be much better to keep it a private issue. Thinking about whether it was right or wrong didn't stop me from doing it. In fact, the urge to touch myself came at the strangest moments sometimes. Like when Anna had walked in on me, when I was getting into the bath. You would think you'd be too embarrassed to think about anything else, but when it happened I felt excited by it. It wasn't like a bad habit you could control, when it happens it happens and there's nothing you can do about it. To tell the truth, I never thought much about the rights and wrongs of it at all. I was too busy acting like a boy with a new toy to be bothered.

I very quickly fell into a great night's sleep but not

before hearing the faint sniffling cries coming through the wall from Gavin's room. I didn't believe for one minute that he was too upset or overjoyed about Margaret to be crying. However, I wasn't going to have to wait to long to find out and be able to understand what had being going on. Dreaming that night was rather scary, I'd not thought much about the hardware shop for a while but boy did my dream that night jog my memory. Just like the other dreams, I was taken back to the shop window, but this time I seemed to be drifting closer and closer to the large man. Like a ghost, I was floating though the stands and shelves that stood in my way. I tried with all my might to pull back and prevent myself from going any further but I couldn't. As if being controlled like some kind of puppet, I moved onwards until I suddenly stopped dead. In front of me, I could see the figure standing over what laid on the floor. As he bent down to pick it up, I could see the shadow of what I presumed was me at the front window cast over the far wall. I was only a few feet away from the man but the darkness still managed to drape him in mystery. A few seconds passed before I heard the sound of me falling against the window and dropping into the snow. I watched on in horror as the man dropped the body onto the floor and took a step towards me. I could see him; his eyes pierced straight through me with pure unchained evil. After a slight pause, he ran directly through me and towards the main door. The second he moved through my body my hair stood up on end. I felt ice cold and visions of a man walking down a cobbled road with a dog ran into my mind. It was as if the moment we touched he'd left a memory with me. As the lock in the door turned and the bell rang out, I woke up.

It was pitch dark and I found myself jumping from the bed and running to put the light on. I was scared; much more scared than the previous dreams had ever made me. My heart was beating and my lungs were working overtime to supply enough oxygen to keep me from passing out. I felt different in some kind of way, but I didn't know how. I just knew I wasn't the same as I was before climbing into bed.

I stood with both hands clutching the light switch for ages. My legs had stopped shaking and my breathing and heart rate gradually returned to normal. It wasn't that I was scared to get back into bed; I was scared of falling back asleep. I didn't know why my dreams kept returning me to that place and I didn't really want to know why. I just wanted to sleep without being scared out my wits. For the third time in a week I had to get changed out my pyjamas. Instead of putting on a new pair I left the light on and climbed into bed naked. For some reason, I'd never been to bed naked before. We had always been brought up to wear pyjamas. It was a very strange feeling to say the least. It was like being released in some way. I stretched out like a starfish on the bed and remember moving my arms and legs in and out. Only a few minutes ago I was scared out my wits and now I was feeling happy whilst enjoying the pleasure of a new experience.

From that night on, I never wore pyjamas again. It was only something extra to wash and they never really served a purpose unless you needed to go to the toilet in the middle of the night. Eventually, I fell back asleep and woke up what felt like a few moments later but was actually six hours on. It was ten thirty in the morning and boy, had I overslept! Getting out of bed, I found another reason why most people wear pyjamas in bed: it can be quite cold in the morning and that doesn't improve self-confidence when looking down at something that disappears in the cold. After taking a roasting hot bath, I got changed and made my way down stairs.

It wasn't until I entered the kitchen that I noticed that the snow had stopped. It was a clear blue sky and the sun was shining, sending a blinding glare into the room. After adjusting my eyes to overcome the sunlight I saw the kitchen was empty. The dirty plates from breakfast and a teapot sat rather untidily on the table. I about turned and walked into the main room and found it likewise empty. Stopping and turning around I wondered what was going on.

"Gavin! Dad! Gran!" I shouted out, but no one responded. A slight panic started to fall over me and so I started to shout even louder. "Anyone here? Hello!" I felt like a stranger in my own house and my first ever sense of loneliness crept over me, as if I was lost in the woods. Making my way to the dining room I could feel tears start to build up behind my eyes and emotions began to thrash about like a storm at sea. As I pulled the sliding doors apart, my legs almost gave way.

"Surprise!" Right in front of me stood everyone: Mum, Dad, Gran, Gavin, Margaret Mullholland, Anna, Jenny and Jamie.

It took a few seconds to register before it hit me, with all the excitement of the last few weeks I'd forgotten it was my birthday. Everyone stood gathered around the dining table that had been laid with a feast of food and a pile of presents.

"Wow, I never expected this."

"You thought we'd forgotten about your birthday didn't you?" said Dad with a great big smile on his face.

Suddenly, there was a rush of people swarming towards me. The words happy birthday came pouring from every set of lips turning into a song of mixed highs and lows. After the rendition was over and I had wiped the mixed tears of joy and fear away, I made my way to the table and started to rip the presents open. Gran, instead of giving me the usual wind up toy and pair of socks, had given me a ring. It was solid gold with what looked like an old tree on it.

"It's the tree of life," Gran whispered as she watched my eyes glow at the sight of it. "It belonged to your Granddad, and I know he would have wanted you to have it." Taking it from my fingers, she directed my attention to an inscription on the inside of the shank, which read *"Branch out and plant your roots like every man on the good earth should."*

I still had loads of presents to open but I found myself pausing and pondering over the words that had been so preciously engraved within the ring. Gran placed it on my finger to find that it fitted perfectly.

"Open this one, open this one," Gavin shouted at the same time being hushed by Margaret. Gavin never had the best taste in present buying so I never expected much from him. I took the sparkling blue wrapped parcel from him and pulled the paper off to find a little wooden box. I opened it thinking it was some kind of jack in the box, but was surprised to find it contained what looked like a little silver book. As I lifted it out of the box and opening it up I realised it was a photograph frame. Opening it revealed a family photo on the left and a photo of Mum on the right.

"I helped him pick it," said a light fluffy voice over my shoulder. Drawing my attention away from the photographs I looked up to see the voice belonged to Margaret. She was quite a small girl with red hair and a pale face. She didn't look like the kind of girl to give a boy a black eye.

"It's very nice, thank you both."

"You're welcome," she replied.

Looking over the shoulder of Gavin I could see Jamie standing patiently in the background next to Anna but they were not talking to each other. I walked towards him and wondered how on earth he knew to be here.

"How did you know about this?" I asked, at the same time catching a look at Anna.

"Remember when I was here for dinner?"

"Yessss."

"Well your Mum happened to ask me when my birthday was, then she told me she was trying to do something special for your birthday, so I suggested she gave you a surprise party. It was supposed to happen tonight but with the snow and all, your Dad thought it best to have it during the day. So he came and collected me this morning."

"He collected you from Blacksmith Fire?"

"He sure did, right from the front door."

To say that I was intrigued was an understatement, but I was far too happy to think much about it. I picked up a small neatly wrapped parcel from the table. The message read, "To a true friend from a true friend." I'd never seen Jamie's handwriting before and I'd never have guessed he had such neat and curvy writing. It was the kind of writing you found on royal parchment. Opening it I found a little wooden carved boat.

"I made it myself," he said looking rather proud at his achievement. The attention to detail was amazing; it had lots of little windows and sails. On the front of it was a carved bust of a half-naked lady. On each side of the hull was a plaque with the ship's name, 'BROTHER', curved boldly upon it. He'd painted it many different colours and even the rough-cut plaque it sat on was painted to look like waves.

"You never told me you could do woodwork like this!"

"You never told me it was going to be your birthday!"

"No, it wasn't like that. I just forgot all about it."

"If you say so." We looked at each other and just smiled.

There was no way that I was going to win in this conversation; after all, no one normally forgets about such an important day as their own birthday, so I could see why he didn't believe me. Mum and Dad gave me some new clothes and, as they did every year, they deposited money in a bank account for me. They told me when I was old enough they'd give me the bank book, and I often wondered what age old enough was.

The last present to open was that from Jenny and Anna. They didn't fuss like the others did when I started to open it; they just stood and watched. Pealing back the paper, I uncovered two items. The first of these was a massive bar of milk chocolate. I remember thinking it would last all the way till my next birthday. Placing the chocolate on the table, I lifted the second item from the wrapper. It was wrapped separately in a brown paper bag. Opening it, I put my hand inside and lifted the contents out. The blood started to rush to my face as I released what it was. There were three in total in three different colours. It was three pairs of underwear, but not like the normal underwear I wore. It was far more modern looking.

"I hope you like them," laughed Jenny.

"Yes, yes, they're great." I didn't know what to say. Words had escaped me and I found myself speechless.

"Well try them on then and give us a spin," Jenny shouted. The entire room burst into fits of laughter while I shrunk with sheer embarrassment and turned an even brighter shade.

After all the presents were opened and I'd returned to a more natural shade of colour, we all sat around the table and proceeded to eat some of the feast that covered it. As we sat down, I understood how such a small girl like Margaret was able to give Gavin a black eye, as she kept slapping his hand for eating like a pig. Mum and Dad laughed at the sight of Gavin being tamed by the love of his life while Jamie kept trying to take my attention away from Anna. I couldn't help but envisioned myself prancing up and down in front of her wearing the underwear she gave me. My visions were shattered however when I pictured her rolling around the bed laughing. I must admit it brought a smile to my face and I saw the funny side of it.

For the first time in ages we felt like a real family. We were all talking and having fun; there was no sign of the funny goings on, or the low whispers of recent days. Even

Gavin seemed to be happy, and Mum and Dad hadn't argued for a few days. It felt great, and to top it all off, Christmas was going to be here next week. It was then that it hit me; all the whispering was more than likely about today. That's why everyone kept going silent, because they didn't want me to find out. Even Jamie was good at keeping a secret.

By the time we had all finished, it was past two o'clock and the snow had been stopped now for well over two hours. Everyone had started to move into the main room except Mum, who went upstairs, and Jenny, who stayed behind to clean up the mess.

"How would you like to come with me later?" Jamie asked.

"Sure," I replied, eager to find out what he had planned for us.

As we sat down, Anna came closer and closer to where we were sitting and eventually joined in on the conversation. It felt great to be sitting next to her and talking like Gavin was doing with Margaret. I wanted so much to find out if she felt the same way towards me as I felt towards her, but I was scared and somewhat unsure how to ask her. Being so close to her made me very excited and trying to concentrate was proving to be extremely difficult.

After only a few hours, I asked Jamie if it was time to get going. He understood that I wanted to get out the house so agreed. We said good-bye to everyone except Mum who had still not come back downstairs. I didn't think much about it because Mum often stayed upstairs to work with her sewing machine. I shouted goodbye as I put on my coat and we left the house. Walking down the front steps, I thanked Jamie for coming and making it such a special day. He didn't say anything in words, but his smile conveyed what he was thinking.

"Well, where are we going then?" I asked inquisitively.

"I told Mrs Blake that we'd go round and see her

today. I also told her it's your birthday, and she said she'd make a cake."

"She didn't have to go to any bother for me."

"Nonsense, she took a shining to you. She thinks you're a nice boy."

"A nice boy! What does she mean by that?"

"She just thinks you're a gentleman. Somewhat like me."

"Jamie Richardson, I can tell you now, both you and me ain't no gentlemen. Men like us are simply good decent folk."

"You know what? You're right."

CHAPTER FIFTEEN
Christmas Death

We travelled through the snow until we reached the street that Mrs Blake's house was on. From here we were able to see a group of people standing outside the house. A look of panic appeared on Jamie's face turning our walking into a jog. Just as we approached, Linda came running out from the front door.

"Jamie, I've been looking for you all day!"

"What is it Linda, what's wrong?"

Linda looked pure white, her expression dead and almost ghostly. Listening to her dry throat and sticky lips, it was obvious she was finding it hard to talk. Jamie's voice rose as he asked again, still making our way up the steps and into the house.

"Well, Linda, tell me! What's happened?" Just as we entered the house, she stopped us in the hall and gave me a look as if wondering who I was. "Don't worry Linda, he's a good friend, he can listen." I respected Jamie for allowing me to stay, but I wasn't so sure I wanted to hear what Linda was about to say.

"She's been asking for you Jamie."

"What do you mean?" he asked in quick reply, his voice now starting to break into a high pitch.

"She's not well, Jamie. Not well at all. I've been trying to find you all day, but no one knew where you were."

"What's wrong with her?"

"The doctor's still in the bedroom with her. She's relly sick."

Jamie had now turned the same pale colour as Linda. His eyes glazed over and his body shook uncontrollably. He made off in the direction of Mrs Blake's bedroom; it was situated just of the main hall on the ground floor.

"Wait, Jamie, you can't go in there yet!" yelled Linda, running behind him. Jamie completely ignored her shouts and barged straight into the room. I stood in the doorway and watched as Jamie fell to his knees at the side of the bed and grasped Mrs Blake's hand.

"What on earth?" called the harsh voice of a man as he took to his feet from the corner of the room.

"Sorry, Doctor, I tried to stop him," gasped Linda.

"What is the meaning of this, boy?"

The now bloodshot eyes of Jamie turned in the direction of the doctor. His mouth had already started to move before his feet had the chance to lift him up. "What is the meaning of this? The meaning of this?" he shouted, crunching up his fists and shaking more violently than ever. "Who exactly do you think you're speaking to, Doctor?"

"Jamie, the doctor's just trying to help," Linda cried as the two of them drew within inches of each other. The Doctor was a very tall man and dressed very similarly to that of an undertaker. Seeing Jamie look up at him with such anger in his eyes, I knew instantly he was capable of toppling such a giant.

"I, doctor, am the only person in this town except Linda here who cares for this woman." I knew my exclusion from the list of cares was not to be taken personally. I understood very well that Jamie was trying to make a point, and that he was.

The doctor was taken aback by Jamie's outburst and took a step backwards as if expecting Jamie to throw a punch at him. Realising how concerned Jamie was about

Mrs Blake, he changed his attitude suddenly and completely. "I don't mean to offend, Mr?"

"The name's Richardson, Jamie Richardson."

"Excuse my ignorance, Mr Richardson, but I was under the impression Mrs Blake had no acquaintances."

"But Doctor!" called Linda, "I told you about Jamie, You know Mrs Blake's been asking for him!"

You could see the hesitation in the doctor as he considered his answer very carefully, but before he had the chance to respond the frail poorly voice of Mrs Blake spoke out.

"Jamie, Jamie, is that you?"

Jamie rushed back to Mrs Blake's bedside and grasped her hand that lay idly on top of the pink flowered covers. "I'm here Mrs Blake, right next to you."

She turned her head and as if with a lot of struggle she opened her eyes. "My dear boy, you're here."

"Yes Mrs Blake, I'm right here."

"I thought I'd lost you again."

A puzzled look appeared on Jamie's face and he looked at Linda and me as if looking for an answer.

"I'll explain later," said Linda, who seemed to know what Mrs Blake was talking about.

"I'm not lost, Mrs Blake, I'm sitting right here, right next to you. Everything's going to be just fine."

As if trying to keep her strength, she re-closed her eyes but continued to speak. "I don't have long, Jamie. I know what's coming and I'm not scared."

"Don't be so silly, you've got loads of time, you're just feeling under the weather, that's all."

A slight smile appeared on Mrs Blake's face as she strung a further sentence together. "Always trying to help me, now it's time for me to help you." Her voice had started to fail and what little colour she had in her face when we'd first entered the room had now almost totally drained from her skin. Like an egg timer about to drop its last grains of sand, she lay helpless and weak, ready to accept death as it slowly led her away.

"Mrs Blake, you're going to be just fine, even the Doctor will tell you, won't you Doctor?" Jamie looked towards the doctor who had re-seated himself in the chair in the corner of the room, but the doctor never took his eyes from the floor or opened his mouth to give any words of encouragement.

"Won't you, Doctor?" Jamie repeated in a more raised and angry voice. But the doctor stood firm and unshaken. Looking at the grasp Jamie had on Mrs Blake's hand, it was clear to see her life was almost over. Jamie's hand appeared bright pink against the cold grey looking skin of Mrs Blake's.

"Sorry, Jamie," said the frail spiritless voice.

"You don't have to be sorry, you haven't done anything wrong. Just save your energy." He bowed his head in sorrow.

"You made me so happy," she whispered, every word weaker than the last. "Jamie are you still there?"

"Yes, Mrs Blake, I'm here."

"She's starting to hallucinate." Everyone looked towards the doctor as he stood up and walked around to the other side of the bed. Her hair looked tatty and wet caused by the sweat that was pouring from her and soaking the pillow she lay on. Looking at her face, she resembled a stone statue standing still in a winter garden, rather than a living being.

"I love you Jamie."

"I love you too, Mrs Blake."

After a pause the doctor placed two fingers on the side of her neck. Almost simultaneously, with his left hand he swept down across her stone like face, closing her eyes completely. "I'm sorry Jamie, she's passed away."

The doctor stood looking down at Jamie, whose grip showed no sign of loosening from Mrs Blake.

"No, no, Mrs Blake, wake up, Wake up, Mrs Blake. Please wake up," Jamie started to cry as he tucked his head into the covers next to his hand.

Apart from Jamie and Linda's cries the room felt and sounded dead. The doctor bent down and lifted his bag from the floor and proceeded to walk quietly towards the door. With one last glance behind he moved past me and out of the door with his head hanging low. As he went out of the front door, I could hear the voices of the gathering outside dull down in respect at the doctor's news.

Jamie moved himself onto the bed beside Mrs Blake, as she lay dead. Linda knelt down at the foot of the bed clasping her hands. In a weak and shallow voice, she started to pray. For some reason, I wasn't able to cry, and, even though I wasn't religious, I bowed my head and contemplated the words she spoke as she prayed for God to take Mrs Blake's soul to a better place.

Not knowing quite what to do, I closed the door to the room and walked quietly into the kitchen and put the kettle on the stove to make a pot of tea. Linda and Jamie needed a while to themselves and I couldn't think of anything else to do. I felt a strange kind of numbness fill my bones and a deep sensation of sadness had somehow washed over me, yet I didn't feel like crying. I'd never seen a dead body before but Dad's words the day when I watched the doe being killed gave me a different outlook on death. I watched out of the window as the people who'd gathered around the garden started to disperse. Obviously satisfied in their quest for gossip, they were armed and ready to spread the tale of the lonely old woman who died all by herself, or rumours to that effect.

The kettle started to hiss and whistle as the roasting hot water jumped from the spout. After searching the cupboards for cups, I placed everything on a tray and proceeded back to the bedroom. Balancing the tray on one hand, I knocked the door and waited a second before Linda came and opened it.

"I've made us a pot of tea."

"Oh, thanks."

Jamie sat on the side of the bed, his head in his hands, and only looked up as I placed the tray on the dressing table. It didn't feel like the time to ask who took milk and sugar so I poured three cups and place two teaspoons of sugar and some milk into each of them. Without having to ask, Linda picked up a cup and immediately started to sip the roasting hot contents. Picking up the other two, I moved over to Jamie and offered one out which he took using his two rather shaky hands.

The room fell into a sudden and somewhat eerie silence only disturbed by the occasional slurp of tea and sniffling nose.

"You know, I did love her," said Jamie out of the blue. "Not like real love, but like a mother and son love. From the minute we met I knew there was something special between us, like a bond of some sort. It sounds stupid I know but..."

"But nothing," I rudely interrupted. "I know how much she meant to you, and you don't need to be ashamed for the way you feel."

Jamie turned and looked down at the body that lay innocently under the covers of the bed and gazed opened eyed. "What do we do now?" he asked.

We looked at Linda, whom we both presumed would know because she was much older than us, but the bland and somewhat stupid expression she held told us she didn't know either. As if springing to her own defence, she burst into speech. "I've never had to bury someone before!" I remember thinking Linda wasn't the kind of woman who was tactful and ladylike, and by this demonstration I was right.

I stood for a minute before I realised the best person

to speak to was sitting in the main room of my house. Dad had been to many funerals over the years and was sure to know what to do.

"Jamie, if you like I can go and ask my Dad to come round. He's sure to know what to do."

A slight look of relief and appreciation came over him and without waiting for his full reply I went from the room and ran towards the house as fast as I could without falling and breaking my neck on the ice. On the way, I considered everything that had taking place over the last hour and wondered why life played the way it did. I mean, everything in life has a reason. A stove is used for cooking and shoes are used to protect your feet, but what are humans used for? When considering the role we have to play in the big bad world it's hard to figure it out. Surely the world would be a much better place if we never existed. That way there would be no wars or destruction, no murdering or hatred. The only thing I was able to come up with was that the earth is just a stepping stone. A place to collect a character and a soul before moving onto a bigger and better place. I wasn't sure if in fact God was the person behind life and death or if it was just a natural progression with all things living. In any case, I wasn't going to contemplate the subject too much or turn into one of the world's great philosophers; I had much more important things to be getting on with.

I entered the house and without taking off my hat and coat I walked straight into the main room where Dad was sitting with the rest of the family. Trying to act calm and normal, I gave him a look that suggested I wanted to speak to him. Acknowledging my request, he stood up and followed me out into the hall whereupon he closed the door behind him.

"Is everything ok son?" he asked hesitantly.

"Well, not really, Dad. Do you remember I told you about the lady that Jamie helped to look after, Mrs Blake?"

"Yes."

"Well, she just passed away."

"Dear God, I'm so sorry."

"We were just on our way to see her when we noticed a group of people standing outside her house. Linda, the lady who also helps to take care of her, came and told us she wasn't feeling too good. When we got in the house we found her in the bedroom with a doctor. After a short time of speaking to Jamie she just slipped away."

"Is Jamie alright?"

"Well, he's rather upset but he doesn't know what to do next and I was wondering if you could come over and help him?"

"Of course, I'll just grab my coat and tell your mother we need to pop out."

Dad wasn't a young man any more so I thought it best to walk instead of run, and anyhow, it gave us a chance to talk and catch up. We never talked about anything in particular other than how Jamie must be feeling really upset and what we'd been getting up to lately. The walk seemed to last for ages. By the time we reached the house, the sun had almost disappeared completely, leaving a cloudless and pink sky residing above. On entering the house, the piercing silence and lack of light was the first indication that death had a strong presence. We walked along the hall until we reached the bedroom door. I looked up at Dad, and with a raise of his eyebrows I knew we were ready to go in. Dad took the forefront and knocked the door lightly whereupon the face of Linda appeared as it opened. Inside the only light came from a small bedside table lamp, its frilly shade matching the flowered bedcovers which still enshrouded Mrs Blake.

Jamie had taken up residence in the chair, which was previously occupied by the doctor.

"I'm so sorry Jamie. I can only imagine how you're feeling."

In response, Jamie stood up and looked at Dad. Even

though his face was covered by shadows, his red eyes and flushed face were still visible. "Thanks, Thomas, I appreciate you taking the time to come round."

"Make that your first and last appreciation, Jamie. I'm here because I want to be, because I want to help."

"Would you like a cup of tea, Sir?" asked Linda.

"Yes, that would be great Mrs...?"

"Oh sorry, Dad, this is the lady I was telling you about. Dad meet Linda, Linda this is my Dad."

"Pleased to meet you, Linda."

"Likewise, Sir."

"Linda, please the name is Thomas!" "Thank you Thomas."

Linda left the room taking a tray of empty cups with her, while the rest of us moved closer to the bed.

"I'm a little lost at the moment; I just never thought anything like this was going to happen."

"That's the unfortunate thing about life. We never know what's around the corner and the strangest things can happen at the drop of a hat." I wasn't quite sure if this was an appropriate time for one of Dad's meaningful and slightly spiritual conversations, but by the look on Jamie's face he seemed intrigued by the words of wisdom.

As Dad and I stood, Jamie sat down on the side of the bed and lifted Mrs Blake's hand, which had now taken on a blue-toned colour and a heavy-looking appearance. "I'd never spoken to her about death and funerals. We didn't talk about how she'd like to be taken care of after she passed away."

Just before Jamie had finished, Linda had re-entered with the tray of tea. She slipped it back into place on the top of the dressing table then proceeded to open the top drawer. She'd only opened it a couple of inches before slipping her hand inside and pulled out what looked like a white envelope. Everyone including Jamie had turned their attention to Linda's hands. She moved towards us holding the envelope strongly and close to her body.

"Here Jamie," she said in a light, careful voice. "Mrs Blake asked that I give this to you if anything ever happened to her."

"She told you she was dying?"

"No *honest*, she never told me anything like that. Just that if anything did ever happen I was to give you this."

Rather suspiciously, Jamie took the envelope and examined it loosely. On the front was written Jamie's name in bold black sweeping italic letters, whilst on the back was a small red seal. I wasn't quite able to make out the impression of the seal except that it bore the name *Blake*. With his hand still shaking and everyone standing there watching him, he began to open the seal, but before he had the chance to lift out the letter Dad spoke.

"Would you like some time to yourself, Jamie?" Although I could sense we all wanted to know what writings it contained, I knew Dad was right. This was a time for Jamie to contemplate what Mrs Blake, perhaps in her last days before death, had wanted him to know.

"Please, I'd prefer if you'd all stay." No one said anything else as we stood and watched as he lifted the letter out. He placed the envelope on the bed beside him and stared at the still folded pieces of paper. "Thomas, would you?" Jamie had put out his hand containing the letter and was directing Dad to take it from him.

"Could you read it please?" he asked. In a rather slow and painful looking transfer, Jamie handed the letter to Dad. Treating it with every ounce of care, Dad unfolded the few pages and took a deep breath before starting.

My Dearest Jamie

I'm so sorry if right now I'm causing you a great deal of pain and suffering. I don't mean for you to be feeling that way. I know you'll be wondering why I didn't tell you or Linda that I wasn't well, but I hope you'll understand when I say I didn't want you to feel sorry for me, or devote any more of your time to me. I have known for some time now that my life on this earth was drawing near to a close. In fact I knew even before we very first met. The doctor has been amazed I've lasted so long. The last few years of my life have been some of the best I've ever experienced, and I want you to know that it's because of you I've lasted far longer than expected. You gave me a new hope to live, a new lease of life and for that I'm eternally grateful. For someone so young you carry with you a great responsibility to care for others, a responsibility that you don't have to carry but one that you choose to out of love and care for the people around you.

I once told you that my children died when they were young, but something I never mentioned was that my oldest son was also called Jamie. You reminded me of him so much that day I found you sitting on the steps to the house. From the second our eyes crossed paths I felt a strange attachment to you. I know you weren't a replacement for him, but I know God had gifted me my last wish before taking me away, and that was to feel special once more. Like the special feeling of receiving a present from your child on Christmas Day. Or like giving a boy a reward and finding he hadn't spent it on himself but had secretly given it back. I always knew that Linda wasn't a helping hand from the government, and it was only after much arguing that she finally told me the truth, the truth about how a young boy thought more about an old crabby woman than himself. Your deed was a very noble one, Jamie, and I know your mother must be very proud of you, as I am.

I ask that you don't look at my death as a sad event, but would rather you treat it as a glorious one. For glorious it will be when I'm reunited with my children and husband again after passing through the gates to

Heaven. You should know that I shall always be with you in your heart. Always ready to talk to you and comfort you when you need a shoulder to cry on. In your moments of sadness and happiness I shall be there to assist or rejoice with you. Until the day we meet again I hope that the earth will be a good home to you. I know you'll make a great husband and a loving father and hope that children bring you a world of happiness.

As a dying wish I ask that you have me buried in the grave of my husband in the town cemetery. I don't want to see any tears and hope you'll be brave enough to keep your head high. Over the years I haven't gained many friends so don't expect it to be a busy occasion. There's no need for an elaborate ceremony, so keep things simple and straightforward. You should contact William McNorton Undertakers to prepare me for my rest. They should be very helpful as they assisted in my husband's funeral. I would further instruct you to take this letter and that you ask your good friend to escort you and go to see my solicitors, Henry Jacobson and Sons. They can be found at 11 King Street in Edinburgh. You should ask to speak to Henry senior; he shall take care of you.

Remember, Jamie, I shall always love you, and I shall always be with you. Although your life may change in the near future I know you'll follow your heart. I end with saying good-bye and wish you every success in your life. Until we meet again,

> *Love*
> *Mrs Yvonne Blake*

P.S. Please take care of Joe for me.

As Dad's hands lowered and his head looked upwards, the room fell into a dull silence. We had just listened to what could only be described as one of the most beautiful things

I'd ever heard in my entire life. The words penned by Mrs Blake as she was dying came straight from the heart. They were pure and unadulterated loving words. Her letter was so correct and precise. She had managed to capture Jamie's spirit and soul and chained them into words.

Looking at the others in the room, contemplation rang out from every face. Quite what they were contemplating I wasn't sure. I suppose if it wasn't about death it would have been about God and religion. No one actually broke the silence, or at least not that I remember, it just sort of happened. One minute silence, the next talking voices.

Although Mrs Blake had told us what was to happen, we still didn't really know what to be doing next. Dad handed the letter back to Jamie and he slowly placed it back into the envelope.

"Linda," Dad asked, "do you know where to find McNorton's the undertakers?"

"Yes, Thomas, they're just off the main street across from the church."

"Would you like to go there and explain what's happened? I'm sure they'll know what to do next."

"Yes, of course." At that, she about turned and left the room looking as if she was about to carry out some kind of top secret special mission. Dad walked over to the door and switched on the main light, sending the room from darkness into colour. Jamie had taken to his feet and had joined us at the foot of the bed where we looked down at Mrs Blake, lying cold and dead in front of us.

"I know she said to be brave and not to cry but I just can't help it." At that, Jamie turned to Dad and began to cry. I watched as he tried to comfort him by placing his arms around him, his words trying desperately to drown out the sound of tears.

"Everything's going to be ok Jamie, you'll see."

As I watched I couldn't help but feel slightly redundant. I felt as if I was floating in the corner of the room and watching down at everything that was going on. I had a bird's eye view of the entire room. Somewhat like being the only person sitting in a theatre house and watching a play being performed. From the opposite corner of the room I could see something coming towards me. I wasn't too sure what it was but I remember feeling extremely calm considering. As it came closer it became clear what or should I say who it was, it was Mrs Blake!

She, like me, was floating in the high ceiling above Dad and Jamie below. In normal circumstances I would have been screaming at the top of my voice but something inside was telling me there was nothing to fear. She came to stop about a foot away. From this distance, I could see she was dressed in pale coloured clothes with a hat that had feathers sticking out the top. It was as if she had just come home from church or something.

"My dear boy," she said in a rather peaceful voice. "I can't say how much I'm pleased to be talking to you. Only now that I've departed from my mortal body, am I able to see how much pain others keep stored inside. I see you hold very little pain although confusion hangs over you. Jamie, though, holds much pain and suffering, far more than he deserves. A life of heartbreak and misery controls him. I fear that I've given him the key to unleash his demons and set right what was wrong."

I didn't understand what she was telling me. Immortal bodies! Unleashing demons! What did it all mean?

"You must look after him. Take care of him and be there when he needs you the most."

"Be where?" I shouted, but just then she vanished and I found myself standing back on the bedroom floor, Dad still embracing Jamie as he cried.

Mrs Blake had told me confusion was hanging over me and she was right. I was so confused I didn't know if I was coming or going. Had I just been daydreaming? Or had I

163

really just seen and talked to the ghost of Mrs Blake? Her words jumped about wildly in my mind as I tried desperately to make sense of them all. The key to unleash his demons. It sounded like something you'd find in book banished by the church to a sacred vault in the cellar never to be seen by human eyes.

"Thanks for being here, Thomas," Jamie said to Dad.

"Here, use this." Dad took a white hanky from his coat pocket and gave it to Jamie. As he dried his eyes, there was a sound from the front door, which was closely followed by the bedroom door opening. Linda had returned and behind her were two men. Both of them were dressed in black from head to toe. On entering the room they removed their top hats and looked at the ground while Linda introduced them.

"Jamie, this is Mr William McNorton and his brother David."

"Sorry to be meeting you under such unfortunate circumstances," said William while his brother nodded in agreement.

"Thanks for coming at such short notice, it's really appreciated."

"A demand our business requires, unfortunately. This must be the recently departed Mrs Blake." William said as he and his brother moved to the side of the bed. "If I could ask that you all leave the room while we make the preparations." The four of us left the bedroom and found ourselves stopped in the hallway.

"Joe!" Jamie shouted. "I forgot all about him." Jamie ran into the main room and switched on the light. "There you are, boy." As we entered the room Jamie was sitting on the floor next to Joe. "I'm sorry Joe, I forgot all about you, didn't I?"

As if sensing what had happened, Joe just lay on the floor with his head sitting between his legs and his eyes transfixed on the carpet. Jamie looked up as we stood gathered around him and sighed. "I think he knows."

I tried to help by talking but to no avail. "Animals are normally pretty good at sensing things. I learned that at school." My knowledge of animals and their sensory powers didn't seem to impress anyone or help the situation any. I decided to vet any further outburst I might consider saying and decided to offer my assistance by making some more tea. "Would anyone like a drink or something to eat?" This definitely received a different response. Everyone looked delightfully pleased at the offer of food.

I left Dad and Linda sitting in the chairs while Jamie stayed sat on the floor and made my way to the kitchen. However, just before I had the chance to reach the entrance, the McNorton brothers blocked the way, forcing me back into the main room as they walked past with a coffin. It was dark brown with brass coloured handles on it. I watched as they passed by, struggling to manoeuvre it through the bedroom door.

As the door re-closed I made my way to the kitchen. I filled the kettle and put it on the stove to heat, then went in pursuit of food. It was now late and I hadn't eaten anything since I left the house earlier in the day so the thought of food had made my stomach start to rumble. I opened the larder door and peered in to find the light switch. After pulling the cord and viewing the shelves, all I could find was a loaf of bread, a few vegetables and some pots of preserve. I took the bread and a jar of some rather old looking honey and put them on the near by worktop. After searching the drawers, I managed to find a knife to cut the bread and one to spread the honey. I opened the sticky lid and looked inside before deciding it was okay to use. My bread cutting skills weren't the best by any means and each slice must have been about two inches thick. That easily increased to three inches after the honey was put on.

As the kettle whistled, I took it off the heat and placed it on the cold side of the stove. I looked around for the teapot and remembered we'd left it in the bedroom. I paused for a second wondering if I should disturb the undertakers or not, then decided to knock and ask them. So I walked back along the hall past the main room and stopped outside the bedroom. I could hear the brothers speaking inside but couldn't make out what they were saying. I knocked lightly as a mark of respect and waited for a second. There was no reply so I knocked once again, but still no reply.

Taking the doorknob in my hand I turned it slowly and looked inside as I opened the door. On the bed lay the wooden coffin with its lid propped up against the wall. Mrs Blake's absence from the bed suggested she was now lying inside the coffin. This was confirmed when I could see William McNorton holding her hand and looking at the rings she wore.

"She loved wearing her rings; I don't ever recall her ever taking them off. I suppose she'll want to be buried with them." Of course, I was talking utter rubbish, I never knew any such thing about Mrs Blake and her rings, but I could see the glare in William's eyes as he stared at the gem encrusted golden rings. I knew instantly the professionalism of the McNorton Brothers wasn't as Mrs Blake had suggested or had been led to believe. I likewise knew that given half the chance they'd have taken the rings and sold them.

"Of course, young sir," William muttered.

Spotting a small jewellery box on the dressing table I handed it to William and asked if he'd kindly remove the rings and place them in it. He knew that I knew what he was about to do, but the both of us just acted normally. As William slipped the rings off Mrs Blake's hand and into the jewellery box, I noticed the drawers on the dresser that were previously neatly closed had been ruffled. Knowing William was watching me very closely, I drew his eyes and attention towards the dresser.

"Tell me William, is searching through a dead woman's belongs a demand of the job?"

"What exactly does the young sir mean?" he answered, trying to sound as honest as possible.

"What I mean, Mr McNorton, is that you and your brother here haven't been giving Mrs Blake your undivided attention now have you? I don't see why on earth you'd find the need to go rifling through Mrs Blake's belongings." My anger that was now raging inside had become very clear in the tone of my voice, although I was trying very hard to keep my voice just above a whisper.

After a few seconds of still silence, William spoke, "We were merely looking for something more appropriate for Mrs Blake to wear."

This was a very feeble excuse and a blatant lie. "Well, tell me, did you manage to find something more appropriate then?"

"Em well, well..."

"No, I didn't think so. I'll tell you once Mr McNorton, anything you and your brother have taken from this room better be returned to where it belongs. And let me assure you, if I find so much as a hair out of place I'll have the police here quicker than you can move an inch. Am I making myself clear?"

"Very clear, young sir, very clear." As the two brothers moved closer together in defence, I stepped forward and took the jewellery box from William's hands and moved over to the dressing table. Before lifting the tea tray I stopped and looked at the two brothers as they stood eagle eyed at me.

"Can I say that you two should be ashamed of yourselves. Put in a position of trust, you've violated everything holy about your vocation and you ought to think very carefully the next time you ever attempt to carry out such shameful acts of theft and dishonesty." At that, I lifted the tea tray along with the jewellery box and left the room.

As I walked out of the room I found Dad to be standing in the hallway. "That was a very brave thing you've just done, son."

I looked past him to see if Jamie or Linda was standing close by before answering. "I take it you heard?"

"I sure did, not that I was being noisy, it's just I noticed you walked past and presumed you went for the tea tray, only when you didn't come straight back past I knew something wasn't right. I was going to come in but I could hear you had the situation under control."

"Please don't mention this to Jamie, he's had a bad enough day as it is." With a look of agreement, Dad turned and went back into the main room while I made my way back to the kitchen. I placed the kettle back on the stove to heat while I washed the cups and refilled the milk jug. As I poured the hot water into the teapot, I heard the bedroom door open and the shuffling of the coffin coming out into the hallway. I could hear the sound of William McNorton talking to Jamie before they walked past the kitchen with an evil stare and then out through the main door with the coffin.

A sudden sense of relief rained over me making me feel twenty pounds lighter the minute I heard the door close and I knew the McNorton brothers had gone. In a fine balancing act, I carried the tea tray and plate of honeyed bread into the main room. With assistance from Linda, we placed the tray and plate on the table. The atmosphere, although it was to be expected, was very sombre but that was about to change. I lifted the plate of honey bread and offered it out to Jamie followed by Dad then Linda. Each holding a piece in their hand they burst into laughter. There was no sign of tears of sadness only those of joy, even Joe lifted his head from his paws and started to bark.

"Alright, alright it's not that funny," I shouted whilst laughing myself. Sure, my sandwich making skills weren't perhaps the best but at least I tried. The laughter only increased when everyone attempted to eat. Honey wasn't only covering everyone's hands it was also dripping all over the carpet, something that Joe didn't mind as he licked it up.

Looking at the large clock that sat on the mantelpiece, I realised that the time was now twelve forty. Before I looked at the clock I was feeling bright eyed, but the minute I saw the time my brain went into sleep mode and was telling me to get to bed.

"Thanks for all being here; it really means a lot to me."

"Jamie, we're here because you're our friend and you need us. You'd do the same for us." It was funny to hear Dad calling Jamie his friend but he was right. We were all friends, all friends, sticking together to get through a hard situation. After trying to eat the bread, we all gave up and resorted to finishing our tea.

"Well, I don't know about you lot but I'm washing my hands," Linda said as she walked towards the hallway. One by one we followed her to the kitchen where we washed up.

Staring out of the kitchen window, Dad suggested it was time to think about going home. "Whereabouts do you live, Linda?" Dad asked.

"Down Victoria Road."

"We'll walk you home on our way. Jamie, I think you should stay at our house tonight. I'll get a message to your mother; she'll be terribly worried about you."

"Thanks, Thomas." Linda disappeared out of the kitchen to return a few moments later. "These are the keys to the house, Jamie, you should look after them."

Jamie paused then collected the keys from her hand. "Thanks, Linda."

"Woof, woof," barked Joe, who was sitting in the doorway looking to find out who'd be looking after him.

"Dad, can Joe stay at our house with Jamie tonight?"

"Of course he can, we can't have one without the other now, can we?"

Jamie smiled as he collected the leash that was hanging on the wall near the door. "Tonight's one thing," he said "but what about tomorrow? I'd love to take him home but my little brother's allergic to dogs as we found out many years ago and they make him quite ill."

"Let's not worry about that just yet. Now, if we're all ready, let's make a move," Dad prompted.

"Oh, just a second." Jamie walked back into the house and reappeared a few seconds later. "Sorry, I'd forgotten Mrs Blake's letter."

As we all walked out of the house, I took a hold of Joe's leash while Jamie locked the door. Looking up at the house as it stood in darkness; I could have sworn I saw Mrs Blake watching us from one of the top room windows. But when I looked again I saw nothing, only the dark black abyss of the glass highlighted slightly by the layers of snow that clung to it. As we walked along the snow filled street, the house was swallowed by the night sky that cast a veil of glittering stars above. It was extremely cold that night, so much so that Dad gave his coat to Linda to wear in order to silence the sound of her chattering teeth. It wasn't long before we'd reached Victoria Road and we were saying goodnight to Linda. Dad seemed very grateful when she gave him his coat back and he immediately put it on. As we reached the start of our street, Dad told us to go on and said he wouldn't be long before he followed. I knew what he was about to do but said nothing. Jamie, Joe and I just walked to the foot of the house and then up the marble steps into the main hall. Dad, of course was, making his way to Jamie's house. He knew where it was because Jamie had told me Dad had picked him up from there this morning.

We'd only been in the house a few seconds before Mum, Gran and Jenny appeared. "Oh Jamie, I'm so sorry to here about Mrs Blake, you must be so upset," said Mum.

"Thanks, but I'm ok, honest."

"Where's your Dad?" she then asked.

"He's letting Jamie's Mum know that he's staying here tonight, he said he wouldn't be long."

"Oh, ok." It was obvious by Mum's response that she wasn't too happy with Dad going to see Jamie's Mum but I couldn't quite understand why.

We sat in the main room and talked to Mum and Gran while Jenny made us a quick bite to eat and a drink. It was clear Jamie didn't want to talk much about the day's events, as he tried his hardest to avoid most of the cross examination from Gran and Mum. Trying not to add to the conversation, I gave them both a wide-eyed stare which stopped Mum in mid-speech.

"So who is the third person in your company?" Gran asked, looking at the side of the chair where Joe was lying with closed eyes.

"Sorry, Gran, that's Joe, Mrs Blake's dog," With a lift of his head and a slight glance, Joe looked up at Gran then returned to his sleeping position.

"Oh, don't worry Miss, he's well house trained," reassured Jamie. "It's just Thomas said it would be ok for him to stay tonight! I hope that's ok?"

"Well of course it is, Jamie." Mum smiled compassionately.

"It's been a day of both celebration and commiseration," sighed Gran.

"Oh yes," Jamie yelped. "I've kind of spoiled your birthday, haven't I?"

"Nonsense, it's not your fault it turned out like this. Granted, it might not have been the best day of my life, but it surely was one of the most educational ones." Everyone looked rather queer at my expression of the day's events, but I understood what I meant. After all, it's not every day you get a surprise birthday party, a death, a ghost and dealings with two rather dodgy criminals. All in all, this was an extremely eventful day, surely one that I wasn't going to forget in a hurry and one that hadn't finished yet.

Just after we'd finished our eating, the front door opened and Mum marched out to the hall pulling the door closed behind her. Knowing the time, I gathered it must have been Dad returning from Jamie's house. It wasn't like an argument but I could hear them speaking in raised voices. Why on earth they'd be having a disagreement at this time of night I didn't know. They weren't at it long however because in no time Dad was walking into the main room with Mum following closely behind him.

"Jamie, could I speak with you for a moment please," Dad asked, at the same time smiling as if intimating nothing was wrong. Jamie took to his feet, followed by Joe, and signalled for me to tag along. We followed Dad out of the main room and into the kitchen. Dad lifted the kettle and proceeded to make himself a cup of coffee. It must have been almost five hours since the last time he'd had one, so he must have been feeling slightly anxious. We took up seats at the table and waited until Dad had joined us.

"It's just to let you know, Jamie, that I've spoken to your mother and I asked her if it was alright for you to stay the night. She was obviously upset and worried because she hadn't heard from you all day, but I've explained what happened. I told her we'd take you round first thing in the morning."

"Thanks, Thomas, that's very kind of you."

"There's another reason why I wanted to speak to you. In her letter Mrs Blake asks that you contact her solicitor. It's better that these kinds of matters are dealt with as quickly as possible. So your mother agreed that, if it's alright with you, I'll take you into Edinburgh tomorrow."

"Oh, well, to tell you the truth I hadn't thought much about it, but I suppose you're right."

"You'll also have to consider going to the funeral parlour and arranging Mrs Blake's funeral. We can speak about it in the morning but for now I think it's best if you two get some sleep, you'll have a long day tomorrow."

The word sleep was enough to trigger an uncontrollable wave of yawns from both Jamie and me. "Goodnight Thomas, and thanks again."

After saying goodnight to the rest of the family, we made our way upstairs to bed, still being followed by Joe.

On entering the room, Jamie stopped and looked at me. "Thanks for today. It was a true test of friendship; I'll never forget what you've done for me today."

"Jamie, I haven't done anything special, and anyway I know you'd do the same for me."

"Let's hope we'll not find that out in a hurry. I don't want to have another day like this for a long time."

"Yes, let's hope not." We started to get changed while Jamie rolled out the covers that Mum must have placed in the room while we were in the kitchen. The thought of getting changed in front of someone never even entered my head. Before I knew it, I was naked and jumping into bed.

"I thought you were a proper pyjama boy," Jamie laughed.

Not quite sure how to reply I considered my words carefully before responding. "Let's just say I'm into new things. There are pyjamas in the top drawer if you want some?"

"You're alright, thanks, I've only worn pyjamas once in the past five years." We both laughed and that's about all I remember about that night until we were woken up by Dad in the morning.

"Come on boys, I told you we have much to do today." I attempted to open my eyes, which felt as if they'd been glued together, while listening to the groans coming from Jamie on the floor.

CHAPTER SIXTEEN
Journey to Edinburgh

We had only gone to bed at about three and we were now getting up at six thirty. To say I was still very tired was an understatement. My brain was telling me to stay in bed while Dad's banging on the door was saying to get up. I dragged myself out of bed and put on a pair of the rather exotic underwear that Anna had given me as a birthday present.

"Come on Jamie, get up," I called, at the same time giving him a strong kick.

I made my way to the bathroom to get washed. Although having a bath seemed like a wonderful thing to do right now, it didn't seem to be the best idea considering we were already running late. I brushed my teeth and tried hard to wash the sleep from my eyes. Just as I pulled the plug from the sink, Jamie entered. "Come on sleepy, we're running late."

"Um." A rather simple reply, but it definitely confirmed he was still alive and not in the land of the dead.

"I'll put some clean clothes on the bed for you and if you're quick breakfast will be ready for you downstairs."

I opened the closet and looked inside as I decided what best to wear. Mum always loved us to look smart so I had loads to choose from. I picked a dark blue suit and a white shirt for myself and a similar style suit for Jamie but in black with a white shirt. As if looking for confirmation that they were good choices, I turned around and held them out for Joe to see, who was sitting in the middle of the room watching all that was happening. A single bark confirmed it to be a good choice, so I laid them on the bed and pulled a handful of ties from the rack to see what would best compliment them. Tie selection was never my fashion forte and was often my downfall. I took half the pile with me down stairs for Mum to select one and left the other half for Jamie to pick from. Mum was clearly very tired too because she looked dreadful and instead of the usual cooked breakfast lay bowls of cereal and dry toast.

"Mum, what tie do you think I should wear?"

Taking the ties from my hand Mum perused the selection and picked a light blue one with thin white diagonal stripes. "There you go, that one looks best."

"Thanks Mum," I sat down and poured some milk over one of the bowls of cereal and started to eat.

"Well, someone else looks very smart too," announced Mum. Jamie had entered the room dressed in the black suit I'd laid out for him. Although he looked extremely tired, it wasn't really that noticeable dressed the way he was. He looked more like a man who'd just come home after having a really hard day at work.

He'd only just sat down and started to eat when Dad reappeared and was hustling us out of the door. He'd been outside shovelling snow out of the way of the carriage house to get the car out. As he kissed Mum goodbye, we grabbed a few slices of toast and headed outside. Just as he was about to jump into the car, Jamie ran back into the house.

"Sorry for being a pain but I was just wondering if you would be able to take care of Joe for me please, or perhaps Gavin would be able to walk him for me, it's just..."

"Of course," Mum answered, "now be off with you."

The car was already running and warm inside when he returned. He got into the back with me while Dad took up the driver's seat.

"We'll go see your mother first, Jamie, then head to Edinburgh."

"Ok, Thomas," Jamie replied rather groggily. The drive to Blacksmith's Fire didn't take long, and in no time we found ourselves being welcomed by Mrs Richardson. As we left the car and made our way to the front door where Mrs Richardson stood, I could see faces appear in the misty windows that watched open eyed at our every move. I don't suppose they ever saw many cars pull up outside.

"Oh Jamie, come here," Mrs Richardson cried. They interlocked as they hugged each other tightly.

"I'm ok, Mum," gasped Jamie.

"With friends like this, I know you're ok, son," and with those words she outstretched her hand to touch my shoulder, at the same time giving Dad a look of real appreciation. "Come now sit down and I'll fetch you all something to eat."

"Honestly, Mrs Richardson, the boys and I have just eaten, and in any case we don't really have that much time, to tell you the truth."

"I understand, but at least take something with you." At that, she hurried off into the small kitchen area still under lamplight and returned with a small basket. "It's not much, but it should keep you all from eating each other."

Dad smiled as he collected the basket from her hands. "Bless you, Thomas. It's been a long time since I've seen such goodness."

"You should know it's not goodness, Mrs Richardson, but nothing more than I would expect myself."

Sure, Dad was much older than we were, but in his heart he wasn't any older than a boy of sixteen. I knew from his stories he was trying to regain the youth he never had. Making him feel like one of the boys was a real achievement for me. Without spending money or making a big fuss I was able to give Dad something that in many ways was very insignificant, but to him was worth more than gold, and it was nothing more than boyish fun and friendship. Just as we were making our way to the door, I caught a glimpse of Mary as she stuck her head around the kitchen door. She appeared just as beautiful as I remembered her looking when I'd had dinner at Jamie's. She never spoke a single word as her fingers slowly crept around the doorframe and her eyes watched every move made.

We said goodbye to Mrs Richardson as Dad tried to hurry us out of the door and into the car. With all the snow, he was concerned about how long the journey was going to take. Just as my head was being pushed out of the door I gave a smile and a silently spoken goodbye to Mary. Her returning smile was enough to tell me that she understood and enough to make me feel happy and brightly awake.

Jamie and I took a seat back in the car as Dad spoke a few more words to Mrs Richardson. "What do you think they're talking about?" I asked Jamie as he put his hands under his bottom to stop the cold seats from freezing him to death.

"Mum's not used to having guests; if she had her way, she'd talk all day given half the chance." We laughed as Dad opened the car door and climbed in. He was clearly very cold as he cupped his hands and warmed them with a deep warm puff of breath. As the street was very narrow, we had to continue going into Blacksmiths Fire to find a turning point. I'd never travelled as far as this into the Fire and for the first time I was able to see what produced the hard grinding noises that came from within.

As we drove, we came to the end of the rows of houses that sat on each side of the road and drove into what looked like a large town square except there weren't any town house or large houses of the type you would expect to find. Instead, there was a large open-fronted stone building lit up by roaring furnaces. There were large turning wheels in every building that seemed to be not only blowing air but drawing water as well. Men worked hard hammering iron into many shapes and forms. They seemed oblivious of the cold as they walked about wearing only trousers and armless shirts. As the car began to start turning in the open area I finally understood why it was there was no snow lying on the ground. It had all been stock piled in a large heap at the far side of the square. Men were carrying it into the furnace building and dropping it into large wooden troughs. We had just re-entered the narrow street so weren't able to see what it was used for but I presumed they used it to cool down the metal or something.

As we left the snow-less Blacksmiths Fire and drove back into the streets of Rockfield, I watched out of the window and gave thought to the people of the town that we'd just left behind. I felt slightly guilty when considering the things I'd done over the years that had wasted items such as food and toys. Here was a small area of our town that was deprived of some of the most basic items not excluding the lack of food and here was I throwing things away without giving it so much as a second thought. I vowed there and then never to throw anything away again without giving thought to what could be done with it except heaving it among the rubbish. The silence of the car and my thoughts of helping the poor were disturbed when Jamie shouted out.

"Thomas! Could you pull over for a second?"

Without moving his lips, Dad pulled the car over to the side of the road and I quickly realised what was happening. Jamie got out the car and ran down the farm track of mixed mud and snow to where Mr McNeil could be seen herding cows into the milking barn. Even with the window down they were too far away for me to hear what they were saying, but it appeared Mr McNeil was agreeing to something. Mr McNeil patted Jamie on the back before departing and Jamie ran back up the farm track. He ran a little too fast as a matter of fact because just as he neared the end of the track he slipped and skidded in the sludgy mix of snow and mud that lay thick on the road. If it weren't for the fact that he'd just managed to catch onto the large swinging sign that bore the words 'RIVERDALE FARM', he would have landed face down in it.

It took a few minutes after he entered the car for us to go because Dad and I were laughing too much to do anything.

"Okay, okay. So I made a fool of myself. It could have happened to anyone." Jamie's sharp defence and the fact that Farmer McNeil could be seen bent over laughing only made the situation worse. After wiping the tears from our eyes, Dad started the car and off we went. With a wave from Jamie and me to Farmer McNeil who was still standing watching us, our journey had really started.

"Sorry about the hold up, Thomas, but I forgot all about work this morning."

"A few minutes won't make a big difference," Dad answered. "And in any case you did the right thing."

"The right thing, Thomas?"

"You're a very considerate young man Jamie; under very trying circumstances, you still have power to think about others before yourself. I only wish we could find young men with your character to work in the business. As a matter fact that's something I'd like to talk to you two about, but we'll leave it till later." Jamie and I looked at each other with curiosity and wondered what on earth he wanted to speak to us about.

The sun had just started to make its daily rise in the still moonlit sky and was shedding its rustic red rays through the lingering clouds that moved slowly and peacefully above. I didn't often wander out of the door this early in the morning but found myself wishing I'd done it more often. The beauty that surrounded us was indescribable. The trees seemed to change colour with every second while shadows that once covered hill and field had now moved, sending the landscape into a collage of colour and shade. Thinking about the outside was difficult however as the car had not yet reached a comfortable heat. I'd curled my toes up inside my shoes and had wrapped my hands under my armpits in order to keep some warmth inside my body. Jamie, however, seemed oblivious to the cold, and had somehow managed to fall asleep. The recent events had certainly taken a toll on him. It was clearly visible on his face, as his head lay lopsided on the back of the seat. He seemed kind of lonely and sad in a way, as if he was being taken from a cell to the waiting death squad; there to meet his end.

I watched him for a while and listened to Dad singing as he drove along the partly snow cleared roads in the direction of Edinburgh.

The snow so crisp
The ground so hard
The air so cold and sharp
The clear blue sky
The mountains high
Oh Lord I wonder why

Oh Lord I wonder why
Oh Lord I wonder why
Oh Lord I wonder why the earth was made by you for I

The lands of far
The sea so wide
The sand and grains of time
The stone and rock the earth and trees
The flowers and the bees

Oh Lord I wonder why
Oh Lord I wonder why
Oh Lord I wonder why the earth was made by you for I

The years go by
The time to die
The newly born arrives
The child so sweet
The lover's seat
The friends that like to meet

Oh Lord I wonder why
Oh Lord I wonder why
Oh Lord I wonder why the earth was made by you for I

The time to go
The shadow falls
The soul that floats away
The work is done
The widow's song
The coffin and the grave

Oh Lord I wonder why
Oh Lord I did look high
Oh Lord I trust in you from now until the day I die

As I've already explained, we were never a religious family and especially not Dad, but boy did he love to sing the songs that rang from the church every Sunday! I reckoned he'd learned them as a child when Gran and Granddad took him to church. I remember he told me once he hated it. He always felt as if people were watching him and making him feel very uncomfortable. One time he got a glimpse of a friend making funny faces and the Father saw him laugh in response. Thinking Dad was laughing at him, he called him out of the congregation and up to the steps to where he stood. He then proceeded to make an example out of him and made him come back the following week to do a speech on "why the young of today are important to the church of tomorrow". Gran and Granddad had been truly embarrassed by the whole ordeal and punished him severely as a consequence. He never told me what exactly they'd done to him but it must have been bad, because he still remembered it till the day he died.

Over two hours had now gone by and the sun was now firmly in place overhead. The roads seemed to get better the further we went and Dad's singing became as bright and tuneful as the morning that had unfolded around us. On more than one occasion, I had to push Jamie back into position after he slid when rounding a corner, and I was now finding it hard to keep my own eyes open. Although I was feeling tired, I wanted to stay awake, so I interrupted Dad and his singing in order to have someone talk to me. Cars in those days weren't the quietest things, so I climbed into the front passenger seat to get closer.

"Why do you suppose Mrs Blake has asked that Jamie goes all this way to see her solicitor, Dad?"

"In truth, son, I can't answer that, but I suppose it's something to do with her estate."

"What do you mean, her estate?"

"Well someone's estate is what they own, all the possessions they'd collected over their life time."

"Oh, you mean like their house and things?"

"That's right."

"But Dad! What has that got to do Jamie?"

"Well, I remember you telling me that Mrs Blake had no living children or husband, so she has to leave her estate to someone. Maybe she thinks Jamie is that person."

"You mean, you mean she might have left all her belongs to Jamie?"

"That she might well have done."

I sat back in amazement and considered the story Jamie had told me about all the money Mrs Blake took to the bank one day. If she was going to leave all her belongings to Jamie, perhaps she was going to leave all her money to him as well. For the first time I saw a good sign for Jamie

182

and his family. I felt rather guilty about thinking such thoughts when Mrs Blake had only died a matter of hours ago, but perhaps this was the break that would give Jamie and his family their lives back. It was then that I realised death was just a handing down of a lifetime of work and achievement. Sure, the body and soul of a person had gone, and hopefully to a better place, but their life's work hadn't gone. It remained behind, to be passed down to the living family members or to whom the deceased had wished. Perhaps that's what Mrs Blake was talking about when she appeared to me. She said, "I fear that I've given him the key to unleash his demons and set right what was wrong." Although I still didn't fully understand what she meant, I was starting to see the fuller picture.

My mind was wondering round and round that much that Dad thought I was becoming carsick. "Are you ok, son?" he asked, while pulling my face towards him with his hand.

"Yes Dad, just feeling a little bit queasy, that's all."

"Um, we'll pull over in a bit to get a breath of fresh air," he answered, still looking at me with his eyes of concern.

I was keen to keep going to get to Edinburgh, but pulling over seemed a good idea. We continued to talk for a few more minutes before pulling in at the side of the road over looking the Forth. We had stopped quite high up and the view down the hill and into the water of the Forth below seemed utterly pure and innocent. The vast intake of water from the sea seemed still and flat. Nothing stirred, not even a single boat or hungry bird seeking to find food in the cold of the morning. It appeared that we were the only living people within miles, the sole survivors of a terrible yet peaceful war that left the landscape untouched or spoiled.

The lack of noise coming from the engine of the car had stirred Jamie from his well-deserved sleep, and brought him sailing back to the realities of death and painful moments.

That's if he wasn't dreaming about it while his head was tossed from side to side in the car.

"Are we there yet?" he yawned.

"Not just yet, sleepy head, we've just under an hour to go," Dad answered.

Jamie stumbled his way over to where we were standing at the same time rubbing his eyes. "You sure know the nicest places to stop, Thomas. The view from here is fantastic."

Looking down the slopes we could see hundreds of trees thrown along the hillside accompanied by clusters of rocks and boulders, all topped with icing-white snow that clung and sparkled like fairy dust in the dazzle of the sun. At the bottom, amidst the short banks, the water glided out to the other side making a mirror sheet of perfection. It swallowed the features of its surrounding landscape, only to cast them back out upon its face to reflect the harmony that beheld it.

Not wanting to spoil the rich landscape around me but at the same time bursting to have a pee, I decided to make haste to a nearby tree to relieve myself. Dad and Jamie must have been thinking along the same lines because, uninvited, they accompanied me. We each gathered around a large evergreen tree and took stance ready to let flow the water from within. It's strange but peeing in public amongst friend and family isn't the easiest thing in the world to do. Your bladder seems to lock up and refuse to work, it's highly embarrassing, especially when you know you have to go but nothing happens. I wasn't the only one feeling the curse of the dreaded lock pee syndrome, as no sound was being made and no steam was rising from any other corner of the tree. Under those circumstances every second feels like a minute, ever-enduring until either the mind says release or you give up and try again later. Just as my hands reached to tuck away and retreat, Dad spoke through the vale of the tree.

"It's a bloody nuisance when these blasted things don't work properly. I've asked your mother a hundred times to get me a new one, but she always forgets to pick one up when out shopping."

Whether it was with laughter or just because our minds had been taken away from the pressure, the tree's insides exploded with steam and the sound of flowing water. Being careful not to extend our aim to each others' shoes, we tried to contain our laughter 'til we were finished. I'd never known Dad to speak like that or say something so funny before, but one thing's for sure, I liked it.

After we withdrew from our positions and returned to the open area next to the car, Dad directed us to collect a handful of snow and rub our hands clean.

"We might not have tap water, but there's plenty of nature's very own cleaning products", he said. Dad was a strong believer in cleanliness. I think that's one of the reasons I enjoyed taking a bath so much. I was brought up to appreciate water and was always taught of the importance it had in life. After all, water is the main ingredient requirement for living. The best part of our bodies is made up of water and we need to drink it to stay alive. I just loved swimming around in it.

After a few minutes of standing around and feeling the cold creep back into our feet, we got back into the car and headed on with the rest of the journey. Dad restarted to sing and act merry while Jamie and I spoke in the back.

"You getting nervous?" I asked him.

"Is it that obvious?"

"No, no. But I know how I'd be feeling if it was me. I mean it's not exactly an every day thing you're doing."

"Not what I'm doing! What *we're* doing. If it weren't for you and your Dad, I'd never be doing this. What do you think is going to happen?"

"I'm just as much in the dark as you, but Dad reckons you must have something to do with Mrs Blake's will."

"Her will! What would I have to do with that?"

"Well, if you're right and she doesn't have any other living family, she needs someone to take care of her things."

"You mean like Joe?"

"I mean like Joe, the house and all her other valuables."

Jamie sank into some deep silent thoughts after that, and it wasn't until we reached the start of Edinburgh that he spoke again. "I'm home again."

"Did you used to live here, Jamie?" asked Dad. Of course, unless Gran or Jenny had told him about what they had overheard the other night, Dad wouldn't have known that Jamie once lived in Edinburgh.

"I sure did, Thomas, but that was some time ago now, and by the looks of it much has changed since then."

From the open countryside, we had now hit a wall of houses and roads. It was very busy and even the air seemed to be carrying something. I'd never seen so many cars driving about in all my life. All around houses grew tall towards the sky. They weren't like the houses in our town; they had rows and rows of windows going at least fifteen high. I remember thinking, no one single family could be living in such a big house. Dad, noticing the amazement on my face, began to speak.

"They're called tenements. They're just like lots of little houses put together to make one large building but many families live inside."

"What, you mean they all live together and use the same rooms?"

Both Dad and Jamie laughed. "No, they all have a small part of the building which has its own rooms." It took a good few minutes of them explaining before I finally understood.

CHAPTER SEVENTEEN
Death's Fortune

We travelled for some time through the bumpy streets made of cobbles before the car came to a stop. We had pulled up outside a curved crescent of houses. It must have been at least a quarter of a mile long, with large bay windows going the whole length of it. There was a great big black wooden door between every window laden with polished brass ironmongery. It wasn't until we'd got out the car that we realised there wasn't any snow lying on the ground. In fact apart from the fact that it was a little cold, the day seemed very nice. On the other side of the road was a large common green. It was fenced off with black wrought iron, and inside grew large trees and bushes. I could see people sitting on benches feeding pigeons that fluttered about fighting for breadcrumbs. On the very corner of the fence I could just manage to read a street sign which said 'KING STREET'.

"Well I suppose we better go inside," prompted Dad.

At that, we made our way up a stone bridge of steps that spanned a drop at the front of the building. There were windows down under ground level as if the building had some kind of cellar. Just below the large number eleven was a brass doorplate that read the words 'HENRY JACOBSON & SONS'. Dad opened the door and we walked into a large black and white chequered marble hallway. The staircase was made from dark rich oak and the walls rose up to high ceilings accompanied with a large leaf patterned gold architrave. You could tell this wasn't a standard everyday office. It had the hand of a nobleman written all over it. Everything seemed to be over accentuated and contrasted to make a picture of pure harmony.

The sound of feet could be heard coming towards us, and after a second a man appeared from a doorway at the far end of the hall. He was tall and dressed in a grey pinstriped tail suit, with a white shirt and large knotted tie.

"Good morning, dear Sirs," said the extremely well-spoken voice as he moved closer.

Dad took a few paces forward and stood totally erect while he spoke to the gentleman. "We've come a long distance in the hope of finding and speaking to a Mr Henry Jacobson Senior."

"Well you've certainly arrived at the right place. Whom should I say is looking for him?"

Without even so much as a twitch, Dad replied, "Mr Jamie Richardson."

"And your business?"

"That I cannot tell, as that is a matter to be discussed by Mr Richardson directly with Mr Jacobson."

"Very well, wait here until I ascertain if Mr Jacobson is available and willing to speak to you." At that, the man about turned swishing his jacket tail behind him and walked back through the far door.

A few minutes passed, giving us time to admiring the building and the workmanship it possessed, before the man reappeared.

"Mr Jacobson has agreed to speak with you, follow me please." We walked behind Dad who followed on as we were taken past many rooms and up a flight of stairs with hurried speed. Finally, we arrived in a large open room where a petite woman sat behind a desk stacked with files and paperwork. The room was embellished with plants of many kinds and colours. The smell, although strong and sweet, held a peculiar sense of staleness.

"Please wait," the man directed with a sudden halt.

We stopped and watched as he walked over to the lady who tilted her glasses down and glared over towards where we were standing. They conveyed a few words to each other before the lady walked over to the large set of double doors on the other side of the room and gave them three distinct knocks. A deep strong voice sounded from behind the doors before she entered and the tail coated man exited past us and out back along the hall. This room was just as lavish as the others we'd passed on the way up. There was some kind of dark red coloured paper on the walls with a gold regent looking pattern on it. The carpet was likewise dark red and very thick and heavy to walk on. I was just about to speak when suddenly the double doors swung open and the petite woman called to us.

"Mr Jacobson will see you now."

We followed the carpet that flowed into the oncoming room and came to stop in front of a rather fat balding man, who sat in a great big leather seat behind a desk that was extremely low to the floor.

"What a rather curious blend of gentleman now comes before me. Tell me Sir, what brings you such a distance to speak with me?"

"Begging your pardon, Mr Jacobson, but it isn't I who requires speaking with you. I'm merely the guardian." At that, Dad turned to Jamie who had stopped behind him and asked him forward. "Jamie, could you please give Mrs Blake's letter to Mr Jacobson?"

At that, Jamie reached into the left inside coat pocket and pulled out the envelope with the italic writing on it. With his hand shaking, he moved forward and handed the letter to Mr Jacobson who, by this stage, seemed completely bewildered. He lifted the letter from the envelope and unfolded it. Putting on a pair of reading glasses, he began silently to read the contents. I could hear the words being said in my mind as his lips moved to the tune of his writing.

I watched as he paused and read the letter over again. He then seemed to stop and consider the words.

Finally, he placed the letter on the table and rested his hands on it while he inclined his eyes over the top of his half-sized spectacles.

"I must apologise for what I first presumed was a waste of my time. I have heard much about you, Jamie. Much good has been spoken about your name and I am both proud and privileged to be acquainted with such a fine young man. You must introduce your friend and guardian to me."

Jamie was that amazed and flabbergasted by kind words that he found it difficult to speak. "This is my best friend and his Dad, Thomas."

"I am likewise pleased to meet you both. You must all be hungry and thirsty after such a journey under these distressful circumstances? Before we continue with our talks would you join me in some lunch?"

Dad took a step to one side making it obvious it should be Jamie who replied to the offer. "Well, we have travelled and thirsty we are, although hunger hasn't crossed my mind I wouldn't say no to something to eat either."

"Well, that settles it." As Mr Jacobson walked around the side of the desk, I realised why the wooden desk he sat behind was as low to the ground. Although he was considerably overweight he was also considerably undersized. In fact, he was only half the size of any normal man and from the looks of it I wasn't the only one to notice his lack of height as Dad and Jamie's faces also lit up with surprise.

We followed as he led us out of his office and through the previous room with all the plants and back into the hallway. Turning left, we went up a further flight of steps along a short corridor then turned right through a doorway. Suddenly, my stomach started doing back-flips as the smell of warm welcoming food flowed up my nostrils and deep inside. Still following, we were taken through what looked like a house until finally we reached a kitchen area set with a table of food. The voice of a woman singing could be heard but was nowhere to be seen.

A song of flying bluebirds
A sky that's filled with joy
The earth in all its glory
Full of wings that flow afar I see the birds a whistling
Humming tunes of love each day
To keep the sounds of evil
Far away out of harms way

La la la la la la la
La la la la la la la
La la la la la la la
La la la la la la la

The trees in early springtime
Come alive with natures songs
The home for flying bluebirds
As they beat their wings so strong
The innocent will conquer
As the tunes fill up the sky
The sound of flying bluebirds
As the world does come alive

"Well done, bravo," voiced Mr Jacobson, interrupting the sweet voice that we'd discovered was coming from a large cupboard.

"I'll be right there, sugar cup," replied the mysterious voice from within. Mr Jacobson's face had turned a rather flush colour of red at the sound of being called, "sugar cup." Only a second later, a woman, very beautiful but of the same stature in height as Mr Jacobson, appeared.

Being faced with a crowd and realising we must have

191

heard her singing she too turned a rather sensitive colour of red. "You could have told me we had guests, Henry, instead of allowing me to make a fool of myself."

Dad took a step forward. "A fool, certainly not; a charming and wonderful singer, yes. It's a delight and pleasure to hear such a lovely woman sing."

Slightly taken aback and not knowing quite how to reply, she just smiled and threw a look of ingratitude at Henry, whom I presumed was her husband.

"My dear, these guests have travelled many miles and are in much need of a good feeding."

"Well, you had better all take a seat then," she said, at the same time pointing towards the table that sat in the middle of the room.

We gathered around the table and each pulled out a chair that sat around it. It was very obvious even before attempting to sit down that the seats were far too small and low for us to be able to sit in properly. Not wanting to appear ungrateful, we scrunched ourselves into the chairs and tucked our legs under the table rather uncomfortably. Mrs Jacobson walked around the table giving us all a plate. Immediately, Henry, using his hands, grabbed fistfuls of food, and dropped it onto his plate. The three of us just looked in amazement at the sheer greed of such a small man. It was no wonder he had grown to the size he was when he was eating so much. It wasn't long before Mrs Jacobson clipped him around the ear and warned him to behave in front of guests. It was very plain to see who the boss was in this household. Throughout the meal, Henry never asked about Mrs Blake or about how or when she passed away. He talked about the weather, the food and even the watch that Dad had strapped around his wrist. After spending at least an hour watching the fat jaws of Henry munching and chewing away as if food was about to run out, he lit up a cigar and sat back in his chair allowing his stomach to breath as he undid his top trouser button.

"There's nothing better than a great cigar after a wonderful meal. It allows the senses to appreciate the better things in life."

Amidst coughing, I remember thinking how on earth his senses could be appreciating anything; after all, they were being subjected to an overwhelming inhalation of dirty, thick, smelly smoke. I noticed Dad was becoming slightly irate as Henry kept blowing the smoke towards his face in order to allow him to appreciate the cigar as he was. Jamie just sat silent, taking in the surroundings and sampling the mixture of food that lay before us.

"Well I guess we should make our way back to the office and discuss the matters at hand," Henry said blowing a ring of smoke up into the air.

"I think that would be a good idea; the boys haven't had much sleep and weariness will soon be creeping upon them."

I couldn't control my anxiousness to get back to my feet any longer, as my legs had started to fill with pins and needles and were now becoming quite sore. Moving rather too quickly, I stood up and almost toppled the table sending food all over the floor. "I'm so sorry," I shouted, pulling the table back and attempting to save as much food as possible.

"You're quite alright young man; I've warned Henry this table is no good for large men. Haven't I Henry, I've told you a thousand times if I've told you once, haven't I?"

"Yes dear, that you have."

At that, Henry hurried us out of the kitchen and back along the hall through the plant covered room to his office. "Please take a seat," he directed as he climbed into his own. He picked up the letter once more and began to read. "I see, I see, I knew this day was coming, although I'd expected it much sooner. Yvonne was a very nice lady, and a great friend. We'll miss her deeply."

"Sorry, Mr Jacobson," spouted Jamie. "Did you actually know Mrs Blake?"

"That I did dear boy, and very well at that. Her husband was a life time friend of mine; I was the best man at his wedding."

"Not wanting to sound disrespectful Mr Jacobson, but you don't appear to be old enough to know Mrs Blake for that long."

"Well you see her husband was seven years younger than she was and one of the benefits of being a shorter than average person is that you appear to be younger than you actually are. I'll be seventy two on my next birthday." Astounded looks came from the three of us as we looked closely at the man before us. For seventy-two years old, he looked great; as a matter of fact, he looked greater than great. I remember thinking how I'd like to be looking like him if I ever reached his age.

"Well, well, I've heard much about you, Jamie, and almost been caught leaving the house by you on a few occasions."

"I've almost caught you?" Jamie replied, sounding very surprised. "That you have, you were unaware about my visits with Yvonne, and that's the way it was intended."

"But, I don't understand."

"Understanding is something you don't need to be concerned about; you have to trust that all was done to protect both you and Mrs Blake. I was very surprised upon receiving a letter from Mrs Blake in which she wrote about you and asked that I make haste to speak with her. Knowing her to be quite ill, I immediately set forth and arrived to find a somewhat invigorated and younger Yvonne. After several cups of tea and some catching up, she spoke at length about you. She told me how you first met and about all the kind things you had done over the last year to help her. Being a solicitor, my initial reaction to hearing about you was one of caution. Her not telling anyone about you and keeping you a secret could have been a very dangerous thing to have done. It was expected that she only had a matter of months to live when her illness was originally diagnosed. In fact, that diagnosis was only given a few days before the two of you first met. She wrote to me at least once every month or so but always omitted to mention you up until the letter I talk about.

"She solely put her extra time on this earth down to you. You gave her inspiration to go on and keep death at arm's length. As you know only too well yourself, some days were much better than others, but she continued to battle against what she called the reunion. Over the next while, I visited her on many occasions to make sure she was still happy with the decisions she had taken. You need to bear in mind, Jamie, that I'd never met or talked with you, although research gave me enough information to say that you were a good man. I took all that I was able to have gathered about your past and family and took it to Yvonne. I needed to know one hundred percent that she was in fact happy. Without you knowing, she shed tears over your past and rejoiced in your future. It was then and only then that I accepted her wishes and concluded the matters she sought to be done. However, I kept a constant check on the both of you and watched for anything that would sway my judgement. However much I tried, nothing adverse ever happened and for that I'm eternally grateful. And I apologise for not recognising you, Jamie, when you first entered but I'm not used to seeing you in such attire."

At that, Mr Jacobson stopped talking. He removed a small gold key from his waistcoat pocket and unlocked a small drawer on the left-hand side of his desk. He removed an envelope identical to that which lay before him and opened it. "This letter has been in my possession for some time now and I was instructed not to open it until you visited me." There was a pause while he opened the letter using a rather lethal looking knife and began to read. "So it is confirmed, Yvonne is now at her reunion. A sad day that I shall remember for some many years. Yvonne instructed me to pass this into your possession on the day that we would come to meet. Although it pains me greatly to hear of her death, I am pleased to carry out her wishes."

Mr Jacobson lifted a small parcel from his drawer and extended his arms as far past his fat body as they allowed towards Jamie, who was slightly oblivious and required a slight nudge from Dad to direct him to collect it. Quickly coming back down to earth, he collected it and glared opened eyed at the neatly wrapped package.

"It may be a good idea to open it," said Mr Jacobson. Placing the package on his lap, Jamie untied the string and unravelled the pale coloured paper. Inside was a small wooden box carved from what looked like oak. It was a beautiful piece of workmanship detailed all over with flowers.

"MY BOX!" Jamie coughed with amazement.

"My box?" repeated Mr Jacobson, equally amazed.

"Yes, I made this for Mrs Blake some time ago to cheer her up. It's a feelings box. I told her whenever she was feeling really good she should open the box and store some of the good feelings inside. That way on days when she wasn't too good she could open it and take some back to cheer her up again."

Inside the box sat two envelopes, both the same in colour but one appeared much thicker than the other did. Sitting the box on the desk, Jamie opened the thinner envelope of the two. He removed a letter penned on the same coloured paper as those that sat on the desk before us and began to read aloud.

Dear Jamie

Although this may be a sad time I hope you've mustered the strength I know you have to conquer the emotions of grief. Be strong not for me but for yourself. You need to go on with your life and take back the childhood you've so sorely missed out on. Be cautious in the world and learn that people can and will take advantage if given the chance. However don't be too cautious, you taught me that and I tell it back to you. I ask that you take the guidance not only from Mr Jacobson but also from your true friends and your family.

I don't want to leave you with my last words being that of dwelling on times of sadness so will part by saying Thank You. I've returned your box to you today fully filled with all the love and good feeling I could spare. I hope there's enough to help get you through your life and difficult times that all good lives have. Also included is an advance of money to help reunite me with my husband and take care of the house until Henry has all the transfers into your name complete.

Live and blossom a loving family, take each day as it comes and seek only for happiness.

    Your Ever Loving Friend,
    Yvonne Blake

After he finished, there was a deafening silence, only slightly disturbed by the quick fire finger typing coming from the next room.

"Are you ok?" asked Dad in a low voice. Jamie lifted his tear-glazed eyes from the letter and looked around at the three faces that sat watching him. His mouth opened but no words came clearly, only a choked high pitch noise similar to that of a distressed bird. The seconds seemed like minutes while we watched him fight to regain his voice.

"Here, my dear boy, drink this." Mr Jacobson hopped from his chair and handed Jamie a small metal like flask that he took from one of his drawers. I could see Dad about to speak but it was too late. Jamie had rested the flask against his lips and tossed his head back. His reaction came almost instantly. A red flame erupted all over his face engulfing him in a look of anger. His tear-glazed eyes were now like deep oceans as they welled with water. I was convinced the next words he spoke would be accompanied with vicious torrents of flame.

Dad took hold of a glass and the small water jug that sat on the table and quickly poured a glass for Jamie to drink. "Giving a young boy whisky, Mr Jacobson, honestly!"

"A young boy, maybe, but the taste is one that he will be acquainted with soon enough."

"That may be very well, but that will be of his choice, and not that of a thoughtless act."

Seeing the great battle of words that was about to take place I did the only thing that came to mind. "Excuse me, Mr Jacobson, could you please tell me where I'd find the bathroom?" My interruption stopped the both of them in mid flight. I even managed to gain Jamie's attention.

"Oh yes," Mr Jacobson answered. "Go out and into the hall, turn left and then second on the right. Follow the red carpet till it meets with the green carpet and turn left."

I was about to turn when Jamie stood up. "I'll come along too, if you don't mind." At that, the both of us walked out of the room and immediately stopped outside the closed door and listened to hear what was about to be said. We'd only just rested our ears against the door when a sharp cough could be heard directly behind us.

"It's very rude and indecent to eavesdrop," said the small lady who'd been sitting on the nearby desk. Without saying a word, we walked from the room and tried hard to remember the instruction on how to find the bathroom.

It was truly a fantastic building. Jamie admired the pictures that hung on the walls as we walked.

"I think Dad's going to give that Mr Jacobson a piece of his mind, giving you that fire whisky." Not hearing a response, I turned and saw that Jamie had stopped. He was peering up at a large painting of a man that hung proudly on the wall. "What is it Jamie?"

"It's him; it's Mr Blake, Yvonne's husband."

"Are you sure?"

"As sure as I'll ever be, it's got his name at the bottom and he looks just like the pictures I've seen of him."

The plaque read 'Mr James Charles Blake, Appointed to the King'.

"What do you think it means?" Jamie asked, sounding bemused. "I don't have a clue why it would be resting upon these walls."

We ignored the picture for now and proceeded towards the bathroom. Following the instructions we arrived at a large wooden door with bulging brass fittings. Upon entering, the sheen from the polished floor and walls was overwhelming. It was as if we'd entered the inside of a diamond mine. It was almost a pity to use such a beautiful room for doing the toilet. The sinks were covered with little bottles of soap and after-shave. Thick white towels hung from large gold rings attached to the walls and each toilet was contained in its own little wooden cupboard.

"What I'd give to have a bathroom like this," I said.

"You and me both, it's fantastic."

After using up much of the soap and aftershave, we made our way back to the room feeling relieved and in a much better mood. Upon entering, we half expected to see Dad and Mr Jacobson fist fighting. However, we were pleasantly surprised to find them laughing. We sat back down and the laughter slowly turned back to a more serious and solemn tone.

"Well, Jamie, I'm not permitted to offer any more information until I am in receipt of the death certificate and after the burial."

"What more information have I to ask of you anyway? I've done what I set out to do, and that was merely to inform you of the tragic events, as instructed by Mrs Blake," Jamie replied, perplexed.

"I see you still don't fully understand the importance of this visit, but soon you will. Well, time is pressing and, although I'd love to be able to speak more, I've other pressing matters to continue with. I must ask that you return here after the funeral has taken place, accompanied with the death certificate."

Although Jamie still looked puzzled, he placed the envelopes in his pocket, collected the wooden box and joined us in standing up. After saying goodbye, we left the room. Leaving the building and rejoining the outside invoked the senses to awaken again after being subjected to the vile stench of cigar smoke.

CHAPTER EIGHTEEN
The Lion Gate Hotel

The time was late in the day so Dad suggested that we stayed the night in the city, rather than face the long journey home. The chance of staying the night in such a great place was far too good to pass over so we agreed almost instantly.

"Oh, but what about my Mum? She'll be very worried if I don't make it home."

"It's ok, Jamie, I expected the journey may have been an overnight one so I have already spoken to your mother about it."

"Thanks Thomas."

We re-entered the car and watched out of the windows as Dad drove a few minutes before coming to a stop outside a large building with a dark blue, tunnel-like entrance. Barely seconds after we'd stopped a stranger in a uniform appeared and opened the car door. My ignorance was well expressed when I asked the man what on earth he was doing.

"This isn't your car," I barked at him abruptly.

"No, silly, he's opening the door for you so you can get out," laughed Jamie as he pushed past me and out of the car. Feeling slightly stupid, I apologised and followed suit leaving the man to jump into the car and drive it away to be parked.

We walked under the blue tunnel-like canopy and into the large building. The atmosphere was buzzing with excitement. There was music being played on a piano accompanied by the sound of string instruments. All around there sat people drinking from all sorts of wonderful looking vessels, all dressed in fancy clothes and shoes. Dad ushered us along to a counter where a young woman was sitting writing in a book.

"Good evening sir and welcome to the Lion Gate Hotel, how can I assist you?"

My senses had become infused by her looks and smell. She was one of the most beautiful women I'd ever seen. The smell she carried captured and teased the senses. Her body in every possible way was perfect. The words she spoke while Dad explained we needed a room for the three of us was like song. I couldn't help but stare as she penned Dad's name and our address into her large desk book in thick black ink. As if knowing I was watching her, she looked up from the desk and we both paused for a second before I retreated and restrained myself from looking again. Only when I heard the sound of keys being collected from a peg and them being handed to Dad did I look back once more as we walked in the direction of a winding stair dressed in a royal blue carpet.

We followed Dad up several flights of stairs and along a hall 'til we reached room 1253. The room smelled of royalty and glory. The curtains and carpet were rich with colour and workmanship. "Right boys, let's get washed up and make our way down stairs for some dinner."

One by one we took turns to wash up before we made the walk back down stairs to the ground floor of the hotel. It was now dark outside so the fabulous plasterwork on the ceiling was able to come alive with shape and form as the light cast itself upon its every curve. The massive chandeliers glittered and sparkled brightly giving a true feeling of decadence. Dad had obviously been here several times before, as many people were saying hello and calling him by his first name. Dad simply smiled and nodded in response. We eventually walked through a large set of double doors and into a great hall lined with rows of tables. All around the room waiters were hurrying to and fro. It was like watching a fine balancing act as they zipped past each other both coming and going from the kitchen holding large silver trays on the tips of their fingers.

As we entered, a tall man holding a white cloth stopped us. "A table for three sir?" he asked, talking as if his nose was blocked.

"Yes please."

"If you'd be so kind as to follow me sir." We were directed to stop at a small table close to a large window. We'd only just sat down when a menu had been thrust into our hands. "Drinks, sir?"

To our delight, Dad ordered three glasses of red wine, specifically asking for a French Begoni 1877. I'd never taken Dad to be a wine connoisseur but he certainly knew what he wanted, the smile that arose on the waiter's face was testament to that. Looking at the menu was like reading a Chinese newspaper. Or at least it ought to have been. The entire menu appeared to be written in some strange language. I clearly wasn't the only one struggling with it, as Jamie appeared to be looking around the other tables to see if perhaps he'd been given the wrong menu.

Without even having much time for thought, the waiter was back holding three glasses and a bottle of wine. He placed the glasses on the table and poured wine into each glass being especially careful not to spill even the smallest drop. "Are sirs ready to order yet?" he asked placing a glass at each of us.

"Yes, I'd like the Lamb with mint and mild mustard and the boys would both like the rump steak with white wine sauce and vegetable, please."

"Fine choices, sir," he replied with a smile. He then collected the menus and made his way towards the kitchen with a rather straight and uncomfortable looking walk. Dad just smiled as we looked at him. He had found the whole menu saga very appealing.

"Thanks for the wine, Thomas," said Jamie as he clasped the glass in excitement of his first taste of the red grape drink.

"You're both very welcome."

I, too, was keen to taste what the glass contained. I lifted it with anxiety and pressed the rim against my mouth. Its deep fruity smell aired into my nostrils as I tilted my head back accepting the liquid. Initially, it had a warm feeling like licking the blood from a cut. It was then followed by a drying of the tongue and a somewhat fresh and spicy aftertaste. I wouldn't say it was an altogether enjoyable experience because it wasn't, but I certainly grew to like it over the years to come.

Dinner arrived on silver trays covered with silver domed lids, which upon being removed expelled a mushroom of steam into the air and revealing the most mouth-watering meals I'd ever seen. I remember taking a fleeting glance at Jamie's plate to see if his steak was bigger than mine was, but it wouldn't have really mattered because none of us finished it anyway. It was a pure waste I know and the thought of Jamie's family sitting around the poorly lit table eating boiled ham and bread made it even harder to leave, but what you can't eat you just can't eat. Looking around at the other tables, the waste was truly amazing. Had no one ever contemplated telling the cook to make slightly smaller portions? I remember thinking.

We never spoke much all through dinner. I think we talked enough during the day to entitle us to a little break. The silence wasn't going to last, however, because as Dad so rightly told us there was much to do and much to take care of.

After dinner, we took refuge at a small table in what appeared to be a music room. In the far corner of the room I could see a small band playing light soulful music.

After being accosted by a second waiter and drinks being brought to the table we started to talk.

"I expect much of the day's events have passed you by, Jamie," asked Dad.

"I wouldn't profess that I understood all of what Mr Jacobson spoke, so yes, you're probably right."

"I don't wish to meddle in anyone's business, Jamie, but I feel my guidance may be of assistance in some matters. Anything you're not sure about or would like enlarged on please feel free to ask."

"You're a lot of things, Thomas, but you're no meddler. I appreciate everything you two have done for me."

"I dare not speak of riches, but if my eyes and ears don't deceive me, Jamie, I think a great fortune has landed upon you."

"What kind of fortune?"

"One that shouldn't be spoken about just yet, as we have other things to discuss. We have a funeral to arrange after which things may become a little clearer."

"Yes, I've been thinking about the funeral." At that, Jamie reached into his inside jacket pocket and pulled out the two envelopes he was given by Mr Jacobson. He read the letter aloud but only just above a whisper in order to reiterate the wishes of Mrs Blake.

Dad asked that he re-read the third last sentence: "Also included is an advance of money to help reunite me with my husband and to take care of the house until Henry has all the transfers into your name complete."

"What do you think that means?"

"Well, I guess she wants to be buried alongside her husband, he must be already buried in the local graveyard," answered Dad.

"That's right; I remember her telling me she often visited him." Jamie then picked up the second envelope, which was considerably bigger than the first. Instead of it having the usual seal, it had a thick gold ribbon around it with a large red stamp sealing it. Taking his time not to rip the envelope, he cautiously peeled back the seal and removed the ribbon band. Turning the back of the envelope towards him he lifted the flap and gazed in amazement at what he was holding. It was only his innocence that precluded him from hearing the words in Mrs Blake's letter clearly. From the first time he read it aloud, I understood what was contained inside the second envelope and Dad's lack of surprise meant he must have known too. Any other person would have been right into it, but not Jamie. His lack of haste was as genuine as anything I've ever seen or known about him.

"Why, it's... it's money," he stammered, trying not to choke on his own tongue. He slowly pushed his fingers into the envelope and lifted out a handful of ten-pound notes. "There must be a hundred pounds here," he gasped. Looking back at the envelope, he noticed a small piece of paper. Placing the money on the table, he collected the note and unfolded it.

Dear Jamie

This may seem a great deal of money but I assure you keeping a home as a young man is an expensive thing to do and funerals don't come cheap. I hope this will tide you over until all matters are finally concluded. These are the last word's that shall ever be written by my hands so remember them well.

Money doesn't bring happiness, but it can surely help in finding it. Be wise and grow to be an even greater man.

Love
Yvonne Blake

Jamie placed the note on the table and looked at both Dad and me with astonishment etched into his face. "What must you both be thinking about me?" I never quite understood what made him do it, but for some reason Jamie lifted from his seat and ran from the hall leaving not only the letters behind but also the money. Dad quickly grabbed them and ran after him, leaving me sitting whilst everything went quiet and all eyes in the room came to rest upon me. What they must have been thinking I can only imagine. It took a few seconds before the music restarted and people continued with their conversations.

I slowly stood up and made my way back into the main entrance hall. Looking around, I couldn't see them anywhere. I walked through the clouds of cigarette smoke and people, trying desperately to find them. I walked along a wide hallway and into a massive room. The sound of cards being dealt and spinning could be heard coming from all over. There were scores of people gathered around what looked like long tables and sitting on stools. In the distance, I could see a bright light with the words 'BANK' glowing on it in large letters. In the middle of the room stood a great marble statue of a naked winged lady with a wreath on her head. She was a beautiful sight to see and quite stunning.

Moving closer to the crowded tables, I could see they weren't like any normal tables I'd ever seen. They were covered in green cloth with numbers all over them. Right at the top of the table stood a man wearing a red waistcoat with a bow tie. In his right hand he held a pearly white ball that he rolled back and forth in-between his thumb and first finger. I stood for a few minutes watching and listening to the goings on.

"Place your bets please," the waist coated man called, at which people started stacking piles of small, coloured discs on the different numbers on the green cloth. People were shouting all sorts of instructions.

"Tier for neighbours."

"Ten on 11, 16 and 24."

"Fifty black."

The waist coated man swapped the small ball to his

left hand and, with his right hand; he reached onto a large numbered, coloured wheel at the top of the table. Taking hold of it, he gave it a small tug, make it turn round. He then swapped the ball back to his right hand and, placing it inside the walls that contained the wheel. With a little flick of his fingers, he sent it spinning around the outer rim. The ball was tumbling and jumping as the wheel rotated. As the wheel began to lose momentum, the ball bounced a couple of times and, with one last jump, it came to rest on the only green coloured box on the wheel with the number zero on it.

The waist coated man turned to the table and called it out, "Zero!" There was a mixture of responses to his number call. The majority of the people looked quite disheartened and many of them left the table, but one person was ecstatic. He was a rather scruffy-looking man compared to the others and held a small pile of blue discs in his hands that he dropped from one to the other. The waist coated man moved closer to the table and in one large embrace, he gathered in the multi-coloured discs that had been strewn all other the table, leaving those on the number zero. The other discs clinked down a chute, as the red waist coated man lifted the remaining chips about an inch off the table. In a slick, well-practised movement, he stacked them into piles of four on top of each other with the one hand, making a stack of five. He then appeared to look deep in thought as he turned around to a blue waist coated man and said, "*blue two sixty.*" With a quick glance at the blue discs, the blue waist coated man nodded his head in agreement, to which the red waist coated man pushed the pile of discs over to the rather scruffy looking gentleman.

"Looks like my luck could be changing," the scruffy man almost sang, implying he'd been unlucky up till then. As many people had now moved from the table, I took a closer look.

The same routine happened again with red waist coated

man calling out, "Place your bets please... no more call bets... no more bets." At that, the ball dropped again landing this time in the number fourteen. Yet again the scruffy man seemed pleased. Looking back at the table, I could see he had a pile of discs on that number also. For the second time he was the only person to win. By the time he was receiving his second pay out, I'd managed to move right next to him at the side of the table. Looking to the side, he noticed me watching him in amazement.

"You're a bit young to be gambling," he said, giving me a nudge. I didn't reply in words but gave a slight smile instead.

"Pick a number," he prompted with a second slightly harder nudge. "Quick, before he calls no more bets, pick a number." Without giving it much more thought, I pointed to number 33. Instantly, he placed a large pile of discs on it just before *"no more bets"* was called.

The ball seemed to take much longer to come to rest. I watched it spin round and round while the mixed colours of the wheel that had merged together with speed had started to separate into black and red. With a hop and two back kicks the ball landed in the black box number 33.

"Well done, you've just earned me a small fortune, my boy." By the look on the faces of the remaining players I could see he'd won quite a lot this time, they were all saying, "well done," and smiling even though all of them had lost themselves yet again.

The waistcoat man split the discs into stacks and did some calculations in his head before turning again to the blue coat man. *"Blue six, five, eighty,"* he called. With the same look and nod the scruffy man was paid out, but not before he was asked how he'd like the money.

"Five in blacks and the rest in blues please," he answered. I looked up at the large clock on the wall and suddenly realised what I was supposed to be doing. At that, I turned and went to walk back into the main hall. Just as I was leaving the table the scruffy man called out, "You off so soon? Here catch!" I turned just in time to put my hands out and catch what was flying towards me. I stopped and looked down at my hands to find a small black disc. I looked back up and smiled at the scruffy face that was watching me. While the others at the table gasped and cheered but for what reason I wasn't sure "A last number before you go?" the man asked.

Without much thought, I called out a number as I turned and walked away. "Number ten." I never found out what the next number was that the small white ball came to rest in nor do I know how much he gambled on that one thoughtless number. He could have won a million for all I know or lost the lot. But that's gambling, I suppose. You pay your money and take your chance.

I put the little black disc into my pocket without much more thought and made my way back into the main entrance hall to try and find Dad and Jamie. The fact that there were lots of people standing around made it virtually impossible to define where they could be. Just as I decided to walk back to the room, I felt a hand reach onto my shoulder. With a bit of a jump, I turned to find the lady from the front desk behind me.

"Are you looking for someone?" she asked.

I knew all too well who I was looking for and what I was about to do, but the fact that this beautiful woman who spoke like an angel had actually touched me, had taken all vocal ability away from me. I stood mouth moving but nothing coming out.

"Are you ok?"

"Ye-y-yes thanks, I mean I'm ok."

"You looked a little lost standing there, are you looking for someone?"

Now, the right thing to have said was the truth: that I was looking for Dad and Jamie. But some strange power overrode my mind and I quickly found myself adjusting the truth. "Well, yes actually, I was suppose to meet my two friends here but it doesn't look like they've remembered."

"Oh, that's a pity! I'm sure you'd have had something nice planned as well."

"Nothing special, just a few drinks and some time to catch up." If I hadn't lied much in the past, I was certainly making up for it now. I tried very hard to concentrate while all around me there was the hustling noise of people hobnobbing and laughing.

"If your plans have changed, you wouldn't be so kind as to give me a helping hand for a few minutes would you?"

Without even considering my reply the words spilled forth. "Of course." I couldn't believe it, here I was in a room full of people and out of everyone I was the one being asked to help this truly beautiful woman. I learned a valuable lesson that day, a lesson that would change my thoughts and views on offering assistance to strangers forever.

"I'll just leave a note at the front desk in case your friends come back to let them know where you've gone and I'll be right back." She disappeared for a brief second giving me a last chance to view the surrounding crowds for Dad and Jamie but to no avail.

"Are you ready?" came a voice from behind. Turning around, I could see I was being asked to follow this strange woman as she moved her finger back and forth in a somewhat exciting and mysterious fashion. Almost tripping over my own feet, I quickly stepped off my left foot and walked towards her. I followed her down a long corridor like a puppy dog being pulled on a leash as my eyes were engrossed with her long, slim, shiny legs. She was wearing an ocean blue knee height skirt that frilled all along the bottom. She had a matching ocean blue jacket that fitted tightly around a white shirt highlighted by a blue bow tie. Her idle chat while we walked only demanded a yes and no answer. I preferred it that way in order to remember all the lies I'd told. It was at this point when I started to wonder what on earth she could need me for. We came to stop outside a small door, very similar to those that the cleaners could be seen pushing trolleys in and out off. Taking a small key from the right hand pocket of her jacket, she unlocked the door and opened it.

Fumbling around slightly, she clicked a switch turning on a light that revealed a small room; slightly similar to the room we were staying in but much smaller and not as well kept. There was a damp, stale-like smell coming from the carpet and there didn't appear to be any windows.

"After you," she said, at the same time pointing inside.

My naivety was an insufficient shield against my trust in people and I welcomed her invite as if being asked into a sweet shop for the first time. Upon entering, the inside of the room didn't improve much. A few feet inside, the room turned to the left in an L shape. Right on the bend was a closed door leading somewhere and filling the small space was a bed and dressing table.

"It's not much," she said, as if acknowledging the look of pity on my face. "But it's only a stepping stone to better and bigger things." I recall thinking she must have a large river to cross if this was a stepping stone to bigger things. "You don't mind if I get changed first do you?" she asked. Without giving me the chance to respond, she had walked through the small door and closed it behind her.

Through the walls, I could hear a muffled shout "to make myself comfortable." If she meant ease up a little, I could understand her because I had started to feel a little unsettled by this stage. The minutes passed by very slowly and I found myself thinking about Dad and Jamie while all the time I heard the sound of humming and a shower running. I sat upon the bed and looked around the room. On the dressing table stood a small silver picture frame with a photo of a young girl in it. There was an array of makeup and hairbrushes scattered rather messily and a trophy of a dancer took centrepiece. Just as my eyes had exhausted every nook and cranny of the room the door reopened.

Nothing in life so far had prepared me for what was about to happen. As bold as brass and totally naked she walked out in front of me. Here was I sitting on this woman's bed whose name I didn't even know, and she was walking about bare naked. I looked away as the blood not only ran to my face but to other places.

"I hope you don't mind but I forgot to take a towel in. You couldn't reach into that drawer and fetch me one, could you?" Still inclining my eyes to the one side, I stretched out and opened the drawer her hand pointed to. Feeling inside I pulled a large white towel out and passed it out to the side at arm's lengths. "There's no need to be shy, I bet you've seen many a woman's body before."

Her question seemed to hold its own answer. It was as if she somehow knew I'd never seen a naked woman before and was just toying with me. Turning around towards her, I found her to be standing right in front of me. My first reaction was to stand, but I found myself quickly sitting again after my legs gave way. "Is it something in here you want me to give you a hand with?" I asked only to receive a smile.

My heart was pounding at a million beats a second and my breath had become very deep and painful. Suddenly and without warning, she stretched out her hands and lifted mine into them. "Do you think I'm attractive?" she asked, at the same time sending me a long transfixed stare.

"Well, yes... I mean, of course, you're very beautiful indeed."

"Oh you're just saying that."

"No, honestly, you are."

After a short pause, she disengaged the grip she held on my hands and allowed them to fall into my lap. The thoughts that were running through my mind had now turned to confusion. Where was I? What was I doing? Before I

213

had much of a chance to comprehend the answers, I felt her still slightly damp hands reach into the inside shoulders of my jacket, slipping it off and onto the bed. I automatically withdrew my arms while all the time gazing at what stood before me. Her hands had now started to ascend up my shirt releasing each button with ease. Upon my tie being removed, she flicked the last remaining button opened and with the same quick shoulder movement she draped the shirt over my back exposing my naked chest. Taking a hold of each wrist she then undid the cuff button. For the first time in many years, I rekindled the young schoolboy feeling of being dressed by my mother. Sending my arms into the air she pulled the shirt completely off. If the beating of my heart wasn't loud enough to hear, it was certainly visible enough as my chest strongly vibrated with every pound.

Taking to the floor, she knelt directly in front of me, her breast barely inches away from touching my knees. She reached down towards my feet and released each lace before removing my shoes and socks. My hands were trembling with fright and embarrassment, but fear was being distracted by confusion and uncertainty. After the last sock was removed, her hands preceded right to my trouser belt. As if under some sort of mind control, I stood up unwillingly, allowing her to slide the belt off from around my waist and undo my trouser button. Like a stone falling to the ground they collapsed and rested around my ankles leaving me to stand almost totally naked. All that my body now wore was a pair of the rather exotic underwear that Anna and Jenny had bought me for my birthday.

Climbing to her feet, we now stood face to face. Slowly, she reached her head towards me and with exact precision she placed our lips together to kiss. So engaged by the touch of her lips was I to notice that at the same time using her hands she had slid my underwear to the ground. For the last ten minutes or so we'd said absolutely nothing. The room had fallen silent only to be broken by the sound of sliding clothes and the occasional drip of water from the small bathroom.

Suddenly and without thought, I placed my hands on her breast. They never felt as I'd expected them to. They were firmer than I'd imagined they'd be, and they had a somewhat pimply texture to them. We stood for a few seconds and kissed some more before, as if as one body and in one distinct motion, we swept backwards and landed upon the soft covers of the bed. I could feel myself rubbing against her body as we kissed and rolled about on the bed. My excitement was becoming very overwhelming and I could feel my erratic breathing turn my head dizzy. It was that day that I learned kissing didn't only involve the touching of lips, you could kiss almost anywhere!

Just as my body temperature soared, something clicked. With a fleeting glance at the dressing table, I noticed for the second time the photograph frame holding the picture of a young girl, only this time the picture had changed, the person staring back from the silver frame was Anna. Suddenly everything died. What on earth was I thinking of, and what in hell's name was I doing in this small room with a woman whose name I didn't even know and who I was about to engage in sex with?

I recoiled from under her and sprang from the bed. This wasn't right. This should be something special. Something for me to remember and share with someone, not some act of lust.

"What's wrong, are you all right?" she asked, sounding rather bewildered.

Fear had taken control of my voice and caged it somewhere deep, not permitting me to explain my actions. Some sort of self-preservation mode had switched on telling me to get out from this dragon's lair and escape the claws of this intoxicating she-devil of lust. Grabbing my clothes from the floor, I ran from the room and into the hallway. It was only upon hitting the coldness that I was able to take a deep breath and thank God for my lucky escape. Although escape wasn't quite the right word, as now I was standing in one of the main hallways of the Lion Gate Hotel totally naked.

Just as I'd regained my senses and understood my position did I hear the sound of a handle moving and a door opening. I dropped my clothes to the floor and franticly searched for my underwear. Common sense would have told me just to put my trousers on but that would have been far too easy. As I was bent over searching the bundle of clothes, a shadow appeared over me. I stopped and slowly looked up. As I moved my head upwards, I saw two pairs of legs. They appeared to belong to that of a man and a woman. Now looking at head height I found it was an old man and woman.

"My dear boy, cover yourself up, this is a hotel."

"I'm so sorry, sir, madam. I was..."

"It's obvious it's not intentional, come boy, in here and get changed." By this time, a few other people had walked past staring at the sight of a young naked man covering his manhood. I was as red as a lobster in boiling hot water and ready to burst into tears. "I'll get your clothes, just get in and out of view, quickly now."

Still covering myself up, I ran across the hall and through the door opposite that was being held open by the old woman. As I passed her and entered the room, I noticed a slightly wicked look upon her face. The room was large and very extravagant. I stood next to an oval glass table and waited till the old man arrived. He walked in and placed the jumbled clothes on the table.

"Come on, dear; let's give the young man a moment to recompose himself." With the same wicked smile, the woman looked around and gave me a final eyeing over as she closed the door behind her.

I quickly redressed as fast as possible, almost breaking my neck as I fell when pulling my trousers on. Now finding myself re-dressed except for the lack of one sock that I'd clearly left behind in my haste, I walked over to the door and slowly peered out. In the hallway, I could hear the old couple speaking to what looked like the hotel manager.

"We're very sorry sir, but it was dark and our son was making his way to the bathroom. By the time he realised what he'd done it was too late, as he'd shut the door behind him. We can assure you it won't happen again."

"Very well but please make sure it doesn't, we're a respectable hotel and naked men running about aren't very good for business." At that, the manager walked away.

As I opened the door fully, the couple turned round.

"Now then, that's much better; it's not gentlemanly to walk about in a public building with nothing but your hands to cover you."

"It wasn't intentional, I can assure you."

"Well I hope not."

"I appreciate your help, sir; I overheard what you said to that man."

"Oh that, let's just say you've made for an interesting evening."

"I'm glad it made someone happy."

"Well, my dear boy, we have an engagement to keep so we must leave, but it was intriguing to have met you."

"Thank you sir, madam."

They then continued down the hall until it turned and that was the last time I ever saw them. It had been a very disturbing evening, although an interesting and self-learning one. I stood for a few moments and stared at the door that held behind it the woman who'd in some way tried to seduce me. I didn't learn about that word seduce until later on in life, but I'm certain that if I'd known its meaning that day that's what she'd attempted to do. Many a man would love to be seduced by a woman but for me it was a scary and very daunting experience, an experience that's subsisted with me throughout my life.

After a bit of soul searching and contemplation, I realised the woman I loved was sitting at home in Rockfield. I wasn't sure if she felt the same way but I made the decision to ask her on my return. I wandered back into the main entrance hall and stared around looking for Dad and Jamie. Little did I know that they were looking for me?

When Jamie had run off Dad had found him sitting outside the hotel at the side of the road. Dad stood a couple of feet back and gave him a few moments to gather his thoughts. After a few minutes had passed, Dad sat down next to him and they talked.

"Jamie, you'll catch the death of cold sitting out here."

"The death of cold is better than the death of shame and embarrassment."

"Jamie, you've no need to feel shame or embarrassment, you've done nothing to think that."

"I can only imagine what people are thinking, I bet they're all thinking I befriended a little old woman to gain riches then killed her slowly."

"Come on now, such talk is just ridiculous. No one is thinking any such thing. And anyway, why be concerned about the thoughts of people who've never cared for or given you a second thought? You're a good man, Jamie, and an honest man. Such men are a rarity and shouldn't be spoiled."

"You have to believe me, Thomas, I never intended for things to turn out like this. I'd rather have Mrs Blake back than be gifted with all the money in the world."

"That I know only too well, but she's gone and she isn't coming back for any man. However, in her absence hopefully she'll live on because, through you, her money will do good for people."

"I just feel lost, like I've been dropped into a large bubble out at sea with no land in any direction, I can see everyone and everything around me but don't know where to go or what to do, I'm very confused."

218

"Jamie, it's expected that you'll feel lost and confused. In the last few years, I know you've suffered more than most people have suffered in a lifetime. But remember, we're here for you; you've got more people who care for you than you realise."

"I know, but I've always had to try and be strong and brave, I've always been the one to provide, not only by means but by help and caring. I guess it's taking its toll now."

"Jamie, when I was younger my father always told me, a man's problems are like a wrapped box, you never know what's inside until it's opened up. If we keep our problems packaged up, they're only being stored to be opened at a later stage. It soon gets to a point when we run out of storage, and when we start to clear the shelves undoubtedly things are going to fall down on top of us. Life's too short to be carrying loads of baggage. It's better that we chase life as we live it and be happy for what we've been given and not what's been taken away. I fear we all lose things in life and I'm no different, it will soon be me in your position but I don't have time to dwell on what ifs."

Jamie didn't pursue Dad's comment, sensing he wasn't quite ready to speak about it yet, but he knew before me something terrible was soon going to take place.

"What will we have to do in the morning?" Jamie asked.

"Well, after we arrive back we'll have to make our way to the McNorton Funeral Parlour. The arrangements will have to be made for the funeral. Hopefully, most of the details would have already been taken care of but there will be some minor things to attend to. I expect the funeral will take place the day after tomorrow."

"As quickly as that?"

"I'm sure Mrs Blake would rather that than be lying by herself at unease."

"Yes, I'm sure you're right." Jamie turned and grabbed onto Dad. "Thanks Thomas. I mean it, thank you."

Jamie wiped the tears from his eyes and Dad and he proceeded back inside. Their conversation had helped Jamie far more than Dad would ever know. For later on in life Jamie confided in me that while he sat on the kerb of the road that evening he had heavily contemplated ending his life by walking into the path of a moving vehicle. He had reached a low in his life that day that thankfully never returned to him again. For at the trying hour of his life when all he wanted to do was rejoin his Dad and Mrs Blake, he stood strong with the help of those around him.

After establishing that I was no longer sitting at the table, Dad and Jamie went back to the hotel room to see if perhaps I'd made my way back there. Little did they now that during their conversation, I was experiencing the gratification of sexual pleasure. Although it wasn't perhaps the best experience of my life, it certainly ranked highly as one of the most interesting of all time. We finally found each other as I was making my way up the stairs and they were coming down.

"There you are!" called Dad, "we've been looking all over for you."

"And I was looking for you two."

"Well, we've found each other now. It's been a long day, I think it's best we make our way back upstairs and get some sleep. We've the long journey home tomorrow and much to do after that." With no more said, we walked back to the room and got ready for bed.

I was dying to tell Jamie all about my little escapade but decided it would make for a far better tale one night in the future. After we washed, we made our way to the beds. There were only two large double beds in the room so Jamie and I shared while Dad had one all to himself. The beds were very comfortable indeed; we had only just lain down when Jamie had fallen into a deep sleep. I called his name a couple of times but there was no chance of waking him. He was well and truly trapped in the abyss of dreamland. I, on the other hand, although extremely tired, couldn't find the strength to keep my eyes closed. My eyelids just kept popping open to view the shadows being cast on the ceiling by the flickering streetlights outside.

Lying in bed that night I considered the last few days' events with much interest. I had arrived at a point in life where the road ahead had split. On the left strode a long and straight road edged with fields of golden corn. On the right led a twisted and darkened path, shrouded with large dark trees that creaked and whistled. I tried hard to imagine what stood at the end of each path but wasn't able to come up with a fully conclusive opinion. I guessed that the left would carry me to the creative and hard working side of life, using the corn to make the much needed bread to sustain a family, while the right hand side showed the travel of strife and heartache. Every good life is full of pain and equally of love and enjoyment. I knew that I was destined to travel both roads at some point to bear witness and testament to the winding paths of life. No matter what life had in store for me I knew that one-day I'd be a great man. I had a thirst for life and for everything it could throw at me. I was ready and waiting to accept the trials that unknowingly stood before me.

I'm not sure what the time was when finally I fell asleep. I reckon it was somewhere between two and two thirty. But one thing I do know was what woke me up. In sleep I found myself back at the hardware shop. This time wasn't like any of the previous times. This time I felt safe and somewhat secure. It was also much lighter this time and the shop seemed to be open for business. There was a man looking at a glass cabinet in the far corner of the room while I noticed someone moving about at the back of the shop. I wanted to move forward but couldn't muster the energy to lift my legs.

"It's ok," said a voice from behind. I stumbled forward slightly as my body turned to see where the voice came from. Standing right there in front of me as bright as day was Mrs Blake.

"I think it's about time we ended this dream once and for all, don't you?" she spoke.

I could hear as perfectly as I could ever have wished for but when I tried to speak nothing came out. My mouth just appeared to open and exhume silence, but somehow Mrs Blake knew exactly what I was trying to say. Very softly, she placed her finger on my lips then turned me around. Taking me by the hand, she walked me to the rear of the shop. There on a small wooden stool sat a man. His head was bowed and the look of grief was stricken all over his pale grey, oily face. He was looking down at a small wooden grate that held a tattered red blanket and a black leather strap.

My grip on Mrs Blake's hand tightened as the man stood up and placed his hands on the front counter. It was them! It was the hands I saw on the wall at the church the day I was chased. I looked to Mrs Blake and tried desperately to pull but nothing would happen. Like a child in a stubborn huff, I tried to drag myself away, but to no avail. A freeze seemed to travel from Mrs Blake and into every inch of my body.

"Excuse me sir," called the voice of the man who was looking at the glass cabinet. At that, the large man walked from the counter accidentally kicking the small wooden box with his big feet and went in the direction of the cabinet. The wooden box was now only a yard away from me at the most and I could clearly see a small carved badge that was nailed to the front of it. Inside the neatly carved border was a name. A name of an animal I guessed. It read 'SAMSON'S SON'.

It was then I realised the leather strap was actually a leash. Everything started to become clear. A gulp in my throat told me I'd made a great mistake. Still holding me with her left hand, Mrs Blake raised her right one and pointed to a block of white marble that sat on the floor near the back door. The door was slightly open, shedding a ray of light across the block. There were some words chiselled out which had begun to be coloured in with gold paint. Although it wasn't finished, I understood what it was and likewise what it read.

Samson's Son

In a lonely life you stood me proud
Each day and night you watched for sound
A faithful and loyal friend
We travelled right until the end

Your trust in me was always strong
Our journey wandered far and long
For many years we paired the streets
An often sight for most to see

But now you're gone and free to roam
Amidst the winds and rays of sun
To glide and sail the clouds and sky
In my heart you'll never die

It was then, just as a warm tear melted a heated trail down my cheek that I knew. It was no human body the man was lifting that day, it was a dog! The look of realisation must have been glowing all over my face as Mrs Blake could see that I now understood.

"Not everything in life is how it seems and all that seems isn't always all it is. It should do you a lot of good to remember that in future."

Words had failed me. I felt ashamed and stupid. How could I have possibly thought of all those wild things? That night I certainly learned never to take things for granted or to jump to conclusions without taking the time to review the situation. Instead of feeling fear from this man, I now felt sorrow for him.

"I think you know what I'd like to happen, and if you don't I'm sure it will come to you soon enough," said Mrs Blake, still able to give one of her sharp piercing stares. I don't recall saying good-bye to her or leaving the shop. The next thing I knew, Dad was waking me up. Both he and Jamie were already up and dressed.

"Come on, sleepy, it's time for breakfast," Jamie shouted. I quickly got up and washed before joining them to walk down stairs.

"We'll have to book out first then we'll grab a spot of breakfast before we head home." The minute Dad mentioned the words book out a large swelling grew in my throat. I knew that the chances were that illustrious temptress of a woman could be there. She wasn't someone I wanted to meet again in a hurry.

"Dad, why don't Jamie and I make a start on breakfast while you book out? You know how long it can take me to eat sometimes."

I knew Dad could sense something wasn't quite right but he agreed nonetheless. Just as we rounded the last flight of stairs, there standing with her head tilted towards the desk she stood. Now all I had to do was manoeuvre my way across the hall without her seeing me. The hall was extremely empty considering how busy it was the night before. Trying to make it look as if I was engrossed in some meaningful conversation, I spoke to Jamie shielding a serious expression.

"Did you sleep well Jamie?"

"I'm not too sure if it was the bed or the fact that you kept moving and talking all night but I never slept a wink."

"I don't move and talk in my sleep!"

"You most certainly do, and not only that, you talk about the most stupid things."

"Like what?" I asked, hoping I hadn't mentioned anything that would embarrass me.

"You kept talking about a dog and woman."

"What woman?!"

"How do I know? But whatever it is she has belonging to you, I think you should just ask her for it back." At that, Jamie just smiled as if to acknowledge that he knew I'd been up to something. I suddenly remembered something! I touched the outside of my jacket pocket where I could feel where I'd placed the single sock, but I couldn't understand why on earth I'd be talking about it in my sleep. Whether I had been dreaming about it or not, I know there was no way on earth that I was going to ask her for it.

We made our way into the dining hall and took up a small table near to the windows. We were quickly attended to by a waiter and in no time breakfast was served. Just as we'd started to tuck into some ham and eggs, Dad joined us. The smile on his face could have told a thousand stories. He casually sat down before reaching into his left-hand side coat pocket. A gut feeling told me what was about to happen and I could only have wished for the ground to open up and swallow me whole and alive.

"The young lady at the desk asked that I give my young friend this back. I take it seeing as you're the only one without socks it must belong to you?"

At that, Dad handed across the table a black sock. My black sock, the sock that could open up a massive can of worms. I wanted to grab the sock and hide it or deny any knowledge of it, but I found myself slowly taking it and saying. "I hope you said thank you for me?" Then I slipped it into my pocket and continued on eating. I could feel Dad and Jamie staring at me.

"I take it we won't ask any more about it then?" Dad said in a very childish voice. I was trying to keep cool under the pressure, so gave very little reply: "There's nothing to ask." With a slight glimpse upwards, I could see the both of them snigger, but thankfully they were interrupted by the waiter who'd returned to enquire what Dad was wanting for breakfast.

Being first to finish, I left the table and made my way to the bathroom. I wasn't in need of a toilet but I desperately wanted to put my socks back on. I'd only been away a few minutes before returning to find Dad and Jamie had gone. As I stood and looked around I felt a tap on my shoulder.

"Sorry if I startled you, sir, but the others asked that you join them out front when you returned."

I quickly thanked the smartly dressed concierge before making my way to the entrance without looking back once at the front reception desk. As I walked under the blue canopy and out into the street, I could see Dad and Jamie standing.

"Great timing," said Dad just as the car pulled up. The old man who'd been driving it quickly travelled around the car and opened the doors for Jamie and me to get in while Dad got into the front to drive but not before giving the concierge a tip and thanking him. Then we were off and on the way home.

CHAPTER NINETEEN
Preparations

Nothing much happened on the way home apart from a few sneaky sock remarks and some sniggering from Jamie and Dad. Jamie, whom I'd obviously kept awake all night, quickly fell asleep, leaving me to stare out the windows and give thought to many things. Dad, being very predictable, began singing to himself, making it all in all it a very peaceful journey.

It was a great feeling to be walking up our front stairs and into the house. Just being home always gave me a sense of security and warmth. All seemed very quiet on entering into the hall. We hung up our coats and made our way into the main room. The fire crackling away was the only sound that could be heard until all of a sudden sounds of laughter came from the direction of the kitchen. Dad was first to enter with me closely behind. Everyone was sat gathered around the kitchen table.

"Thomas," Mum shouted as she ran toward him and landed him a great kiss. I didn't quite know why but Dad was looking at her rather strangely, as if he never expected her to be there, or to have been so energetic. Nevertheless, he hugged and kissed her in return. Then came my turn. I too felt slightly strange as she wrapped her arms around me. It was as if she hadn't seen me for years, like I was her long lost son, finally returned. Jamie also received the same welcoming treatment.

"Come and sit down, and I'll sort you all a quick bite before dinner." She dragged both of us to the table.

Before our backsides had even managed to touch the chair there were questions coming from all angles. Everyone wanted to know something about our adventure to Edinburgh; all, that was, except one, Anna. She just sat there as quiet as a mouse and looking at nothing other than the plate that lay before her. She was looking beautiful; in fact, she was looking more than beautiful. The firing questions just flew into the depths of my mind while I watched her. I imagined what her skin would be like to hold and touch, how her hair would feel and what it would be like to kiss her.

Suddenly, all those nice thoughts evaporated upon receiving a blow to the side of my ribs from Gavin. "It's rude to just ignore someone, you know?" his attitude somewhat grumpy.

"Sorryyyy," I half-shouted back as I tried to regain breath. "I was thinking about something. What did you ask?"

"Oh, nothing, if that's the mood you're in."

Just as Jenny was dishing out some broth, Gran asked how everything had gone. "Very well," Dad replied. And at that everyone's questions were answered.

After lunch but before moving from the table Dad told of where our journey had taken us and what we'd done, but at the same time keeping much of the personal matters concerning Jamie to himself, including the whole sock incident, for which I was very thankful. Dad and Jamie may have given up the chase for information on that subject, but the likes of Mum and Gavin wouldn't have been so easy to fob off.

After a lunch of broth and bread, I signalled to Jamie that we had to go out for a walk. I had suddenly remembered something I had to do.

CHAPTER TWENTY
Surprises Come in Threes

I shouted "Joe" and waited a second as I heard the dog's nails clicking on the wooden floorboards as he came rushing at the sound of this name, tail wagging nineteen to the dozen.

"What're we doing" Jamie asked, pulling on his coat. Before I answered, I collected the leash that hung on the coat stand and attached it to Joe's collar.

I wasn't quite sure how I was going to explain to Jamie what I wanted to do, or if he'd even agree, but I was sure of one thing, it had to be done. Not because I wanted to do it, but because Mrs Blake wanted it that way, and that I was sure about. Just as we got to the bottom of the stairs Jamie asked again, "Come on then, what are we doing?"

"You must swear that you won't think I'm crazy or stupid."

"Ok, I swear."

"No really, *you must swear*."

"Alright, I swear. Now, for Pete's sake, tell me what we're doing."

"I think I know what we have to do with Joe."

"What do you mean, 'do' with Joe?"

I started to explain about the dream I'd had on the night we'd stayed in the hotel and how Mrs Blake had taken me to the hardware store. I told how I watched with her holding my hand and what I'd seen on the floor, namely the leash, kennel and the head stone belonging to Samson's

Son. I recall Jamie looking at me in disbelief as though my imagination was getting the better of me, but I knew, deep down inside I knew, what I'd seen wasn't my mind playing tricks with me. It was real. I continued to speak and, although Jamie didn't totally believe, he followed without interrupting.

"You see, as I was standing there totally frozen, seeing and hearing everything that was going on Mrs Blake spoke to me."

"What did she say?" Jamie now asked eagerly.

"She told me I knew what she wanted me to do and after that I don't remember."

"You mean she disappeared?"

"Well, all I remember after that was being woken up by Dad for breakfast."

"So if we walk in here and find that this man has never owned a dog, you do understand we'll be making complete fools of ourselves, don't you?"

"Yes, perhaps, but if he did have a dog and I'm right, what then?" Even to me this was quite a puzzling question.

We trudged on in silence for a while, both lost in our own thoughts. The sun was shining so hard you could feel it burn against your face but still the snow stayed firm and crunchy underfoot. Its crystal-like twinkles were like an army of mirrors fighting hard to keep the evil heat rays away. Finally, we reached the shop and stopped outside, looking at each other uncertainly.

"What now?" asked Jamie as we came to rest at the shop window. "We might be making a big mistake, just acting on a dream you had."

"I am sure this is what we have to do."

Make no mistake about it, I was petrified. There wasn't a single part of my body that wasn't shaking uncontrollably; even my lips seemed to move by themselves. I clasped the golden door handle and pushed forward into the shop with Joe hearing the bell ring above our heads. The shop was empty inside and the silence was only shattered by a voice shouting from out back.

"I'll be right with you."

Just like in my dream the shop looked and smelled exactly the same. We stood for only a matter of seconds but, boy, did it feel like forever! As we gazed around the shop, the sound of footsteps could be heard coming towards us, and big footsteps at that. From the darkness of the back door, we could see someone emerge. His face and hands were the first things to be highlighted by the little sunlight that was left to come in through the shop windows.

My voice sank further and further with every step until the man came to rest at the counter. "How can I help you boys?" he asked, his voice being exactly how I'd heard it in the past although it didn't sound quite as scary now.

With a push from Jamie, I stumbled forward 'til I was almost right at the counter, tripping over poor Joe. "Hello sir," I started. "I'm very sorry to be disturbing you on this fine evening but I was wondering if perhaps I could speak with you for a moment if you'd be so kind?"

"You mean you want to apologise for being a sneaking individual who has nothing better to do that frighten people half to death."

As you can imagine, I was totally taken aback by this. God only knows how he knew it was me at the window that day. "Well, yes, that does have something to do with it."

"And right it should do an' all, if you'd given me half a chance instead of running away I could have explained what you'd seen quite easily."

"Well y, yes, I realise that now."

"And so you should. Now come on and say what you've got to say and be done with it, I'm a busy person when I'm not a mad murderer, you know."

From behind, I could hear Jamie sniggering whilst the extra glow in the shop must have been coming from the warmth of my face. Just as I was about to say sorry and explain, the man interrupted.

"Before all your apologies, I'm thinking you should be introducing your friends, should you not?"

"Oh yes sorry, this here is Jamie my best friend and this here is Joe."

"Jamie and Joe, ah. So be out with it then, what's all this talking you want to do"

"Well you see sir; it's actually Joe that we've come to speak to you about."

"And why exactly would that be?"

"Well it's a long story and to tell the truth we haven't the time to go into it at the moment but, needless to say, it involves you and Joe."

"Oh, does it now?"

"It sure does. The matter is, sir, that Joe here is now homeless. A lady called Mrs Blake owned him, but sadly she passed away a few days ago leaving Joe here in something of a predicament. You see, Jamie's brother is allergic to dogs and, unfortunately, my Mum hasn't much time for animals so we're in some need of help."

"Well how do you suppose I'm able to help in such a predicament?"

"Yet again, sir, without giving too many explanations, I was under the impression that you liked the company of dogs but that you were without one at the moment."

"So much may very well be the case. How you comes to know about it I'm not sure but one thing I am sure about is this. Any animal who professes to have been owned by the good Mrs Blake of High View Road is certainly welcome to stay with me."

I looked at Jamie in amazement, as he did the same to me. There was obviously a lot more to this situation than met the eyes. "So sir, does that mean that you'd like to be Joe's new owner?"

"Well, owner's not something I would say is quite appropriate keeping in mind that he seems to have at least two of them standing right here in front of me, but that isn't to say I wouldn't say no to his staying here. You two would have to look in on him once in a while and continue to look after him, but as for his sleeping arrangements he's more than welcome here."

"Oh thank you, sir, and thank you."

"And another thing, boys, the name's not sir, it's Adam. There ain't no airs and graces with me."

"Thanks, Adam," said Jamie from behind, at the same time giving me a tug and pointing to the clock on the wall.

"Oh damn it, we're late!" Walking around the side of the counter, I handed the leash to Adam and after saying thanks for the tenth time we left.

"That was amazing," screeched Jamie excitedly. "We ought to be calling you mystic man from now on," he laughed loudly. I'm not quite sure what it was but something was telling me that Jamie knew a little more than he was letting on. If he did, he never ever told me but he often made hints to that effect. We ran back to the house as quickly as we could, over-excited and overwhelmed by the fact that my dream had been strangely true.

As we walked up the stairs and into the hall, we heard a lot of noise coming from the main room. On pulling the doors open, we found out why. Inside the room, as well as Mum, Dad, Gran, Anna, Jenny, Gavin and Margaret were Jamie's family, each of them dressed rather finely and all talking to one and other. Upon seeing our two little heads popping through the door, Dad clapped his hands.

"It appears that we won't be eating that late after all, now that these two have arrived." As he spoke, a smile rolled over his face. "Now go and get washed before we start without you, off you go."

At that, we raced up stairs and into the bathroom.

Taking turns, we washed as quickly as possible and headed down stairs. It appeared we were having dinner in the dining room, as that's where everyone was now sitting and chatting away. Dad was sitting at the head of the table, to his left sat Mrs Richardson with Mum on his right. Working from left to right after that sat Jenny and Gran, Paul and Anna, Gavin and Alice, Margaret and Mary followed by Jamie and me when we took up our seats. All the food was already sitting on the table piping hot, steaming and looking fantastic. There was no saying of grace or anything like that, just a shout from Dad for everyone to tuck in.

It was a very interesting dinner to say the least. Everyone seemed to be enjoying themselves and the food wasn't long in disappearing, which pleased Jenny I can tell you. There were conversations flying in every direction and I remember at one point just sitting back and listening to some of them. The grownups were talking about how the last few days had been terrible and how the snow didn't look to be going away. Jenny and Gran were talking about the estate and hoping that all was ok. Paul and Gavin talked non-stop about anything and everything. The girls were very much into small talk and chitter-chattered away, while Jamie sat for the most part thinking away to himself.

"What are you thinking about, Jamie?" I asked, giving him a slight kick at the same time.

"Well, I've only got till tomorrow and I need to know what's going to be said at the funeral."

"Ah, you mean the songs and things. I'll give you a hand after dinner and we'll come up with something, don't panic."

"That's easy for you to say," came his quick reply. Although I never gave it much thought, there were two or three occasions that I found Mum staring at Mrs Richardson. It was as if she was trying to remember her from somewhere. The evening closed in very fast and before long the pudding had been and gone and everyone was sitting and chatting away in the main room to the sounds of the fire cracking and hissing.

I was just about to ask Jamie if he wanted to go upstairs and have a look through a book of songs when he stood up. "Sorry if I've caught your attention at a bad time but I'd really like to speak to you all if you'd be so kind as to spare a moment please."

All the conversations went dead and all eyes and ears were now resting firmly on Jamie.

"It's just that you all know about tomorrow, and I know that Mrs Blake asked for a quiet funeral. And I know that none of you knew her that well, but all the same I'd really like it if you could all come along tomorrow and be there. I understand it if anyone doesn't want to, but I'd really appreciate it if you could manage it." With those few words he sat back down again. The conversation took a few minutes to gather pace again after that.

Giving Jamie a tug, he followed me up stairs and we spent the next few hours looking through the songbook trying to find something useful. Eventually, we settled on one song and decided to try and write a reading ourselves. After many notes and drafts, we finally had something. It was meaningful, polite and above all personal. Not something that had been used many times before, but a one off.

We went back down stairs where Jenny was just going around dishing out hot mugs of chocolate. Mum had arranged for Jamie's family to stay the night instead of going back home so late. There were plenty of spare rooms so it made perfect sense. The only person not to stay was Margaret whose Dad came and collected her at around nine thirty. Poor Gavin was pretty annoyed by this but nevertheless got on with things. Just around eleven o'clock, Dad signalled that it was time for bed and at that we all made our way upstairs. Paul slept in along side Gavin whilst Alice and Mary slept in one of the top bedrooms. After getting washed and into bed, all we could hear for the next hour was Gavin and Paul messing around next door until Jenny was asked by Dad to go up and give them both a talking to. All seemed to go quiet after that and I found myself not the least bit tired.

"Jamie! Are you still awake?"

"I sure am. You finding it hard to sleep also?"

I considered my answer carefully before offering a reply. You see, although the funeral was playing on my mind, that wasn't what was keeping me awake. It was the fact that both Anna and Mary were staying in my house that was preventing me from sleeping. The thought of them being only a few rooms away and probably half-naked was making my mind work overtime. I presumed Jamie wouldn't take offence with me telling him the truth, so that's exactly what I did.

"Well as long as you're thinking more about Anna than Mary I don't reckon I mind that much. And even if that ain't what you're thinking I'm thinking that's what you should be telling me whether it's the truth or not." We both laughed loudly at the almost tongue twisting words Jamie had spewed, causing us to receive a knock on the door from Jenny.

As in most cases when it's dark, people tend to be able to speak not only more honestly to each other but they also ask each other things they wouldn't normally ask if they could see each other, if you know what I mean. In this instance the talk turned to girls and sex, a subject I was becoming quite an expert on.

"What do you suppose it's like to have sex, Jamie?" I asked, keeping the noise down so as not to pass the conversation through the wall to Gavin and Paul. There was a slight pause then a release of air followed by a response.

"Well, not having done it, I'm not entirely sure, but I reckon it's very much a soft and gentle kind of thing. You know, like all lovey-dovey." I pulled up visions of my brief encounter at the hotel and I assured myself that lovey-dovey wasn't the best way to explain it. "Anyhow, it should be me asking you that question shouldn't it?"

By this I knew exactly where Jamie was coming from. Should I tell him about my happenings or not? I knew he obviously guessed something with the sock saga, but the chances were that even if I did tell him he wouldn't believe me.

"I'm waiting, or are you going to keep it a secret forever?" I had no choice, if I didn't say it meant I was keeping secrets from my best friend and that's not the way best friends carry on. I explained what happen but adjusted some bits a little so as not to look totally stupid. Jamie was so intrigued that he wanted to hear again. We laughed for a while and then, without knowing, we were both asleep.

Morning wasn't the first thing to awaken me from sleep that night. Stirring rather restlessly, I awoke to see Jamie and his shadow staring out the window. I kept laid back and still and watched for a few moments.

"The snow's started to fall again," said Jamie, surprising me.

"Is it falling fast?"

"As fast as their little wings will allow," he followed softly. "There's been something bothering me of late, something that I may have to ask your assistance with if you don't mind."

"Like what?"

"Tonight is neither the time nor the place to discuss it, but I'm hoping that no matter what you'll understand."

To say he was acting just a little bit strange was an understatement, but I could see quite easily that cogs in Jamie's head were turning at rapid speed. With no more said, the naked body of a boy and his shadow climbed back onto the floor, rolled under the covers and drifted off back to sleep. I could only wish to tell you the same happened to me, but Jamie had my mind working overtime. I was

imagining all sorts of strange and wonderful things he'd
perhaps wanted me to help with. None of which was
correct, as in time you'll find out.

CHAPTER TWENTY-ONE
First Funeral

There is something about the day of a funeral; the deadening silence of the house, the denseness of the atmosphere, the sharpened sense of observation. I noticed it as soon as I woke up. There was no noise from the house. Jamie had gone, leaving his covers and clothes neatly piled up on the chair. I got out of bed and for the first time I felt the bitter chill of winter not only in the air but all over my body. I washed and dressed, listening for sound of life but heard none.

Throughout every room there was no one to be seen. Everyone had vanished as if by some sort of powerful magic. In the kitchen, however, sat a single bowl on the table filled with cereal and a milk jug standing guard next to it. There were also some large slices of bread with a selection of jams and honey resting on an oval plate at the centre of the table. Presuming everyone was doing something; I sat myself down and began to eat. It was only just as I was starting my second slice of bread and honey that I heard a noise. I could hear footsteps trudging up from the cellar below, and finally Jenny emerged. We said good-morning in a sombre way.

Finishing what was left of my bread and honey, I causally asked Jenny where everyone had disappeared too. She gave me a vague and implausible explanation about getting hats for the funeral. I could sense that something wasn't as it seemed.

Just as I opened the doors into the main hall the large clock that sat on the mantle struck ten. And only a few seconds after that did the main door open and Mum, Gran, Dad and Jamie walked in, each having feet covered in snow and all looking rather cold. Jamie stood in the hall, looking very preoccupied within himself.

"Are you ok?" I asked taking a few steps towards him.

"Yes, I'm fine, just a little bit tired, perhaps," he said, not meeting my eyes. I knew something wasn't right, but didn't feel now was the time to press for answers. We all sat in the main room for the next hour, drinking tea and not really talking much. There was a feeling of sadness which matched the look on most of the faces that were sitting there. Jenny and Anna entered the room, shortly followed by Gavin and Margaret who'd just arrived. The minutes ticked by until Dad stood up and said it was time to leave.

We arrived at the cemetery in several cars, emerging onto the snow-covered ground. The churchyard was dotted with black figures, dark against the white snow and grey skies. The wind was quite brisk and brought a bitter bite to the face if standing in its direction for long. Only after everyone was out of the vehicles and standing in the yard did we begin the walk down into the cemetery. All around, the snow glistened and sparkled, aided by the rays of the sun that rested upon it.

We followed a straight path that had been cleared until we were about halfway down when it started to turn left and continued for maybe fifty or so steps. As we got closer we could see many people gathered and I for one presumed that another funeral must have been taking place. It wasn't until we were almost right before them that I recognised some of them. Standing there was a whole host of people; there was Mr and Mrs Jacobson and two other shorter

240

than average men whom I didn't recognise. There was Linda and the doctor who'd attended Mrs Blake the night she died. Standing nearest the tombstone was Adam from the hardware shop accompanied by a woman who I didn't know and, last but not least, Joe.

Looking back over my shoulder, I could see the coffin arriving. Six men in black carried the dark-scrolled coffin with its brass handles. They moved towards us in a slow, co-ordinated procession, lifting the left leg first and placing it firmly on the ground before lifting the right leg in the same deliberate fashion. Slowly but surely they arrived and in a single motion, they turned and stood tall and erect, three either side of the grave. The Reverend took his place at the foot and we all turned, heads bowed for the ceremony. The service began, and afterwards each person collected a handful of earth, dropping it lightly down as they paid their last respects.

"You okay?" I asked Jamie.

"Sometimes I just feel so tired," he said in a detached way, staring up at the heavy, grey skies. "Tired of so much and so little... of life's constantly changing hand... never knowing what is coming next."

I scuffed at the ground, not too sure what to say in the face of such life-weary statements. "You'll be fine," I said finally, before stepping forward to give him a hug of moral support. We stood silently for a moment, and I could sense Jamie's relief of knowing he had support.

CHAPTER TWENTY-TWO
The Turning

Just as we had almost arrived outside the church, I could
see Dad walking towards us. "Jamie, I've told everyone
that they're more than welcome to come back to our house
for tea and coffee, I hope you don't mind?"

"Mind? I really appreciate everything you are doing
for me, Sir... sorry, Thomas," Jamie said, correcting himself
quickly.

Dad grabbed Jamie's hand and shook it firmly. "Happy
to, son. Happy to." Then he turned away quickly, as though
embarrassed.

Once back at the house, the solicitor Mr Jacobson
requested a private conversation with Jamie. What
happened after that I found out when Jamie told me?

"Mr Jacobson had two other men with him whom he
introduced as his sons Adare and Maxwell Jacobson. Then
he began talking rather seriously, which unnerved me
slightly," Jamie said, and put on an upper class, deep voice
as he narrated Mr Jacobson's words. "'Rather than have
you travel all the way back to Edinburgh I thought perhaps
we could conclude the matter of Mrs Blake's will here and
now. That is if you don't mind?' I concurred, and Mr
Jacobson took from the inside of his coat pocket a sealed
scroll and a pen. On breaking the scroll's seal, he unrolled
the paper and began to read:

I, Mrs Yvonne Blake, residing at 112 High View Road, Rockfield, do hereby and hereon the second day of September Nineteen Hundred and Twenty Two declare in the presence of my solicitor and long time friend Mr Henry Jacobson that I am of sound mind and the fullest of body. It is and shall be my last will and testament that I bequeath all my life long possessions to one Mr Jamie Richardson residing within the Blacksmith Fire of Rockfield including my home known as 112 High View Road, Rockfield and contents. All other properties in my name and their subsequent contents, all monies both deposited and not, all vehicles, jewels, gold, silver and all other items both valuable or not included in my estate. I likewise give to the above Mr Jamie Richardson, my twenty percent share in the company known as Henry Jacobson and Sons of Eleven King Street, Edinburgh, likewise the several rental buildings in and around Rockfield. I wish there to be no clause as to any of the above and that a speedy conclusion should be sought.

Signed	*Witnessed*
Henry Jacobson	Linda Lamb
Henry Jacobson	*Linda Lamb*
11 King Street	*9 Victoria Rd*
Edinburgh	*Rockfield*

Mrs Yvonne Blake'

"As you can image, I sat for a few moments dumbstruck. If I'd just heard right, Mrs Blake had left me in her will everything she ever owned. No one said a word. I stood up and gazed out of the window for a few moments whilst trying to gather my thoughts. 'You're a very wealthy man, Mr Richardson, a very wealthy man indeed. In my estimation going by the current bank accounts and the total assets, I expect you've more than likely become a millionaire.' I turned from the window and looked at Mr Jacobson, who was now standing and waited for him or someone to say they were only kidding, or that it was a big mistake or something, but they didn't.

"'If you'd kindly sign your signature on here for me, Mr Richardson, I think we ought to be giving you some time to yourself.' I walked around the table and collected the bright golden pen with inscribed markings and signed the long letter that sat on the table, and then with a hand shake Mr Jacobson and his sons left, closing the door behind them. I tell you I thought I was going to be sick. I couldn't stop shaking and all I could do was walk back and forth. I suppose a good few hours must have gone by before the first knock came on the door.

"'Jamie, can I come in?' Instantly I knew it was Mum. I walked to the door and opened it; we sat for the next 30 minutes and talked. I told her everything that happened at least three times and then some. For the first time in years, I saw a movement in Mum I hadn't seen for a long, long time. Her eyes turned brighter and her whole face seemed to polish with real colour. Of course, as she explained, Mr Jacobson had already been and seen her this very morning, and had made her somewhat aware of what was to happen. She thought it was best that I spoke with them alone and so waived the right to be there with me. We didn't speak much after that; we just hugged each other. I never thought in my wildest dreams something like this would ever happen to me.

"After Mum had left, the next knock on the door was you and here we are. It's like once again I've been picked up and thrown to the lions, but one thing's for sure, I think I've discovered how to tame them."

I was never too sure what Jamie meant with those words and nor can I say it gave me much thought, but what I can say is, Jamie was reborn that day. It wasn't a sudden thing or something that happened over night but surely it happened all the same.

After sitting a little longer and noticing the sun had now started to fade, we left the study and rejoined everyone in the main room. There was a slightly strange feeling in the air. Almost like the calm before the storm. Everyone seemed to have a kind of buzz about them. Everyone except Jamie's family and mine had gone, and Jamie was somewhat annoyed with himself for not having said goodbye. Dad insisted that once again Jamie and his family should stay the evening and likewise have dinner. Although Mrs Richardson argued that she was being a pain, she stayed and that evening we ate a meal fit for a king. Young Paul was the last to leave the table; having started his third piece of apple pie, his mother insisted he finished it before leaving as punishment for being so greedy. Dad just laughed and herded everyone back to the main room where Jenny already had the tea and coffee ready.

It's funny when I think back, because although everyone wanted to know what had happened in the study, especially the younger people, no one asked or even dared hint about it. Everyone just waited until they were told.

The night quickly ran in and in no time my eyes were beginning to drop. A sudden sense of sleep was upon me and the bedroom was calling.

"Goodnight everyone," I yawned before heading up stairs. After going via the bathroom, I headed to the bedroom where my bed was now shouting out. As I got into the room, I barely had the energy to get undressed let alone switch the light on, so standing in the middle of the room I got changed. It was only as I lifted the covers from the bed that I noticed someone standing just out of the shadows of the window.

"You tired as well, Jamie?" I called in a half yawn, but he never replied. I stood for second and looked harder and it was then I realised it wasn't Jamie who was standing there.

Through the moonlight pouring in from the window, she passed and stopped directly in front of me. Placing a hand on my chest, she whispered to me. "Like a true friend you were today, a true friend."

Taking her hand away she lent forward and our lips touched. My hands and legs trembled. My heart roared and my mind melted. All within seconds my body had been slain and captured in every way by the beauty that stood before me. Oh how much did I just want to take her in my arms and never let her go! I captured my breath and held my hand towards her still shaking violently. Interlocking our fingers we drew closer together. This time I could smell the sweetness that swept from her skin with every rub. With my other hand, I touched her face and as if it were butter my hand seemed to melt upon its softness. It was then that something strange happened, something for what I have no explanation other than mind over matter. I moved my head closer and closer until finally for the second time our lips had reached each other's. Somehow my body had taken control, it seemed to know what it was doing and I never had the want or the will to prevent it. As we kissed our arms had now wrapped around each other's bodies.

The touch of her hand as it swept across my back shot a wave of excitement tingling through me, and then suddenly we stopped. Sliding her hands down and across my buttocks she stepped to the side. "Not now," she said. "Not here," and with that she was gone.

For a glimpsing second she looked round as the hall light entered the room and lit me up, then as the door closed the darkness returned.

Standing there, I asked myself if I was dreaming or was the night and my mind playing vicious games with me. But there in my hand held the answer. It was near impossible to see but I knew what it was. A single strand of hair, its length was immeasurable and its importance greater than anything I'd ever known. I walked over to the table that sat on the far wall and carefully opening the largest book that sat there I dropped the hair upon it and closed it again.

As I passed the window I could see the snow was still falling but paid little attention and followed forward to the bed in front of me. Lying in bed, I felt somewhat strange. I was surely happy and not in the least a bit tired now, but all the same I felt different. It wasn't long before I was touching myself and feeling even better. My senses had truly awakened and within seconds I found myself rushing to the bathroom. Boy, did I really painfully want more to happen that night! Even when Jamie eventually came to bed that night I was still awake although he never knew it. On the same day as Jamie had rediscovered wealth, I'd discovered something far greater, I discovered me.

CHAPTER TWENTY-THREE
A New Home for Christmas

The next morning came all too soon and there was only one thing on my mind, Anna. All in all, I was very happy and excited about what happened those few hours ago and as if to reassure myself I opened the large book that was laying in the same position as I'd left only hours before. Opening its heavy front cover was like unwrapping the world's largest present. Slowly I peeled back its pages one by one till there, on page thirty-two and under the chapter heading of butterflies did it lay, one single strand of hair. Golden was its look and more enchanting than any of the butterflies that sat pictured in its foreground. I dared not to touch it nor disturb it in any way but just stared at it. It was only after a groan came from Jamie as he slept neatly curled up on the floor did I lower somewhat back to the realms of normality. I remember thinking how strange I'd have looked if Jamie had awoke at that moment and found me standing there naked and gazing at what he would have initially thought to be butterflies.

I quietly gathered some clothes, slipped into some pyjamas and headed for the bathroom. It was still rather dark outside and although the house was still quite peaceful I could hear sounds coming from the kitchen. I entered the bathroom and waited while the bath filled almost to the point of overflowing before slipping inside. I don't remember what I'd been thinking about during that short time that saw the sun rising high and the house awaken but I know one thing, I was happy. It was only after the third knock came at the door that I decided it was best to get dressed and let everyone else get washed.

Making my way downstairs and into the kitchen, I sat silently at the table while Jenny hurried back and forth around me. Ten or fifteen minutes must have passed before anyone else joined us and the first to enter was Dad.

"Good morning all," he half shouted feeling quite lively himself.

Jenny answered in a harassed voice. "Breakfast will be ready shortly, Thomas, would you like a cup of coffee?" Seeing Jenny to be very busy, Dad declined her kind offer and proceeded to make it himself. Although I was well aware of what was going on, I was still rather wrapped up in my own thoughts and never cared to speak much that morning. Most would have presumed that I was in a mood or was being childish about something, but Dad knew that wasn't the case. He never knew what the exact reason for my daydreaming was, but he certainly knew I wasn't in any mood.

The morning passed very quickly that cold Friday and all too soon lunchtime had come and gone. It was at around two thirty that Dad asked Jamie and me to go for a walk with him. Jamie's brother and sisters along with Gavin were out in the back garden playing with the snow while Mrs Richardson, Mum, Gran and Jenny sipped tea and chatted in the main room. I hadn't seen Anna at all so far that day and only hoped she wasn't feeling embarrassed about what had happened between us, but Dad hurrying us outside didn't allow me to dwell on it much. We walked along the street and headed out of town along one of the old roads that ran parallel with the old canal. It hadn't been used for a long time and we were mostly warned not to play near it when we were younger.

We must have walked about a mile before Dad started

to speak and by that time my feet were not only wet but also very cold as the snow lay thick on this road and hadn't been walked on that much by others.

"So Jamie," Dad asked quite ominously, "have you considered much about what you're going to do from here on?"

Jamie looked a little confused by the question and hesitated somewhat in his reply. "Not really, Thomas, although I'm not really sure if I know what you mean." For even after all that Jamie had been told by Mr Jacobson, he still never really understood and appreciated his new circumstances.

"Well, with all due respect, Jamie, you're now a very wealthy young man, and without any disrespect your home in Blacksmiths Fire isn't really befitting such a man or family as yours." Jamie paused, taking the time to consider his words. Seeing his reaction I think Dad thought it best to lead Jamie to the obvious conclusion of where all this talk was leading to. "I think under the circumstances it might be better that you and your family move into 112 High View Road, don't you?"

Before he even knew what he'd said, Jamie's mouth had already spoken. "But that's Mrs Blake's house!" And then finally realisation hit quicker than that of a bee sting or the whip of horse's tail. "Ah, I see what you mean." After the entire house did now belong to him and I'm sure Mrs Blake would have wanted him and his family to live in it, it was certainly big enough.

"We can organise to have all your things picked up tomorrow and have you settled before the end of the week, all going well."

"Thanks for all your help, Thomas. I mean the both of you. I can't repay you enough for what you have done for me, honestly I can't." Dad with his usual manner just smiled.

"Mr Jacobson has also left in my care the safety deposit box. Not being sure of its contents I didn't want to bring it along with us, but I'll fetch it the minute we get home."

We turned back on ourselves and started heading back for home, everyone busy with their own thoughts about how Jamie's life had so suddenly changed.

It wasn't too long before the warmth of the house was soon surrounding us again and first thing we did was change our socks that had nearly frozen themselves to our feet. Just as I started to get feeling back in my toes, there came a knock at the door.

"Come in."

At that, Dad entered the room holding a rectangular metal box. It was shiny from the outside and had a small keyhole in the end. Placing it on the bed nearest Jamie he took a couple of steps back. "That's the box I'd talked to you about, Jamie. I believe the key should be in one of the envelopes you were given."

Jamie rushed for his jacket that he'd previously placed at the foot of the window and searched the pocket for the envelopes. Quickly finding the right one, he sat back on the bed and tipped its contents out. Sure enough, three rather small but important looking keys fell out. Two had a scrolled end and were of a brownish looking colour while the third looked more like a doubled-ended key and was of polished silver appearance. Taking the last he eagerly placed the key against the mouth of the lock and slid it perfectly inside.

With a turn of the wrist and a single click from the box, the lid popped up slightly. Jamie hesitated before finally stretching out his hand and pushing the lid back till it rested firmly on the bed. The box was quite deep so from where I was sitting I wasn't able to see directly inside. Jamie first peered inside before placing his right hand in and removing a small red velvet bag. I could feel the tension mount with every unravel of the golden cord that held it taut, quickly the top was open and Jamie was turning it upside down to empty its contents into his other hand. What then fell out I would never have guessed in a million years.

There in his hand he held a dummy, just an old, somewhat dirty, standard child's dummy. We all looked in bewilderment but Jamie knew what it was. He knew it belonged Mrs Blake's children and as a result was a highly treasured item of hers. Placing it back into its little red bag, he proceeded to remove the next item. This perhaps would have been an easier item to have predicted. For after removing the lid from the small silver box Jamie held in his hand a small stack of photographs. The first was clearly that of Mr and Mrs Blake's wedding day while others were of their children and various other family style pictures.

There now remained only one item. It was a small leather bound box about two inches square and seemed to open in the middle. Taking the box firmly in his hand, Jamie pushed the lid back to reveal two rings. The one on the left was a highly polished plain gold band while that on the right, although slightly similar, held a large bright white diamond in a claw on its top. The diamond truly glittered as if for the first time in a hundred years it had seen the light of day. Removing the rings Jamie noticed and inscription on the inside of the bands. The first read "To My Loving Husband" while the other read "To the Woman of My Dreams May I Never Awake." I immediately thought back to the ring that Mr McNorton had removed from Mrs Blake's finger on the night she had died, but that was obviously just a gift of some sort.

After a short time Jamie replaced the rings and pushed the leather case closed, once again shielding the rings from the light of day. No one said anything while Jamie placed the items back into the metal box and locked it once more.

"All we have left to attend to is a few signatures for the bank accounts and that's almost everything taken care of," said Dad as he stepped forward and collected the metal box from Jamie. "This is better locked away for now, or at least until you have a safe enough place to store it yourself." At that he left the room and could be heard heading downstairs where he was more than likely going to place the box in the safe.

We talked for a while after Dad was gone, and also read through the list of assets a good few times as well.

"So what do you think you'll do?" I asked, interested in what Jamie was thinking about. His face seemed curiously blank and devoid of emotion - as though there was a mask covering his feelings. I felt the closeness we had shared up to now slipping away from me slightly. I was confused by this.

"I'm not sure; I mean the whole thing hasn't really sunk in yet. I guess I'll try and fix things for Paul, Alice and Mary. I mean, I'll try and give them back everything they had before. And it'll be nice to see Mum happy again, but other than that I'm not sure yet."

It was as good an answer as I could ever have hoped to hear: yet again, Jamie's first interest was that of his family and that only endorsed the kind of person he truly was.

After a lot of talking we made our way down stairs, Dad was napping in the large chair while Mum, Gran, Mrs Richardson and Jenny all sat looking through needlework patterns. I could hear the other kids playing upstairs in Gavin's room before we came down so that only left Anna who I'd still not seen all day. We sat about for a bit until dinner was ready, before I knew it the clock was striking eleven o'clock and yet another day was nearly at a close.

That night Jamie and I sat at the window and gazed outside at the stars. The snow hadn't fallen for a good few hours now and the sky was crystal clear. The stars were brighter that night than they'd been in a long time, and every inch of black was full of them. Without thinking first, I asked Jamie what he'd wish for if given the chance and although he answered I knew that somehow everything he'd ever wished for had already come true or at least everything except one.

"If I only had one wish, just one, I'd wish my Dad

would coming walking through that door, pick me up, and say, "how's it going, boy," but that's more a miracle than a wish."

I had no words to comfort him with, nothing in the world could bring that wish true and we both knew it. Although it dampened our moods somewhat, we still managed to stay awake a while longer and laughed about some of the strangest things, till slowly we both nodded off.

Saturday morning started with a buzz. Dad, Gran, Jenny, Mrs Richardson, Gavin, Paul, Alice and Mary arrived, to give Mrs Blake's house an air of excitement that it hadn't seen in ages.

The buzz echoed around the rooms and the excitement filled the large open ceilings. Dad co-ordinated what little furniture was on the large green truck inside while Mrs Richardson along with Mum looked in every nook and cranny. The house never knew what'd hit it and I reckon by midnight it was glad of the peace and quiet it received. No more fighting over this room and that. No more bumping into this wall and that as furniture was moved backwards and forwards. No more whistling of the kettle that had been going constantly all day. All that now was happening was centred in the living room on the ground floor. It was long since we'd all gone home and Jamie's brother and sisters were now snuggling into their new beds in their new rooms, which they had one of each. The only ones who remained awake were Jamie and his Mum. They sat together in the one chair, the one chair that Mrs Blake had so loved to sit in, and said nothing. The only sounds came from the hands of the clock that were moving strongly on the mantle. What their thoughts were that night I'll never know. But for once they were happy, the whole family was happy.

The day had turned out to be such a fuss that Anna and where she currently was had totally slipped my mind. I lay in bed and often contemplated getting up and asking

Jenny, who I was sure was still up, where she was. I knew Mum and Dad were awake because I could hear them dancing to slow music down stairs, and it was to those soft lulling tunes that I drifted asleep.

The morning arrived sharp and to the sounds of excitement. "Bang, bang, bang" The door rattled as Gavin stood shouting outside it.

"Come on, come on you have to see." I quickly put on some clothes and headed down stairs. With the week's events I suppose I'd forgotten all about it. I mean, it's quite easy to forget something if you're never given the time to think about it. But there, taking up almost the whole of the far side of the main room it stood. Tall, towering almost to the ceiling and sparkling in all its wonder. All around it dangled the usual trinkets and pieces that were gathered over the years, and boy, did it look good. We stood for ages and absorbed all the good feelings it emitted and watched as the tiny little lights twinkled and flickered one by one. With this one mighty statue that stood proudly before us we knew! Christmas! Christmas was coming! With all its glitter and bounce I'd never even noticed that under its largest fan of branches close to its base lay gift upon gift. Each wrapped ever so preciously and clutching onto its own little bow. For if ever I'd seen a Christmas tree, this was one to surpass them all.

Amidst all our excitement we didn't notice Mum and Dad standing behind us. Although rather tired looking, their faces shone with delight at our happiness. After receiving a large hug from the both of us they disappeared back to bed; from the kitchen came the noise of the kettle blowing full steam. My first thoughts were of Anna, so quickly I turned out of the main room and straight into the kitchen. Standing there however was only Jenny. She seemed to whistle to the sound of the kettle as it now coughed and spluttered hot water all over the stove.

"Jenny," I asked. "Where's Anna?"

Her whistling came to a stop as she lifted the kettle from the heat. "She's upstairs sleeping. Why'd you ask?"

"Well, it's just that I don't remember seeing her at all yesterday, and, well, with all the excitement I'd have thought she'd be up to see what all the noise was all about."

"Well now, where do you suppose that big old tree came from, eh?"

To say I was puzzled was an understatement. "You mean Anna got it?"

"Well, with a little help and some instructions from your Gran, she sure did."

"Who's help?"

"Now that would be telling, wouldn't it?" Although I only had a half answer to my question, I could see there was no point in asking Jenny any more about it, instead I hustled neatly into one of the kitchen chairs and waited for breakfast.

It was quite late after breakfast that the rest of the house came alive. Gran was the first to come slowly downstairs, followed by Mum who was now looking ten times worse than she had this morning. Although she walked and talked fine, there was something strange. A sort of ill look drew her inwards and her eyes seemed poised and wearisome.

"We're having a special dinner tonight," said Mum, just as I was leaving the house to make for Jamie's. "So don't be late."

The walk to High View Road took a little longer than usual that morning but only because there was a thickness to the air. It wasn't quite the same as fog but still it had the heavy look and feel to it. I strolled carefully along making sure to avoid any icy patches that sat cold and polished, ready for their next victim to slip on. The Richardson's household was alive and kicking. Rounding the back I watched while Paul and Alice attempted to murder each other in the snow,

256

then gave the doorknocker a swinging blow.

Mrs Richardson answered the door with such a fuss you'd have thought I was some kind of royal visitor, but I expected the excitement of her new home was still making her quite excited. I followed her into the kitchen where along with Mary she was making what looked like mince pies and some kind of meatloaf or stuffing.

"Jamie will be right with you," Mrs Richardson said, "that is, if he can drag himself out of the bathroom, he's been in there for hours." With that, she disappeared into the hall to call him.

Only a few minutes past before he joined us all in the kitchen. "Well thank heavens for that, I almost thought you'd gone and dissolved up there, you've been in the water that long."

"Motherrr," he replied.

We sat down in the kitchen while Mrs Richardson fetched us a cup of hot chocolate each and forced a second, although somewhat late, breakfast down my throat.

"So how did your first night in the new house go?" I asked as an open question.

"It'll take a little getting used to but I slept like a log all night," answered Mrs Richardson.

Mary just continued to smile while Jamie replied, "I never slept much but I think that was mostly to do with all pine needle in my skin."

A strange look from me was enough for Jamie to drag me off into the main room. Likewise standing tall and bright was a Christmas tree. "But how? I mean when?"

"There was a knock at the door last night, not far after midnight I reckon. I was expecting you'd forgotten something so opened up to find this man standing there."

"Who was he?"

"Well, that I'm not entirely sure. You see, all he said was that he'd been sent round by a young lady to deliver something, and with no more to say he pulled at something and in pops the head of a Christmas tree. He gave me a hand to get it in and stand it upright, Mum offered him a cup of tea, but he refused. Said he had lots of people to be making happy and that he had to go, so he did. Mum and I stayed up late to decorate it and that was that."

I explained that the very same thing had happened at ours and I told him about what Jenny had said. We sat down both looking a bit puzzled and still had no answer we could think of. We'll just have to wait and see, I thought.

CHAPTER TWENTY-FOUR
Warnings

For the rest of the morning, I rustled about the house with Jamie putting the finishing touches to the rest of the rooms and making a list of all the materials we needed to get to sort a few minor repairs and such. Once we'd done, we grabbed our coats and headed outside.

"I think I'm due a big thank you to someone, don't you," Jamie asked, although it seemed he was telling himself more than he was asking. Anyway, knowing what he meant, we made our way to the cemetery and along the path leading to Mrs Blake's grave. The ground had been refilled and the whole covered with a thick layer of crisp virgin snow. Jamie walked around the side of the grave and wiped the snow from the headstone.

As he knelt down, I suddenly felt out of place and a little intrusive. Slowly and quietly, I backed away down the path heading further into the depth of the cemetery. I couldn't help thinking that for such a small village we had a great big cemetery. The further I walked the more I became aware of the fact that there were many more trees. In fact at the very front of the cemetery there were none at all, only a few shrubs and bushes that you wouldn't have even noticed as they'd all be covered in snow. But here, there were plenty. Some of their trunks were massive and their branches spread outwards and upwards. I'd never thought of a cemetery as being a tranquil place, but it was. It was certainly far from the cries of being a spooky and horrible place, although this was daylight and I wasn't making my assumption in the dead of the night under only stars or, if lucky, moonlight.

Most of the headstones in this section of the cemetery were large. From above they would have looked like the pieces of a chessboard in mid battle. I walked slowly, trying to read any writing that was visible or not covered by snow. I quickly realised that many of the graves belonged to young children and babies. In fact, every second and third belonged to someone under the age of ten. No flowers were laid in the section, only the overgrowing ivy that was visibly swamping the cemetery's right hand side and slowly creeping onwards to engulf the almost certainly forgotten about souls that lay below.

I was almost two thirds of the way down the cemetery by now and with a quick glance behind I could only see up to the brow of the hill I'd walked down. From here, I could now see the back wall of the cemetery and beyond. It was well over eight feet high and in almost perfect condition. Suddenly and without warning, the wind picked up. The snow was being whisked from the ground and well up into the air. A hissing noise sounded all around and trees started to rattle their bare branches. I turned and started to walk back to Jamie, but a sense of strangeness overcame me. I felt as if I was being drawn and carried along the snowy path towards something, something not harmful, not dangerous, but something willing and strong. Everything around became still and white. Everything that is except one. From the swirling still whiteness came movement. I wasn't scared or even alarmed. I felt a sense of calmness, a sense unchallenged by that of fear or alarm. Before I was able to see clearly what or should I say who was in front of me, their voices echoed all around mixing with the stillness and drawing closer and closer. Emerging from the haze appeared two figures. The one on the left was clearly

Mrs Blake but to her right was a man. Watching as they came ever closer, I puzzled over where I knew the man's face from, and then suddenly it hit me! It's Mr Richardson, Jamie's Dad.

The time in which it took for them to be standing in front of me seemed like ages, yet I didn't have time to think. Mr Richardson was a tall man, very proper looking, and from the way he was arguing with Mrs Blake he spoke like a gentleman.

"He's my boy and he shall do as he feels fit, I tell you. He doesn't need your interfering!"

"Well that's gratitude for you; I would have thought you'd be pleased for him and not longing for him to seek such a vendetta of hate."

"*Vendetta!* How dare you speak to me like that, woman? I wish for nothing more than retribution and justice for the evil that destroyed my family and my boy's heart. I long for nothing more than what's owed to me, what's owed to my family."

"What's owed to you... owed to you? Well I never. You, mister, are owed nothing. You gave up everything you were owed the day you left your family in the lurch, the day you walked away and, and ohhh."

"Hum hum," I sounded, standing perfectly straight and looking as if I'd hadn't heard a word of their conversation.

"Oh, my dear boy, I'm so sorry we arrived with such a commotion," she said. Floating closer towards me, Mrs Blake reached out. "My dear boy, Jamie is in grave danger."

"How?" I asked.

"His mind is taking him places he ought not to be going. He seeks for revenge."

"But how? Why?"

"*Why* I think we both know, but *how* is something only Jamie knows. His thoughts have taken him places that stir with hate and evil. Places that control the mind and churn the soul. He's in danger of doing much harm. He needs your help whether he thinks it or not."

"What should I do?"

"My dear boy, I only wish I could answer you. I only wish..."

"Well, if you've quite finished I think it's about time I'm given the chance to speak." At that Mr Richardson, barging forward, pushed Mrs Blake out the way and came within inches of my face. "My boy needs you, yes that much is true, but he doesn't need you interfering or placing doubt in his mind over whether he's right or wrong. He must do as he sees fit and recover the honour that was stolen from us, from him. I only ask that you remain strong for him and keep your friendship bound by justice and truth, such, my friend, is how the future must be carried forward for his own sake. You understand more about how he feels than you know."

All the while Mr Richardson was speaking I could feel myself walking backwards until I couldn't walk any further. As I pushed against the tall headstone behind me, I could feel its coldness pour into my body and echo the tone and feeling of his words. Although I tried to listen, I found myself thinking about Jamie. I cast my mind back to a few days prior and remembered Jamie telling me he was going to need my assistance: *There's been something bothering me of late, something that I may have to ask your assistance with if you don't mind... Tonight isn't the time or the place to discuss it, but I'm hoping that no matter what you'll understand.*

The next thing I remember was Jamie pushing my shoulder. "Are you ok?" I felt my eyes opening at the sound of his voice and found myself laying on the cold snowy path staring up at Jamie who with his hand still firmly on my shoulder was kneeled over me. "Are you ok?"

"I think so!"

"You must have slipped and bumped your head; I've been trying to wake you for a few minutes. Are you sure you're all right?"

Climbing to my feet I shook off the snow that clung so coldly against me. I didn't feel sore but still, as if by a natural instinct, I ran my hands around the back of my head feeling for bumps and cuts, but nothing. Had I actually slipped and dreamt everything I thought I'd seen, or was this just a way of coming back to reality after such a ghostly visit? Everything was very confusing indeed.

Being watched very closely by Jamie we started to walk back up to the brow of the hill and towards the church. We didn't talk much but I had the strangest feeling that Jamie was dying to ask me something. Just as we neared the large black gates that hung at the entrance, Jamie noticed the Reverend walking in through the side door of the church.

"Wait here a second, I've something to ask the Reverend."

As he ran after the Reverend I continued to walk towards the main entrance and rested myself against the wall whilst waiting for him to return. I watched intrigued as the sun made its daily descent from the sky. The powerful rays it emanates providing life for all. Throughout the years it's clear to see why so many artists have captured its beauty. Could it be that the sun is God himself? A mighty power that watches over us and provides. And just like God, who no man has ever seen, nor has any man been able to stare at the face of the sun. For the penalty of blindness would be imposed on he who did. It's as if the sun is openly broadcasting itself by saying "I'm here, but don't look at me. Feed from me, be guided by me, grow strong and live long, but don't raise your eyes." In many ways, to me that would just about round up what most people would think about God.

I was just starting to feel the cold when Jamie reappeared.

"You get the Reverend?"

"Yes, sorry it took so long but I had to convince him that I was right."

"You were right, right about what?"

"I'm not sure I can tell you yet. I mean, it's not that I don't trust you, it's just, well, I'm not a hundred per cent sure myself if what I want to do is the right thing. I mean, look how long I had to speak to the Reverend, and he should have been the easiest of people to understand."

"Sometimes it's better to think with two heads than one!"

"You're more than likely right, but promise me, promise me you'll give me the truth, the truth as you see it the moment I tell you?"

"I'll try." For the life of me I couldn't see what Jamie was about to tell me coming. But I tried to be as honest as possible.

"Well, I told you all about my Dad and what happened, right? There's been a gap in our family since Dad, you know, died. You see, the thing is that since that day no one's ever been to see him. I mean no doubt we all think about him, but he's just been left alone, all by himself. As I stood at Mrs Blake's grave, I got to thinking how strange it was that here I was speaking to a woman who'd been so kind to me and so generous, but yet I'd never done the same with my own father." At that, Jamie paused. Almost in tune we turned to each other. "I think it's time Dad came home."

I listened to his words; I now understood what he was talking about. The visions of an exhumation ran wild in my head, but somehow, just somehow, I could see where Jamie was coming from, and he was right. His Dad didn't belong in some forest in the middle of nowhere with no one to remember him. He belonged nearby where his family could go for comfort and support. Where they could go to talk to him and feel close to him. Looking back at Jamie, I could see how poised he was while waiting for my answer. However, instead of speaking I just smiled. A smile that said a thousand words and which with just a few controllable pulls of muscles expressed my feelings.

As we walked Jamie talked more about his Dad. He told me stories of things they used to do and some of the funny things they'd done together. I cast my mind back to my ghostly visit in the cemetery when I saw Mr Richardson. He looked just like he did in the photograph, yet there was something strange, it was as if I knew him from somewhere else.

"Come on, I'll race you!" Jamie shouted, at which he sprinted off down the road.

"Watch you don't fall and break your neck," I shouted back as I ran after him. We stopped just before arriving at the main street. "Mum's cooking a special dinner, Jamie, so I'd better get home but I'll come round later if you like."

"Yes that's fine; I've a few things I need to get done anyway. If I'm not back when you arrive I shouldn't be long behind you, ok?" He walked off with a backward wave.

I took my time walking the rest of the way home and listened as my stomach started to rumble and gurgle. A fog-like mist lingered and hovered just above the ground while the night drew quickly in. By the time I reached the house, the moon was just appearing bright and waxen in the sky. Upon entering the house, the smell of food was overwhelmingly good, so good that my stomach was now doing somersaults in every direction. I might have eaten two breakfasts but the cold must have taken a lot of energy from me, or at least something had.

Dad was sat in the main room reading a paper with a cup of coffee. Mum was reclining on a chaise longue, and somewhere in the dark recesses of my mind I observed that she was looking frail and somehow smaller. Seeing me staring at her, she smiled brightly and I banished my thoughts and went into the kitchen where Gran, Jenny and Anna were all fussing around putting the finishing touches to dinner.

"Oh, he's back," said Jenny cheerfully.

"I hope you're hungry?" Gran laughed at the same time as looking at the food spread on the kitchen table.

"I sure am, starving as a matter of fact."

"Good, well you better get upstairs sharp and get washed."

"Okay. I'm going."

Dinner that evening was great. We all sat around the kitchen table and ate like kings. The kitchen was so hot that the windows were thick with condensation and the dinner never seemed to go cold. Although I remembered Mum saying it was going to be a special dinner, it didn't seem like anything special, and no one made any important announcement or anything. It slipped my mind by the time pudding arrived and I thought nothing more of it. The clock was striking seven o'clock before dinner was over and we'd all finished chatting.

I'm going to pop over to Jamie's house, but I won't be late." Everyone was too talkative to have heard me apart from Mum who glanced over as I went through the door and blew me a kiss.

"Bye." And at that I was out of the house and walking up Jamie's steps in no time. I knocked on the door and within seconds was being greeted by Mrs Richardson for the second time in one day.

"Hi there, Mrs Richardson, is Jamie back yet?"

"No, I've not caught sight of him since you both left this morning."

"Oh, he did say he had a few things to be doing and that I had to wait for him if I got here before him."

"Well, you'd better come in then and get some heat into you, it's freezing out there. Would you like a drink or a mince pie?"

"No thanks Mrs Richardson I've just had dinner, but thanks anyway."

"You're more than welcome. Settle yourself down in the main room if you like, as you can see I've still much cleaning to do."

I left Mrs Richardson to her cupboard cleaning and walked into the main room. The Christmas tree shining brightly in the left hand corner while on the large seat lay Paul and Alice fast asleep. I sat down in what was Mrs Blake's favourite chair and watched them. They looked so sweet and comfortable. The heat in the house was more than enough to keep them warm so they needed no blanket. They lay contentedly huddled together presenting a more peaceful picture than you could ever have painted.

CHAPTER TWENTY-FIVE
The Macmillan Estate

I was almost falling asleep myself when out of the corner of my eye I saw movement. Springing to attention, I peered into the dark corner of the room trying to make out what made the sudden jerk.

"Sorry if I startled you, I never meant to do that. I thought you'd fallen asleep."

Perhaps I couldn't see the person but I sure knew the voice, although I'd only heard it a few times before. "Hello, Mary, I didn't see you there."

"I know, I was doing the very same as you before you came in, I mean, watching them, Paul and Alice that is. They look so happy; I don't ever remember them looking like that, not ever." She came towards me, stopping less than a foot in front of me.

Her long hair shimmered with the twinkling of the lights that were now behind her. Her thin body was now sheathed in new clothes. I could see her lips yearn to open and speak. It was as if she wanted to tell me something, something important but she either couldn't or wouldn't. I'm not sure why but something told me to stand up. Pushing myself from the chair, we now stood almost face to face. I so wanted for her to tell me what was playing on her mind, what it was that sat poised on the tip of her tongue.

"What are you two up to?" It was Jamie. He was standing just inside the doorway and looking straight at us."

"We were just talking about you," answered Mary calmly.

"I hope it was all nice things," he replied as Mary walked past him and out the door.

"When did you get back, I didn't hear the door?"

"Mum was outside in the garden so the door was open. More to the point, what were you two doing?"

"Nothing, we were just talking about you and um, Alice and Paul." Both of whom were still asleep. Although he had a look of suspicion, I hadn't lied to him.

"Did you get everything done you needed to do?" I asked him, trying to change the subject. Jamie nodded cheerfully.

"I think I've just about taken care of everything. I've spoken to the Reverend, to the McNorton brothers. I've had a telegraph sent to the paymaster, now what else? Oh yes, and Farmer McNeil helped to organise a truck and a three man team."

"Jamie, calm down a minute, I can't make head or tail of what you're saying."

"The door," he said to himself, and at that he got up and closed it. "It's a surprise. I don't want Mum to find out yet."

"Find what out, Jamie?"

"*You know,* about Dad. He's coming home for Christmas."

Now I realised, like being hit with a brick on the back of the head I understood. I knew he was wanting to have his Dad's body brought to the cemetery, but I didn't realise he was doing it so quickly, we'd only just spoken about it this morning, but in saying that Jamie had more than likely been thinking about it a lot longer. "So you've arranged everything?"

"I sure have, been busy at it for hours." Now, to say I felt a little left out was an understatement, but I understood that this was something Jamie wanted to do himself. He looked so pleased and happy, there was a fire burning inside him. It was somehow as if like a phoenix he was reborn in an explosion of flames.

We talked about where he'd been and who he'd talked to. He certainly had been busy that late afternoon, that's for sure. It seemed he'd thought of everything right down to the littlest of details, or had he? By the time we knew it, it was nearly eleven thirty and time to get home. I insisted on walking it myself although Jamie was more than happy to walk half way.

"No, there's no point in us both getting cold, and anyway we both need to get to sleep, we're up early. I'll see you in the morning. Goodnight Mrs Richardson."

"Goodnight."

It was a cold, cold walk home that night and very quiet. With my hands in my pockets I walked along quite the thing. It wasn't long till I was thinking about what had happened with Mary. I was excited by it. A feeling spread throughout my body and I liked it. It wasn't until I was scared half to death by a cat that I realised I'd been touching myself through my trouser pockets. I looked around making sure no one had seen. I would never have dreamt in a million years of doing something like that in public. Yet here I was making a spectacle of myself for anyone to see. Admittedly, it was rather exciting to think about it afterwards though.

I'm not sure whether it was the cold or just the late hour but I felt very tired. On getting home, I could hear music from the main room. On opening the door, I could see everyone sitting except Gran who was entertaining everyone with a song. For the second time in one day, Mum gave me a strange kind of smiling look and nodded me over to her. I sat down with the rest of the family and listened. I'll say one thing; Gran didn't half know how to sing. Her vocal cords may have diminished slightly with age but her songs had great lustre. After a while, I found myself going upstairs and laying in a bath. The hot water penetrated every ounce of my body and gave strength to my chilled bones. Going to bed after that felt great. All the covers had been changed giving the bed that crisp, alive feeling you only get from something that's new.

"Come on sleepy, it's time to get going."

"What? Where?" I peeled open my eyes and rubbed furiously at the sleep that was trying to heal them closed.

"Jamie, what time is it?"

"Just after seven I reckon, now come on." With a quick swish of the blanket, Jamie left me cold and exposed on the bed with no other choice than to get up. I got changed as fast as possible only just dipping my face in the sink. Downstairs, Jamie was sat with a mug of hot chocolate while Jenny was busy kneading what looked like bread dough.

"You'd think some people never sleep the way this one was banging the door this morning and the way you kept everyone up last night with all your shouting. We were almost calling out the doctor, you looked that bad."

"Who, me?"

"Well, who else do you think I'm talking about?"

"But I don't understand."

"Well, there's not much to understand. At about half past two this morning, I could hear someone shouting and screaming. Just as I was entering the hall, so too was the rest of the house... except you that is. We stopped outside your door because for a few seconds all had gone quiet, and then suddenly you started shouting again. 'No, no' and 'don't die' amongst other things. Your Dad opened the door and turned on your light, but he quickly went in and closed the door when we all saw how you were laying." I could feel every square inch of my face explode with embarrassment. "Your Dad was in there with you for quite a while before he reappeared. For the last ten minutes or so everything seemed quiet except a few groans.

"'He's alright,' he told us. 'A bad nightmare I suspect, but there's no sign of fever or illness.' Although everyone was relieved, we were all still very intrigued by your goings on. I don't think your poor Dad's been to bed all night, what with him checking up on you every hour or so."

"But Jenny, I don't remember anything at all. I mean I remember going to bed, but the next thing I know is Jamie waking me up. However, I do feel really tired."

"Just get this into your stomach," and with that Jenny pushed a large bowl of cereal in front of me and a mug of hot chocolate. I could see Jamie was just dying to ask me questions, but even when Jenny was away I wasn't going to be able to tell him anything. My thoughts just kept flicking back to the thought of everyone seeing me lying naked. Even Mum hadn't seen me like then since I was three or four. I just wanted to get out of the house before anyone else got up. I threw the cereal down my throat while blowing the hot chocolate to make it cool enough. Within minutes I was grabbing my coat and was leaving the house.

"Jenny, can you tell Mum and Dad that I've got business with Jamie most of the day so won't be back till late?"

"Sure, you run along now and have fun."

We were only out of the house a second when Jamie started with his interrogation-like questioning. "Well? What was all that about?"

"As I told Jenny, I don't have a clue, honest. I really don't know. I got out of the bath last night and into bed and the next thing I know, I see you standing over me."

"So you don't remember anything at all, not one little bit?"

"I've told you, nothing. I only wish I did, perhaps then it wouldn't be so embarrassing." At that, Jamie just laughed, but I could see the whole situation was teasing him, not to mention me.

We made our way to Riverdale Farm in the still

darkness of the cold winter morning. We didn't talk much about how the day was going to unfold, but more about what the future would hold. I reckoned I'd be working with Dad within the next year and would be married within the next three. Jamie however said nothing much about the future, well not much that anyone would make either head or tail of.

He just kept saying, "I reckon I've planned out my life for the next while. I'm just filling in a few gaps right now." There was a certain look in his eyes. A look unmistakably like that you'd expect to see in the eyes of a condemned man or an innocent man charged with murder. Not pity nor remorse, but more like a sharp piercing glare of intent.

We arrived at the farm to find an old blue truck in the yard ticking over without sight of a driver. The engine coughed and spluttered as if it actually felt the coldness against its blue metal body. I could see lights on inside the farmhouse, and the shadows that were moving about gave it a busy, hive-like appearance.

Jamie turned the large door handle and pushed the door open. Instantly the smell of food engulfed us. "Good morning, boys, you're just in time." Just in time for what, I remember thinking, but it was soon very apparent.

"I did want to tell you," giggled Jamie. "But I was so interested in what Jenny was saying that I didn't want to stop her."

As we were pushed into the large kitchen and directed to take a seat I found out what he was talking about. On the table lay large great plates, between which were stacks of buttered bread, jugs of milk, pots of jam and much more. We'd only been sitting a few minutes when Farmer McNeil came into the kitchen along with three rather large looking men very similar to his own appearance.

"Good morning boys, ye'd better eat well, ye have a busy day ahead of ye."

As the four of them sat around the table, Jamie saw

that I was wondering who they were, but before he could introduce them, they did so themselves.

"Nice to meet you young man, I'm Robert, this here is my second brother Alistair and that's my third brother James, and, of course, John's my fourth brother."

As I looked at John, everyone knew what I was dying to ask.

"Yip, we're quadruplets," said James.

"You can all make yourselves acquainted later," called Mrs McNeil as she placed piping hot food on everyone's plate. Golden brown bacon, sausages, fried eggs that were perfectly shaped, mushrooms and tomatoes. The list went on and on. I might have eaten five breakfasts already that day but boy would I have still wanted to have eaten that food!

Only, after we'd all had seconds, and when all the milk was drunk we moved into the main room where the fire was lit. We gathered around a large table which had a map rolled out on it. Keeping the map down was a set of compasses, a square, a pencil and a twenty four inch ruler which were placed figuratively at each corner.

"Now from what I remember and what you tell us Jamie, the work on the estate had only reached this area when you were there. We know that the first two hundred yards of trees were never felled, and you reckon it was only a ten minute walk to where the spot is, so that puts us somewhere in this area. The re-plants won't be all that big but it's still going to be hard to find it."

At that, James interrupted his brother Robert who was obviously the leader of the four. "Jamie, is there anything at all that could help us, I mean like a headstone or something?"

Jamie thought before answering. "We planted an oak tree, but apart from that, nothing. We thought it best not to leave anything just in case an animal tried to dig him up or a person would take a chance at digging in case he was wearing anything valuable, but there was something someone said."

"Go on," Robert pushed.

"I remember a few of the men talking. They said something about the forest, but I never got the whole conversation as they went quiet when they saw me."

"What did they say?" asked Alistair this time, trying to push him along as if he was running out of time.

"They said something about 'Cameron Squad Passes' and 'Fears Omens'".

"Um," sounded Robert, "I think that perhaps your father wasn't buried by himself after all."

"Why'd you think that, Robert?" asked Jamie queerly.

"Well, if we put two and two together, that would mean your Dad was buried somewhere within the Cameron squad passes."

"What are they?" Jamie asked.

"Well, many years ago there was a great battle to take over the estate from the McMillan family. News came of the plan to the McMillans well before the battle so they enlisted help from Camerons. They were a group of men who liked nothing better than to fight for reward.

"You see, once they were all employed in His Majesty's service but they broke away. Although the king made a heavy search to find and hang them, they could never be tracked down. Most people thought they couldn't be found because the men trying to find them were their friends at one point and more than likely still were.

"Years went by without anyone being able to find them. Until one day the king hatched a cunning plan. He knew the men had become somewhat like hired killers. So through some of his most trusted fellows he spread word of a takeover of the McMillan estate. He knew the chances were that the McMillans would try to enlist help, and he was right. Word soon came straight back that the Camerons had been called to defend the estate. The king had planned to take over the estate by the use of the passes that were cut though the vast forest.

"There were three in total, all meeting up in the shape of a triangle. The reasons for them are still somewhat unknown but they were there. The Camerons in their wisdom formed themselves into three squads each taking up a point of the three passes that lay in the east, south and west of the forest. This way whichever direction the attackers came they would be prepared. In the event of anyone getting past at either the south or west, they would be slain at the east. To anyone this may have sounded like a good plan, and it was. However, the Camerons could never have known how many people they would be up against. It was on a bright summer's morning when they were taken by surprise. Overnight, the king had mustered two and a half thousand men to the outskirts of the forest. One thousand rested at the south and likewise at the west, while the remaining five hundred stood in reserve.

"The king knew fine well that the Camerons, who had already lost many of their men through minor battles, were now only about three hundred strong. But still he wasn't going to take any chances. They slowly moved in on the two forward squads and surrounded them. Without so much as a single shot, the squads, who were only a hundred men strong, and seeing they were out numbered ten to one, gave up. Stripped of weapons and all clothing, the men were forced bound and naked to the centre of the forest. A rope for each man was strung across the many branches and each had a noose placed tight around their neck. With three men to each rope, the Camerons were strung up and left hanging in the whistling wind of the forest.

"Those in the east were left untouched and never heard so much as a scream that day. It was only two days later that they found the dead, blue bodies of the friends dangling like acorns from the trees. The smell was such that the men could hardly bear to cut them down. It took them almost a week to bury all the bodies, but bury them they did. In the very shape that the devil fears himself, they laid out the graves. Since then the area has been known as "Fears Omens", meaning the very sign of fear itself."

"Do you think that's where they buried Dad?" panted Jamie. "Well, it kind of makes sense now that I think about it. I mean, taking the distance into account and what you've told us, I reckon it's a good starting place."

"But, what about all those bodies? I mean, we can't just go and, well you know."

"If we've to go any further Jamie, I don't think we might have any choice."

All went quiet as Jamie contemplated what we could be setting out to do. You could almost see his brain steaming ahead on full coal as his mind decided what to do.

"Well, we'd better get going then."

And at that the sound of chairs moving restored the air.

"The truck's packed and ready to roll," said Alistair.

"Now you all take care and be sure to come home safe and well," fussed Mrs Mac as she proceeded to give us all a hearty hug.

Squeezing into the truck didn't prove easy and only worsened when James realised he'd forgotten something and had to squash us all as he climbed out and back in again, but in no time we were off and running.

"How long will it take to get there?" I shouted over the sound of the angry engine.

"About three hours in this weather, all going well," Jamie hollered back.

I don't remember much more about the journey that day, only that I had a sore head when I arrived. I reckoned it had something to do with the engine noise although the others thought it had more to do with my head hitting things when I fell asleep. Either way, I wasn't feeling like the sharpest tool in the box.

Getting out of the truck and seeing the forest was like something indescribable. There wasn't much snow but still it twinkled and gleamed. I'd half-expected to see a forest dead and bare from all the descriptions I'd heard about it, but that couldn't have been any further from the truth.

"Well, the rest will be walking from here," smiled Robert as he looked at my feet and wondering if they'd be up to it.

In a somewhat determined fashion I started to march onwards. "I'll show him my feet are up to it," I thought.

"Here, where you going?" I stopped and looked round to find everyone staring at me. "We've supplies to carry and anyway, you're heading off in the wrong direction." Everyone started to laugh, everyone except me that is. I made my way back, where Robert helped a large backpack onto my shoulders.

"Jesus, Robert, what's in this thing?"

"Just a few bits and pieces that could come in handy," he replied after which he about turned and stomped off in the direction of the vast forest.

We all just seemed to tag along and within minutes we were submerged by large trees, shrubs and darkness. All around me the forest seemed to be alive. Energy spilled from the bark of the massively overgrown tree trunks. They seemed to be growing taller and taller with every step we took, and the remnants of years of pine needles and broken twigs lay inch thick on the ground.

It took a few minutes but slowly my eyes adjusted to the lack of light, although my senses of smell and hearing more than made up for their loss. My comprehension of time seemed somewhat disturbed from the point of entering the forest. I wasn't sure if that had something to do with the fact that I'd slept for a considerable length of time or just because of the lack of light. Either way, time disappeared.

No one talked much that morning, perhaps because they weren't quite sure what to expect, or maybe just because, like me, they were listening to the trees. It might seem a strange thing to say, but that day I could almost swear I could hear them. James was the first to really break the silence. With the use of his booming lungs and large mouth he began to sing.

Trees so small and trees so big
Trees of maple and trees of fig
Rising tall to greet the sky
Reaching out to heavens high

Seasons come and seasons go
Sun may shine and wind may blow
But as the years go rolling by
Your mighty heart does never die

With colours great and colours dull
With little seeds or acorns long
Your branches spread to one and other
Your roots grow down to tie each other

Many homes you hold up high
Many meals you do provide
For creatures small and creatures big
A mighty shelter you do give

But one day you will come to fall
By man's own axe or thunderstorm
Then to the saw your trunk will go
And made to fit man's humble home

I wasn't quite sure if this was a good song to be singing to the trees or a bad one. I mean, I wouldn't like someone to be telling me I was going to be made into furniture. But the brothers seemed to have a kind of fellowship with the trees, in as much as they cared for them. The way they touched their trunks in passing was like how a mother would touch her stomach to feel her unborn child. They certainly had an understanding with the trees, an understanding I would never know or truly comprehend.

We kept walking for some time without stopping for rest. It must have been close to one o'clock when we finally sat down. In a small opening where the sun just managed to pierce the canopy of trees shedding a glimmering ray of light to the floor we reached for the flasks of water.

"Boy, I needed that," said Jamie, wiping the running water from his mouth.

"We don't have far to go," pointed out Alistair. "But it's better to rest here for a few moments than rest at Fears Omen; we don't want to be spending any more time there than we need to."

No one disagreed and after a while we made tracks again. Boy, did I feel stiff! We'd only rested just a short time but my bones didn't appreciate being disturbed. We carried on still with little talk ever onwards and into the depth of this great living creature that surrounded us. It was only when my feet were about to fall off and my back was almost bent in two with the weight of the backpack that we came to stop again. Forming into a straight line, we stood upright and stared open eyed at the sight that lay before us.

For the first time in hours we had light, a full circle of it to be exact. Although there were trees, they had no leaves. Thirty or forty trees stood before us. Each large and each bare. It was a strange and spooky feeling. The trees at first glance appeared dead but they weren't. I can't explain how I knew they were still living, but they were. Jamie was the first to walk into the ring of light. We all watched as the rays of the sun covered his body and gave strength to his appearance. Nobody else moved. We all just stood still like the trees that stood tall and dumb in front of us. Jamie moved around looking up and all around. He seemed somewhat lost and totally alone, like he was a boy in a box of darkness and searching for an exit.

"This is it, we're here. It's different somehow but I'm sure."

Slowly, the rest of us moved into the light and a sudden change in temperature was instantly noticeable. My skin tightened around my face and my eyes strained in the brightness. I stood still and silent at what swept around me. For those few seconds whilst my eyes adjusted to the light, I saw things, strange things. Swimming in the air around me were souls, ghosts of men, all speechless and blind to our presence. I reached out but then all seemed clear. I could grab nothing but warm, still air that carried a smell unlike any I'd ever smelled before. I'd only been there for a few moments but I quickly knew I didn't like this place.

For some unexplained reason we all came to stop not far from the centre of the circle, all except Jamie, that is. With three small steps, he walked forward and knelt down with both knees on the ground. Placing his palms down on the level earthly forest floor he bowed his head. We watched on and listened as Jamie spoke to his Dad for the first time in all the years since his death. It was quite strange but if I didn't know better I would have said his Dad was actually there that day, penetrating from the ground and straight into his heart. It was one of the most powerful reunions I'd ever seen in my life.

Telling you his words of that day would only bring tears to your eyes. They were far too personal for me ever to repeat to anyone. Needless to say, they came straight from the heart and were in no way at all altered by our presence. No one attempted to disturb Jamie in any way. It was he himself that was the first to speak.

"This is the spot, right here."

"You sure?"

"One hundred percent."

With a helping hand, I removed my backpack and took

off my coat. James brushed away the light covering of moss and lichen that lay at Jamie's feet.

"We should get started then," said Jamie, bravely. Robert grabbed a shovel from the top of one of the backpacks and passed it to Alistair, then another to James, John and finally me. Standing square to each other we started to dig, but being careful not to dig too deep with any strength.

We'd only removed a couple of feet of earth when we came across the first signs that we were digging in the right spot. Protruding from the disturbed earth was cloth. Although dirty, it was unmistakably white cloth. Two of the McNeil brothers then descended into the grave, the first of whom moved the rest of the remaining earth by hand, while the other traced the corners of the white cloth material ready for it to be lifted. With the cloth now fully exposed a third brother then descended into the grave, who with the assistance of the other two managed to remove the body from its resting place and out onto the ground adjacent. John, who had been watching, fell to his knees and prayed while Jamie looked high into the sky and in a light whisper spoke the words, "Thanks be to God."

I wasn't sure how to react. I stood for the most part and just watched. I don't recall it being a sad moment or even scary. Everyone, however, seemed to act slightly differently. Jamie seemed happy while John appeared somewhat fearful. Alistair looked rather ill while James and Robert seemed rather shocked, as if they had never really expected to find a body. No one wanted to break the silence, that much was clear, but there was a sense of haste. Alistair had already intimated we shouldn't spend much time here.

Placing down the large canvas wrap that he'd been carrying, Alistair started to unravel the material to reveal four wooden poles. I didn't pay much attention to how they assembled the items, but they did, and when they were finished we had a perfectly made stretcher. With a glance towards Robert and James, they moved in on the body and lifted it neatly onto the stretcher, and in the same instant covered the whole with a dark blue, heavy looking cotton sheet. Without wasting too much time, we re-covered the ground, packed up the backpacks and made haste to leave. Alistair and Robert took the first turn to carry the stretcher while John, James and Jamie walked up front.

I'm not sure what it was but something attempted to keep me there that day. Just as the others had left the circle of light, a dark cloud passed overhead sending the place into a deep depression. My feet were telling me to walk on with the others but my head was saying stop. I wanted to leave, but something was holding me. All around me was now dark and death-like. In the light this seemed a safe place to rest but in the hazy darkens it seemed evil and nasty. I could feel the ground moving beneath my feet, the air became heavy and moist, then suddenly all around me they came. Surrounding me in every direction, they came closer and closer. Squeezing not only the breath from my lungs but also the soul from my body. I felt like I was being crushed by a mountain and drowned by the sea all at the same time. I fell to the ground, choking in pain. I tried in vain to crawl from the centre of the circle, but still they came. Pulling at my ankles with their cold silky hands, I was taken nearer and nearer to the recently exhumed grave.

Lifting me up, I could see them. They swarmed all around in their hundreds. Faceless souls with dark hollow eyes, they swam in the air like flies. Not a word they spoke, but the feelings they expelled were clearly evil. Looking down, I could see the ground opening; it was then I realised what was happening. We had taken something and they wanted the space refilled. But I wasn't dead. I mustered every ounce of strength possible and struggled, but to no avail. It was just then, just as death had a firm grasp of me, did she arrive. Moving the cloud and returning the light she cut me loose from the silky hands and crushing power that held me captive, and set me free. Like a felled tree I hit the ground and all went dark.

No dreams filled my mind, just nothingness. I don't recall anything of what happened after that, only waking up. My head was pounding and dizzy, the world seemed upside down and moving below me. I glared with open eyes before daring to move a single muscle, but then I understood. Lifting my head, I could see the feet of others walking behind me. Lifting my head higher, I could see Jamie with John.

"Hold on he's awake," Jamie shouted. At that, I felt everything come to a halt, and my body being lowered to the ground.

"So you're awake then?" I looked up to see Alistair standing over me. "I'll tell you boy, you're not as light as you look."

I was slightly lost to say the least. "What happened?"

"Well that's what we were going to ask you. We noticed you had disappeared so went back to find you. When we did, you were lying on the ground unconscious. We tried to wake you but you were out cold. I've carried you for the last three miles."

By this time everyone had gathered around me and was dying to find out what had happened. Now, although I knew something had happened, I would have been crazy to have told them all. Instead I just played dumb. "What's the time?" I asked in an attempt to divert the conversation. "Is there any water?"

Jamie reached into the backpack of John and pulled from it a water flask. "Here you go." I took the flask and drank.

"So you're okay then?" asked John.

"Well, I think so! I must have tripped or something."

"Tripped? Well, let's get you to your feet then, I ain't carrying you if I don't have to."

With a little help from John, I climbed upright. I looked

for my backpack but Robert who was carrying it made me go on without it. In no time we were back at the truck and ready to leave. The stretcher was carefully loaded in first, followed by Jamie.

"Well Jamie, this is where we part, and anyway there ain't enough room for us all."

"But Alistair, how will you all get home?"

"Home," Alistair chuckled. "Look around you boy, we are home."

Jamie looked just as confused as me but none of us argued. I climbed into the truck and we waved goodbye to Alistair and Robert. John sat up front with James who drove, leaving only the two of us in the back along with the body.

Jamie and I talked for a while but the sound of the engine drowned out any speech, so in no time Jamie was crouched on the floor next to his Dad and sleeping. I was by no means tired; I was the exact opposite. There were too many questions wriggling through my mind. What had just happened to me back in the forest? Who or what were the things trying to catch or kill me, and how did Mrs Blake know to save me? Like an angel in the night, she came to me. In my moment of need she came and saved me from what I could have only described as hell, but why? How was it possible that I was able to see these things, including Mrs Blake? I'd seen her too many times now for it to be in my imagination. I couldn't quite understand it all, and I wasn't going to admit that I could see ghosts and spirits. Everyone must have been thinking I was already crazy.

CHAPTER TWENTY-SIX
Another goodbye

The drive home didn't seem to take too long, so in no time we were driving down the track to Riverdale farm. With a splutter and backfire the truck came to a stop and the engine ceased its high pitched noise. Touching his shoulder, I woke Jamie up. "Jamie, we're back."

"Oh, okay," he muttered, yawning.

Just then John's big head appeared at the rear of the truck. "That's us, boys." And with that he lowered the truck's tail door and we climbed out. We entered the house, leaving the body still on the stretcher in the truck.

"Welcome home, welcome home." Mrs Mac cried.

Looking at the clock, I could see the time was nearly seven o'clock. No one really talked much about the day's events as we sat in the kitchen and ate. Boy was I hungry! Chicken had never tasted so good, and I could feel the milk chill my insides as it sank deep into my stomach.

"Mmmm, Mrs Mac that was great."

"Well thank you, I try my best." Mrs Mac smiled as she swept away the plates that now lay licked clean on the table.

"Well, the day's running out and we still haven't finished."

"Yes, you're right John, if you would be able to drop me and Dad off at the McNorton Brothers I'll take care of everything else from there."

"Well, Jamie, if you're sure?"

"I am John, but thanks for all your help today, all of you. I could never have done this without you."

As Jamie looked at me, I just smiled. I might not have been the best helping hand but at least I was there, and I knew Jamie really appreciated it. We got back out to the truck and Jamie stopped me. "Look, I hope you don't mind but it's best I carry on from here by myself."

"Of course, that's fine."

"I mean it's not that..."

"You don't have to explain, I understand."

"Thanks for being here; you're a true friend, *a true friend.*"

Nothing more was said and before John took Jamie to the McNorton brothers they dropped me off at the house. "Well, I'll see you tomorrow then, Jamie?"

"Sure, I have something to do first thing but will come round after that." With a sudden cough, the engine of the truck revved up and drove away, carrying a cargo that most would never have imagined in a million years. I walked up the steps and into the house feeling rather exhausted and tired. It had been a long and rather strange day.

All seemed quiet in the lightly lit hall. A smell of baking lingered heavy in the air and small damp patches were still visible on the carpet from snow-ridden shoes. I quickly took of my coat and made for the main room. On opening the doors, I found, to my surprise, no one. Just a ticking clock, a crackling fire and a bright sparkling Christmas tree. Although the room felt warm it carried a strange sense of unease. I went to the kitchen but still no sign of anyone. Just as I was turning from the kitchen, I heard a door closing upstairs. I walked up holding the large bulky hardwood handrail in trepidation. Why would everyone be upstairs? My heart upped a pace and my fingers tightened around the handrail. Wild thoughts started to tear through my mind. I reached the first landing and listened, but nothing.

Continuing upward, I reached the fifteenth step and halted before stepping into the next hall. This was the third and last level to the house. In the roof above was a great glass dome with patterned coloured glass. It had pictures of a cornfield surrounded by deep valleys and a running stream. The hall had only one doorway in it, belonging to Mum and Dad's bedroom. The doorframe itself was made from dark oak. To the left and right stood two great pillars with the most intricate artwork. Each pillar held a large globe and was linked together with a bold chain. I stood outside the door and clenched the handle with one hand on top of the other. I listened for a few seconds before pushing it down. With a click, the latch gave way and the door crept open.

There was little light on inside and all seemed quiet. Just as I moved strength into my arms to open the door Dad's face appeared.

"Hello son," I looked up to see his face was pale and fearful.

"What's happening, Dad?" I knew something major was wrong. His face had shed its colour and his fingers trembled as he put his arm around me and walked to the edge of the stairs. We sat down on the last step and looked at each other. "It's Mum; she's not well, is she?"

Although he answered I could tell I was right before his lips moved. "Sorry son, she's not well, not well at all." I knew by his speech this was no cold or 'flu, this was serious, very serious. Without any more words, I got up and walked back to the door. With a slight pause, I gathered breath and entered.

Mum lay on the bed with the rest of the family gathered around her. The sudden shock of how ill she actually was hit me. No one said a word. The flickering of the bedside light gave no added colour to her face. Her face was so white it was as if she had been dipped in flour. Her hands seemed old and cold. I walked to the side of the bed where Gavin and Gran had made a parting for me and stood aghast.

Mum, who first appeared asleep, turned towards me and smiled. I so much wanted to speak but something inside anchored me from doing so. A lump slowly moved from my stomach and rested large in my throat bringing with it a glaze of water to my eyes. I slipped my hand across the recently ironed bed sheets and clasped her hand. Her weak fingers hardly clutched as we made contact. I looked up from the bed and stared deep into her eyes. The black of her pupils enlarged like the night sky and glistened as if they were full of stars. Although we passed no words and never mentioned the words love or goodbye, I knew that night was going to be the last night of her mortal life. With a last smile, she closed her eyes and drifted off into an everlasting sleep.

Everyone cried, everyone except me, that was. How was it I didn't know about Mum's illness? All the signs were there: Gavin crying, Mum sleeping more, Gran staying for so long, the list just went on and on. Why didn't I see? Or was it just that I didn't want to see? I stood and watched as Dad and the others knelt around the bed. Gran seemed angry and sad, while Gavin just cried with his head smothered into the blanket. I walked towards the door, stopped and looked back at Mum as she lay, before opening the door and leaving.

As I left the room, I felt pain, a pain that swept across every inch of my body and made me shiver from head to toe. My head became swamped with questions, and suddenly I exploded inside with anger. "Why." If there were a God in this world, would he subject me to so much death, pain and heartache? I couldn't think. Looking around the hall, I noticed the small cupboard hatch in the far sidewall which went to the attic. Without giving it much thought, I found myself opening the hatch and climbing in. The wind whistled through the darkness and bitter chill that hung inside. My eyes stretched as they searched for light. Shadows of the unknown circled all around me, climbed upon me and for the second time that day sent me dizzy to the floor.

I landed in a stream of moonlight that sank in through the small round window in the apex of the house. As my eyes stung with the sudden change, I became transfixed on the moon. It somehow seemed to be coming closer and closer. Laying numb and breathless on the cold dusty floorboards it became clear. As she separated from the mangle of spirits, I saw her. Glowing bright and with a smiling face she floated inches away from me.

"Don't be sad," her first words were. "For there's nothing to be sad over." I was about to speak but her translucent fingers somehow sealed my lips tight as she stretched out her hand to me. "You must be brave and remain strong; you've always been the strongest. I'll always be near you and will always be there for you, but as I'm there for you so too must you be there for me. Your brother and father need you; you must go to them and help them. They're not blessed with your gift and so can't call on me as you can, and, although they will always feel me near, they will never see me as you do."

It was right then, at that precise moment I realised. I was gifted, all my life I'd seen things, things that perhaps I never questioned at the time but things I considered to be strange. All the moments of recent days where Mrs Blake appeared to me were real. Up until then I wasn't sure, but now, now I was.

I looked up at Mum and smiled. I felt good as a sense of heat poured over me. I no longer suffered pain or hate, no longer searched for answers why, and no longer, above all, felt loss. Mum had died but only in body, her soul was more alive than ever. I climbed to my feet and stood as she drifted backward, out of the window and returned to the mass of swirling moonlight that hung high in the dark night sky and I smiled.

CHAPTER TWENTY-SEVEN
A Gift for the Family

I sat and dreamt a little before going back into the main body of the house. Nothing much seemed important that night and little had really changed in my life, or so I thought. As I climbed back out of the hatch and into the hall, I stopped, listened and soaked in the sounds of grief and distress that echoed off the tall walls in the hall. Instead of going back into the bedroom, I made the decision to go downstairs. I entered the main room, taking up the seat where Mum would usually have sat. I slipped off my shoes, curled up tight on the chair and fell asleep.

Nothing and no one appeared in my dreams that night. I don't remember waking up or even stirring at all. The next thing I recalled was hearing a voice somewhere between the realms of sleep and wakefulness. I opened my eyes at the same time as stretching out and saw Dad sitting on the floor next to me. He turned to me and looked in silence. His eyes puffy and skin damp, he pulled as much strength as possible to his cheeks in order to pull a smile. Looking around, I could see that Dad wasn't the only one who adorned the room. Everyone was there, everyone except Mum that was. They all lay strewn across the chairs and floor asleep.

"Merry Christmas, son." I looked heavily at him and gave thought to his words. "Merry Christmas, Merry Christmas." I quickly tried to add up the days. It couldn't be Christmas. I mean, it just couldn't be.

I moved my head and eyes over to the Christmas tree that still stood proud against the wall and the realisation hit me. *It was Christmas.* I suddenly felt really happy, happier than I'd been in a long time. I looked once more at the tree and even more at the neatly wrapped presents that sat under its great twinkling branches.

"It's Christmas, wake up everybody, it's Christmas." I jumped from the chair, over Dad's head and landed in front of the tree. I first scanned the boxes looking for labels holding my name and then grabbed the biggest one. Pulling it from under the tree, I knew it must have been a good present, not just because it was heavy but because of the way it was wrapped. Every Christmas, Mum would always wrap one present differently. Its paper would always be deep blue, there would be a four-inch perfectly knotted red bow tied tight around it, and its name card would always read "To a Special Boy."

I sat on my knees and placed both hands on its shiny paper. I was excited, so excited I could feel the blood gushing through every vein. As I began to rip off the paper something stopped me. I looked behind and there, stood Gavin, Gran, Jenny and Anna. Their combined look was one of scorn. I pushed the present back under the tree and stood up. Like the accused standing in court, I faced a jury of discontent.

"He's right." Everyone's head turned to Dad who was still sitting on the floor facing the door. "It's Christmas today, as it will be next year and the year after that. Diana would never ask that the boys miss such a day, and I'd never have that either." At that, Dad stood up, walked over to the tree and lifted from its branches a small burgundy paper wrapped box. He paused before unwrapping its delicate paper and turned around. "Well come on."

Everyone moved in and gathered a parcel. "This is yours Gavin," said Gran, while Jenny and Anna swapped what they held. Dad sat down on the floor crossing his legs. He held the ever so small box tightly before beginning to peel back the paper. I sat and watched as his eyes became laden with joy. Placing the box on the floor he held its contents between his fingers. It took a few seconds before I realised what it was but then it was clear. He was holding a small perfectly rounded stone. It had been painted almost the same colour as the box that held it, and in gold letters had the word forever spelt on its warm surface. Picking up the box again, Dad took from its lid a small note of paper. I didn't peer over his shoulder there and then, but later had the chance to read its words. In Mum's handwriting she'd written,

My love I've placed in solid stone
A humble home to keep it strong
A shell that now will never break
Or care about the night or day

My love I've wrapped in deep, deep red
A love that never will lay dead
For when you hold me in your hand
You'll feel me echo all around

This stone I give for ever more
In hope that you will love once more
For lonely you must never be
Enjoy a life of joy for me

I wasn't any more confused by her words than I was over the fact that she had written them knowing well fine she wouldn't make it to Christmas Day. Dad seemed to know exactly what those few words meant. I could tell by the way he perked up and kind of glowed around the face. I'm not sure if he ever showed anyone else that stone, but I know he carried it with him to the day that he died, and was even buried with it in the pocket of his favourite dark blue trousers.

I never really thought much about Mum that morning, and everyone seemed to somehow instantly move away from me whenever I went near them. The only person who really spoke to me was Dad. It was around ten o'clock and I was half asleep in the bath when there was a knock on the door.

"I'm in the bath."

"Can I come in?"

"Yes, ok."

Dad crept in the door as if he didn't want anyone else to know. After he climbed through the thick steam, he sat on the side of the bath. "Are you ok?"

I gave a moments thought before giving him an answer. "I am, are you?"

Placing his hand on my wet hair, he smiled. "It wasn't that I didn't want to tell you, I hope you know that? Your Mum, well, she asked me not to say anything. She made me promise. I wanted to tell you, I think you should have all known, but I had to follow her wishes."

"Dad, it's ok. I understand. Well, kind of understand. All the signs were there and Gavin knew."

"How?"

"I'm not sure, but I suppose he heard you and Mum speaking at some point."

Dad paused and didn't say anything for a minute or two. "Your Mum already made all her own funeral arrangements with your Grandmother. The funeral director came and collected her early this morning."

"So what will happen now?"

"Well, there isn't much for us to do. I'll hold off informing her friends till tomorrow. I don't think it's a good day to bring sadness to people's lives." With that, Dad stood up and made his way back to the door. Just before leaving he turned back around. "Don't worry about the others.

They'll understand. It'll just take longer for them."

After he pulled the door closed behind him, I pulled my body under the water and held my breath tight. Still under the water, I opened my eyes. From here, the world seemed more alive than normal. The stirring bubble topped water gave shape and form to the bathroom ceiling. I felt as if I could just float away into a different life, a new life. Although I popped back out of the water that morning and didn't drift away, my life still changed. It perhaps wasn't new or suddenly different, but it changed.

I never thought about Jamie that morning or about what he was doing. I kind of thought about very little. However while I was having the worst Christmas in the world Jamie was having the best Christmas he and his family had had in years. That morning he woke his family up by shouting the house down.

"Ho, Ho, Ho Merry Christmas." He ran from bedroom door to bedroom door banging. "Merry Christmas." Quite quickly, the pyjama wearing sleepy eyed faces opened their doors. "Well, come on then," Jamie shouted as he started to run down the stairs, by which time Mrs Richardson had entered the hall. The house had gone from peaceful bliss to hurried excitement sprinkled with the feeling of love and happiness.

Gathered in front of their Christmas tree they held each other's hands and stood silent. They gazed at what laid around the tree and all over the floor of the room. Stacked high and wide were presents, loads and loads of presents, each one being wrapped, some with bows some with frills and even some that had their own box. The unusual thing about the presents was that none of them had any names on them, not one. I would have thought that someone had forgotten to have done it, but in fact it was done on purpose. Jamie, in his wisdom, took the decision just before wrapping the presents to leave all the nametags off them. He thought it best to let his brother and sisters share the presents between them and give to each other as they thought each other would like. Mrs Richardson sat back in old Mrs Blake's chair and watched as for the first time in years her children had a great Christmas. She never attempted to unwrap or open a single box. Just the fact that her children were happy was all she needed.

Alice, Mary and Paul weren't even half way through the presents when Mrs Richardson made her way into the kitchen. Jamie followed behind her and watched as she lifted the kettle from the stove, filled it with water and returned it to the black heat. Jamie walked in and handed his Mother a small parcel. As he reached out, she collected it in his hands and held tight.

"Thank you, Jamie. Thank you." She then leaned forward, kissed his forehead and looked down at the present she now held. Undoing the small bow allowed the loose fitting paper to give way. She placed the wrapping on the table and removed the lid from the top of the small box. Her fingers trembled as she reached inside and collected its contents. Placing the rest of the box on the table she held in her hand a ring. A ring that she'd once owned and pawned to keep food on the table, a ring that was given to her the day she got married. It was later on at some point that Jamie had told me that his Dad wouldn't let his Mum or him sell their wedding rings. They were the only valuable items they managed to keep when things went bad. But at that point when life was at its hardest, Mrs Richardson had no choice but to let it go.

Upon seeing the ring she cried, but not with sadness, she cried with excitement. The sound of tears somehow called the other children into the room. As they gathered at the door wondering why their Mum was crying, she walked towards them, hustled them into her arms, and hugged them.

"I've got something for you all to see," said Jamie.

"What? What is it Jamie?" cried Paul.

"First we need to eat, and then I'll take you all."

Everyone looked amazed; they'd already had the best Christmas money could buy, so what on earth could Jamie possible have in store for them? It wasn't going to be long before they found out. As Mrs Richardson cooked a Christmas breakfast Jamie and the others got changed. Around the table Jamie could see and feel that everyone including his Mum was dying to find out what he had planned. With all the excitement, it was clear that they weren't going to be able to eat very much. Jamie swore he could just about hear the sound of the butterflies humming about in their stomachs.

"Ok then, let's get going. You all better wrap up well, we've got a walk in front of us." Without saying anything else, everyone leaped from their seats and was at the coat stand in seconds.

All being wrapped up tight they made their way outside into the snow. Following Jamie, they eventually arrived at the graveyard. Jamie pushed open the large black gates leading onto the recently cleared path. Looking back at the others, he invited them in. "Come on then." Walking one in front of the other Jamie led them to the side of a grave.

"Oh Jamie I forgot, poor Mrs Blake."

Jamie advanced to the headstone and brushed from its face the snow that had covered it over night. Upon noticing the words Mrs Richardson fell to her knees and gasped.

"Oh, Glory to the most High." Words failed her; her expression was like four seasons in one.

"Now we're a real family this Christmas," cried Jamie, who at the same time offered out a hanky to his Mum. Alice and Mary helped her back to her feet. "It's Dad, Paul," said Jamie.

"I'm not stupid Jamie I can read," and so he did.

Here Lies Mason Richardson loving Husband
of Emily and Caring Father of Paul,
Mary, Alice and Jamie

You grow not old as we that are left grow old,
age shall not weary you, nor the years condemn
At the going down of the sun and in the morning
We will remember you

From now and forever

"See I told you."

Jamie just smiled. He wiped his eyes, joined his two sisters and mother and hugged. Although the day had only just started, this was the best day of Jamie's life. For the first time in years he and his family felt together. They were in the cemetery that morning for nearly two hours, each taking time to have a personal moment alone. Jamie didn't listen to what the rest of his family said that morning. He only knew what he said himself.

It was only when their fingers were blue and their feet were frozen to the bone that Mrs Richardson hurried them back up the road.

It wasn't until a few days later that I found out that Jamie had visited my house that day. His knock on the door was answered by Jenny.

"Hi Jenny, Merry Christmas"

"Merry Christmas, Jamie."

There was slight pause as Jamie studied the expression on Jenny's face. "Is everything ok, Jenny?"

"I'm sorry Jamie, it's Diana, she passed away last night." Silence hung from the porch and covered the two of them. Jamie's day that had started so happily had been struck down in flames. "It's not a good time for visitors at the moment, sorry Jamie."

"No, I understand, but how? When?"

"Jenny, Jenny," called Gran.

"I'm sorry Jamie, I have to go, please call round again in a day or so." And with that she closed the door softly and quietly and went to Gran's call.

Still standing on the porch, he stood frozen and dumbstruck. He, like me, had never expected that Mum was suffering from an illness. He, like me, never noticed the blatant and obvious signs, and he, like me, never for one minute thought Mum would be dead before Christmas. He walked home that morning in shock. As he neared home, he did the right thing by pausing outside the house and thinking strong about whether he should tell anyone. After a few moments of decision he opened the door to his house and entered with a smile. Even though he so much wanted to tell his Mum the tragic news, he knew deep down inside that would have been the wrong thing to have done. Instead, he acted as if nothing had happened and continued to have a joyful and fun filled Christmas with his family.

CHAPTER TWENTY-EIGHT
Comfort at Night Time

That Christmas day was the longest day of my life. No one talked, no one smiled, hardly anyone moved from their seat in the main room. It was like no one had the will to live any more. Lunch came and went and all too soon the night had drawn in as we sat around the kitchen table to eat dinner. Capped in anger and strangled by silence, we sat poised. I could sense everyone's need to talk, cry and shout with anger. I could feel the vibrations that ripped through the thick wood of the table caused by their rapidly beating heats. I could have sworn that the mist on the windows came from the   anger of their body heat. Dinner couldn't have finished any quicker that day than it did. Without asking, I left the table and walked upstairs. I couldn't understand why everyone was acting so strange, and I certainly wasn't going to be a party to their sadness.

Lying on the bed I tried hard to think of anything other than family, but it was useless. Mum's dying had somehow killed the house. The walls looked dull and the ceilings seemed sad. It was as if somehow the house knew Mum had died, either that or my imagination was working overtime. Not   having anything to do, I just wanted to fall asleep. There was no point saying goodnight to anyone, they would have more than likely ignored me if I had. Instead, I pulled off my clothes, turned off the light and climbed into bed. I watched as the shadows on the walls swayed back and forth. Their movement often created recognisable shapes and patterns.

Some time passed when somewhere between the realms of being awake and asleep I heard a light knock on the door.

"Are you awake?" It was only when she asked for the second time that I understood who it was.

"Come in, I'm awake."

As the door crept slowly open she entered. "Are you ok?"

"I think so." At the same time as Anna took her place on the side of the bed, I pulled the bed covers up past my neck, covering the fact that I lay naked below. "I never thought she would die so quickly. I mean, she looked fine."

"I take it you knew about Mum's illness then?"

"Well, not really. I heard your Gran and my Mum talking one night. Your Gran was very sad and kept crying so Mum said she was going to see what was wrong. I sat alone for ages before I decided to go and find out what was happening. As I got outside your Gran's bedroom, I stopped for a moment. I could hear them talking inside so stood there and listened. I couldn't believe what they were saying. Even up to last night I never believed it, who would?"

"I never knew. I never even suspected Mum had a cold, let alone anything else."

Anna appeared shocked at what I'd told her. I'm not sure if that was because she felt guilty about her knowing and me not or just because she thought I should have been told.

For some time that night we sat and talked, throughout which I found myself avoiding questions about Mum. It wasn't that I didn't want to speak about her, it was just I didn't see the need to. I learned a lot about Anna that night and so too did she about me. It was easy to speak to her. I felt some kind of attachment that allowed me to speak freely.

"Oh look, it's snowing again."

Anna got up and went to the window. She stood still for a few moments before saying anything. "I love the snow, I love the way it falls from nowhere and disappears the same way. I love the way it's so much fun yet so dangerous at the same time."

I remember watching her stand that night in the light of the window, and she was so beautiful. Her hair folded down over her shoulders like a flow of water running down past her ear. "Come watch the snow," she called quietly. To start with I acted as if I hadn't heard her. "Come on, watch the snow with me," she called again.

Now, I could have made up some excuse or I could have quite easily have lied, but for some reason I wanted to watch the snow with her. I wanted to be close to her and smell that sweet smell that she had, so I got up. I left the covers on the bed and walked naked towards her. I wasn't really able to see what her reaction was as the night darkened her face, but she never moved, screamed or even flinched. I stood directly behind her and slowly wrapped my arms around her.

We'd only watched the snow for a matter of seconds before we became interested in other things. Anna turned around to face me and without thinking I kissed her. The touch of my lips against hers was fantastic. As if an animal instinct had came over me I changed. Suddenly I was holding her tight in my arms. A single soft kiss had turned into a long, strong and meaningful moment. I stopped and pulled my head back for a second to see if she was okay, but before I had the chance to view her expression she grabbed me. With her hands on the back of my head, she pulled me closer than we'd ever been before. The feeling of her hair between my fingers was great; the warmth of her body gave me heat. For what seemed like forever, we clung to each other. In no time I could feel the back of my legs resting against the bed. I was either somehow without knowing pulling Anna towards the bed or she was pushing me. Either way I wanted it, I wanted her. I wasn't sure how to take the step from standing to being on the bed, so without thinking too much about it I just sat backwards onto the bed and Anna followed.

Goose pimples had erupted all over my body. Each and every muscle became tense and aware of even the slightest touch. We lay facing each other on the bed; our arms wrapped around each other's body. My mind raced over things I'd talked about with friends about girls and sex, but lucky for me I didn't have to do much that night. As we lay there touching each other's arms, Anna made the first move. From touching my arm, she moved her hand around my chest, then slowly downward. I immediately reacted to her touch. My heart rate quickened along with my breath as she held and fondled me with her hand. I could never have imagined sex would ever have felt like this.

With a little bit of encouragement from Anna, I placed my hands on her breast. They were soft and warm. They were welcoming and interesting. I moved myself to be kneeling over her body. With her hands on my thighs I unbuttoned the tiny little buttons that held her shirt together. Sweeping each side over her shoulders her breasts lay bare before me. What little light that came in through the window highlighted their shape and form. I reached out and held them softly. They were wonderful. Like holding cold, cold ice, my hands and body shivered. I moved off her legs and sat to the side of her. All she now wore was a small dress. Just as if she knew what I wanted, she stood up, removed her dress and underwear and then joined me back on the bed. We were now both completely naked. My excitement hadn't died in the slightest. Pushing me flat on the bed she moved upon me and by taking me again with her hands she entered me inside her. That very moment was like no other moment I've ever experienced in my entire life. That timeless moment has stayed clearer in my mind than any other memory I've ever owned. That night I became a man. We made love longer that night than I've ever done since and ever will. If ever I had the chance to go back in time or re-experience anything I've ever done, it would be that day, that moment, that very second.

Afterward, I found myself staring wide eyed at the ceiling. I wanted the night to happen time after time again. I must have had a smile like a Cheshire cat that night, but all too soon it was over. At some point I must have fallen asleep and woke late the next morning. Stretching out to feel Anna I found she was gone. For a second, I questioned myself over whether it had actually happened or not, but I only had to look at the window to know the truth. There drawn in the condensation was the slowly dissolving pattern of a flower. My heart warmed at its sight and my stomach flipped with butterflies at what it meant. I quickly took refuge in the bath and gave thought to what would happen to our family now that Mum had died. I wondered if perhaps she had watched me last night as I entered into my first sensation of love, but surely not, I mean are spirits allowed to watch anyone and anything in the land of the living? Surely even spirits must obey certain rules and regulations.

While my head was ducked under the water, I could hear every sound that was being made down stairs as it travelled through the water and directly into my ears. Although I could hear voices, I wasn't sure who they belonged to. There were also a lot of banging and loud noises. I got dried off and then changed quite quickly that morning. As I made my way down stairs I found Gran polishing the side table while Jenny was cleaning out all the kitchen cupboards, and Anna was cleaning the ornaments that lay strewn around the house. Although I walked down the stairs almost silently, everyone seemed to hear me. Gran stood upright from her bent over position, Jenny paused and turned around and Anna just glanced around and smiled.

"Good morning, come here and give your Gran a hug."

I looked at her and hesitated before moving down the last few steps towards her. "Good morning Gran."

"My dear boy, I'm so sorry. I should never have treated you like I did yesterday. It was just..."

"Gran, it's ok, I understand, honest. There will never be a day that goes by when I don't think about Mum. But just because I don't cry or just because I'm not sad doesn't mean that I don't care. Mum told me to be happy, she told me to live as long as I can and to never look back or spend time being sad over something or someone. No matter what happens to me in life from now on I'll always live by that."

Gran held my shoulders and looked deep through my eyes. She saw something in me that day. For some reason she shuddered at what she'd seen. It was as if she had peeled back every layer of my body and found something magical or amazing inside. I also felt something strange. It was as if I had passed something from me to her, a little bit of something that made her eyes twinkle and her cheeks colourful. She hugged me after that as if I'd just given her the best present in the world then turned and picked up the duster that lay on the side table and continued cleaning. Jenny's grin said all that she was thinking.

I walked into the kitchen and sat down. "Would you like something to eat?" Jenny asked, handing me a large mug of ice cold milk. "You must be starving after last night."

My face instantly and uncontrollably exploded with several shades of scarlet, while at the same time I almost choked to death on the milk. I looked at Jenny with disbelief. I mean surely Anna wouldn't have told her Mum about us, about what we'd done.

"Jesus Christ boy, what's wrong with you?"

"Nothing, nothing, I'm okay, just fine."

"Well?"

"Well what?"

"Do you want some breakfast? You hardly ate any of your dinner last night."

A wave of relief washed over me, but her half hidden smile made me suspect she knew something, maybe not everything, but she was teasing me.

CHAPTER TWENTY-NINE
Written in Ink

I didn't eat much that morning, maybe because I was excited. Maybe it was because I was nervous at Jenny's remarks, or it could just have been because I was in love. In love with the most beautiful girl in the world. What actually caused my excited nervousness, I don't really know and I don't really care. That day, I could have lost an arm and I wouldn't have noticed.

I wanted to ask why everyone was working hard at cleaning, but something told me not to. I looked in the main room to find Gavin but he wasn't there. In fact, he was nowhere to be found, neither was Dad. Seeing all the cleaning that was going on, I decided to go back upstairs and do a bit of cleaning myself. It had been a long time since I'd cleaned my room, and I wasn't going to be able to rely on Mum doing it from now on. It wasn't that I was a messy boy, it's just well, when someone else will do it for you why do it yourself? I cleared most things away just like Mum would have done and even attempted to tell myself off for being lazy. I swear if anyone had walked into my room at that moment they would have thought I was crazy, I mean who in their right mind tells himself off like his mother would do?

I lifted up the suit that Jamie had been wearing the day we went to Edinburgh from where it had been left laying over the desk chair. Just before hanging it back up in the cupboard, I noticed some paper sticking out of the inside pocket. I paused for a second before reaching in and taking it out. I hung the suit upon the rail and placed the pieces of paper on the table. I hesitated as I turned around. Should I or shouldn't I? My fingers tapped repeatedly on the side of my leg as I pondered before swinging back around and re-lifting the papers. There were three pieces in total, all folded together. I opened them up and started to read. My hands trembled faster and faster the more I read. I couldn't believe what I was holding, what I was reading. Why? My mind was racing back and forth not to mention side ways.

There was a sudden knock at the door. "Just a minute." Quickly I pushed the papers back into the jacket pocket and closed the cupboard door. "Come in."

"Hi, son," Dad said upon entering the room, "how you keeping?"

"I'm ok, thanks, just been doing a little cleaning."

"So I see. I've been away to see your Mum and arrange the last few funeral arrangements. All will take place tomorrow at ten thirty."

"That's quite fast."

"Yes, but I feel it's better that way."

"Um, you're probably right."

"You're a young man, son, a very brave young man indeed."

For some reason everything everyone spoke to me that morning seemed to have a kind of warning entwined in it or some other kind of special message.

"Dad."

"Yes?"

"I was wondering." A knock I hadn't expected sounded at the front door, interrupting me.

"Oh that will be the reverend," Dad said, "he said he'd be arriving about now. We'll speak later?"

"Ok." I'm not all together sure what exactly I was going to ask Dad that day, but one thing I knew I had to ask him something, if only he could have seen that in my eyes. As he pulled the door closed behind him, I collapsed on the bed. I wanted so much to go back to the suit and take a second look at those pieces of paper, to read those words that had been so neatly written in solid jet-black ink. But I couldn't. Instead, I tried hard to seek some kind of reasoning behind them. To make what was so clearly wrong into something that could be right. No conversation I'd ever had with Jamie could lead me down a path that could provide real reason, no path that could offer pardon for such a plan. I lay back and hoped that I was wrong.

What was left of that cold day melted away into deep thought and soul searching. Every five minutes there was a knock on the door and a new visitor offering their sympathy for our loss. It was only after about the tenth visitor that I realised why everyone had been up early cleaning the house; they wanted it to look nice and pretty for everyone who came around. Mum was dead and all they cared about was making the house look presentable. And the sad thing is, had the house been a mess the people visiting would have left and talked about it. It seems people have a thirst for gossip, a hunger for belittling their neighbour and starvation of common decency. I'm glad that I never ventured down stairs that day. I would more than likely have been sick at the sound of hearing them and watching them as they wept tears, perhaps false, perhaps from fear of the unknown. For I strongly believe that in life people are only sad at death as a result of not knowing what lies beyond the realms of lifeless death.

It was that same day in which I'd questioned Jamie's plan that I found myself agreeing with it. Jamie was one hundred per cent correct in what he'd written, in what he sought above all other things in his life. He was right in wanting revenge for his loss and wanting some kind of payback for the cruelty that had suppressed him and his family. It was at that precise moment that I took in my hands for the second time the three pieces of paper that contained Jamie's deepest thoughts, his strongest desire and the one thing he'd wished for over the past years. In my hands I held a plan that would make all those people responsible for his father's death and the poverty of his family responsible for their actions. Although I found myself agreeing with most of what he'd written, there were some parts that needed changing. I gave thought to every single part and slowly but surely rewrote it. As I held the finished plan in my hands, I smiled. Right before my eyes was the most perfect test of friendship ever imaginable. Throughout writing every single word, I knew I was capable of carrying it into execution.

I folded up the two plans and placed them both inside the suit pocket. Before closing the cupboard door, I paused. For the second and last time, I questioned everything, but my mind was made up. It's strange and somewhat hard to explain but for some reason I felt strong that day. Looking out of the window and judging by the fact that no one had come chapping on the door for a long time I knew it was late. Feeling a little hungry, I travelled down stairs to the kitchen. After getting a little to eat and a mug of hot chocolate, I went to the main room. Only Dad, Jenny and Anna were there.

"Hello son," said Dad in a rather sleepy tone.

"You must be starving, boy," Jenny said quickly after. "I'll go and fetch you some supper."

Just as she was getting up I waved what was left of a thickly buttered slice of bread. "I'm fine, thanks, Jenny."

"Well if you're sure."

"I am."

Dad yawned and stood up. "I'm away to bed. It's been a long day. Good night all."

"I think I'll join you," said Jenny and then, thinking about what she'd said, quickly tried to correct it. "I mean, not that I'm going to actually join you, I just mean..." Dad laughed and so too did Anna and I. It wasn't often that Jenny got herself into a fluster, but in any case we all knew what she actually meant to say.

I learned that night that Dad had moved into one of the guest bedrooms, not wanting to sleep in the room he had shared with his wife. As a matter of fact, from the night she died he never so much as entered the room.

Dad and Jenny had left the room, leaving Anna and me alone. With her feet tucked under her body, she sat in front of the fire looking lovely. The flickering of the flames somehow brought a real sense of liveliness to her body. Standing right next to her I bent down and collected her hair. It carried heat from the fire giving it real warmth. I stroked it several times before we so much as whispered a word to each other. "Anna," was the only word I had said when she reached out and placed her fingers on my lips.

"Watch the fire," she said. "Watch the energy consume all around it." I looked deep into the roots of the whistling red flames as they moved tirelessly. There at its base where it was the hottest of all I saw it. Like a gathering of naked dancers entwined together, the fire possessed its power. Eating inwards into the pile of wood and coal it stopped for nothing. It never rested or halted at all. It just kept eating away until at last there was nothing left to eat, and then and only then did it start to die in the ashes and remnants of all it had eaten till at last it just disappeared.

I sat down on the floor beside Anna and took hold of her hand. As if I'd just been struck by lightening, I became very energetic. I wanted to dance and jump around. I felt as if I could run ten miles or swim the Forth. Anna, too, seemed somewhat powered up. I got back to my feet, turned off all the lights and closed the heavy curtains before rejoining Anna on the floor. I reached out to her and gathered her head in my hands. There was no need to pull her towards me, as she came all too freely. This time I wanted to be the one in control. I wanted to be the one making all the first moves, and this night I did.

Moving towards the floor, we leant back holding each other. I felt her eyes pulling me towards her and within seconds our lips were touching. In the heat of the fire we slowly undressed each other 'til we lay naked and cuddled up on the floor. She looked amazing, as if posing for an oil painting; her body appeared ripe and ready for picking.

After some time of running my hands over her body, I moved on top of her and we started to make love. Like the previous night, the feelings were fantastic. The passion we felt for each other was strong and powerful. This night during making love a cold breeze suddenly entered the room. Anna never seemed to notice but I could feel the waves of coldness ripple across my feet and back. Glancing from under my arm as I moved, I could see the distant sight of eyes peering in through a small gap that appeared in the door. I knew only to well who the eyes belonged to but for some reason I didn't mind them watching. In fact it made me feel good. To some that might sound perverted or strange, but not to me.

I allowed him to watch for several minutes before making it obvious that I knew he was there watching. At which point he very slowly closed the door and tiptoed upstairs. Gavin never mentioned that night to me, nor did I to him. But I had a funny feeling that I'd added something special to his knowledge that night.

It was well after three in the morning that Anna and I parted company for our separate rooms, although I so wanted to keep her close to me. I fell asleep that night to the feelings of greatness. My dreams were filled with good thoughts and nothing else.

CHAPTER THIRTY
Flying with Angels

Although I'd gone to bed late, I awoke bright and fresh around eight the following morning. The smell of cooked ham hung lightly in the air as the sun started to make its steady climb into the sky. Pulling back the covers, I could see the sun wasn't the only thing making a climb that morning, so I spent a further ten minutes in bed before making my way to the bathroom.

My hope for a long hot bath was ruined by Dad's shouts, "Come on boys, hurry up."

I'd only just got under the water when Gavin came barging in. Half-dressed in a pair of black trousers with a white shirt and black tie, he dived for the sink. It wasn't until I spoke that he even realised I was there.

"Gavin, throw your tie over your back before it gets covered in tooth paste."

"What're you doing there?"

"Um let me see? Having a bath, perhaps?"

"Very nice, you know what I meant. We don't have long so you best hurry up."

"Ok, ok, pass me that towel." While I got dried, Gavin brushed his hair, taking the time to make sure every little strand was accurately positioned. By the time he was finished, I was onto cleaning my teeth.

Dad's shouts for quickness were now getting louder and carried a hint of anger in them. I cut short my stay in

313

the bathroom and quickly got changed. I reached into the cupboard and collected a black suit, a pair of shoes and a tie. Feeling slightly pressured, I got dressed as quickly as possible and made my way down stairs.

"What is it with boys? They're never in a hurry. If you need breakfast, you better be quick and get into the kitchen. There's warm bread in the oven and ham on the grill but it's getting cold."

To tell the truth, I wasn't really all that hungry, well, at least not for food. The only hunger I felt was for Anna. Every minute we spent apart, although we were under the same roof, was unbearable. Gavin tucked into some breakfast while I sipped at a large mug of hot chocolate. Watching Gavin eating was like being in a barn of hungry pigs, all snorting and grunting. With that thought in mind, I left him alone and went into the main room. Here, Dad and Gran were sitting talking while Anna sat brushing Jenny's hair. Just as I sat down, the clock struck nine thirty. Dad and Gran's conversation stopped and so too did Anna's brush strokes. For a few brief seconds, time in the room seemed to halt, kind of like it just froze in time and then quickly and without warning restored itself. It was strange to say the least, but no one else seemed to even notice it.

Dad stood up, and with a sharp intake of breath spoke.

"Well people, it's time to go."

Everyone made their way into the hall where we adorned ourselves with coats, hats and gloves. At the sound of us all in the hall, Gavin quickly joined us, after which we made our way outside where there were two large black cars waiting on us. Dad, Gavin and I got into the first one, while Gran Anna and Jenny got into the second one.

Although it had crossed my mind that we were leaving a little early I didn't really give it much thought. It was only when the cars came to a stop and I looked outside that I understood why. Dad was the first to get out, followed by

Gavin then me. Gran, Anna and Jenny remained behind as we walked along the narrow path that led us to where we were going.

Although I'd never really spent much time here before, I always remembered Mum telling me about it. The path came to a stop at the top of a cliff. For miles around, you could see everything. I take it that's why the Romans had used this very spot as a look out all those years ago. Mum and Dad used to come here when they were younger. Well before even Gavin and I were born. I remember Dad once telling me during one of his secret talks that it was here that he and Mum had their very first night of passion.

As we stood on the cliff that morning, Gavin on Dad's left and me on his right, he reached and took hold of our hands. "Your Mum made me promise that when she died I would bring you both out here. She never said why and I never asked. I think she wanted you both to understand why for yourselves."

Gavin, who was obviously finding the whole situation very difficult, couldn't hold back any more. He began to cry and was quickly comforted by Dad who gathered him in his arms and held him. I walked out to the very edge of the cliff and listened to the wind. I swear I could almost hear it talking to me, and it was then that I understood, or at least found some kind of reasoning to why Mum wanted us to come here. Mum had brought us to the very edge of the border of life and death. It was here that the angels learned how to fly. In this very place where the air was clean and clear did the dead first come and learn to be free. Closing my eyes, I felt as if I could just fly away, carefree.

As I reopened my eyes, I stood agape. All around me I could see people flying, I could see angels. Hundreds of them surrounded me, and there right in the middle, shining brighter than any of them, was Mum. She shone brighter than light itself. I so much wanted to fly out there to meet her, but it was as if I was being held back, as if there was a line just inches in front of me that I wasn't allowed to cross yet.

As I watched in amazement, I felt myself being pulled backward.

"Don't stare into the sun like that, son."

"What?"

"You're staring directly into the sun, not to mention standing tiptoed on the edge of a seven hundred foot cliff."

Suddenly, everything changed. The air was no longer strewn with angels and the feeling of freedom. All I could now feel was Dad's hands as they held me rather tightly, stopping me from stepping over the edge.

I don't know why, but Dad felt something that morning. I could tell by the way that he looked at me. Something had happened that he wasn't sure about. It wasn't until many years later that he actually asked the question to which he supplied the answer. And by that time it was too late, as he died less than an hour later, to do anything about it. As for me, that day supplied me with more than enough proof as to whether there was an afterlife or not.

We made our way back along the path to the cars. Gran, Anna and Jenny sat patiently while the two drivers stood talking to each other. At our arrival, they quickly got back into their driving seats and then we were off.

As we drove along the main street, I noticed lots of people making their way in the same direction as us. On arriving at the cemetery, I realised where they were all going. As we entered the main gates for our second funeral in such little time, I was shocked at the amount of people. It appeared that the whole of the town was there.

The main wall that ran around the cemetery was covered by children sitting upon it, many of whom were friends of both Gavin and me. The car was reduced to a walking pace as it attempted to advance through the crowds. I knew Mum was always well thought of throughout the town but I never in my wildest dreams expected Mum to have such a large turnout. I suppose almost all of them never had the chance to say goodbye and more than likely wanted to be there for her. The cars came to stop just outside the main doors of the church. Upon the doors being opened, we got out and moved inside.

The great hall bellowed with the sounds of organ music. All around stood great big vases of white lilies containing a single red carnation in the centre.

We were directed to seats at the very front of the church where Mum lay within her dark cherry coloured casket, which had been draped in Mum's familiar chequered blanket that Gran had sewn for her as a child. As we sat down, the church started to fill behind us. I looked back a few times to see that there weren't enough seats. Many people were standing in the isles, and crowding in the doorway. I felt proud that day, proud that so many people had come to see Mum, my Mum.

We'd only been seated a few moments when the music slowly came to cease and the Reverend appeared from a small side door at the front of the church just under a great big statue of Jesus Christ.

"Good morning. It is with much sadness that we are gathered here today, to bear witness to the passing above of a truly extraordinary woman, a woman who led a life as a life should be led, a woman who gave just as much as she received and a woman who above all gave love to a family who will now miss her dearly. For such was this woman that it's clear to see by the overwhelming gathering she has to see her away today. Although Diana was not a religious person or dependent on God or Jesus, she knew that deep down inside that when her time on this earth was to come to end, she would ascend to the Grand Heavens Above where the world's Great Creator lives and reigns for ever. As was her desired request, I shall not say many more words or reflect on Diana's life. I would just ask that everyone be upstanding and join with me in singing a song before proceeding outside to where Diana will be finally laid to rest."

We were about half way through the song when four large men came and collected Mum. I watched to the sounds of singing and crying as Mum was lifted and taken from the church out through the gathered crowds to her grave.

As the song came to end the Reverend signalled for us to follow him. Dad comforted Gavin and Gran as we walked the forty or so steps, past the full pews and the crowds and along the snowy path to where Mum had come to lay. Although it was cold outside, I didn't feel it at all. My body was riddled with pins and needles that made my feet itchy for the want to walk.

By now the entire graveside was compacted with people. I stood as the Reverend began once more to speak, only this time I didn't hear his words. Instead, I could hear whispering above me. I looked up but could see nothing. The whispering seemed to drift off down the graveyard with the wind. It was at that time that I actually looked at the faces of the people who surrounded me.

The first face that my eyes came to rest upon was that of Jamie. I could see that like Gavin he had been crying. But there was something about the expression on his face that gave him a look of fear. It was as if he'd just seen a ghost, and perhaps he had, for it was then that I remembered. Only as his eyes penetrated the black fabric of the suit jacket I was wearing did I understand why his face grew a look of horror. I just sent a smile back in return and continued with my look into the crowd. I noticed some people that wouldn't look directly at the casket and instead turned their heads and eyes away, while others just bowed their head in sympathy with our family's suffering.

Very quickly, the Reverend's few words were over and he was calling upon people to step forward. Around the grave stood Uncle Simon and his son, along with Dad, Gavin, Jamie, the Reverend and, when called forward, me.

318

Each of us held onto gold coloured cord that was attached to the casket. The four men who had taken Mum outside stepped up to the grave and removed from under the coffin the large wooden beams that prevented it from entering the ground. On the Reverend's signal, we slowly lowered Mum into the ground, where her mortal body was returned to the very earth that gave it strength and beauty. Here would remain the shell of her mortal existence while her spirit would fly free in the skies above.

CHAPTER THIRTY-ONE
A Few Days to Go

After Mum was lowered and those who wished to had dropped a flower onto her casket, people started to disperse. Mum had prearranged that the church community hall should be used instead of the house for the tea afterwards. The minute the doors were opened and the warm smell of coffee came pouring out did everyone start pouring in. As for me, I drifted off down the graveyard in search of the whispers.

Dad was occupied with sympathisers while Gran and the others made their way inside. I came to a stop at the foot of a massive oak tree that grew strongly in the centre of the cemetery. Looking upwards, I knew that for some reason I had to climb it. Although I had never been good at climbing trees, I managed to climb this one with ease. Within no time, I'd become rested within the bosom of the tree and the eerie feelings that hung from its cold branches.

All seemed quiet at first, but slowly the shallow voices arrived. All around me came the sounds of whispering that got louder and louder and louder, then, suddenly they were there. Each taking a seat in the tree and looking towards me as if I should have been surprised at their arrival. In fact that couldn't have been further from the truth. I was expecting them to appear, although a puff of smoke or some lightning wouldn't have gone amiss. The three of them sat before me, Mrs Blake, Mr Richardson and Mum.

"I believe you now understand what Jamie is looking to achieve," said Mr Richardson.

"Well, I guess so."

I hadn't even finished when I felt my jacket pull open and out flew Jamie's plan. I watched as the three pieces of paper began to unfold in mid air. Mum and the others read the words that had been written very closely. The looks on each of their faces were varied. Mrs Blake laughed as she read while Mr Richardson seemed angry. The veins in his forehead started to bulge and pump rapidly. His face exploded in red blotches before suddenly he disappeared.

The smell that lingered behind him was terrible. Mum and Mrs Blake seemed very happy at what had just happened. "I better go after him," said Mrs Blake. "I'll see you later young man."

Then with a second ping she was also gone, leaving just Mum and me. "You liked the Roman cliffs?"

"I sure did. Did I really see what I thought I saw?"

"Well now, what do you think? When have your eyes ever deceived you before?"

I gave thought to what she said before answering. "But if I did really see those things that means Heaven and God and all the other things must be true?"

"That may well be the case but unfortunately that's something for you to decide." Her smile told me not to ask any more questions, so I didn't. "You put a lot of thought into your words."

"What do you mean?"

"The words upon the paper, it was you that wrote them."

I looked towards the three pieces of paper that still hung unaided. Sending a light blow of air from her lips the papers slowly turned to face me. She was right! The plan that had come from my pocket was mine, and not Jamie's, but how? I placed my hand inside the suit pocket and inside sat Jamie's plan.

"Good will always ride before evil. That's why yours preceded Jamie's. Now all you have to do is convince Jamie that you're right. Remember, he's waited a long time for this and it's cost him more than money can replace. His new life means nothing unless he feels at one with himself. You two are much closer than you know. I must go, but before I do I need you to do something for me."

"Yes."

"Tell your father that he must follow the path that took him to the Roman cliffs all those years ago. He'll understand what I mean."

"Ok, I'll tell him." I so wanted to ask why but just as I was about to speak there was a noise, a loud 'crack!' As I looked down so too did Jamie look up. He looked up just in time to see three pieces of paper fall slowly towards him. My heart jumped into my throat as I watched him bend to pick them up. One by one he collected them. I didn't dare move a muscle as I watched him read.

A few minutes had passed before finally he looked up again. I couldn't bring myself to look at him. I felt ashamed, embarrassed that I had gone behind his back.

"This isn't quite what I had planned!"

I turned and looked down as he spoke. His voice wasn't angry, just somewhat surprised. As my hands grabbed firmly onto the branches I summoned the power to speak.

"I hope you don't mind. It wasn't that I was prying or anything, but when I saw what you'd written I couldn't *not* do something. If you'd gone ahead with what you wrote you'd surely be locked away in prison for years, I don't want that to happen."

"Don't panic," he replied.

"Just because I wrote it, it doesn't mean that's what I was actually going to do. In a way, I wanted you to know. I don't know why but it feels better, now that I know you know, but you do understand I have to do something?"

I knew what the answer was to the question but that didn't stop me from pausing. "Yes."

"So can I count on your help?"

"Yes."

"Well, come down from there and tell me who on earth you were speaking to." Before answering his question, I knew I couldn't tell him the truth. I mean, how on earth could I tell him I was speaking to two of the people he most loved, when in his dreams that's all he ever wished for? I never kept many secrets from Jamie, but this was one.

On reaching the tree's roots and solid ground, I could see he was waiting for an answer. "Well, who do you think I was talking to? It was only me up there."

"Well, you shouldn't talk to yourself; you could get carted off for that."

On the way back up towards the church we didn't speak. The inside of the hall was stuffed with people, all eating and sipping at hot cups of tea and coffee. I could see that Dad was being constantly covered by people passing on their sad respects, while Gavin sat with Margaret, Gran, Jenny and Anna. Looking around, I knew I had to go home; I'd never been the kind of person who liked big crowds, not even on birthdays or other special events. I much preferred a small select group of people to share in celebrations, Mum always understood that while Dad always encouraged me to mingle: "Knowing many people is what brings bread home to the kitchen table," Dad would always say.

I knew Dad enjoyed the company of large groups of people because he was a member of many organisations. He was proud of the fact that he had gained great respect in many of these. I never asked where he went or why but religiously he would leave the house on every second and fourth Thursday of the month dressed in a dinner suit and carrying a rather overlarge black case with the number

1253 upon it. I remember one time just as he was leaving the house he turned and spoke to me,

"In a few years time, you'll understand, son," and with that he was gone. To say that his words were cryptic and mysterious was an understatement.

I waved in Dad's direction to try and get his attention. It was only after the third attempt that he finally noticed. Making an excuse, he pushed his way through the crowds to get to me. Seeing I needed to speak with Dad, Jamie made his way towards his family. Dad and I walked outside away from all the noise and hustle of the hall.

"You ok?" I asked.

"It should be me asking you that. I forget just how much you've grown up." Dad brushed the snow from a nearby bench and we sat down. We talked for some time but all the while I was thinking of how to bring up the subject of Mum and what she wanted me to say. About ten minutes had passed when suddenly my mouth opened and I began to speak.

"Dad, I don't want you to think I'm crazy but I have to tell you something, something Mum asked me to tell you." I could see the look on his face change, but I didn't give him the time to ask or say anything. "Mum said I've to tell you that you must follow the path that took you to the Roman cliffs all those years ago."

He seemed stunned and shocked at what I'd told him. It was clear to me that he so wanted to ask me how, where, when and every other possible question that entered his head about how I knew. He sat in silence; his stunned appearance turned to that of blank and expressionless. He took hold of my hand and turned to face me.

"Son, there's something I need to tell you. Something I should have told you the moment I knew. It's just..."

"Thomas, do you think I could possibly speak with you for a moment?" asked the Reverend who had appeared from nowhere.

"I'll speak to you later, son. There are things we need to talk about." With that, Dad stood up and followed the Reverend into the old manse house.

I walked back into the hall to look for Jamie and puzzled over what it might be that Dad had to tell me. Jamie was standing alongside his Mum drinking a cup of tea. "Hello, Mrs Richardson."

"My dear boy, I'm so sorry, so, so sorry about your poor mother. You must be devastated."

Although I thanked her for her kind words, they really couldn't have been further from the truth. I would have been more devastated if I'd been to the larder cupboard and found we were out of hot chocolate than the fact that Mum had died. You see, in my eyes Mum wasn't really dead, she was just kind of different now, and different isn't dead. Before we were able to leave, Mrs Richardson forced the both of us to have some tea and a slice of fruitcake. I'm not sure if it was because she felt sorry for me, but for some reason just as we left she gave Jamie a kiss goodbye and then me. I wasn't really embarrassed by this but it did make me feel kind of strange.

We left the hall and made our way out of the churchyard and back into town. Along the way we had a snowball fight and made a few jokes, but all too soon the tone would change back to a more serious note. The town itself was very quiet. Most people, I presumed, were still at the church. Most if not all of the shops were closed, leaving the air fresh and untouched. It was at that moment I wished I were back in Edinburgh, there the air never stood still; there everything   hustled along with a certain kind of tension. I liked that sense of hurry and chaos, a sense that would grow inside me and scream to get out.

It was nearly one in the afternoon when we arrived back at the house. The first thing to be done was to boil some water to make hot chocolate. We sat and said nothing while the kettle hissed and spat on the warm stove. Even after the water was boiled and the chocolate was made, we still sat in silence. Like someone had stripped us of words, we appeared dumb to the room that enclosed us. I think we both knew what we had to talk about but who was going to be first to start?

Jamie placed his now empty cup on the table and turned to face me. We were virtually sitting next to each other when he turned but for some reason he felt the need to come closer. My grip around the cup became tighter as I felt his eyes pierce me. A ripple of unease swam over me. For the first time since we'd known each other Jamie had put me in a position that made me uncomfortable. The moment he noticed just how uncomfortable I was, he retracted and said nothing. The kitchen buzzed with excitement. I knew Jamie had wanted to tell me something important, something that he had held onto tightly and for a brief second had almost let slip. If only I had just kept steady he might have told me, but the moment had passed and it didn't seem right to ask.

I reached to the middle of the table and uncovered some ginger cakes that had been baked by Jenny. Pulling two from the pile, I re-covered them, offered one to Jamie and then quickly ate one myself.

"We only have a few days," said Jamie.

"If I miss this chance, another will never be available. Now is the time that actions speak louder than words. Now I have to put into play the thoughts that have controlled my dreams over the last years. Now, now is the time."

I heard each word that he spoke. I understood each word that he spoke, but there was a darkness that surrounded him, something that overshadowed him.

We sat at the kitchen table and spoke for hours. We had made a list of everyone who would be able to help. Jamie explained the layout of the school and where everything was. All we had to do now was convince the others that we needed their help, but without harming the

326

plan by giving away too much information.

It was about three thirty five when Dad and the others got home. They all looked exhausted. Jenny offered to make some tea but Dad said no and retired upstairs, so too did Gran and Anna. Jenny, although she looked tired, stayed in the kitchen and started to prepare dinner.

"I'd better be getting home for a while but I'll come back round later and we'll sort out the other things."

"Ok."

"I'll take this lot as well, that way it's not lying around." With that, Jamie collected the plan and all the other pieces of paper we had written on and I walked him to the front door. I watched as he walked down the stairs and along the road. Closing the door, I could feel someone watching me. On turning around I found Jenny propping herself against the kitchen doorway,

"I hope you two aren't getting into any mischief?"

"Em, no, of course not."

"I can smell mischief and I'll warn you now. Your poor father has suffered enough let alone you two going and causing him heartache."

I just looked at Jenny then slowly lowered my eyes to the ground. When I looked back up she was gone. It's true what they say, "everyone has a mother whether they want one or not." Jenny might not have been my mother but right about now she was certainly acting like it.

I made my way upstairs to the sound of silence, even the clumping of my footsteps dissolved in the pile of the thick carpet. It's strange how one minute you can feel wide awake and the next moment you can be that tired that all you want to do is sleep. That's exactly what happened to me the moment I entered the bedroom. I barely remember lying on the bed. Face down and still fully clothed, I melted into the soft pillow and a world of dreams.

I found myself walking through the corridors of a large building. I could see that it was still daylight outside yet the halls were dark and musty. There were no pictures on the walls that were decorated with dark oak panels. The floor was formed from a mixture of randomly laid Granite and marble of various colours and sizes. Each door that I passed was closed.

I found myself drifting down the hallways uncontrollably, turning one way then the other then the other again until finally I stopped. Facing me was a door that stood slightly open, but not enough as to be able to see inside. I remember there being a thick smell in the air that carried a kind of mist or heavy sweatiness. My arms slowly pushed the doors, but they swung open with a mighty crack as if I'd thrust them. Looking inside, I could see a figure in the distance but it was not recognisable, due to the mass of steam that swirled around the room and the bright light that shone through the high up windows. The figure seemed somewhat cautious but oblivious to the fact that I was standing there.

I moved closer but as I did the person moved behind a large wall that divided the room. Everything seemed familiar as if I'd been there before, yet I didn't recognise anything. I moved a further few steps into the room and then froze. I now understood where I was. As if looking to God for help I moved my head and eyes up towards the ceiling. There I didn't see the usual light fixtures or decorations. What I saw was Jamie. His pale white face was blank as he slept. Somehow he'd either invited me into his dream or I'd found a way in myself.

Everything was happening so quickly. Jamie's pale face now radiated with fear. The sound of his heavy breathing filled the room giving a sense of danger. It was then it began. As if by magic, the first of the conspirators moved straight through me, followed by a further two. It was a strange feeling to say the least, very similar to a tickle only much deeper.

I watched as the three boys now entered the shower block. I could hear the sounds of voices and laughter. From out of nowhere a further person appeared. He seemed to talk to the others then walked back to the main door. I knew only too well what was now going to happen. I covered my ears as I heard the first scream and suddenly I was awake. My heart raced and my hands trembled in fear. Still ringing in my head was the sound of Jamie screaming. I couldn't close my eyes for fear I would see more.

I got up from the bed and looked down. My trousers were wet and so too were the bed covers. It was then I realised what had happened, I'd wet myself. A sense of embarrassment didn't even cross my mind, as I was still far too upset to think about it. I just stood there. Ten or fifteen minutes must have passed before I did anything. The warm feeling had now turned cold and damp. I removed all my clothes along with the bedding. Jenny would never suspect that I was asleep at this time of the day so it was easy for me to tell her I had spilt something. I took some clean clothes and entered the bathroom where I ran a hot bath and soaked for an hour. Now I was able to appreciate first hand the pain Jamie had felt. Now I was able to understand why he was prepared to kill the boys who had tortured him, ultimately killing his father and at the same time wrecking his family life. Now I was able to help in curing Jamie by putting into action Jamie's plan, Jamie's real plan.

CHAPTER THIRTY-TWO
Family Secrets

All sense of time that day had evaporated, and before I knew it dinner was served. The house still felt lost and quiet. I knew it would be some time before it would return to normal. The smell of roast pork and sweet apples lifted my spirit somewhat and brought a smile to my face. I loved roast pork and apple; there was something about that first crunch you got when biting into the deep, golden crisp skin. It's funny how the small things in life can make a man feel good.

Around the dinner table that night there was an air of unease. For some reason, Gran and Dad never seemed to speak much and hardly even looked at each other. Jenny handed round the bowls that spilled with piping hot vegetables while Gavin eagerly carved the pork.

"This looks great, Jenny," said Gavin in an attempt to break the silence.

"Well thank you."

Although I gave it much thought, I couldn't think of anything funny or even interesting to say that would assist in changing the atmosphere, so instead I just sat there and said nothing. The longer dinner went on the more I could see Gran was worried about something.

I placed my knife and fork down upon the table rather heavily and sat back. Immediately everyone turned and looked. "Well, is someone going to tell me what's going on?"

"Thomas, please don't," said Gran who now looked like she was about to pass out any second.

Dad lifted his eyes from the table and looked at Gran. Although his lips moved and it was easy to see what he was saying, no sound came from his mouth. In silence, Dad had whispered the word "sorry". Tears welled in Gran's eyes just before she moved from her chair and ran out of the kitchen. Jenny, grabbing Anna, chased after her leaving only Dad, Gavin and me.

Gavin seemed more worried than me at what was about to be said or done, but he wasn't going to find out at the same time as me.

"Gavin!"

"Yes Dad."

"Would you leave me and your brother for a while, please?"

Without asking any further questions, Gavin placed his cutlery on the table, removed his napkin from his lap, got up and left, closing the kitchen door behind him. For what seemed like ages, Dad sat at the table with his head in his hands. I watched as he shed tears that fell directly from his eyes onto the scraped surface of the table filling the deep groves in the wood. Finally, he got up and moved over towards the window. With his back towards me, he started to talk with an extremely shaken voice. His hands trembled as he clutched the cold white porcelain of the sink.

"You told me something today that I've feared ever since the day you arrived in my arms. Something that I've hidden from you all these years. Something that makes me ashamed of who I am. But no matter what I'm about to tell you, you must promise that you forgive me."

Dad had somehow managed to tear himself away from the sink and was now kneeling in front of me. His head bowed, he appeared a poor and crippled man. Now to say I was scared at what he was about to say was not just an understatement; I was terrified. What could have been so bad as to make Gran run from the room in tears, and reduce someone I thought of as such a strong man to nothing more than a blubbering baby?

"Ok, I promise Dad, honest, I promise."

At my words Dad looked up. Wiping the tears from his eyes he stared at me. "Ever since the first day that I saw you I vowed that I'd tell you when you were old enough, it's just that I never, ever found the right time or the right moment. I know deep down it was because I never had the strength to say for fear that you'd never speak to me again, and now I've left it too late. I should never have left it as long as this. Your mother always said that deep down inside you knew. She always knew you treated her differently to how Gavin did. I always said it was her imagination but maybe she was right."

Dad had now rested his head comfortable on my lap while clinging on the chair with his both hands.

"When I met your mother I was dating a young lady called Emily. For me, Emily was the love of my life and I knew she would have done almost anything for me. The only thing that stood in our way was one man. You see Emily's family were very upper class, which meant they didn't want her having anything to do with me. I tried many times to speak with her parents but they weren't having any of it. I was forced to leave her alone and was warned of the consequences of a refusal to do so. So one night she crept away from her house and we met at Roman cliffs. For hours we made love, until the sun eventually forced her to leave, and we said goodbye. For months I couldn't eat or drink thinking about her being with Mason. He was a long time friend of Emily's family who Emily had known for years. They were destined to be together and her family was going to make sure nothing stopped him from getting her."

"It was a few months earlier that I met your mother, boy was she funny! No matter what kind of mood I was in she would make me laugh. Although we weren't seriously involved, we had become very close and intimate. I made it so that Emily would find out about Diana in the hope that she would become jealous enough to disobey her family and come with me to Edinburgh. In fact, it did the exact opposite; it made her fall in love with Mason, leaving me on the sidelines. Although I was upset, I had your mother to comfort me. She never said if she knew about Emily and me and I thought it best never to mention it to her. However, later that July I received a message from Emily saying she must speak to me as a matter of urgency. I was getting ready to leave when Diana arrived. She seemed overly happy and desperate to tell me something: she was pregnant. I was extremely happy at the news, so, like you do, I immediately proposed. Within five minutes, I'd found out that I was going to be a father and that I'd be married in less than five months. I was doing fairly well in business and I knew my father, who was then alive, would be more than willing to help out a little. I made an excuse and left Diane to go and meet Emily. Boy, was I in for a huge surprise!"

"I arrived once more at the Roman cliffs only this time to find Emily in tears. It took me over half an hour to calm her down enough to speak. As we sat she told me that she was also pregnant. I was dumbstruck, not to mention in a rather precarious situation. Emily didn't know what to do. She had made love with Mason so it would have been easy to say the child belonged to him, but I knew as well as her that her morals would interject. She was a woman who had pride and principles. If she was to pass off this child as Mason's, she would have to forever let go of these principles. We talked for hours and eventually we agreed. Emily would have to return home and hope that Mason wouldn't ask any questions about the child. I later found out that she didn't tell him about the pregnancy until mid September. When he found out he was over the moon. For the first time in months everyone seemed happy. Emily married Mason in November that year while your Mum and I married in late October. Ours was a modest wedding compared to theirs. We had a select amount of friends and family while they had a massive affair with lavish food and drink and hundreds of guests. But, on the whole, we were all happy.

"It wasn't until February that things went drastically wrong. On the 11th February your mother didn't feel well. I called the doctor who after examining her said she was in extreme danger. Immediately, he called for assistance and throughout that night they tried to save both your mother and the baby, but unfortunately the baby didn't survive and your mother remained in real danger. It was that same night while Mason was away on business that the doctor was called out to Emily's house.

"They hadn't long moved into the house so there was only one maid. The doctor arrived just in time to find Emily giving birth to a beautiful baby boy, my baby boy. While the maid was away cleaning the baby the doctor was telling Emily about the death of Diana's baby. She was very upset at hearing the news. I don't know why the following happened but it did. Seconds after she heard the news something strange happened. She felt the same sharp pain she'd experienced when giving birth only moments before. The doctor quickly examined her to find that she was about to give birth to a second child, and only seconds later she did. There in the doctor's hand lay a second baby boy, just as beautiful as the first. Without so much as sparing a thought and before the maid returned, Emily asked that the doctor take the child to me. The doctor, who was a long time family friend to both families, asked no questions. He double-checked that Emily was safe and well and left. Covered in a small tartan shawl, you were placed in my hands that very night. Your mother who was grieving over her loss found healing in your presence.

"I had no choice but to tell your mother everything, but to my surprise she already knew. I had kept letters from Emily hidden in a small box in a downstairs cupboard where I thought no one would ever look, but she had found them.

"The doctor told Diana that no one would ever know and he swore fidelity and secrecy. In an attempt to keep people from connecting the two of you, we changed your date of birth to a few months earlier with the help of the doctor. All through your early years, we never drew attention to your birthday. By the time you were old enough for parties, no one could have ever guessed. The dead baby girl was placed in a grave marked with a small heart shaped headstone. The headstone simple read 'Emily, a life that hasn't lived but was loved as much as one that did.' Although you never knew, your Mum visited that grave every week. Even when she wasn't feeling too well she went. It was your mother who named the baby girl Emily, after she blessed us with you.

"A few months after you were born, your mother and Emily met for the first time up on Roman cliffs. They talked for a while but neither of them ever told me what about. After that day they never spoke again. Emily and Mason moved away to the city and that was the last I ever seen of her until I saw her one day in the town a few years ago. She was old-looking and very ill. I took her to see the doctor and over the next couple of weeks we met very regularly. Without making it obvious, I gave her money and food. She wouldn't let me get too close, although I wanted to so much. I never told your mother about Emily's return but the day you brought Jamie home for dinner I could have died. I tried to act as normal as possible for fear that your mother would notice but it was too late. The moment he entered the house she knew, so too did Emily when she first saw you. You may not have noticed that you two look alike but you do.

"All that night we argued. She wanted to know how long I'd known and what I'd done about it. As much as I tried, I couldn't lie, not now, not after so much had happened. I explained how I'd seen her walking along the street and that I'd visited her almost every day. Your mother was so upset, but being the kind woman she was she understood, and even made sure that I kept going and making sure they were ok. Jamie never saw me visit the house but he almost caught me a few times. I had to reacquaint myself with all the back streets that I used as a boy. Your mother would often bake bread and food for me to take. She even gave me clothes, as she knew she would no longer need them. In her dying days, your mother cared more about other people than she did about herself. That's one of the reasons I fell in love with her. She was so special yet so ordinary.

"Although we had given up all hope of ever having our own baby, we never stopped trying. I remember getting home one day and finding your mother upstairs with the doctor 'It's a miracle,' she shouted 'A miracle!' I knew straight away what she was shouting about, she was pregnant. That day was one of the best days of her life. We tried to do everything in our power to make sure the baby would be born without any complications. The doctors couldn't understand how it was possible. There was so much damage caused in the first birth that to conceive was truly a miracle. As each month passed, we hoped and prayed that everything would go well and finally the day arrived. After six hours of rather scary labour we had a baby boy, we had Gavin.

"The both of your grew to be good healthy boys but, despite our continued attempts, we never had another child. For years, I've wanted to tell you this; I would find myself in your room in the middle of the night trying desperately to tell you, but no matter how hard I tried I could never do it. I thought you'd treat me differently if I did. That you wouldn't want to be here, that..."

I placed my fingers upon his lips. My head was travelling back and forth over my life. On one hand, I'd had a great life with a great family, but on the other hand the life I'd led was a sham, a life of lies and deceit. How could I reject a family that had loved and cared for me all my life? Yet how could I love a family that stole from me the right to know how I was born? My eyes that had slowly filled with tears now rested on the brink of overflowing. My body felt as though it was shutting down or taking a rest. Everything around me became blurry and hot, and then suddenly I felt peace.

My body felt light and free. All around me was light, masses of light. The air was filled with the smell of honey and hot chocolate. It took a few moments before I realised where I was but then it was clear. I was sitting in my favourite seat in Mrs Cook's tearoom. The warm feeling I had in my hands was coming from the overly large mug of hot chocolate that I held. It felt great just being there; it felt calm and safe. I'd been sitting for a while before I started to look around. In the far corner of the room I recognised some people; it was Dad, Mum, Gavin and me. Before I had the chance to give anything thought I was joined by Mrs Cook. "There're a lovely family, don't you think?" she said as she glanced with her head towards the table they sat on. "Always kind and considerate, always caring. You know them parents would do anything for them children, just look at them, two adorable young men. I remember this one time many years ago when the oldest boy wasn't feeling too well and his father made the trip all the way out here just to pick up some of his son's favourite cake. Now, if that's not love, I don't know what is. It's a special thing to have a family that truly loves you, a very special thing indeed. I see and hear lots of things in here you know, but anyone can see and hear. What's the use of hearing if you don't understand? What's the use of seeing if you don't believe? You have the strength to forgive, the strength to understand and the strength to believe things can be better. Don't waste what life you've lived on a life that you cannot restore. Live for tomorrow because today will always take care of itself."

As she touched my hands I drifted from the light and all went still and dark.

CHAPTER THIRTY-THREE
Forgiveness Opens Many Locked Doors

I don't remember having any more dreams. The next thing I recall was waking up in bed. Above, I could hear and see people. Their faces were a blur at first but then slowly they became clear. The closest person was Dad; he was sat on the side of the bed holding my hand. The other person I'd only seen a few times was the doctor who'd been at Mrs Blake's house the night she died. I didn't feel as if I was dead or unwell so I was surprised to see him.

I pushed myself upright and looked around. The doctor immediately rushed over and looked at me.

"How are you feeling?"

"I'm ok, I think."

Dad got up from the bed and moved over towards the window. I could feel the tension he carried with every step that he took. For the first time ever, I watched as Dad stood helpless and at the mercy of someone else. As I slept in the darkness, something had taken me and washed me. When I awoke I no longer felt strange or distant. I couldn't blame Dad for the events all those years ago. How could I judge a man who did nothing more than follow his heart and gave me nothing but love? He might have done wrong by not telling me sooner but we all make mistakes. I only had two options: I could either hold this against him for the rest of his life or be unhappy or I could carry on with life still having the love and security I'd grown up with. In any case, it wasn't just Dad who knew about this. There was a whole chain of people I would have to hate and that wasn't going to do anyone any good.

I walked over to Dad and stood next to him. As I took hold of his hand, I heard the door closing. On looking around, I could see that the doctor had left the room. Outside the window it was night time. The stars were bright and clear in the sky, as they lay scattered around the glow of the moon. The streetlights glittered and sparkled, sending rays of warmth in every direction, but Dad felt cold. It wasn't difficult to know what to say to him but it was hard to know how to start.

"I do understand," I began. "I know what you did was full of every good intention and I've never suffered in any way because of it. No matter how I was born I'll always know that it was you and Mum who cared for me, fed me, gave me clothes and a happy life. Nothing you've said will ever change that. But life is somewhat different now, and there's one thing that we have to do. Something that we have to do together."

"I know, Jamie"

"Yes, he has the right to know. He has the right to know about you, about me."

"I must speak with Emily first. She must be part of any decisions that have to be made. I'm sorry, son, but I must speak to her myself."

"I understand."

As he about turned to leave the room, I called to him. "Dad, I love you."

Instantly, he returned and grabbed me. His arms were like a locked cage as they held me tight. "I love you too, son."

With that, I pushed him towards the door. "Go." And he did.

I ventured downstairs feeling rather thirsty, where Jenny was kind enough to make me some hot chocolate and a ham sandwich. I sat down at the table where I was quickly joined by Gavin.

"Hello," he said rather quietly.

"Dad told me everything. I don't know what to say."

"There's nothing to say, Gavin. I haven't had a great deal of time to figure everything out but one thing is clear, nothing will change. I'm still the same person I was when I woke up this morning and so are you."

"Yes, but it's not fair."

"Gavin, listen to me, if there's one thing you learn in life it's this, life isn't fair. Life doesn't come with its own little rule book or guide through its intricate mazes. Life comes with no guarantees or helpful advice. Life is purely what you make it. We all choose our own paths, we all choose our heights and levels, we all choose how we live."

Gavin said nothing after that; he simply gave me a hug and a few simple words. "You'll always be my big brother."

"I know."

After I'd finished, I placed the dirty mug in the sink and went through to the main room. Anna was sitting next to Gran who was still visibly upset in front of the open fire. As I entered, neither of the two looked up. It was time to clear the air and disperse any tension or bad feelings. I walked over and sat on the floor next to Gran. Without looking at her, I spoke into the fire.

"I understand why you're upset and I want you to know that I'm ok. I realise that you were only trying to protect me and for that I'm grateful. But now is the time to move on. Let's not waste time being sad or unhappy; I know Mum would never have wanted that for any of us."

"Your mother was right about you, you are an angel," said Gran as her frail hands stroked my face.

I wasn't tired but for some reason I wanted to go back upstairs. Jenny had remade the bed with fresh covers and blankets. Staring out of the window, I slowly got undressed.

The world outside was massive. Looking into the darkness of the sky, I got the sudden urge to travel. I wanted to see far beyond the mixed landscape of Scotland. I wanted to see further than what Britain had to offer. For the first time in my life, I had direction. I wanted to travel the world. I wanted to learn first hand about all the places that I'd been taught about in school. Then it hit me! My ideal job, a career that I actually thought I could do and do well. I wanted to become an archaeologist. I couldn't wait to tell Dad, I was so excited. Dad had asked me many times what I was interested in doing and I had never been able to tell him, but now I was. It was as if by opening my eyes to life, life showed me the way to view who I was in a totally different way. I was given the key to unlock my destiny in a way that I never thought possible.

I went to bed that night full of hope. I didn't hear Dad coming back in so it must have been really late before he got home. I looked forward to waking up and starting the next day, fresh and with a different outlook.

CHAPTER THIRTY-FOUR
Revenge Prepared

The following morning came much sooner than I'd hoped for. "Son, wake up."

At first I thought I was dreaming but then the shaking became stronger. As my eyes opened and tried to adjust in the still darkness, I could hear Dad. "What's wrong?"

"Come quickly, you need to get dressed, I'll be downstairs. Be quick." A sense of panic could be felt in Dad's manner. His alarmed voice had awakened me to the brink of fear and worry. I quickly got out of bed, picked up the clothes from the floor that I'd worn the previous day, including underwear, and got rapidly changed. The house was in nearly complete darkness as I made my way down the stairs so I knew it was still really early. The only light that was on was coming from the kitchen where there was the sound of voices. On entering, I could see Dad sitting at the table speaking to Constable Irwin, while Jenny, who was looking rather tired and half dressed, was boiling the kettle. On my moving from the dark hall into the kitchen, the talk died.

"What's wrong Dad, what's wrong with Jamie?" God only knows how I knew something was wrong with Jamie but I did. All of a sudden I felt a real sense of danger and was immediately sick. I ran for the sink just in time before making a mess all over the floor.

Constable Irwin with his sniffer dog nose automatically

picked up on the fact that I knew he was there because of Jamie. "So you know Jamie was going somewhere?" His deep voice probing for an answer before I had the chance to think confused me. Dad stepped in and asked that he gave me a moment.

"Here, drink this," said Jenny at the same time casting an evil eye towards the Constable. "It's warm milk; it'll settle your stomach." I held the milk but before I got the cup to my mouth I was sick again. Something was terribly wrong. I could feel something unfamiliar deep down inside, something I'd never felt before. But although I hadn't felt it before, I knew what it was; it was danger, real danger.

After a few minutes I became steady. I was able to drink the now not so warm milk along with the thick skin that had formed a seal over its top. Sitting down at the table, I looked at Dad.

"Son, if you know anything, anything at all, you must tell us."

The only thing I knew was the plan, but that wasn't going to take place till the next day.

"Look young man, we don't have the time to be sitting around waiting on you making up some kind of cover story for your friend. Now be sharp about it and tell us where Jamie was going."

Constable Irwin's words had insulted me. I was enraged by the way in which he spoke and I found myself not being able to hold back. Standing up and pushing my face across the table to where he was sitting I began. "Firstly Constable, this is my home you're in at the moment so that means you'll be courteous when you're here. Secondly, my so-called friend is in fact my brother and I have no need to make up any cover story of any kind to tell you or anyone else." Straight away I could see a look of shock and surprise cross the Constable's face. Even Dad was taken aback by my sudden outburst. "I think I do know where Jamie has gone and he's only going because people like you failed to do what was right in the first place. He's going to do what anyone in his situation should do. He's going to get his revenge."

It was on the last word that suddenly the light in the kitchen went out. Jenny opened the door to the stove which helped to shed a little light into the room while Dad went to check the fuse box. Within moments, he was back. "It's not the fuse box, I've looked outside and all the street lights are out, there must have been a power cut." Jenny collected some candles from the cupboard and placed them on the table lit. "Son, I know that Jamie was wronged but we can't allow him to do something stupid that he might regret. We need to know where he is going."

Suddenly, I thought about Gavin and what I would have done if he had been placed in similar circumstances. Dad was right; I wouldn't let my brother carry out something that would affect him for the rest of his life in a bad way. I left the table and went up stairs to the bedroom. I opened the drawer to the table where I kept the plan then remembered. I hadn't put the plan in the drawer at all; Jamie had taken the plan and all the other pieces of paper away with him yesterday. He also said he would come back round later. I quickly went back down stairs to the kitchen. I found I was asking myself lots of questions.

"Jenny, did Jamie call round last night at all?"

"No, the last time I saw him was when you two were acting rather suspiciously in here yesterday afternoon."

I placed my head in my hands. How could I have been so stupid? Jamie never had any intention whatsoever of taking me with him. This was always something he was going to do on his own or with help I didn't yet know about. No wonder he was so easy to convince when changing the plan. All he was doing was pacifying me. I was left with no choice but to tell Dad and the Constable what was about to happen at Sir Richard's boarding school. I briefly explained what I remembered about Jamie's initial plan and why he was going to carry it out. I could hear the shock in their voices as they inhaled a deep breath at each sentence. After I'd told them there was a deadly silence.

"We have no time to lose," said Constable Irwin, and at that we all stood up.

"What should we do?" asked Dad.

"We need to make contact with the school and warn them that Jamie is on the way."

"But how? If the power's down so too will the phone lines."

"Damn it, you're right."

"We have no choice but to drive there." Everyone made their way to the front door including me.

"Where do you think you're going?" growled the constable.

"I'm coming too." I could feel his face grimacing at my reply but he didn't say any more. After we had wrapped up, Dad gave Jenny a light kiss on the cheek, said a few words and then we left.

The snow was falling fast in the sharp easterly wind. All around the trees whipped back and forth in a hurried and excited dance. "We have to go and see Emily first. She needs to know what's happening," said Dad in a concerned voice. We entered the cold interior of the new police car and made forth for 112 High View Road. As we approached the door, Mrs Richardson was already there. "Come in, come in." We made our way into the main room where it was filled with dozens of lit candles. As our eyes crossed paths, we both paused. Although we didn't exchange any words at that time, she gave me a smile that only a mother could give. I wasn't quite sure how to return the gesture and so replied with something more like a grin than anything else.

"Have you any news?" she almost begged.

"We think we now know where he's going and why,

but we don't have time to talk. By the looks of it, Jamie's already had a good head start on us." It was just as we were about to leave the room that something struck me. Horror filled the now empty space in the cabinet where they should have been. "*Mrs Richardson,*" I shouted.

Everyone poured back into the room. "What is it, son?"

"Mrs Richardson, the gun cabinet, have you taken anything from it?"

"No! Why?" I lifted one of the lit candles towards the cabinet. As I got closer it was clear to see. Missing from two of its polished brass holders were two weapons, one shotgun and a pistol. I knew Jamie was more than able to use both of these weapons as he'd told me he'd used them with Farmer McNeil. My heart sank as the seriousness of the situation became apparent. Fear now possessed every person in the room, including me. Immediately we left the house and made for the police car. The sun was now just appearing in the background of the snow-laden sky as we pulled away from the house and away from Rockfield. The journey was going to take over three hours if we didn't stop even once. As the car made its way towards Sir Richard's, I couldn't help but think about what Jamie was doing. If only I'd tried stopping him, if only I knew who he was, before all of this started.

By the time we knew Jamie was away, he was arriving at the great towering gates of Sir Richard's. Two days earlier he had arranged to be collected and driven the one hundred and thirty miles to the village of Queenslie where the school was situated on its outskirts. The village itself was small. There were all but a hundred or so people living in it. There was no law enforcement for miles, so on a good day it would take at least an hour for a constable to arrive and even longer if he was unavailable or already on a call. As Jamie left the blue Ford car and entered the gates, he took in a deep breath. Carrying a large backpack, he made his way through the trees and towards the main building. It was eight in the morning and he knew most of the residents would still be fast asleep, including the teachers. The steam from the kitchen part of the building rose into the daybreak sky giving the only sense that the building was occupied. The gardens were filled with crisp white snow that sank three inches with every step. As he neared the tree line, he took a long look to see if anyone was around. Feeling confident he calmly crossed the open lawns until he came level with the high stone walls and stained glass windows of Sir Richard's Grand entrance.

Being careful to make as little noise as possible, he made the walk that would bring him to a side entrance of a large hall-like building. He paused for a second and listened before giving the door three small but distinct knocks - knock, knock knock. From the other side of the door came a similar reply. The knocks were the same in number and equally spaced, knock, knock, knock.

Slowly the door began to open. The hand that clasped the inside handle was small. As the door opened wider, a figure emerged from the darkness.

"Ian."

"Jamie, it's so good to see you again, quickly, come in."

As he entered, Ian pulled the door closed behind them. Although it had been over three years since they last met, Jamie thought that it felt like yesterday.

"Well, look at you. You're still a scrawny little thing, ain't you?" Ian laughed.

"You haven't changed all that much yourself."

"Maybe not physically but mentally I'm a different person. I'm stronger now. But, anyway, tell me a bit about you. Your letters have always been vague. But from the sounds of them life hasn't been that great. I was sorry to hear about your father."

"Thank you, anyway, you know I've never been one for letter writing." The both of them hugged while Jamie laughed nervously.

"Are you sure you want to help?" Jamie asked, holding Ian by his shoulders and staring directly into his light green eyes. "It's not too late to back out."

"Remember, what we said in our first year? Friends together you and me, together we will always be. Where one goes the other follows, always there when trouble's calling. Do you remember?"

"Of course, I should never have asked."

"Come, you must be hungry, I have some food at the back of the stage."

The boys walked across the main hall and down a flight of side steps leading to the bottom level of the stage. Ian had gathered a mixture of food from the kitchen that morning along with some milk and apple juice. They talked about many things, including me. Ever since he was expelled from school, Jamie had kept in touch with Ian by writing as many letters as he could. Sometime he would only be able to write once every week or so because he couldn't afford the postage. However, in the last two weeks Jamie had written almost every day. By writing in a schoolboy code that they had designed they were able to discuss the how and where of Jamie's intended plan.

After they had eaten some of the food and drank most of the milk they began to put the plan into execution. The previous day Ian had managed to sneak into the headmaster's office and acquire half a dozen permission slips. One of the things Ian was good at was forgery. Imitating his parent's signatures from correspondence to the school Reverend, he was able to neatly and precisely place their mark upon anything. On this occasion, all he had to do was forge the headmaster's signature and a brief note asking that the named person attend the large sports hall at a certain time.

After running over the plan two or three times they were ready. "Well, this is it then," said Ian. Jamie gave just another nervous laugh. They exchanged a firm handshake followed by a hug then Ian left. All they now had to do was exactly what they had discussed. Any deviation whatsoever could spell disaster. They both knew everything had to be precise and on time. Jamie watched as Ian made the fifty yard walk across the hall and out through the large double doors at the south side of the building.

The closer we got, the harder the snow fell, impeding our progress. We had been driving for little over an hour when the weather conditions became an almost whiteout.

"Do you think he'll do anything really silly?" Dad asked me uncertainly.

I paused. "They, in effect, killed his father." I said slowly.

"Keep driving, constable. We are running out of time!" shouted Dad over the sound of the engine and high winds that crashed upon the car windows. The constable didn't reply, but he must have heard as the car started to go faster. As we ploughed our way though the snow, Jamie was now entering preparation stage two.

Opening the large backpack he had taken with him, he removed its contents one by one and placed them spaciously on the stone floor in front of him. There were four lengths of thick rope, three small heavy lengths of chain, each with a key turn padlock, one pistol, one shotgun, four small lengths of sharp coarse rope, one tub of bright red paint with paintbrush and half a gallon of fish oil.

Picking up the chain, Jamie walked up the side steps for the second time and made his way to the west doors. Here he wrapped a chain around the wrought iron door handles and clicked a padlock over the joining links, sealing the door closed. He then did the same on the north doors, followed by the small exit door located back where he had been seated under the main stage. There was now only one way in and one way out.

Jamie had intimated in his plan that he was going to carry it out on New Year's Day; however, he knew all along he would be carrying it out on New Year's Eve. You see, it was the school's custom that once a year on New Year's Eve at the hour of high twelve, more commonly known as twelve noon, the pupils and their parents would attend a celebration to Sir Richard. Sir Richard designed and built the school and they would be celebrating its one hundred and fiftieth anniversary that very day. Because of this, he knew almost every parent would be in attendance for this momentous and historic date in the school's history. After all, most of the boy's fathers had attended the school themselves.

Standing over the spread of items on the floor, Jamie then collected the four lengths of thick rope. Placing each neatly over his arm, he made for a small doorway to the right hand side of where he was standing. As he entered the doorway, he was met with a steel ladder that climbed up into the open ceiling, above the main stage. Slowly, he climbed the cold steel ladder until eventually he reached the top. Using his hands to see, he carefully followed the thin banisters that were raised on each side of the narrow lighting platforms. Everything up there was dark and spooky. The smell of damp from the semi rotting roof trusses above his head gave the feeling of neglect. By now, his eyes were adjusted to the lack of light and he found himself now standing at the very edge of the front lighting platform. Placing the ropes carefully over the banister, he collected them one by one. Although he'd practised tying the knots several times before, he'd never considered trying it in the dark. This proved to add valuable minutes on the times he had so carefully worked out. He was just placing the last rope through its second loop when something happened. There was someone coming.

Although it was dark, Jamie knew he'd be seen. Just as the south doors burst open, he jumped in a shadow cast by the dark red wine coloured curtains of the stage. Peering out, he could see two boys. "Why is it it's always us having to do snappy McDonald's dirty work? Quite frankly, I'm sick of it: go here, go there. Anyone would think we were his slaves, for Christ sake."

"John, will you just shut up and let's get a move on? My parents will be here any minute and I told them I'd meet them at the main entrance. You know what my father's like if you keep him waiting."

"Look, there they are." The two boys moved over to the far corner of the hall where some tables had been stacked. As Jamie peered over the side of the platform to see what they were doing, one of the ropes started to slip. Quickly, he reached out but it was too late. The rope slipped over the banister with a heavy swishing noise and landed with a thump on the stage below.

The sound of the boys crashing about the tables ceased.

"Andrew," whispered John. "Did you hear that?"

"I sure did. Go and see what it was."

"Why don't you?"

"Oh go on and stop being such a baby," Andrew hissed.

John cautiously moved toward the side steps leading up onto the stage. Almost tiptoeing, he quietly scanned the darkness. Jamie could see he was getting closer and closer to the rope. His heart pounded at a thousand beats a second. All this work, all this planning, was going to go to waste for nothing, he thought. Right then there was a scream.

"AHHHHH!" John cried and Andrew immediately ran towards the stage. "Help me Andrew, help me," John cried, sounding in pain.

Andrew ran up the stairs, tripping up at the same time and crashing forward on his nose. Quickly, he got to his feet, wiping the blood that now poured down his face. "A snake!" John screamed, "A snake, quick, get it off me."

As Andrew neared the centre front of the stage, he could see John lying on the floor fighting. "I'm here John," Andrew called, at which John burst out laughing.

"Ha ha ha ha! If only you could have seen your face."

Andrew exploded with anger. As the adrenaline had so quickly flushed into his body so too did it quickly drain away. With a hard stiff kick, he launched his foot right into the side of John's ribs. "Ouch, that hurt."

"Well, now you know what it feels like. I almost broke my flaming neck running up those stairs." John got to his feet, dropping the rope to the ground, as Andrew stormed off back down the stairs towards the tables. "Hurry up, my Dad's going to kill me. Look at the mess I'm in."

"Sorry!" The two boys lifted the table and quickly took it back through the double doors and away.

Jamie breathed a sigh of relief. "That was close," he whispered to himself. With more caution than before, he climbed back down the steel ladder and entered the stage. Collecting the rope, he quickly went back up and finished what he started. Everything was almost done. Back downstairs, he collected the half-gallon of fish oil and made for the front of the stage. Unscrewing its large metal top, he poured it all over the polished cherry floor boards, making sure not to get any on his feet. Moving to the side of the stage, he then pulled the curtains closed. He gave everything one last check before proceeding to the fourth and final stage.

His stomach turned rapidly with butterflies and his hands shook as he reached down upon the floor for the remaining items. Placing the coarse ropes in the backpack, he swung it over his shoulder. He then slid the pistol into the back of his trousers, making it clear for anyone to see that he had it. With the shotgun in one hand and the paint in the other, he made his final trip back up the stairs to the main body of the hall. Taking one last deep breath, he made for a small alcove to the right hand side of the south doors.

All he now had to do was wait.

Our progress, in the meantime, was getting better. We had reached well over the halfway mark and the snow had started to die down. No one said much at all during that journey. It was as if each of us had sunk within his own little world of thoughts. Dad was especially quiet and somewhat withdrawn from the whole situation. Jamie, however, was on the brink of carrying his plan into execution.

The time was just approaching ten a.m. The entire school had now awoken and the sounds of people talking and laughing rang throughout. The pipes that climbed the walls in the small alcove where Jamie was standing whispered as they carried the trails of conversations from elsewhere in the school. Jamie listened as the whispering somehow sounded like singing. His early morning travelling had started to take its first effects. As he stood upright on the wall, he felt his body slipping. His eyes twitched repeatedly as they screamed to stay open. His body now wanted to rest, but Jamie fought it. Using every ounce of strength, he stayed upright and awake. Although his senses had died somewhat, he knew what he heard. Coming towards him, getting faster and faster, was the sound of footsteps. Just as he hoped, the hall was now filled with bright light from the early morning sun. Within seconds the doors were about to burst open and the final stage of his plan would be nearly complete.

The footsteps were now only a few paces away, three, two, one, and then the doors opened. They needed to walk about six paces before he would see them. Six, five, four, three, two, one, and there they were, all four of them. Ian had carried out his part of the plan precisely. The animals were now in sight. As a hunter sets a trap for the wild bear so do did Jamie set a trap, a trap that would see him reach the goal he sought for the last three years, the goal of revenge.

"What did your note say, Stephen?" asked William. Stephen rummaged inside his dark blue school blazer and removed a small piece of paper. "You are requested to be present in the main hall at ten a.m. sharp, signed headmaster."

"That's exactly what mine says," said James followed by Stuart.

"Well, we'll just have to wait and see why," William said.

The ball was now firmly in Jamie's court, but he needed them to enter the hall a little further before he could continue. His wait wasn't long because in no time they started to move around. Watching very carefully through the haze of the sun, he stepped out. At first, nobody noticed as they were too busy playing around.

But then Stuart turned around. "Hello Sir," he pronounced, thinking Jamie was the headmaster. The others quickly quit their childish behaviour and stood still.

"Not the kind of behaviour we expect to see from sixth year students now, is it?" Jamie admonished in a loud and overly abrupt voice.

The boys straightened up in acknowledgement of the stern arrival of who they still presumed was their headmaster. "We're sorry, Sir," spoke Stuart who was still at the forefront of the boys.

Jamie tossed the backpack towards Stuart's feet. "Well pick it up," he shouted in the still stern voice. As he did, Jamie walked forward across the beam of sunlight and into direct view of the boys. No one spoke; no one even dared whisper a word. Their bodies had become stunned and numb.

"It's been a long time... Stuart, William, James, Stephen," Jamie pointed at each one deliberately as he uttered their names. "Oh, and we'd better not forget your father, Stuart, yes we'd better not forget about him. I'm sure he'll be arriving here very soon, *very soon indeed.*"

"What do you want?" whined James.

"I would have thought that was obvious, James, wouldn't you?" Jamie lifted his left arm that had been holding the shotgun semi-hidden behind his back. The boys would have screamed if only they could have mustered the power.

"Move to the stage, *now,*" Jamie hissed. The boys walked backwards slowly until they were almost touching the front of the protruding stage.

"You're not going to kill us, are you?" Stephen whimpered. "Please don't kill us."

Jamie gave no sign of an answer to Stephen's insolent attempt to grovel. He was now fully acting out what he had dreamt and prayed for. He was now going to get what he deserved, no matter what.

"Well, come on now, Stuart, empty the bag out."

Slowly, Stuart opened the lid to the backpack peering inside for something that would perhaps bite or sting.

"Well we don't have all day," Jamie raged. Seeing the situation was heating up, Stuart plunged his hand deep inside the bag and removed the ropes.

"Now, the four of you, get undressed."

"You what?" said William, feeling a little brave. That was, until Jamie raised the shotgun and he backed down. The boys, frightened and fearful for their lives, did as he said. Removing their shoes and uniforms, they stood half-naked.

"I *said* take your clothes off and that means *all* of your clothes. After all, it's nothing we've not all send before now, is it?" Jamie's mood was starting to change. He was now more aggressive and mean-spirited. The boys removed their vests, socks and underwear, leaving them to stand cold and completely naked. "Well boys, nothing much has grown about you since the last time we met?"

Chalk white from head to toe, James bent over and was profusely sick. "Get him up now!" The others pulled James up while he brushed the mess from his face. Jamie then took a few paces forward and placed the tin of red paint on the floor.

"You pick it up," Jamie pointed and said to Stephen. Slowly, Stephen edged forward and collected the tin from where it sat.

"Now open it." As Jamie had already loosened the lid it came off quite freely. "Now, this is important so listen carefully. Take the paint brush and paint a cross on each of their chests then paint their faces."

"Please, Jamie, don't do this." Stephen sobbed.

"You didn't stop when I cried, did you Stephen? You didn't stop when I was screaming in pain, DID YOU?"

Stephen said no more and retreated the few paces back to the others, where he started to carry out Jamie's demand. Dipping the brush into the paint, he stood at the front of William and applied the bright red paint in the form of a cross on his chest. As the paint dribbled its way down his body Stephen took the brush to his face. Finally, the three boys were painted leaving only the artist himself.

"Now Stuart, you have the pleasure of painting Stephen *and hurry up about it,* we're running out of time." The boys seemed to quiver at the word time. It was as if it suddenly hit them that they might not have much of it left. "Just one more thing now before we move on," Jamie laughed. "The ropes, pick them up."

The boys bent down and each collected a rope. "Who's the strongest out of you all?" Jamie demanded but no-one answered. "You've all turned modest I see. William, tie everybody's hands behind their backs."

It took a few minutes and Jamie watched carefully to make sure everyone was tied tightly. "All done. Now aren't you the lucky one?"

William understandably seemed more frightened than

ever. "Come here, and bring your rope." Jamie snapped. William approached with extreme caution. Jamie knew he had no fear of William attempting any sudden retaliation. He was far too scared to disobey him. "Kneel down and put your hands behind your back." As William did as he was told, Jamie placed the shotgun on the floor, but, at the same time, he made it perfectly clear to everyone that he possessed a handgun. In moments, William was tied and back with the others.

As they stood cold and dripping with paint, Jamie was ready to carry on. "Up onto the stage. Move it!" Jamie directed them to take the row of steps to the left-hand side of the stage. As the last of them moved upwards, Jamie followed. Just as he stepped off the last step, he flicked three switches on the wall. Suddenly the stage was engulfed in light. As they walked around a dividing wall onto the main stage area they viewed their fate before them. Strung from somewhere in the ceiling were four ropes. Each appeared equally spaced and hung at the same height from the ground.

"Move forward."

With the shotgun placed behind each of their backs, Jamie moved them into position. The boys shook, helpless with fear. Jamie placed the shotgun once more down upon the floor. Moving carefully behind each boy, he placed a noose around each of their necks. All the preparations were now complete. Now it was do or die.

CHAPTER THIRTY-FIVE
A Healing Stage

The town of Queenslie was now in sight. The constable estimated that we were only fifteen minutes away. I could feel a tremendous sense of achievement. It was strange, to say the least. I hadn't done anything except travel in a car yet I felt as though I had just won something or the sort of feeling you get when you know you've done your parents proud. The tension in the car was almost exploding out of the windows. Dad couldn't stop tapping his foot while the constable kept clutching the steering wheel in a rocking motion with his large hands.

Jamie was ecstatic. He was almost there. He felt achievement; he knew nothing now could stop him. The only uncertainty he had was not knowing when we would arrive. I was right in thinking Jamie had no intention of ever taking me with him. But he did count on me somehow finding out he was away and fitting two and two together. He hoped that any minute we would arrive at the school and raise the alarm. All he had to do was sit, a luxury that the four boys didn't have – as Jamie so elegantly informed them.

"I hope you're all comfortable. I think now would be a good time to point out your situation. At the other side of this curtain is a five-foot drop. A drop big enough that should you fall over the edge you would be hung. The chances of accidentally falling can be minimised by not moving. The oil under your feet is enough to send you right over the edge." Jamie laughed. "Let's see how long you can last on the edge; I've been lucky, I've managed for over three years so far. But I have a funny feeling you four won't last anywhere near that long."

"Jamie, we're sorry, we should never have done it. It was stupid, we understand that."

"Dear, dear William, if only you had told me that long ago, that way we could have avoided this nasty mess. But, seeing as how you didn't, that makes things rather tricky. You see, whilst you've enjoyed life here and with your parents, I haven't had that luxury. Instead, I've had to suffer my own father killing himself because of you. I've had to suffer living the life of a beggar eating scraps in the outer reaches of hell. And why? I'll tell you why." Jamie moved close behind William and placed his hand against his back. "I've lived the last years of my life in a constant nightmare because of you, because of the four of you. I never got the justice I deserved. Instead, I lost everything including myself. Ever since that day, you've controlled my life, my every move, but not now. Now I control everything. Now I say what happens and at what pace."

Jamie prodded William making him slowly edge back and forth." Please, Jamie, I'm begging you."

William's pleas fell on deaf ears as Jamie walked to the side of the curtain and peered out into the hall. "Not long now."

The school was now visible in the distance. Its great clock tower stood tall over the tree covered landscape. Soon we would be there. The closer we got, the more I could just make out the time on the clock face. As we rounded the last corner onto the final straight before turning into the wide long drive, I could see it was nearly eleven o'clock. As we drove up the driveway to the front entrance we saw lots of cars. I'd never noticed before but there were quite a few cars behind us as well. The constable never even attempted to park the car. As we arrived outside the front doors, he just stopped. Dad was just about to get out when the constable stopped him.

"Wait, we mustn't rush in, it could cause panic and we don't know if we need to panic just yet." Dad quickly agreed and we exited the car calmly.

As we made our way up the stairs I felt a sudden urge to turn right.

"Excuse me, boy, would you point me in the direction of your headmaster," the constable asked a passing student.

"Well, to tell you the truth, I'm not too sure. I last saw him in the dining hall but that was half an hour ago." Seeing the change in the Constable's facial expression, the boy quickly added, "But I'll go and find him for you."

"Well, hurry up, boy."

My urge to turn right was now getting stronger and stronger; something inside was dragging me along. "Dad?"

"Yes, son?"

"We have to go this way."

Dad looked at me but asked no questions. "Come on then."

As we walked along the corridors, the feelings got stronger. Seeing a policeman in the school was starting to attract a crowd. Everywhere we went we could see pupils with their parents.

"Down here." It was only when we turned down a long corridor that I recalled the dream I'd had the previous day. Everything I was seeing was identical. The doors, the floors, the windows, everything. Reason told me that I hadn't been here in the flesh before, but somehow I felt as though I had.

"What's the meaning of this, Constable?" hollered a loud deep voice from behind. The constable tuned quicker than a spinning bottle to find a tall man swooshing towards him in a large black cloak.

"Headmaster, I presume?"

"Your presumption may well be correct but it was I who asked a question."

"I haven't the time to talk and even less to listen. You must follow us and listen as we go."

It was plain to see the headmaster wasn't accustomed to being spoken to in such a way and he certainly didn't like it happening in front of the ever-growing crowd. I remember looking back and guessing there must have been close to a hundred people behind us. As we walked, the constable tried to inform the headmaster of the possible situation in as few words as possible. The feeling inside was now at its greatest. We had come to a large set of doors with no other way to go but through them. Everyone had stopped and the corridor fell silent. I knew Jamie was on the other side of these doors, and so too did he know about us.

"He's inside." Everyone was watching me. The headmaster didn't even know who I was let alone how I knew my way around his school.

The constable looked at me with his policeman eyes and asked, "Is it safe to go in?"

If I'd been asked that question under any other circumstances I would have said I didn't know, but there and then I knew. "Yes, yes it is."

Without further seconds being wasted, the constable placed his bulging hands on either door and swung them open. The sun shed a blanket of light across the room, giving us very little to see. As everyone slowly moved inside, the hall echoed with gasps of horror. As I stood, my heart sunk to the lowest levels it could have possibly found.

As the curtains drew apart, there in front of us were four naked boys. At first everyone presumed they were dead, for they never moved a muscle. First appearances were that they were covered in blood, victims of some kind of ritual killing or sacrifice, but suddenly, one of the boys spoke. "Please don't come any further. He wants our parents to come in or we'll all be killed!"

The boy furthest to the right of the stage could be seen wetting himself. Fearful was a mild way of expressing how they appeared. The headmaster directed an older boy in a black robe to go somewhere. The hall stood silent until he returned. As he entered, so too did a group of men and woman. Instantaneously, the women in the group started to scream. On seeing what was before them, the men attempted to send them away.

"They need to stay," called a voice from the stage. "They need to see the kind of children they have. Some need to see the kind of husbands they have."

I knew the voice belonged to Jamie. Dad held me tight as we watched him walk out from the side of the curtain. He looked calm and at ease as he carried himself and a shotgun in front of the now two hundred strong onlookers. "Now, when I call your name I want you to ask your parents to step forward.

"James." Without hesitating, James did exactly as he was asked. "Mother, Father." Everyone watched as Mr and Mrs Williams stepped forward.

"Please come closer." Jamie prompted the couple to within a few feet of the stage. Any embarrassment they may have felt over their child being naked wasn't showing. Taking his time, Jamie asked that Stephen did the same followed by William and finally Stuart.

"So at long last I have the pleasure of meeting Mr Grierson. Tell me, Mr Grierson, do you still hold a position within the Royal Bank of Scotland?"

Pushed forward by his anxious wife, he replied, "I don't see what my position has to do with this or anything else. If it's money you want just say. I can have any amount here within hours."

"Now, now, Mr Grierson, I haven't asked you to come forward in order to extort money from you. And in all honesty I'm quite surprised that that's what you're even thinking."

"Well if it's not money, tell us what you want."

"*What I want!* You no longer have the power to give me what I want, but you sure had the power to take it away. That's right, you, Mr Grierson, you used your power to destroy what I needed. Now it's time for me to destroy something that's irreplaceable to you."

"*No, please!* Don't do it," Mr Grierson cried.

"What I now do lies in your hands. If you need a clue I'll give you one, but one only, after that it's *do or die*. Do you understand?"

"Yes."

Slowly and clearly Jamie spoke his clue: "Mason Richardson." Mr Grierson stumbled in a wave of emotion. The look on his face was revenge enough for Jamie, but it had to go further. It had to finish once and for all.

"So now the picture is painted. Now you understand why I'm here before you on such a day. This day you thought would be full of happiness and fond memories. This day you thought would be filled with pride as you watched your son write his name upon the roll of Sir Richard. Such a day, with all its goodness, was what my mother and father should have had the chance to experience and treasure. But you saw to it that they didn't, you and the four that stand ashamed and broken before you. Now is the time for you to confess, if not for me but for the sake of your child and those of the parents who stand next to you.

"I'm not even sure if the other parents know what happened to me at the hands of these four. So what I need you to do is tell them."

"Please, Jamie, don't do this."

Jamie spat at the floor in discontent at Mr Grierson's plea.

364

"We're running out of time, Mr Grierson."

"Alright, alright.

"They did it." As he spoke, he pointed his hands towards the stage and looked back at the crowd. "Three years ago these four boys, one of whom I'm ashamed to say is my son, abused and raped the boy who now holds them. Out of love or guilt for having reared such a monster of a child, I added further punishment to the boy by framing his father, for a crime he didn't commit. In trying to protect what was mine, I ruined a perfectly happy family."

Mr Grierson buckled at the knees, gulping back his shame. The other parents looked shocked and horrified, including Mrs Grierson who had been kept from hearing about this certain family secret. No one went to his aid. The hall fell to a deathly silence, only being disturbed by the occasional whimpering of the ashamed boys.

"Jamie, it's time to go home, son." Dad stepped forward and offered his hand towards the stage.

"I'm sorry, Thomas, but the stage is set and the play is yet to finish. I've still to hear from the accused themselves." The look on Jamie's face was sadness. He appeared heartbroken and sunken as he moved slowly to the front edge of the stage. "Now I'm ready. Now I want to hear from you. Whichever of you chooses to speak first shows great courage, and forgiveness is awaiting him."

Somehow, Jamie seemed older and wiser. He gave depth to his words, making them sound out of place in his boyishly thin body, but they were nevertheless listened to with open ears. As Mr Grierson remained cowering on the floor reduced to that same state to which Jamie had been abandoned in the shower block all those years ago, William began to speak, telling the story of how that night over three years ago when after returning from a later than usual run, they happened upon Jamie in the showers. He hadn't heard them as they entered nor did he hear when they whispered about what they could do. William told of how, prompted by James, they entered the shower where they found Jamie and raped him. He told, without choosing his words, of how they molested and taunted Jamie for over an hour. He told about how finally they left him bleeding and hurt. The shock and horror of his story brought anger to the room, but he wasn't finished. Continuing, he explained how Stuart was able to convince his father that they needed his help. Mr Grierson agreed on the one condition that he met with the boys and they told him the truth. Having no choice and finding all other chances of help cut off, they confessed their guilt. Knowing what his son and the others had done, Mr Grierson stood firm to his word and immediately implemented a way of getting rid of the problem by cutting it off at its roots.

The other boys' cries became more noticeable as William stopped. Mrs Grierson couldn't even look at her son or the others. Suddenly, she moved. Everyone watched in amazement as she bent down and collected the tin of paint that still sat opened on the floor. No one could have guessed what she was about to do. Her frail little hand held the handle of the paint pot tightly as she made the few paces back to her husband.

Looking down she slowly raised the tin, tipping it upside down and pouring its contents all over him. "Now you get up on that stage with them where you belong." Her hand was pointing directly at the headmaster. "You're the reason this whole matter was swept under the carpet. You're the one that made this out to be some trivial matter when it was raised at the school board. Now you get up there with them where you belong." The hall immediately broke out in cheers. The headmaster ran from the hall as Mr Grierson crawled to the foot of the stage.

Jamie had achieved his goal. He had received complete and utter revenge. "Excuse me," he called out. The cheers died away promptly and all eyes returned once more to Jamie. "I have one last departing scene before the end.

366

Placing the shotgun on the floor Jamie moved up close behind the boys. Standing with his arms open wide he suddenly pushed them off the edge of the stage.

Everyone's screams turned to laugher as they saw that the ropes just gave way sending the boys dropping to the floor. Perhaps through exhaustion or maybe just because he was overwhelmed, Jamie simply sat crossed legged in the centre of the stage. I watched in amazement as he casually looked around the hall. Like a sponge, he soaked in every ounce of emotion that lingered in the air. As everyone talked and Jamie sat, no one noticed the movements of Mr Grierson. Suddenly pulling himself upon the stage, he grabbed the shotgun that Jamie had left on the floor. Everyone shouted for Jamie to move but he simply closed his eyes and lay back on the stage floor. As Mr Grierson walked towards Jamie, the constable tried unsuccessfully to clear the room. No one seemed at all bothered at the fact that Mr Grierson was unstable and appeared very capable of shooting at them.

"Do you know what you've done? Do you? You've just destroyed me, but if you think for one minute I'm going to go down without a fight you're wrong. I always hated your father. He was always such a *nice* man. Everyone liked him and his happy go lucky smile. He needed to be brought down a peg or two and I'm glad it was me that knocked him down. Now, I have the pleasure of doing it all over again." By this stage, Mr Grierson was standing over Jamie. The shotgun was barely inches from his head, yet still Jamie kept silent. "Just like your father I see. He never had much to say at his downfall, either."

With a sudden jolt Jamie got to his feet. The rather startled Mr Grierson took a few steps backwards. "Some people just never learn," roared Jamie in a boiling rage. His face exploded with anger and his words spat with a fiery zest. "Even when broken you still manage to work. Defeated you still persist to be king." The shotgun shook violently at

Jamie as he neared. "Well go on. Shoot. Pull the trigger and show us all what a man you are. Maybe you could call your son up onto the stage and it could be a family occasion."

"Dad please don't, we brought this upon ourselves. I brought this upon us." Stuart was the only boy out of the four still to be there. The others had quickly run out of the hall the minute they were free. Although he clearly heard his son's words, Mr Grierson showed no change in his posture.

"Well, come on then. I tell you what. I'll make it easier for you shall I?" Jamie reached round his back with his right hand. As quick as a flash, his hand returned adorned with a pistol. "Now that you feel threatened, it should be easier for you. *So do it.*"

Mr Grierson screamed then click. Death fell upon the hall. As if the air had been sucked out by God himself everyone stopped breathing. "No, it can't be."

"Do you honestly think I came here with the intention of killing anyone? I knew I was capable of carrying out today with words and sight only. The human senses are far more powerful than bullets. The guns don't even work for Christ sake. The firing pins were removed years ago. But at least now we all know the kind of man you really are, the kind of man that will rot in hell. Get out my sight."

As Jamie was about to walk off down the side steps of the stage, something stopped him. Pausing, he then turned round and walked straight back to Mr Grierson. We watched in anticipation. The tension was like nothing I'd ever felt. Jamie stared at Mr Grierson for a second then said, "Boo!"

Suddenly, Mr Grierson jumped backwards. He jumped backwards straight into the oil that lay invisibly on the stage floor. His footwork was hysterical in his attempts to stay upright. As he danced on the stage everyone laughed, and they laughed even more when he crashed on the floor. Jamie dropped the pistol and made his way off the stage to the sound of hysterical laughter.

For the first time as he stepped onto the hall floor he looked at me. Dad grabbed the constable by the arm as he made forth towards Jamie. "Don't you think the boy's been through enough? With a sigh the constable just looked at Dad then proceeded. As he neared Jamie, he stopped. We couldn't hear what he said to him but it was short. We expected him to remove his handcuffs and place Jamie under arrest, but he didn't, he continued to walk past him and up to the stage to where Mr Grierson was still sliding around on the floor.

"Mr Grierson, you're under arrest for the attempted murder of Jamie Richardson and in connection with conspiracy to cover up a crime, for the theft of monies from the Royal Bank of Scotland and for perverting the course of justice. You have the right to remain silent but anything you do say will be taken down and may be used against you in a court of law. You have the right to an attorney. Do you understand these rights?"

"*Yes, yes.*"

As the constable bent down to pull Mr Grierson from the ground, he saw Stuart standing watching. "You'd better go get washed and changed because you're next along with your friends." The naked boy retired from the hall looking bewildered. For the last three years, he'd presumed that he and his friends had escaped their crime and were free. Only now did he realise a crime never goes unpunished. The two hundred strong crowd parted, forming a straight path towards the doors. Shaking and in tears Stuart left the hall, surrounded by jolts of verbal abuse and shouts.

Jamie slowly made the short walk to where Dad and I were standing. His body was exhausted and pale. It was hard to think of something to say, so Dad did the next best thing. "Come here."
Standing in the middle of the hall the three of us hugged. Jamie cried and so too did Dad while the crowd that showed

no sign of dispersing clapped. Our hug only broke because we were disturbed.

"My dear boy, I hope you'll accept my sincerest apologies. Words can't express how sorry I am for how my family has treated you and the pain that they have caused." In her hand, Mrs Grierson held a book, a book that brought a huge smile to Jamie's face. "My son doesn't deserve a place in this book, but you do." Dad pre-empted Mrs Grierson's question by placing in Jamie's hand a gold pen. Jamie gave us all a proud look before he neatly scrolled his signature upon the dark brown leather bound book. His hand shook as it pulled back revealing the jet-black signature. Jamie's plan had worked out far better than he could have ever dreamt. Seeing he was stuck for words, Mrs Grierson said nothing more. She leaned forward and gave him a kiss on the forehead. "May God be with you," and with that she walked away.

The three of us made our way out the hall and along the winding corridors towards the front entrance. Our steps were short and all conversation was non-existent. With Dad in the middle of his two sons, we walked proud and strong. There was now only one thing left to do. Dad had to tell Jamie that he was his father. With every step, I wondered not only how Dad would tell him but also how Jamie would take the news.

We neared the entrance to the sound of voices. Making the last right turn onto the marble floor, we found the parents of Stephen, William and James. As we neared, their talking stopped. It was clear they were very upset. "It's ok," said Dad confidently and in rather protective manner.

We continued walking and were met half way towards the doors by the boys' three fathers. Mr Turner stepped to the forefront. "Mr Richardson, I speak on behalf of all our families when I say sorry. What you just did took courage and amazing strength. Although I don't agree with all of

370

your methods, I congratulate you and promise that our sons will be severely dealt with. I'm not sure if our families will ever repair after this, but I certainly hope you're now able to move on and find happiness."

Jamie extended his hand and both he and Mr Turner shook.

CHAPTER THIRTY-SIX
A New Year Begins

Dad walked us outside where he asked us to stay for a few moments, while he went back inside. Over five minutes had passed before he returned holding a set of car keys. "This way."

We followed him as he walked through the snow towards a car. Without asking any questions, we got inside and made forth on the journey home. Within minutes of turning out of the drive, I'd fallen asleep. The day had been just as exhausting for me watching as it was for Jamie. I remember dreaming during that sleep about Mrs Blake and Mr Richardson. They were sitting at the side of a riverbank watching the water. This time our meeting wasn't quite the same. Although I felt as if I was there, I was merely floating on the river as a picture. It was as if the river was a kind of doorway to the land of the living.

"You did well today under the circumstances. Like Jamie, you showed great strength and courage. Now you must go forward with your new life just as you did with your old one. If you need any help you only need call and we'll be there. You have a gift. A gift that many would like and don't have and a gift that many have and they don't know."

I now understood what she meant. Her advice had come at the end of a year in which I'd experienced a number of emotions consisting of good, bad and in-between. All in all, it had been a difficult year, but at the end of it I was still alive and very prepared to go onwards.

"Take care of Jamie for me," said the rather depressed looking Mr Richardson. "You've fulfilled a wish of his since he knew you, and I know as brothers you will help and care for each other, but please promise me something. Promise me you will never lie to each other or keep secrets. Your lives have been constructed on a foundation of lies and secrets; now that you have an empty field, grow your lives as straight as corn." I promised without hesitating and have lived by those words ever since. Anything after that promise I don't remember, I simply drifted off down the water to a place where my body found rest.

As for Jamie and Dad, well, they had a lot to talk about. Keeping his eyes firmly on the road with one hand on the steering wheel and the other on the gear stick Dad began. "I think there's something we need to talk about, Jamie. Something that concerns the three of us in this car."

Jamie didn't seem startled by Dad's serious sounding words. "I was kind of hoping you would bring the subject up, *Dad*." On hearing Jamie's reply, Dad instantly took his eyes from the road and stared straight at him.

"I've known. I've known for the last three years nearly. My Dad told me all about it not long after we moved. I'll always remember it. It was a cold Sunday afternoon in late February. We had been working really hard on this farm, digging fresh drainage trails that led into a burn. Dad was tired and hungry so we stopped and had some of the bread that Mum had baked. Dad started to cry and tell me how sorry he was. How he felt ashamed for not being able to protect and provide for his family. As he pulled me closer, I could smell he had been drinking liquor and heavily.

"'I have to tell you something,' he said, 'but you mustn't tell your mother.' After I agreed he told me how I wasn't his real son. How for the last thirteen years he had been a substitute out of love for my mother. I was upset and confused at what he was saying. He then explained how on the night I was born he came home and was sitting outside in the car when he saw the doctor leaving the house with a baby. He knew it was a baby by the way the doctor carried it and placed it in the car ever so carefully. After seeing that, he followed the doctor to your house and watched as the doctor entered with the baby and came out empty handed an hour later. Although he didn't understand what was going on, he quickly found out. That night he stayed away and didn't return home till the following morning. Without beating around the bush, he confronted Mum and they argued until finally she surrendered and told him the truth. That morning Dad found out about you and Mum. He was so angry words couldn't express it, but he was caught between a rock and a hard place. If he said anything to anyone he could be considered as someone who'd been taken as a fool. That was just as difficult to live with as a child that wasn't his. They agreed that no one else would ever know about what happened and that Mum would have to get reassurance from Diana that she would keep it a secret also.

"At some point, Mum and Diana met where they agreed that none of them would ever speak about what happened that night. They separated after that meeting and were never supposed to meet again. Dad thought it best to move away to prevent the two families ever meeting and he and Mum slowly but surely kept loving each other. It's funny now that I know and look back, because I remember times when I distinctly remember thinking there was something wrong between Dad and me. Don't get me wrong, he loved me, I know that, but there were days when that loving bond wasn't there. I don't suppose it did me any harm but finding out was a bit of a shock.

"I never got to know any more as the farmer arrived and fired us because he suspected Dad had stolen whisky from the cottage. We had to walk for a day before we found new work. I was hungry and physically cold while Dad was hungry and cold mentally. I watched as hour by hour and day by day as he became severely depressed. I knew deep down inside it was only a matter of time before something happened and I was helpless to do anything. I think Dad was trying to clear his conscience before making his supreme sacrifice and that's why he decided to tell me, even if it was whilst under the influence of drink. As I kept my word and never let slip to Mum that I knew, so too did she keep to her word by never attempting to tell me. Some people would think what she did was wrong and disgraceful, but not me. I respect her for what she did, it took strength under extreme pressure and under the circumstances she made the right decision. I just hope I'm never placed in trials of similar circumstance."

Jamie had shocked and stunned Dad. Was there no end to the heartache this boy kept inside? Dad thought.

"I know you'll never be able to consider me as being your real father but I want you to know that no matter what, I'll always be there for you."

Jamie's hand extended out to meet Dad's on the gear stick. "Ever since I've known you, you've been there for me, you've been a like a father to me already." A tear welled in Dad's eye that day. All the secrets had now been let loose and for the first time in sixteen years Dad felt freedom like he'd never felt before. As he turned to Jamie he noticed he'd fallen asleep. "I love you son, I love you both."

Dad made the rest of the journey home with no one other than himself to speak to. We didn't wake till he slowly shook us. "We're home, boys."

It was slightly dark and, although the sun had just about fallen completely from the sky, the air still held some warmth. We made our way up the stairs for the last time that year. As we entered we could hear laughter and fun coming from the kitchen. As we hung up our coats and removed our shoes, no one came to welcome us. Little did we know that Dad had made a phone call during his brief absence before leaving the school to let everyone know things had turned out just fine. One of the other things he'd done was to get Gran to sit down with Gavin and explain the situation. I think Dad felt as if he'd done enough explaining for one day.

As we entered the kitchen we found everyone there, Jenny, Gran, Anna, Gavin, Mrs Richardson, Alice, Mary and Paul. They didn't stop what they were doing as we entered but instead pulled us into the room to join in with the fun. There were no questions asked and no sense of unease lingered at all. For the next hour we completely forgot about the day's events and had some good old-fashioned fun.

After dinner I headed upstairs for a bath. With the long trip I felt grubby and smelly. My bath, however, turned out to be more of a war than anything else, I was half-dressed when there was a knock at the door.

"Can I come in?"

"It's open."

Jamie walked in and took up a seat on the floor. "It's been a long day."

"It sure has."

"We haven't had much time to talk."

"Nope, but we've now got the rest of our lives for talking." Jamie smiled just as yet another knock arrived upon the door.

"Can I come in?"

"The door's open." Just as Jamie had done Gavin stuck his head around the door then came inside. He looked as if he was struggling for words so I thought it only right to help him out a little. "You ok?"

"Yes. What about you two?" Jamie and I both smiled and simultaneously replied, "We're ok."

"You know it's a bit strange finding out you have another brother, but you know what? It's great to find out it's you, Jamie."

"Come here." The three of us stood in the middle of the bathroom pulled together by Jamie and we hugged. Everything was going great until suddenly Jamie pushed me backwards and straight into the water. That's when the water fight began. For ages we played like children ought to play, like brothers ought to play, and we had fun.

We all stayed up that night as a family and waited anxiously as the Grandfather clock struck on twelve. The next ten minutes were full of New Year kisses and toasts. We were never a family for long speeches and this New Year was no exception. Dad was the one who neatly wrapped up the occasion "Here's to Life, to family and to Diana and Mason," and with that the year was over.

I often look back on that year in my life and reflect upon it as perhaps the best year of my life. Although I had many great times and adventures after that year, nothing quite came close. As the years went by and love between Anna and me blossomed so too did a lot of other things blossom, but they're another story.

In life people often ask your name. People like to know who they are speaking to or socialising with. I was asked the very same thing a hundred times, but each time I was asked I simply replied, "me."

The End